Praise for Glen Cook

"Glen Cook's dark and gritty series of fantasy novels tracking the history of the mercenary band known as The Black Company had a huge impact on post-Tolkien fantasies. They marked a turn away from Tolkien and back toward such models as Leiber and Howard, and, with their starkly realistic portrayal of soldiers and war, became themselves models for a new generation of epic fantasy writers like Steven Erikson."

—PAUL WITCOVER, *Locus*

"Glen Cook is a rare beast of a writer—he can vacillate between military fantasy, space opera, epic fantasy, mystery, and science fantasy with great ease. His writing is often marked by a purity; that he is depicting life in its most real sense, from the thoughts in a character's mind to the wind rushing across his or her face."

—ROB H. BEDFORD, *sffworld.com*

"Glen Cook has been credited with single-handedly changing the face of fantasy in the late twentieth century. I'd argue with that—there are too many antecedents for contemporary heroic fantasy noir to give credit to one writer. What Cook has done is build on them very effectively, sometimes brilliantly, to the point that if you don't know Cook, you don't know fantasy."

—ROBERT M. TILENDIS, *The Green Man Review*

"Glen writes a mean book."

—JIM BUTCHER

Praise for Glen Cook
(continued)

"Cook's talent for combining gritty realism and high fantasy provides a singular edge."

—*Library Journal*

"Cook provides a rich world of assorted races, cultures, and religions; his characters combine the mythic or exotic with the realistic, engaging in absorbing alliances, enmities, and double-crosses."

—*Publishers Weekly*

"*The Black Company* is a wonderfully amoral book, often dark and containing violent battles and fantastic characters. Glen Cook changed the face of the fantasy genre forever... and for the better."

—*Fantasy Book Review*

A Path to Coldness of Heart

OTHER BOOKS BY GLEN COOK

The Heirs of Babylon
The Swordbearer
A Matter of Time
The Tower of Fear
Sung in Blood
The Dragon Never Sleeps
Winter's Dreams (forthcoming)

Dread Empire
A Fortress in Shadow:
  The Fire in His Hands
  With Mercy Toward None
A Cruel Wind:
  A Shadow of All Night Falling
  October's Baby
  All Darkness Met
An Empire Unacquainted with Defeat
The Last Chronicle
  Vol I: Reap the East Wind
  Vol II: An Ill Fate Marshalling
  Vol III: A Path to Coldness of Heart

Starfishers
Shadowline
Starfishers
Stars' End
Passage at Arms

Darkwar
  Doomstalker
  Warlock
  Ceremony

The Black Company
The Black Company
Shadows Linger
The White Rose
The Silver Spike
Shadow Games
Dreams of Steel
Bleak Seasons
She Is the Darkness
Water Sleeps
Soldiers Live

The Garrett Files
Sweet Silver Blues
Bitter Gold Hearts
Cold Copper Tears
Old Tin Sorrows
Dread Brass Shadows
Red Iron Nights
Deadly Quicksilver Lies
Petty Pewter Gods
Faded Steel Heat
Angry Lead Skies
Whispering Nickel Idols
Cruel Zinc Melodies
Gilded Latten Bones

Instrumentalities of the Night
The Tyranny of the Night
Lord of the Silent Kingdom
Surrender to the Will of the Night

A PATH TO COLDNESS OF HEART

THE LAST CHRONICLE OF
THE DREAD EMPIRE: VOL III

GLEN COOK

NIGHT SHADE BOOKS
SAN FRANCISCO

Cover design by Claudia Noble
Interior layout and design by Amy Popovich

First Edition

ISBN: 978-1-59780-331-1

Night Shade Books
www.nightshadebooks.com

Chapter One:

YEAR 1016 AFTER THE FOUNDING OF THE EMPIRE OF ILKAZAR:

The Price of Hubris

The prisoner clamped his jaw on a shriek. He had moved too suddenly, turning. He did swear softly. He could not work his muscles, could not build the strength to escape if his wounds did not heal. And they would not if he kept trying before the meat was ready.

A clatter rose outside. This austere suite might be his entire world for the remainder of his existence: a reward for having befriended a woman and having saved the life of a man.

It was the middle of the night. Darkness with stars filled the single foot square window high in the east wall, well beyond his reach. He should be sleeping.

He lay in bed, back to the doorway, feigning sleep, when the visitors arrived. Three, from the sounds of it: one large, one small, one delicate. Female, if fragrance did not lie.

"He heals slowly," one said. "The physician blames his despair."

That voice belonged to Lord Ssu-ma Shih-ka'i, commander of Shinsan's Western Army. It was by Shih-ka'i's grace that the prisoner lived.

A second familiar voice said, "The physician should look closer. He's clever. He'll show you what you expect to see till you relax. Then you'll be dead."

The prisoner's exact strategy. If only his body would heal!

Shih-ka'i said, "The physician says his wounds pierced his soul. He overreached—and it cost him everything."

Mist, Empress of the Dread Empire, considered before she replied. "It can't be easy, living on after making so many bad decisions."

The prisoner, who thought of himself only as "the prisoner" because of his shame, compelled himself to relax, to breathe slow and deep. But he could not stop tears from leaking.

Thousands had died because of his decisions. A kingdom might be destroyed by civil war. His family would be fugitives already. The child-woman he had loved… Who knew? If Sherilee was clever she would insist that she had known him only as someone who visited her friend Kristen, widow of his son and mother of his grandchildren.

He thought about Inger, his wife and queen, seldom. When he did, though, it was with a grand ration of guilt. That love had died.

Inger came to mind when the pain was bad. They met the last time he lay just outside the Dark Gate, she a volunteer nurse helping heroes injured while holding the wolves of the Dread Empire at bay. In his loneliness he had asked her to become his wife.

He had lost another wife, Elana, and another lover, Fiana, before Inger.

Women who loved him did not fare well.

"Were I in charge here," said the woman who had been a friend, and a wife to his best friend's wife's brother, "and I was sure that he would recover, I would brick up the doorway."

Lord Ssu-ma said, "I bear the man no love but that is excessive. He's a cripple. He'll never recover fully. And he's nowhere where he can cause any grief."

The prisoner had no idea where "here" was. Inside Dread Empire territory, certainly. Though Shinsan had suffered severely lately, not one inch of ground had been abandoned

How were Shinsan's wars coming? He had helped facilitate the conclusion of one and had been the loser in another. The Matayangan front must have turned favorable, too. Mist had time to visit.

She observed, "O Shing was a cripple."

"As you say. Vigilance is required."

The night visitors withdrew, to the prisoner's frustration. He had hoped to hear something more heartening.

Despair led to self-flagellation. Then, finally, feigned sleep segued into the real thing.

...

Inger watched her captains bicker over a map. They were getting nowhere. She was too tired to scold them. Too tired to ask what new disasters had them bickering.

Ethnically, three were Nordmen from Kavelin's old ruling class. Two were Wessons, freemen, descendants of long-ago immigrants from Itaskia. Inger was Itaskian-born, as was the sixth man, whom she had borrowed from her cousin Dane. Dane's little army was wintering fifty miles west of Vorgreberg, too far away to provide quick support. Regions nearer the capital were less friendly. Dane's men suffered virulent guerrilla attacks if they moved nearer to Vorgreberg. That forced them to cluster in stronger bands. Those became a strain on local resources, which, in turn, left the locals more sympathetic to the rebels.

Inger refused to let Dane move into the city. She said she did not want to cede the countryside. In truth she did not want her uncontrollable cousin in position to control Kavelin by controlling her.

He would try, given the chance.

Power was his reason for having come to Kavelin. Power was why she had wed Kavelin's lonely king.

Inger sipped scalding tea.

She was a tall, handsome woman whose blond hair had begun to streak grey. Time was not the thief of her beauty. Stress, fear, and lack of sleep were the demons responsible.

The hot tea wakened her fully. "Silence! Thank you, gentlemen. Using the term loosely. Mr. Cleary, you talk. Everyone else stay quiet."

Cleary was the senior Wesson, a stout, sturdy man of thirty-three who had served King Bragi faithfully and remained loyal now that Bragi had fallen. Inger trusted him. The Nordmen and

Nathan Wolf, borrowed from Dane of Greyfells, she trusted not at all. In Wolf's case it was no secret that he was here to watch her because Dane no longer had faith in Josiah Gales.

"Ma'am. Your Majesty. The contention arose because General Liakopulos has gone missing. No one knows where, when, or how. He was polling units out west to see where they stand, now. Our discussion concerned possible hows and whys of his disappearance."

Inger's heart sank. This was bad news indeed, though not a surprise. Liakopulos had had little interest in supporting her. He had been Bragi's man. He considered her incapable of, or uninterested in, pursuing Bragi's reforms. "What are the theories? Mr. Wolf?"

"He deserted. He didn't want to be here anymore."

"And the rest of you disagree?"

Two Nordmen, Sir Rengild and Sir Arnhelm, thought the truth more sinister: The Guild General had gone over to the Marena Dimura strongman, Credence Abaca. Sir Arnhelm insisted, "Those two were always cozy." Which he found repugnant because, as a class, Nordmen considered Marena Dimura less than human woodland savages. Colonel Abaca and his henchmen had developed massive pretensions during the reign of the lost king—a savage himself who would not distinguish between noble and ignoble.

The third Nordmen, Sir Quirre of Bolt, said nothing. With a slight sneer and shake of the head he expressed contempt for his fellows. He believed in King Bragi's vision.

Inger turned to the Wessons. Boyer disagreed completely with Cleary. Neither considered Liakopulos a villain. Cleary was sure the General just did not stop heading west when he saw a chance to leave. Boyer was sure that Liakopulos had been murdered. "And rebels didn't do it. It will be Greyfells when the truth comes out. It's a matter of who stands most to gain, Your Majesty."

"Spoken like a true money-grubbing merchant," Sir Arnhelm snarled. "Everything comes down to a balance sheet."

"Yes, it does," Inger said. There was no love for the General here. Liakopulos had kept these men in check, favoring no one, contemptuous of them all because he considered them adventurers and plunderers who cared nothing for Kavelin. Bragi, Queen Fiana, and her husband the Krief, who died when Fiana was a teen, had all stretched reason to breaking to create a nation in which all the peoples had a stake.

Inger covered her forehead with her left palm, rubbed, thumb and little finger massaging her temples. "Jokerst, find Colonel Gales. I want him here for a working breakfast tomorrow."

Gales would replace Liakopulos. He had been understudying, with the General's assistance. The move was expected. And might be what Dane wanted to see.

Was he behind Liakopulos's disappearance? He was capable. But would he dare the hostility of the Mercenaries' Guild?

Inability to predict consequences accurately was the bane of the Greyfells line. Again and again they dropped stones on their own toes while trying to be clever.

"The rest of you. No more speculation. Get me facts. Find out what actually happened."

Several faces went pale. It was dangerous out there.

"One thing can't be denied," Sir Arnhelm said. "The break with the old regime. Liakopulos was the last."

Inger suspected that pleased the man no end. "All of you, go away. I need rest before I go mad."

They went. She sent for Dr. Wachtel, an overlooked holdover from the old regime. But Wachtel was a holdover from every regime. He was Castle Krief furniture. He had tended Kavelin's rulers for sixty years, whoever they were.

The doctor provided a draught to make Inger sleep. The medication sometimes had a harsh side effect. It caused vivid, often prescient dreams, some of which would be nightmares.

Inger wakened less rested than she had hoped. She did not remember her dreams but met the new day afraid.

...

Credence Abaca's Marena Dimura partisans kept their political prizes in comfort but there were limits to what could be managed in the wilds of the Kapenrung Mountains. Kristen and her companions learned the cost of commitment to a cause, though the privations were social, intellectual, and circumscription of movement rather than a dearth of food, warmth, or shelter.

The children, including young King Bragi II, did not mind. They ran wild with the Marena Dimura urchins, getting every bit as filthy and bruised while having just as much fun in the ice, snow, and forests. Kristen tried to convince herself that this was good for a boy who would become king of all Kaveliner peoples, including the disenfranchised Marena Dimura.

Which was their own fault, Kristen believed. They would not leave the wilderness and become part of the nation, though some had done so while Bragi was king. Abaca had been one of the army's top commanders.

Kristen and Dahl Haas shared a bench inside a cozy cabin equipped with the blatant luxury of a huge glass window. Kristen often wondered where the forest people had stolen it. Snow fell outside. Big chunks hit the window, melted, slid downward as they perished. "Winter here is harder than it is in Vorgreberg."

"Think so? How about during the Great Eastern Wars?"

"That was one bad winter." She frowned. It had been more than one winter and had been unimaginably worse than this. Hunger, danger, fear, and sickness had been constant companions.

Haas leaned close, no longer discomfited by his affection for the girl who had been the wife of his king's son and who was the mother of Bragi's legitimate heir. Kristen had abandoned reticence long ago. She knew her father-in-law approved.

She said, "Sitting here like this, I don't think this is such a bad life."

"How much better the world if everyone were equally content."

"You ought to be content. You've got me."

"Somebody is getting a big head."

Sherilee came for the fire and to watch the snow. The couple said nothing. Speaking to Sherilee gave her license to vent her unhappiness. She could be tiresome.

Sherilee was young, small, beautiful, almost porcelain in her perfection. She looked years younger than she was, which was only Kristen's age. In his absence she had become pathologically enamored of King Bragi, based upon a brief, furtive liaison with a man older than her own father. In her dramatic way she had reconstructed her life around what she thought she had lost when the King had fallen.

Sherilee sighed dramatically.

Her performance drew no response. After further vain sallies, the tragic doll declared, "There must be something we can do to rescue him."

Sherilee was one of a tiny number of people who knew King Bragi was alive and a prisoner.

Kristen sighed herself, then plunged into the game. "Michael Trebilcock and Aral Dantice got away with that once, when they rescued Nepanthe. It won't work again. He's being held by the Tervola, not some dinkle-brain queen of Argon."

She played loosely with history but facts did not matter here. What did was the undeniable futility of any effort to free the King. To start, no one knew where he was being held. Unless, maybe, Michael Trebilcock or Aral Dantice knew. But Michael was out of touch and Aral no longer haunted Kavelin. Trebilcock might be dead. He had not been seen for months.

But Michael was his own man. He went his own way. And that worried everyone.

Since coming to Kavelin Michael Trebilcock had created his own hidden realm of dedicated friends and allies who disdained the small-minded politics of the Lesser Kingdoms. Those people believed in the welfare of the whole instead of that of the partisan.

Michael Trebilcock had remained faithful to Bragi while Bragi was king but Bragi was never fully confident of Trebilcock.

Sherilee asked, "Do you think Aral is in touch with Michael?"

Those two had been friends since their school days in Hellin Daimiel. They had shared several fierce adventures in Kavelin and abroad. Dantice occasionally visited the Marena Dimura during more clement seasons. He lived in Ruderin nowadays but remained in the family business, being part trader, part smuggler, part gangster. Once upon a time, before the wars, his father had been a trader, too. A more legitimate trader.

Aral had one foot firmly in the shadows. Many of his associates over there had spied for Michael Trebilcock.

Dahl said, "Maybe. But Michael would come to him. Michael lives in his own secret kingdom of loyal friends. I couldn't guess their ideology, if they have one. Probably something like what

Bragi's was. They aren't after power. They collect information, then dispense it where they think it'll do some good. And they hide each other when there's a need."

"He did support the King."

"As far as we ever saw, he did. He took extreme risks on Bragi's behalf but Bragi never trusted him completely. Inger is sure that Michael cleaned out the treasury."

Kristen caught something. "Dahl? You know something about that?"

"How could I? I was way far away."

"Dahl. Talk to me. I'm your Queen Mother, remember?"

Sherilee stalked in from the other side, looking ferocious. "Talk, soldier boy! This is something you shouldn't be hiding."

"I'm not hiding anything. I don't know anything. I just remember what contingency plans there were. It's just a gut feeling."

Kristen said, "Talk to me about your digestive troubles."

"Michael might not be innocent, but that's only because he was involved in the planning. Emptying the treasury was up to Cham Mundwiller and Derel Prataxis. A merchant prince and a Rebsamen don with an abiding interest in economics."

Both women held their peace but glared in a way that demanded further commentary.

Dahl said, "Prataxis sometimes talked about how a lack of specie could inhibit economic growth. He believed in a money economy. Meaning he thought we'd all live better if there was a lot of trustworthy coinage circulating. You can't build a state on the barter system. It always made sense when Derel talked about it. He always had examples. Kingdoms like Itaskia, where a lot of money is always in motion, grow strong economically and militarily. In the Lesser Kingdoms, where there isn't much money, nothing good happens because nobody can pay for it. Kavelin has been an exception because it controls trade through the Savernake Gap."

"We don't have that trade anymore," Kristen said.

"We don't," Dahl agreed.

"The theft of the treasury fits how?" Sherilee asked.

"Inger doesn't have a copper to pay her soldiers. And soldiers don't usually want their pay in chickens or corn."

"Ha-ha," Kristen said. "That may be. But I haven't heard of any regiments who declared for Inger falling apart because they haven't gotten paid. And we can't pay the men who stuck with us."

"Troops on both sides are on partial pay donated by the wealthy. The Estates for Inger, the merchants of Sedlmayr and the west for us. Inger claims new money is coming from Itaskia. Our friends say Kavelin's silver mines are pledged to us. Nobody has been asked to fight. Any showdown between men who fought side by side before will probably cause mass desertions."

Sherilee proved she was not just a gorgeous face and damned fine everything else. "We can't mine, refine, and mint enough silver to support production and an army, too."

"When you get down to it, neither side can afford to pay soldiers who aren't fighting for what they believe in."

Kristen said, "So most of them will go home, whether or not they loved Bragi. We should find the treasury money."

Haas said, "My love, the girl genius. One problem. Everybody who knew anything about it died in the riots after the King's fall."

"Except Michael Trebilcock. And maybe General Liakopulos."

"Remote and remoter."

"Meaning?"

"Liakopulos is dead. Probably murdered by the Itaskians. As for Michael, I don't honestly believe he survived, either. But if he did he isn't going to help us."

Sherilee and Kristen glared. Haas thought that unfair. Such lovelies deserved to have nothing weightier than fashion on their minds.

Yet another way Kavelin distorted the natural order. Kavelin boasted strong women who made remarkable things happen.

...

Dane, Duke of Greyfells, want-to-be lord of Kavelin, paced before a fireplace. His newly acquired headquarters was large, old, and draughty. It overlooked Damhorst, a key town on the east-west trade route through Kavelin. The castle was the ancestral home of the Breitbarth barons. Claimants to that title had been eliminated.

Greyfells had taken the castle by stealth. He and his adventurers now enjoyed shelter, warmth, and security but seldom dared go out in bands of fewer than a dozen.

The locals were mainly Wesson, ethnic cousins of the Itaskians. Politically, though, they favored the line of King Bragi through his first wife.

Greyfells favored a succession through Ragnarson's latest wife, his cousin Inger.

Dane of Greyfells was not happy. He had come to Kavelin expecting to put the kingdom in his pocket before winter. But winter was here, ferociously, and he was still far from Vorgreberg, hurrying the family decline toward destitution. His troops were melting away, mainly through desertion. Replacements, when he could find any, were untrained, unskilled, and belonged in cells rather than under arms.

His personal attendant announced, "Gales is here, Lordship."

"About damned time. He was due yesterday."

"He had trouble getting through. He's wounded. So are those of his escort who survived."

Though in a foul temper Greyfells did not yield to the unreason that, too often, left him unable to concede that events could, on occasion, disdain his wishes. He said only, "Clean him up, then bring him in." He did not like dirty people. He loathed the sight of old blood.

"As you will, Your Lordship."

The family sorcerer showed up.

"Babeltausque?"

"May I join you, Your Lordship?"

Dane scowled. Fat people were another dislike. Greyfells further disliked Babeltausque because he was expensive to maintain. He was the best paid of any Greyfells retainer, and the least useful, lately.

The Duke was convinced that Babeltausque was a coward and that he knew things he would not share with his employer.

Greyfells was incapable of understanding that *he* was what the sorcerer feared. Babeltausque withheld information he thought might spark the kind of rage that might lead to him getting hurt.

Greyfells asked, "You have a reason?"

"To collect information. I have trouble working in the dark."

"You don't work at all."

"To work I must be given tasks. Plausible, possible tasks. Not pie in the sky, wishful thinking tasks." Babeltausque had found his courage today. "Bridge builders are constrained by the limits of their materials. A sorcerer is constrained by the limits of the Power."

"Varthlokkur never seemed limited."

"Only from outside. He was. He is. He makes what he does look easy because he's ancient and far more talented than me."

Greyfells grumbled but did not send the sorcerer away. Babeltausque found a shadow and settled. He resented the Duke's attitude but understood it. He was just a house sorcerer, under contract. He lacked a grasp of the Power sufficient to make it as an independent. He could help heal scrapes and bruises. He could retard meat spoilage. He read the tarot imperfectly and the stars the same. His divinations were reliable out to about three hours. He did read character well, usually recognized lies, and could anticipate danger's approach, particularly when that included him.

His most valuable talent was the ability to remain calm and bland of expression in the face of fear or provocation. He used that talent frequently. Greyfells was an ambitious beast blessed with cunning and a complete lack of scruples—typical of his line. He was neither the worst nor the best duke that Babeltausque had known. He was mediocre in most ways. He stood out because of his rages.

Those assured Dane's early demise, probably as soon as someone believed he had a chance to get away with it.

Babeltausque's most important chore was to protect the Duke from his own family, which was not that difficult out here.

The tradition of elevating oneself over the corpse of one's father, brother, or uncle had not been much honored of late. Only outsiders had laid the Greyfells Dukes low with any verve the past three decades. But the possibility survived in Dane's imagination.

If this Duke met an early end the House of Greyfells might collapse. There were no relatives suited to replace him.

Enemies in Itaskia must be busy as worker ants trying to make that happen while Greyfells was away. Returning deserters would tell encouraging tales of Dane's incompetence, which explained why he grew ever more testy. Every day of triumph delayed out here was a day when the family lost ground at home.

Colonel Gales entered. He wore clean clothing that did not fit. His hair was stringy wet from an unwanted bath. His face was red from a rough shave. His right arm was in a sling. He limped.

Greyfells, of course, first noted that he needed a haircut.

The Colonel bowed.

The Duke said, "I hear you had some trouble."

"We got ambushed by Marena Dimura. They knew who we were and had our itinerary."

"But you fought through." Stating the obvious.

"They didn't press the matter. They hit us, hurt us, failed to kill me in the first rush, started getting hurt themselves, so they faded away. I didn't chase them. We were all hurt and they would've led us into a secondary ambush."

Greyfells grunted. He was not pleased but he understood. That was everyday life in Kavelin.

Gales said, "Abaca is content to wear us down a man at a time."

"Too true. Josiah, I'm starting to think I miscalculated when I decided to do this."

"Don't feel badly, Lordship. This kingdom ends up making everyone over into a pessimist, whether you love it or hate it."

The man in shadow studied Duke and soldier. Gales enjoyed remarkable freedoms. He and Greyfells had known each other since childhood. Still, the Duke looked like he wanted to hurt somebody. He controlled the beast within. "Tell me why I'm still out here, Josiah. Why am I not enjoying a cozy fire inside Castle Krief?"

"I can put no kinder face on it than to tell you that Inger wants it this way. She doesn't trust you. She's determined not to let you in till she knows you won't steal her throne."

The watcher thought that would waken the beast for sure.

The Duke did puff up and turn red but controlled himself again. He managed better with Gales than with anyone else. "I can see that from both the Kavelin disease and family familiarity angles. What she's been through since we got her to marry Ragnarson has made her leery of everyone."

Especially family, the sorcerer reflected.

"There lies the matter's heart, Lord. We talk frequently. Lately, she has been concerned less with Wesson resistance or Colonel Abaca than about your intentions. You mention the Kavelin disease. I think she's caught it. She believes it's possible to come to terms with her local enemies. She has started hinting that she wants me to find a way to get you to go home."

"Really?" Surprised. Greyfells could not imagine a female cousin defying him.

"Really. She doesn't know my true loyalties. She thinks I'll support her in anything because of an obligation between me and her father. She is inclined toward sentimental thinking."

"I see." Sounding less than convinced of Gales's faith. But he *had* to be paranoid. People *were* out to get him.

Gales said, "Inger has no friends and few sympathizers. She has no one to count on in the narrow passage. She's alone except for Fulk."

Greyfells stopped pacing. He placed himself at parade rest, back to the fire. "It doesn't matter a whit who controls her son, does it?"

"No, Lord. Fulk is King. Confirmed by the Thing and the Estates. I've been thinking..."

"I think I know, Josiah. My cousin is in grave danger. This kingdom is renown for its intrigues. Her family should put her under our protection for her own sake."

"Exactly, Your Lordship!"

Babeltausque smelled a king-size load of what, technically, was called bullshit. But which man had tipped the cart?

Gales stayed the evening and night, mostly heads together with the Duke.

Babeltausque suspected that success at gaining Vorgreberg and Castle Krief would mean less than Greyfells hoped. His writ would extend no farther than he could see from the capital's wall. And that might be problematic.

Other forces were at work.

†

Chapter Two:

1016–1017 AFE:

Mountains Far

Fangdred bestrode one of the highest peaks in the Dragon's Teeth. Who built the castle was a mystery, as was how the engineering had been achieved. Fangdred had been there for countless centuries.

Its current population was miniscule and included several mummies. Many of the living would not, strictly appraised, easily pass for sane.

The sorcerer had worn many names, including Empire Destroyer, but, commonly, was called Varthlokkur. He employed his arts to spy on the wider world while he wrestled the demands of love, honor, and pride. He observed carefully, painfully aware that mortals were subject to manipulation by puppet masters unseen and driven by imperatives that might not make sense even to them.

He spent hours every day looking for puppeteers, with little success.

He was able to track factions in Kavelin, where everyone acted on best guesses while guessing wrong. His successes elsewhere were less clear. The lords of the Dread Empire were wary. Getting anywhere near the Empress was problematic. What he did see might be staged for his eyes.

He did manage one triumph beyond the Pillars of Ivory. He stumbled across a man he had thought long dead, a fugitive who had escaped from Lioantung during its destruction by the Deliverer. That man was headed home, now.

The wizard did what he dared as the man's guardian angel.

Varthlokkur's mad pride had done irreparable harm during the business of the Deliverer. He had yet to understand what had driven him to such stubborn excess. His excuse had been his fear of losing his wife, but common sense saw that battle won well beforehand.

On the other hand, that fool Ragnarson had been just as stubborn… "Damn it!" His blood was rising for no sane reason.

He could not back down. He could not admit that he had been wrong. Yet he had cost Kavelin dearly. Protecting Haroun during his long journey west was slight recompense but it might pay off in time to come.

Haroun carried his own guilt burden.

Varthlokkur's wife let herself into his Wind Tower work chamber, unannounced and uninvited. She found him focused on his monstrous creation, Radeachar the Unborn, that he used to ferret out secrets and to terrify villains.

Nepanthe was pale of skin and dark of hair, brooding and shy. Sorcery kept her looking young, as it did her husband. Varthlokkur appeared to be in his early thirties but was centuries older. He considered Nepanthe the most perfect woman ever to live. She was his great weakness and absolute blind spot. His love was fierce. That psychosis had so tormented him that he had let it shape today's shattered world.

Nepanthe said nothing. She watched Varthlokkur spy here, send Radeachar there, then enter the blazing construct of the Winterstorm. His manipulation of brilliant floating symbols shaped changes far away. Snow might melt early and raise waters enough so an army patrol would not discover the fugitive from Lioantung. An icy gust might assail the camp of some of the Itaskians trying to take over in Kavelin, starting fires. An agent of Queen Inger might be about to stumble onto the loot from

Kavelin's treasury when something stirring in a sudden darkness so terrified him that he would never go near that pond again. An avalanche might block the route of an ill-advised winter raid by Colonel Abaca's Marena Dimura partisans. A bridge collapse beyond the northern frontier might abort an equally ill-advised winter incursion from Volstokin.

He watched Hammad al Nakir less determinedly. There the daughter of the Disciple, Yasmid, pursued a sporadic, fratricidal civil war against her son Megelin while her father sank ever deeper into a permanent opium dream. There was a special need to watch the son. Megelin's key ally was the dark sorcerer Magden Norath, who might be as powerful as the Empire Destroyer himself. No one knew what moved Norath. He created monsters that were almost impossible to destroy, for no more obvious reason than a lust for destruction.

Norath was weak now, though. He had become the principal target of El Murid's suicide killer cult, the Harish. He thwarted every attack but only after it got close enough to hurt him. Damage was accumulating.

Varthlokkur turned to something of no interest. Nepanthe moved on to the shrunken stasis globe where once the Princes Thaumaturge of the Dread Empire had been trapped, then had murdered one another. Why had Varthlokkur kept that in this diminished form? Why had he not ground the princes to dust, then burnt the dust? Would that be impossible? Could be. It had taken the Star Rider's power to capture them.

She had been there, but that was all she could remember clearly—other than that it had been a terrible night. She feared that she had done something she dared not remember.

She shied away. Those days were gone. Horrible times, they had been followed by more horrible times. It had taken many ugly seasons to bring her here, to a remote place and a life with a man she respected deeply but did not love, nursing her insane son by her first husband and raising an eerie daughter by the second.

Nepanthe drifted round the Winterstorm, as ever wonderstruck. Once Varthlokkur had filled her hair with those glowing symbols… Another memory she did not want to relive.

She turned to her husband. They had been at odds for months

because he had been so determined to shield her from the pain of learning that her son Ethrian had become a monster. He had been that insecure.

Enough! She teetered at the brink of a slide into a hell that existed only in the bleak realms of What If? and Might Have Been. This was now. Now was here. They two had to act as one. Innumerable divinations were iron about that.

Varthlokkur left the Winterstorm. He was exhausted. He took a seat. Nepanthe moved in close, to support him with the warmth of her presence.

In a whisper, he said, "Every day I drive myself to the verge of collapse, trying to hold back the night. But I don't do any good."

"Let it go. Turn away. Focus on us and the children. The fire will burn itself out without you."

"Am I resisting the tide of destiny? Are my efforts pointless?"

"It may take everything you have just to raise Ethrian and Smyrena to be marginally sane adults."

Varthlokkur nodded. The children were in his thoughts always. All four, not just Nepanthe's babes. "I wish. But bad things happened. Some were my fault. I can't help trying to make that right."

Nepanthe did not argue. There was no changing his mind, be his choices good, evil, or just stubbornly unreasonable. And it was true that he had unleashed some of the darkness stalking the world today.

She asked, "What's the situation now?"

"They've moved Bragi to Throyes. He'll never break out, now, and even I couldn't get him away from this place."

"And Haroun?"

"One day at a time. Still headed home. Still sheltered by the fact that nobody knows he's alive."

"And you're helping."

"Not so he'll notice. He's hard. He's convinced that he can go anywhere any time because he's a master shaghûn now."

Today's Haroun resembled Varthlokkur at a similar age. Prolonged observation left the wizard feeling an eerie *déjà vu.*

Haroun had no boundaries. He could kill or be cruel without thought, remorse, or regret. He did terrible things to people who got in his way and lost not a minute of sleep. He would do the same on behalf of his friends. Or to his friends if they became silhouetted against his destination.

Varthlokkur did not sleep much anymore, not because of demands on his time. There were long stretches when his body felt no need. But there were other times, for a week or two, when he would sleep twelve hours a day. At present he needed only the occasional nap.

Of late, in his manic stretches, he had begun using Radeachar to probe the mysteries surrounding its creation. The key points were known. In a mad, complex scheme involving the Captal of Savernake, Yo Hsi, the Demon Prince of the Dread Empire, had impregnated the barely old enough Queen Fiana with seed specially prepared in Shinsan. Though the truth had surfaced only recently, Old Meddler had had a hand in it, too. The scheme had collapsed. Fiana bore a daughter instead of the devil the conspirators wanted. So they switched that daughter for their own child, at the time unaware of the girl's sex.

Years later, following the death of her husband, the King, Fiana enjoyed a liaison with Bragi Ragnarson. She became pregnant. That had to be concealed for political reasons.

Fiana died in childbed, birthing the thing the conspirators had planted in her womb years before. Some twist in time had transposed her pregnancies. Varthlokkur suspected the Star Rider.

The horror within Fiana was too large for her birth canal. Her belly had been opened. The monster passed into Varthlokkur's control and became his terrible familiar, Radeachar.

All that was known to a few survivors of all the war and wickedness since, including, possibly, the dark wight creeping westward through the Dread Empire, sometimes in stages of only yards a day.

Recently, while trying to winkle out anything more about how the Unborn had come to be, Varthlokkur had stumbled across an ugly truth. There had been a day when the King Without a Throne thought it necessary to dispose of a prince named Gaia-Lange, and then a little princess, convinced as he had been that they were instruments of the Dread Empire.

How Old Meddler must have laughed.

Haroun had made two cruel choices and both had been bad. To this day no one suspected. Especially not Bragi Ragnarson.

Since then the King Without a Throne had done the unexpected several times by hurling his Royalists at the enemies of Kavelin's King Bragi. No one could fathom why. Some thought that was because several young Mercenary Guildsmen—Ragnarson, his brother, and friends—had saved Haroun repeatedly when he was a boy.

Haroun could not confess the greatest misjudgment of his life. He could not confess a sin that never stirred a feather of suspicion.

Varthlokkur had stumbled onto the truth and had been appalled. He, who could justify his own foulest deeds, could not understand what had moved Haroun to murder those children.

The guilt that shaped what Haroun had done since was no mystery. Varthlokkur knew guilt well. Guilt was a lifelong, intimate companion.

...

The fugitive's life was narrow and small. He was unique in his ability to focus on himself and his surroundings. He always saw the needful thing where survival was concerned. He had long-term goals, medium-term goals, and goals that did not go beyond the moment. Every moment negotiated led to another, then another. Enough conquered moments became a successfully completed short-term goal.

While no match for the Tervola of Shinsan, Haroun was a trained shaghûn, a military sorcerer, the best of recent times. That was not saying much, though. The Disciple had forbidden the practice amongst his followers. His enemies disdained shaghûnry as unmanly.

Haroun employed his skills sparingly. Feral sorcery, if noticed, was suppressed quickly and lethally inside the Dread Empire.

Haroun's strengths were will and patience. He had endured trials that would have crushed most men. And the miracle was not that he had come through but that he had come through every time. Even the heroes of the epics managed only once or twice.

He knew nothing else. Settling down with his wife to raise a crop of grandchildren was beyond his capacity to imagine.

He was obsessed. He was driven. He was the King Without a Throne. This was the life that his God had ordained.

There were few viable passes through the Pillars of Heaven and Pillars of Ivory, from Shinsan to the broad plains between that double range and the Mountains of M'Hand, the latter forming the shield wall of the west. He dared not be seen in those high, tight, narrowly watched passages. He crossed the hard way, sometimes even avoiding the game trails favored by smugglers.

There came a day, though, when he relaxed in the shade of a giant cedar and congratulated himself on having crossed all of the Dread Empire without getting caught.

But... This was still territory Shinsan ruled. The epic must continue, with the going a little easier. Hazards would be fewer and less determined.

While resting he indulged in thoughts of his wife, his son, and possible futures.

He shut all that down and resumed moving. He could not relax till he reached Hammad al Nakir, and then never till he found Yasmid.

The instant he relaxed his vigilance would be his final moment of freedom.

He was certain that of all the lonely people in his world he was the loneliest. And the most significant. He was a linchpin of history. He would, if he survived, definitely shape tomorrow.

He did not just have a powerful will. He was not just driven. He had an obsessive sense of destiny.

He did, perhaps, overvalue himself. There were lonely operators out there who made his mortal moment look like a lone spark of a lightning bug in springtime. Of those Old Meddler was the foremost and oldest.

Haroun gave the Star Rider a lot of thought when he did not have survival on his mind.

...

"Is that Haroun?" Nepanthe asked.

"Yes. He's finally through the Pillars of Heaven."

"I thought he was dead."

Varthlokkur frowned. Was she having memory problems

again? "He was a prisoner in Lioantung. Caught trying to rescue Mocker." Her first husband, his son, now dead, slain in a failed attempt to murder Bragi Ragnarson.

Would this failure be permanent? Or would the memories return one more time? "He escaped in the confusion when the Deliverer came to Lioantung. He would've been home long since if we'd known that they had him."

"He went to rescue Mocker? All the way to Lioantung? Why?"

"He did. Because he was deceived by the Pracchia."

"That's so hard to believe." Nepanthe had loathed Haroun forever. His ambitions had had a brutal impact on her life. Haroun had pulled her first husband into one cruel saga after another. Again, "He went there to rescue Mocker?"

"Yes. Haroun bin Yousif is unique, darling. He abandoned his own dreams to save Bragi, too, because of a debt of honor." Nepanthe knew nothing about the horrors Varthlokkur had discovered. She would not learn. He would keep that to himself forever.

He did fear that Old Meddler might know and would not hesitate to spread the news if that would stir the pot of action and hatred.

The Empire Destroyer spent a lot of time pondering how best to misdirect or tame that ancient wickedness.

"But..."

"Dear heart, this shouldn't surprise you. These men have all done mad things on behalf of those they value. Michael Trebilcock and Aral Dantice twice trekked all the way to Argon to effect your rescue. Ragnarson risked an army to get you back. That nobility of purpose is who they are." But they could be mislead.

"All right. But... Varth, I don't remember things so good anymore."

True. Her twitchy memory left him impatient when she asked the same question over again. More frustrating was the fact that the problem was intermittent and unpredictable.

"You're helping him get back, aren't you?"

"Yes. Haroun may be the last hope of the west."

"What?"

"The Dread Empire is approaching the end of its terrible trials. The threat from the east has been eliminated. The talismanic focus of defiance in the west, Bragi Ragnarson, has been swept from the game board. The war with Matayanga is winding down. Matayanga has exhausted its resources and will. And, as always, Shinsan remains willing to fight for as long as it takes. Stability exists at the Imperial level. Mist has eliminated everyone willing to challenge her."

Nepanthe wondered about her sister-in-law's personal life. What did Mist intend for the children Valther had fathered?

Varthlokkur said, "If bin Yousif gets home in time, and reclaims his place, there'll be a strongman who can resist the next onslaught."

"Will you be involved if that happens?" Nepanthe's gaze was hard. She was unhappy with Varthlokkur these days, though she did not always remember why.

He had made choices, on her behalf, without consulting her. Neither those choices nor their results pleased her, when she did remember.

"I will play a part."

That offered a chance to carp. She let it go.

She wanted desperately to stop fighting about things that could not be changed. She wanted to make him do the right thing from now on.

...

The Lady Yasmid stood atop the wall of a fortress her father had built as a boy, on deciding to establish himself here at the place called Path of the Cross. War had not troubled Sebil el Selib after El Murid moved on to Al Rhemish. But time had seen him disestablished there. War was back.

War's aftermath was back.

The survivors of the conflict with Throyes and Shinsan had assembled below. The fighting had been unkind to them but they considered themselves the victors. The invaders had gone away.

Yasmid knew the truth. The enemy had gone because of a shift of political wind inside the Dread Empire. Bragi of Kavelin had penetrated the Roë Basin, forcing the enemy to realign his assets. Shinsan's Lord Hsung had been replaced by Tervola interested in concluding the wars Shinsan already had elsewhere.

But let the warriors believe. Let them be proud. Another enemy was coming. Her son, Megelin, was coming. That stupid boy, with Magden Norath skulking through the shadows, behind monsters sent to spread terror and destruction. Magden Norath, who was the maddest and possibly most powerful sorcerer in the west.

Megelin. Her son. The King of Hammad al Nakir.

What insane whim had driven Haroun to pass power to the boy? He had known that Megelin was unfit.

Three men shared Yasmid's vantage. The nearest, physically and emotionally, was old Habibullah, who had been her bodyguard when she was a child and was her closest conspirator as an adult. He had helped purge the Faithful of the worst lapses of her father and his fellow founders. Habibullah's clarity of vision had become the foundation of her rule. Without Habibullah, she feared, she would be lost.

A second man was an enigma.

Elwas bin Farout al-Souki was a self-made champion. His mother had been a prostitute in the foreign quarter of Souk el Arba, beyond the Jebal, on the coast of the Sea of Kotsüm. Elwas had risen from recruit to commander of ten thousand by acclamation of the men with whom he rode. He won battles and brought his followers home. That overrode all else with the war fighters.

Yasmid knew little about Elwas. His rise had occurred while she was elsewhere. He was a solid Believer. His coloring and shape said that his father was a black man. Other characteristics suggested that his mother had been a refugee from over the Sea of Kotsüm. Those things mattered little in the forest of swords. They did matter at court, where men of old families felt slighted if an outsider received honors.

Yasmid refused to be distracted by pettiness, nor did she tolerate it.

The third man, able to stand only with assistance, unable to communicate rationally, was El Murid, the Disciple, Yasmid's father, the salt trader's son whose calling had set the west awash in blood. Whose inspiration, invoked, could send thousands to the slaughter even now.

El Murid was old before his time. He was crippled. He was

partly blind. Incessant pain had led him to opiate addiction. He was so enslaved by the drug he could no longer be drawn into the real world long enough to generate a useful thought. He had no say anymore but remained a powerful symbol. He could be shown and men would gallop to their deaths screaming his name.

That the Disciple was in bad health was no secret. But his appearances were staged to leave fanatic rank and file convinced that their prophet could not be overcome by mundane evils.

The warriors looking on today had not yet recuperated from the Throyen campaign. They had not had enough time with their families. They were tired of war but war was not tired of them. They were pulling themselves together for one more campaign. If they did not, war would devour them and theirs.

The King, Megelin, son of Haroun, son of Yousif, would show his mother and grandfather no mercy. He would attack till he ended the long contest between Royalist and Believer.

Yasmid prayed that her son's followers were more war-weary than her own.

In an introspective moment she wondered how much responsibility for the state of the world lay with her family. Of late, every people, every nation, every kingdom seemed to be at war all the time, indulging in civil strife when no other war was available.

Warfare had been much less common before El Murid began to preach.

†

Chapter Three:

WINTER, 1017 AFE:

Scattered Views

Inger had schooled herself to be cruel when that was appropriate. Her attempt to produce a fierce face for her regime failed. Most supporters still thought she was too soft toward her opponents and too entangled in her husband's reforms.

Her enemies called her a tyrant determined to eradicate all the good that Bragi had done.

She had support amongst the Wessons, regionally. That largest ethnic group had liberated themselves from feudal concepts in place since the Nordmen imposed themselves as the ruling class.

The Siluro were almost extinct. They played no significant political role anymore. The Marena Dimura had abandoned the cities after Bragi went down. They ruled the forests and mountains and made themselves obnoxious by supporting Bragi II. Inger's advisors thought they would be nothing but a nuisance.

When it came to the day to day, only Wessons and Nordmen counted. Sadly, too many Wessons in the eastern and southern provinces allied their ambitions with those of the Marena Dimura. Only the Nordmen Estates and Inger's cousin backed Fulk. And the solidity of that might be more show than iron fact.

Rage seized Inger. This chaos existed only because one wild man had not been able to control his dick.

Heat filled Inger's cheeks. She reddened further, recalling a rumor that Bragi had found yet another lover when his lust for her cooled down. A brat barely old enough to bleed if the gossip was true. A girl younger than some of his children.

His dead children. The survivors were pre-adolescents. *If* they survived. Dane had tried to kill them.

Inger's conniving Greyfells blood considered starting a rumor that Bragi II had been sired by the King on his own son's wife. She laughed. There was no chance that was true but it was the sort of canard that spread from border to border overnight. If she could produce one believable witness…

"Josiah, I can't believe the ugly things I find inside my head."

Gales grunted, rolled over. Only his eyes shone from beneath the covers. It was freezing. Servants did not visit the Queen's bedchamber during the night.

He was not interested. He was being courteous because his lover was speaking. All he wanted was to sleep. But that was impermissible. He could not be here when morning brought Inger's dressers.

"Get up. You have to go."

Grumpily, groggily, Gales dragged himself out, got halfway dressed. A peck of a kiss and he was gone, sliding out via one of the hidden passages that worm-holed Castle Krief and had played so large a role in the stronghold's checkered history. Even the late Krief had not known them all.

Inger watched the panel shut, heard the catch click. She was not quite sure of Josiah. She did know he loved her. He had since she was a maid. But she was a Greyfells and the Greyfells reality consisted of layered schemes, schemes within schemes, and conspiracies so convoluted the conspirators themselves lost track of what they hoped to accomplish.

Josiah said he was working for her. But he told Dane the same thing. He told each of them that he was setting the other up. He admitted that Dane was no longer confident of his loyalty.

But she was in no position not to rely on Gales.

Josiah was her best hope for maintaining herself and Fulk.

Inger was not religious. Few of her people were. The Greyfells outlook was that God helped those who forced their way to the head of the line. But now she got down on her knees and prayed.

...

The Empress looked too young for the role. Her appearance did not deceive her associates. Her vanity was legendary. Her seventeen-seeming had aged only a year in centuries, though she had borne two children.

She was exhausted. She had not had a good night's sleep in months. Neither had anyone else amongst the soldiers and lords of the Dread Empire. Top to bottom, frontier to frontier, wars and scrambles for power had imposed intolerable stresses. Only the hardy remained.

Beautiful even in distress, Mist asked, "They want a truce?"

Lord Ssu-ma said, "They want to negotiate an armistice."

"That got lost in translation. Grant them twenty hours of peace. I'll pull rank and get some sleep. The rest of you should indulge yourselves, too."

Lord Ssu-ma said, "An indulgence I mean to urge on everyone, Illustrious. The Matayangans have no capacity to take advantage."

"Can we get up and moving again if we lie down?"

"In a limited fashion. Locally. After further rest."

After a lot of rest, Mist suspected. Even the most hardened veterans had reached their limits. That Matayanga had begun to collapse was due entirely to the stubborn warrior culture of the legions. Matayanga had spent every treasure, every sorcery, every soul, trying to swarm and swamp its enemies before Shinsan, already battered and distressed, could steel itself on that frontier.

"I'm quitting now," Mist murmured. She wanted to ask if she dared demand unconditional surrender. She wanted to ask if anyone had heard how her children were. She had not seen them in months. Most of all, she wanted to question the Tervola about the potential consequences of peace.

She did none of those things. She collapsed. Lord Ssu-ma Shih-ka'i, the pig farmer's son, placed her on a field cot.

...

Queen Inger's liaison with the commander of her bodyguards was a deep secret, yet there were those in the know. The far sorcerer Varthlokkur knew via the Unborn.

Another who knew was the invisible Michael Trebilcock. Michael had been out of sight so long he had been forgotten by most people. But he was not far away. People who knew him saw him all the time without recognizing him.

He appeared to have aged considerably.

...

In far Itaskia interested men within the War Ministry noted that most rumors about the Greyfells party were proving to be true. It was an excellent time to squeeze that clutch of troublemakers. That wicked, traitorous family appeared unable to withstand sustained financial and political pressure with Duke Dane off on a mad, expensive adventure.

...

The missing Guild General Machens Liakopulos, having gone unseen for months, came to the attention of outsiders while crossing a courtyard at High Crag, the mother fortress of the Mercenaries' Guild. He had just spoken to a council of the Guild's old men.

The witness who recognized him and cared enough to ask questions learned that the General had retired in one of the grand apartments that had come available when High Crag cleansed itself of the Pracchia disease.

The General felt badly about abandoning Kavelin but he felt no compulsion to sacrifice himself on the altar of kingdom worship that had claimed so many old companions. The King was dead. His dream died with him.

Wicked Inger could fry in her own drippings. Machens Liakopulos was old. He was tired. And he was done with ungrateful Kavelin.

...

One-time Lord Kuo Wen-chin was weary of exile but only exile let him enjoy any life at all. Once he had been overlord of all Shinsan. Those who had displaced him would eliminate him instantly should they learn that he lived. But the wishful heart will so often not attend the practical mind.

Kuo's world was a lifeless island off a desert coast far from civilization and farther still from the heart of his homeland. It was a storied island but most of its tales were ancient beyond recollection. Three living beings knew what part it played in the Nawami Crusades. A handful more had heard of the laboratories of Ehelebe. The most terrible horrors subsided into still darkness after a few millennia.

Kuo amused himself by learning what he could from his surroundings. But months fled. Learning became tedious.

He had moments when he cursed Lord Ssu-ma Shih-ka'i for having harkened to his appeal for sanctuary.

Kuo Wen-chin appreciated the honor his friend had done him. And Kuo was a patient man. But his patience was wearing.

He was too much alone. Food came unannounced and anonymously, arriving through a one-way portal. Nothing left the island.

Maybe Lord Ssu-ma had fallen fighting the Deliverer, or in the war with Matayanga. Or politics might have consumed him.

Yet someone kept sending supplies.

He shared the island with only one organism more complex than an insect or spider. Or the rare seabird that landed only perforce. Birds neither nested nor hunted here. They fled as soon as they had the power to go.

Wen-chin had found a crazy old man in a cell beneath the fortress that slithered along the spine of the island. The old man was little more than a ghost, physically and mentally.

Wen-chin found some purpose in nursing the ancient, who had suffered a mind-shattering trauma. He did not know who he was nor how he had come to be here, yet he had crystalline memories of things that had taken place thousands of years ago. He could describe forgotten storms of destruction in intimate detail, dropping the names of warlords and wizards whose empires and sorceries were less than an echo today.

The old man also had plenty to say about Old Meddler when Wen-chin questioned him patiently, and could shape his questions cleverly enough to elicit answers that made sense.

Wen-chin never realized who his companion must be. He did

conclude that the halfwit might be valuable. And mining the ancient's memories did pass the time.

...

The King of Hammad al Nakir, Megelin, son of Haroun, held his mount's reins. Dismounted, he stood atop a barren rise, stared across a brown waste, uphill, at el Aswad, the mighty eastern fortress, now abandoned. Beloul and the other old men who lived there when they were young called it the Fortress in Shadow because it had persisted defiantly in the shadow of the Disciple for years. El Aswad was where Megelin's father had been born. The family had countless ghosts up there.

Haroun bin Yousif first walked into the fires that forged the King Without a Throne there.

Megelin was neither bright nor sentimental but emotion did move him now. He had brought his army far out of its way so he could see his father's birthplace. Haroun had dedicated his being to destroying the insanity of a sun-stricken madman so audacious as to declare himself the mouth of God. A madman who became Megelin's grandfather.

The Royalists passed behind their King, headed north. Once the army reached Sebil el Selib it would exterminate the dregs of the madman's fanatics. And Megelin would destroy his surviving relatives.

Those who disdain history eat the same dirt twice.

The trace from el Aswad to Sebil el Selib passed through country where salty lakes had lain in Imperial times. Today those were white pans sprawled at the feet of mountains where the marks of ancient shorelines could still be discerned. Most of the flats were white as swaths of linen. One, though, had discolorations flecking its face. Rust stains. No one in this army had seen the pan before. Rains, though rare, and wind had disguised the evidence of disaster.

That place was hot despite the season. The air was unpleasant. Dust stirred by the horses burned noses and throats. Megelin had a presentiment that the place was more portentous than it appeared.

Maybe he heard the screams of the ghosts.

The animals sensed more than the men. They were reluctant to go on.

The warriors of the Disciple materialized on the far side of the flat. They advanced slowly on a broad front. Their mockeries crossed the salt as though borne by the devils of the air. They numbered half as many as the Royalists men but their confidence was immense. God was at their back.

The King's warriors needed no urging to go punish those fools.

When Megelin's father was a boy still awaiting his first whisker another Royalist army had faced another force of Believers across this same white sheet. Those Royalists had been devoured.

These Royalists reached that part of the lake where there was brine under the salt crust. Through they fell, struggling to avoid drowning and being turned into human pickles. Riders kept piling into the trap from behind. Even Magden Norath's monsters died in the heavy brine.

Times had changed. At the height of the Pracchia menace the only way to deal with Norath's creatures had been to bury them alive in concrete. They had been possessed of a vitality that could not be defeated by weapons or sorcery.

But those beasts had been unable to stand daylight. These, though terrible enough, had given up much to endure under the eye of the sun.

In the earlier battle Royalist forces had pressed forward, taking the fight to the Faithful. This time they had no Guild infantry to stiffen their line. This time the fight lasted half as long.

Modern results matched the historical except that no ambushes had been set to further humiliate those who fled.

Only Varthlokkur, watching from Fangdred, fully appreciated what Elwas al-Souki had accomplished. Magden Norath saw only the destruction of his children, who could not be replaced. His laboratories were gone.

For survivors on both sides the results were sufficient. There had been a winner, there had been a loser, and the loser had suffered badly. The loser would go away but the Faithful would take back nothing they had lost before. Both sides would hang up their swords for a while. Forever, if Yasmid could get her son to listen.

...

One creature somewhere would be frustrated. Wars everywhere were winding down.

He would not be seen much, though, if he understood that a lot of people were thinking about him. His great strength, over the ages, had been that people did not take notice. But that was changing.

His hand had been too heavy lately.

...

The Royalist survivors scurried back to Al Rhemish. They wasted a winter on recriminations. The old men, left behind when the "final campaign" launched, said much less than those who had ridden the salt. They had no need to say, "I told you so."

Was there a chance they would be consulted next time Megelin had a wild hair?

Probably not.

...

Credence Abaca summoned Kristen. The order was couched as a gracious request but the mother of the king-who-would-be knew she had no choice. While she and her friends, and the children, were guests of the Marena Dimura they were beholden and at the mercy of the forest people. They dared not put on airs. The Marena Dimura might just stop filling the extra mouths. And this would be a hard winter.

All winters were harsh after dislocations during the benign seasons.

Kristen did not go alone. That would not have been proper. Dahl Haas joined her trek through the cold forest. He entered the Colonel's family cabin behind her. He was not allowed near the war chief but neither was he deprived of his weapons. He waited where he could see Kristen all the time. He was made comfortable.

Credence Abaca was a small, dark man, famous for his vitality and energy. These days, though, he was bent and wrinkled. He had a palsy in his left hand. Not good. He was left-handed.

"Sit with me," Abaca said. His voice had changed subtly, too, and he had difficulty seating himself.

"Thank you, Colonel. You've had news?"

"News?" Puzzled. "No. No news."

"Yet you asked me here."

"Yes. Pardon me in advance if, on occasion, I become a little brusque. You will understand why as we proceed."

Abaca's tone worried Kristen.

"There *is* news, good and bad, but not of the sort you meant. From my point of view, our partisans have enjoyed considerable success against the Itaskians, who have gone to ground in Damhorst. They have to stick together in groups of a dozen or more. Also, the Nordmen who allied themselves with the Itaskians are starting to reconsider. Greyfells seems unlikely to receive outside reinforcements."

"That means we've won!"

"No, Kristen. It means we may be able to rid Kavelin of the Itaskians, in time. But Inger has distanced herself from her cousin already. She retains the loyalty of the strongest regiments. We have an unofficial truce with them, for now. They don't want to fight us. We don't want to fight them. We stood shoulder to shoulder on the same battlefields too many times." He stopped. His left hand shook badly.

Kristen said, "I hear a big 'But!' Is that the bad news?"

"After a fashion."

Kristen strove hard to remain respectfully patient.

"Kristen, I am the glue that holds your support together. I am, in fact, guilty of pulling you into my politics so I could put an acceptable figurehead out in front of my ambitions for my people."

Kristen nodded, surprised by his bald honesty.

"I may have done you a severe disservice."

"How so?"

Abaca was quiet for a time. His daughter brought tea that must have cost the tribesmen dear. Abaca Enigara was young and unattractive even by the standards of her own people. She seemed downright grim.

Abaca finally said, "The monster Radeachar was seen again three nights ago. Scouts report the Hastin Defile blocked by snow."

"That's weird. That's the third time this winter."

"It does happen. Once in a winter, one year out of ten. We haven't gotten unusual amounts of snow."

"Meaning?"

"Meaning I've been slow catching on. But I get it, now. Varthlokkur doesn't want us raiding in the vicinity of Vorgreberg."

"He's taking Inger's side?"

"No. He's keeping me from doing something desperate."

"Why would you?"

"Because I'm dying. Because I want so badly to see things settled before I go. Because I am the glue."

Kristen did not argue. Neither did she spout upbeat nonsense. This was grim news. "I see."

"Again, I apologize for dragging you in when I couldn't keep my promises. I wouldn't have done it had I known then what I know now."

"I do have to ask if you're sure."

"I am. This is in the blood. I deceived myself in thinking that it wouldn't get me, I suppose. Putting a shine on it, I can say that I've gotten four years more than my father did."

"Oh."

"So what shall we do, girl? You don't have to tell me now but you'll need to decide within ten days. I'll beat back the darkness as long as I can but that won't be long. And once I go, everything else comes apart."

Because he was the glue. And there was no one to replace him.

"Credence, there may be a positive possibility yet."

"I could use one. Please explain."

"The interest shown by the sorcerer."

"You think he knows about my problem?"

Had he not said so himself? "Nothing escapes him."

"Perhaps."

"As you say, you are the glue. Attract his attention. Show him that you know he's interfering. He might make contact. Then you can get his views on what you should be doing."

Abaca's face darkened.

"I don't mean ask him to give orders. Find out what's going on in the rest of the world. He knows more than you do. There might be a powerful strategic reason for avoiding hostilities. Maybe Inger's regiments have begun to have a change of heart."

Abaca grunted. "I'll think about that. You think about what's best for you and yours. We can still get you out of the country and back into hiding."

Kristen and Dahl made the slow walk to their own cabin. Dahl asked no questions while they were in the open.

...

The fugitive spent four days looking for a way to cross the Roë River without being noticed. There were no bridges this far south.

Something dramatic had happened upstream. The water was high, filthier than usual, clotted with debris and the occasional rotting carcass with feeding birds aboard. The current was not swift but it was there. The flood was too wide to swim and dangerous in more than the obvious ways. There was a shark in the Sea of Kotsüm that did not mind the absence of salt in the river.

A boat was his only option. That was a problem. There was little westbound traffic. That was all military. He did not feel daring enough to ferry over with Shinsan's couriers.

Hiring a rowboat might work. But with the river in flood no boatman would hazard a night crossing. He would be sighted by day. Someone would ask questions.

He could kill the oarsman on the other side but that would cause excitement, too.

He went back to the swimming option. Suppose he made a float, then crossed on a clear night, steering by the stars?

No. Sharks or no sharks, that was begging for disaster.

Almost despairing, he decided to take the long way. That might take weeks but he was not pressed for time. No one was waiting. He had been dead for a long time.

He headed north.

Eventually there would be a city. It would boast a bridge. There would be traffic and confusion. A foreigner would not be unusual. He could hire on with a caravan. And he could enjoy some real food for a change.

His fourth day headed north, working back eastward in search of a ford across a small tributary, he stumbled onto a coracle hidden in the undergrowth. There was no one around. The coracle was neither booby-trapped nor cursed. It was just a tool belonging to someone with a penchant for going unnoticed. A gift from God.

...

Nepanthe stepped back from behind Varthlokkur's right shoulder. "That was cleverly done."

"I thought so myself."

"I'm going to go bake sweet cakes for the kids."

The wizard grunted. "You do that." He wondered how indifferent a mother Mist could be. She had not yet, insofar as he could tell, made the least effort to find her children or to determine their welfare.

It was possible, of course, that she knew they were with their aunt and were, therefore, already as safe as they could be in this dark world.

†

Chapter Four:

1017 AFE:

Dread Realm

The Empress and two bodyguards left portals in the transfer staging chamber of a tower once owned by the Karkha family of Throyes. The duty section had received a warning only minutes earlier. Men were still scurrying around, trying to make the place more presentable. Officer in Charge, Candidate Lein She, was still fumbling with his laces. He had had no time to don his mask.

Mist's bodyguards made their disapproval obvious.

Mist had no such sentiments. It was unreasonable to expect the tower and garrison to be drill ground perfect at short notice.

She conversed briefly with a portal attendant while the Candidate pulled himself together. "No visitors? Not even a random attempt to come through, or to make contact?" She examined the transfer log. Only Lord Ssu-ma Shih-ka'i had visited since the tower became the place where special prisoners were held.

The Karkha no longer existed. Their tower, which rose without outer defenses, could be accessed only by a ladder that had to be lowered from a doorway two stories above the street. It was invulnerable to the normal city threats: riots, jealous rivals, and local politics. It was not designed to withstand military operations.

Lein She had himself together. The Empress said, "Good evening, Candidate. Your logs appear to be in order."

"Thank you, O Celestial."

Mist was taken aback. Was he making mock? No one had used that title since her father and his twin, the Princes Thaumaturge, had overcome their father. Celestial had been one of Tuan Hoa's many titles.

"I'm not my grandfather, Candidate. Relax. I'm just here to see the prisoner."

"Uh… Which one… Great One?"

"You're holding more than one?"

"Seven. All politicals."

"The westerner."

"This way. I'll have refreshments brought."

She ignored a temptation to be malicious. "Tea and rice cakes. Then show these two to the kitchen. Feed them lots of meat."

Legionary discipline triumphed all round. No one questioned her decision to see the prisoner alone. But, then, no one thought the Empress might need help.

...

Ragnarson believed he understood the caged tiger's mood. In the main, it would be rage.

It had been a while since he had been installed here, wherever here might be. He had fallen asleep in a place where they had healed his war wounds. He had awakened here with no sense of time having passed. The few keepers he saw were strangers uninterested in chatting.

He was not uncomfortable. His cell was an oval room thirty feet on its long axis, twenty on that with the one flattened side. There were three tiny windows. Each overlooked an unfamiliar city. The windows faced north, south, and east. There was no window in the flat west wall. Each window boasted thin bars and a vigorous sorcery that kept out all odor and noise. He thought he was about eighty feet above street level in an area that was sealed off.

Only once had he seen anyone down there, and that had been one of the Tervola.

The room was furnished sparsely but not cheaply. He had a bed, large and comfortable. He had a table for eating, chairs, several quality rugs, and another table where he could sit and read or write. That came equipped with several books, a stock of pens, paper, and ink in three colors. His captors allowed him a penknife.

There was a luxury garderobe. The waste went away when staff removed dirty dishes and cutlery. Meals were regular and adequate.

There were pitchers and porcelain bowls at opposite ends of the room, with ladles. There was a metal tub that could be dragged out and, once a week, filled with warm water so he could bathe. A specialist servant would deal with fleas and lice. His captors had an aversion to parasites.

There was an area for dressing. He had a choice of apparel. Like dirty dishes, soiled clothing went away, then came back clean.

He could shave if he wanted. The tools were available.

Not a hard life. But he could not leave.

So mostly he paced, like the caged tiger, and he raged. Hour after hour, day after day, back and forth, paying little heed to his surroundings, fantasizing about what the world would suffer once he escaped.

Little thought went toward actually accomplishing that. That was work for the rational side of his mind. And the rational side had to operate in the realm of reality.

Rationally, it was obvious that there would be no leaving without outside contrivance.

Rationally, he could do nothing but wait.

The prisoner's routine was rigid. Food arrived at predictable times, virtually taunting him: construct an escape plan around this, fool! So when the door in the flat wall opened at an unorthodox hour Ragnarson was so surprised he actually retreated.

He gawked. He failed to recognize Mist for several seconds. She was radiantly gorgeous. He had not been near any woman for so long that his response was instantaneous and embarrassing.

Then his mind clicked.

Mist, aged in spirit but not in that timelessly beautiful flesh.

He arranged himself so as to conceal his arousal.

She smiled. "Hello. The war has eased up. I thought I'd see how you're doing."

Off guard, disturbed by his response, he was flustered. Neither fight nor flight were options.

"Bragi! It's me! Good gracious. You aren't very good at being a noble prisoner, are you?"

Her tone, the amusement edging her voice, dispelled the intellectual murk. "I got it made," he croaked. "Relatively speaking."

They could have shoved him down an oubliette and fed him spoiled pig manure for the rest of a very short life.

He drew no cheer from the thought.

He glared at the achingly beautiful woman.

"I'm beginning to think you're more than just a man, Bragi Ragnarson. You're maybe an elemental who is no longer sane and still headed downhill."

Ragnarson said nothing. He did not disagree.

A face came to mind. Sherilee. That sweet child, younger than his oldest boy. Their liaison, brief as it had been, had reminded him that he was still alive.

He shook like a dog fresh in from the rain. "I'm sane right now but it won't last."

"I'm pleased. You can't imagine how frustrating it is trying to communicate with someone who can't see that they're caught in reality's trap."

"You have me for now. It may not last. Something shook me off my foundations."

"We weren't responsible."

He got no sense that she was lying.

She said, "I came for several reasons. First, to see how you're doing. We were friends. You helped me."

He kept his expression neutral.

"I tried to support you, too. I failed. Then you put yourself into a position where this was the best I could do."

He thought this was more the work of Lord Ssu-ma Shih-ka'i.

"Cynical response noted."

Ragnarson betrayed a smile.

"I've brought news from home. Which is hard to come by, these days."

"I've known you a long time…"

She stopped him. She knew he never believed much that she

said. "It would be more kind to leave you ignorant. The heart I found while I was in exile disagrees."

Ragnarson focused. Time to be careful. The Empress of Shinsan was going to give him something because she wanted something. "Do tell."

"Last month your grandson Bragi seemed certain to become king of Kavelin, instead of Fulk. It was just a matter of time. The Itaskians were being neutralized. Inger was losing support fast. The Nordmen were distancing themselves from her and Greyfells. Your cronies were dead or fled, but that wasn't hampering Kristen."

"But?" That required no genius to see.

"Credence Abaca died. And everything began to fall apart."

Ragnarson resumed pacing. "Abaca died? Really?"

"He'd been ill for some time, apparently. Once he went the tribes had no recognized chief of chiefs. With them out of it Kristen's Wessons began to waver. There have been massive desertions. The men who haven't yet left the regiments have no good reason to stay. They aren't getting paid. They don't want Inger but Kristen fled the kingdom once she no longer had the Marena Dimura to protect her. Kavelin seems ready to fall apart."

It looked like Shinsan had a fine opportunity—that Mist evidently did not view in that light.

Why give her ideas? She had plenty of her own. And Kavelin's torment was his fault.

"I'm sorry. It's a sad thing I caused. Aren't there appropriate sayings about hubris?"

"In almost every language. It's a popular pastime, small men criticizing the stumbles of giants."

Ragnarson glanced out the nearest window. It would be time to eat, soon. What would it be? Outguessing the cooks was a favorite exercise.

Derel Prataxis said men grew introspective with age. Ragnarson had tried it. He could not get interested in his own interior landscape, nor could he make himself care.

Mist broke the protracted silence. "You have no response?"

"Should I? It's sad. My fault. I said that. It is what it is. I can't do anything about it. Or is that why I'm honored with your presence?"

"In a sense. It was."

"Sense me the sense, woman!"

"Don't make me hurt you, old friend." To remind him who was the guest.

"Sorry." But he was not, and that was obvious.

"I hoped confinement would erode that attitude. That given time you would find your way back to the Bragi Ragnarson who won friends easily and inspired people. But he seems to have gone missing permanently."

He did not respond. But he did pace.

"You haven't tried to figure out how you came to this?"

"No figuring needed. I got too big for my britches, then I guessed wrong. My luck ran out."

"So you've spent all this time, with no other demands on you, doing what? Pacing and being angry?"

The appalled way she said that tickled him. "Pretty much."

"You *are* an animal."

That did not please him. She seemed contemptuous now.

"I was considering sending you back but the Bragi Ragnarson I see here looks no better than Dane of Greyfells, or take your pick of Nordmen." She headed for the door, muttering, "How did he get from that to this in a year?"

...

That same night witnessed an event the tower's denizens considered impossible. There was an attack. It was a complete surprise.

The raiders put a ladder up to the tower door. They broke through, spread out, and started killing. They would have succeeded completely had the Empress not been there, stealing a night's rest.

It was a close thing, still. Mist lost her bodyguards. Two of the kitchen crew survived only by hiding in the larder. Lein She made it, too, but was wounded badly defending the transfer chamber.

He apologized for the disaster. "I should have anticipated an effort to free the prisoners."

The Empress touched the Candidate gently. "The fault was mine, Lein She. How many escaped?"

"I don't know." He went to sleep.

Mist studied her fingertips. Lein She might never waken if she could not summon a healing specialist. The portals were down.

She had not taken stock of the full tragedy yet. There had been damage to the transfer portals despite Lein's heroic stand. That may have been the thrust of the attack.

Nine attackers had died trying to ruin them.

The raid seemed too sophisticated for local malcontents.

Her mind made a grand leap. Somewhere amongst the Tervola was a man who wanted to bring her down.

Phsaw! Of course there was. But no Tervola would recruit, arm, and inform a band of guerrillas. It would be beneath his dignity. Nor would any Tervola believe that cat's-paws like these stood a chance against her.

Again, she was not supposed to have been here. The attack must have had another point.

She bullied the surviving staff into securing the tower, starting with the ladder and door. A census of prisoners followed.

There had been no escapes. Evidently, liberation had not been the intent. Three prisoners were dead. Another prisoner had been mauled. Three remained undisturbed, including Ragnarson, who had remained unaware of the attack.

Mist focused on the transfer chamber.

Her paranoia did not fade because she was occupied. She considered the possibility that Varthlokkur was behind the assault.

Unlikely, though. Varthlokkur would be direct. He would send his familiar monster.

The raiders had had a close knowledge of the inside of the tower but had lacked real-time intelligence. They had not been ready for her.

She moved to the door of the staging chamber. "Bring the dead raiders to me here! Without damaging them!"

None had gotten away and none had been taken alive. But the dead had not been dead for long. Some could still bear witness.

First, though, she had to make contact with her headquarters.

...

Ragnarson heard a click. He faced the door, uneasy. Neither breakfast nor lunch had come. Mist must be messing with him.

The Empress came in carrying a tray. He stifled a rude remark. She did not look healthy. "Are you all right?"

"No. I just spent three hours talking to the dead."

"What happened?" That she was still here and bringing him food told him it was something bad.

"Persons as yet unidentified may be aware of your survival."

"What?" Was she frazzled enough to give something away?

"There was an attack on the tower. By local people. Those I could make talk hoped news that our portals were out would encourage a general uprising. But there were hints that they wanted to free the prisoners held here, too. They expected to suffer heavy casualties. Someone here must have been worth it."

"Me?"

"Maybe. There were other prisoners. Some of those got killed."

"You didn't take any of the raiders alive." Which explained her remark about talking to the dead.

"No. And I didn't get to the dead fast enough to squeeze out everything I wanted. But I can't help thinking some clever soul with a different agenda conned some malcontents. I don't *know* that. It's intuition. Maybe somebody wanted to get you out."

Michael Trebilcock?

He did not say the name. But no one else they knew had the connections. Or the gall.

"Trebilcock does seem plausible," she said. "Or maybe just someone who enjoys a good framing."

"Old Meddler? Why would he sink to that low a level?"

"For the drama?"

"With all the grand drama in this world, he wants to stir up skirmishes?"

"The drama is fading. The war with Matayanga is guttering. I intend to avoid war afterward. It will take Shinsan a generation or two to recover. The Tervola see that. Whatever their feelings toward me, they want to nurture the Empire first. Even dedicated old troublemakers want a healing time."

"So you're getting comfortable."

"Never while I'm a woman trying to control cruel men awed by nothing but superior power. My point is, Shinsan is headed for a time of peace. The whole world is exhausted. There was a battle in

Hammad al Nakir recently. Yasmid routed Megelin. She could not follow up. Magden Norath is in Al Rhemish. He could become a tool of the Meddler again. Kavelin is chaotic and getting more so. If the Meddler was behind the raid here his intent might have been to inject you into that chaos to see the fur and blood fly."

"You said you were thinking that way yourself."

"I was. Because of my fondness for you and my fondness for Kavelin, which was my home for so long. And because it would be useful to me, as Empress, to have a stable, reliable, friendly monarch there."

"You walked out."

"I did. You're no longer the Bragi Ragnarson who built Kavelin. You wouldn't go back and make things right. You would work the Meddler's mischief."

Ragnarson started pacing. He said nothing. He did not trust himself to control his rage.

"As you will." Mist moved to the exit. "Do try to use this time more fruitfully. This has to be a life sentence only if you insist."

Ragnarson's lips pulled back in a snarl.

...

Nepanthe, with Smyrena in her lap, leaned against her husband. "Why is Bragi that way?" The baby cooed and kicked. "What happened to him?"

Varthlokkur knew a broader question was being asked. Identical stubbornness, on his part, had caused the breach with Ragnarson. That rift underlay all the evil that had befallen Kavelin since. "'And the Wicked flee where none do pursue.'"

"What?"

"A not quite apposite quotation from a forgotten book. As to the question, I don't know why Bragi changed. There's always a temptation to think such shifts are sparked externally."

"Somebody cast a spell."

"Possibly. But it's also possible that massive bad cess just twisted his mind."

Smyrena needed burping. Nepanthe moved the infant to her shoulder. She gave Varthlokkur a hard look as she did.

He said, "When you're the one behaving badly you blame

outside forces. Unless you're emotionally invested in being too strong-willed to be influenced."

"You'd then have an adventure justifying yourself."

"You would." The wizard leaned in for a better view of what Ragnarson would do now that he was alone.

Nepanthe said, "Ethrian had a good day. I think he's starting to get better."

"Excellent. Excellent."

"I wish we could resurrect that Sahmaman. He really loved her."

"I'm sure he did. Her behavior showed that she loved him, too. But we can't ignore one iron truth. The real Sahmaman died thousands of years ago. We saw a memory given flesh by godlike power."

"I know. I'm wishful-thinking. I just want Ethrian to heal."

"I understand." The wizard would not dismay her by saying that the boy would never escape his raging insanity.

†

Chapter Five:

YEAR 1017 AFE:

Spring Threatening

The Queen's liaison with the commander of her bodyguard was an open secret. Everyone inside Castle Krief knew. Everyone gossiped and almost everyone pretended complete ignorance to outsiders. Unaware, Inger and Josiah Gales kept going through the motions of a strictly professional relationship.

Inger asked, "Is it time for Dane?"

Gales, never entirely committed to anyone, said, "He could give up and go home. Family interests have suffered. Money is running short. Desertions and ambushes have his force down to three hundred."

"I admire your desire to keep faith with Dane. He doesn't deserve you. Tell his soldiers they could come here. I'd like more Itaskians around me."

...

Dane of Greyfells was not well. He was pallid in the extreme. Any movement caused pain. Gales had been cautioned against taking notice. He expressed strong gratitude when offered a chair beside the Duke, in front of the fire.

"This is so much better than Castle Krief. Inger won't waste fuel on heating." Countless economies were under way. The Crown had a very limited income.

"What news, Josiah? Is there any hope? If not, I should cut my losses. Go home with my tail tucked, to jeers and mockery. I cast the dice but they didn't love me."

"Lord, they don't love anyone here. Kavelin keeps right on heading downhill, taking everyone with it."

"So it seems. Answer my question. Any hope?"

"She asked me to poll the soldiers to see if any would come work for her. Her Wessons are walking away, mainly because she can't pay them. Her Nordmen become less supportive by the day, too. She'll have lost all support outside Vorgreberg soon. Each town, each village, each lord, and each guild that deserts reduces her income further."

"So the enterprise is doomed from both directions. And still she won't let me in."

"She remains adamant, My Lord. She will not trust you."

Greyfells remained quiet. His frame went rigid momentarily. Recovering, he asked, "Why, Josiah?" His voice had gone plaintive.

"She has a touch of the illness that ruled Ragnarson, the Krief, and Fiana. She fears what you will do to Kavelin if you get control."

Greyfells tittered, startling Gales. His normal laugh was an all-out, full-bodied roar. Now the Duke ended up wracked by deep, sobbing coughs. Gales feared for the man's life, briefly.

"Sorry you had to see that, Josiah. No. Never mind. I'll be all right. I've survived all this before. Go ahead. Poll the men. Tell them I'll let them go if that's what they want. Might as well let her not pay them as not pay them myself." He contrived a small, controlled laugh. "Take her an honest answer."

...

"About eighty men are willing to come over, Highness," Gales reported.

"That's all?"

"Some wouldn't give a straight answer. They thought the Duke was testing them. Others said that since they wouldn't get paid either place they'd as soon stay put and save the walk. Most everyone said they intend to head home after the weather turns and the rivers go down."

"And you told Dane what?"

"I answered the questions he asked. I volunteered nothing."

"What will he do?"

"He talked about doing the same as his soldiers. About cutting his losses and heading home."

"But?"

"He will, likely, make one more try, doing what you expected. He'll come in disguise with soldiers who want to switch allegiance. They'll actually be men willing to stick with him."

"I see. Will he expect me to expect him?"

"I couldn't say. My mind can't encompass so much complexity."

Later, Inger asked, "Did you see Babeltausque out there?"

"No. Why?"

"He's been keeping his head down. That's curious. He could be useful here. He might be able to find my missing treasury."

"He's the Duke's man."

"You think he wants to be? I don't. He's been with the family through several Dukes, each one worse than the last. I can see him being loyal to the family but having an abiding distaste for its heads."

"I'll talk to him."

...

Kristen's flight from Kavelin took seven weeks. The Royal party crept from one Aral Dantice acquaintance to another, often enduring cold nights in the forest between times of warmth and decent food. Dantice was determined to proceed with caution, concealing the identities of his companions.

Kristen considered his precautions a waste. The party was too big and too burdened with women and children to be anything but what it was. But she was seeing it from the inside.

Dantice told her, "Only folks I trust with my life see you. I tell them nothing because they might be questioned someday."

"Where are we headed?"

"A safe place. If I don't talk about it no one will hear about it."

"Aral, I appreciate everything. You've gone way out of your way.

You've practically given up your regular life. I don't understand why."

Dantice avoided a straight answer. "The travel will be over soon. So will the cold and the hunger. You'll be safe. No one will know where you are. You'll be ready when Kavelin is ready."

"What about my father-in-law? What about the true king?"

"He still lives. We know that. We also know they've stashed him where he won't be able to escape."

Kristen noted his "we" but did not question it. Aral Dantice was much too useful to be challenged.

He said, "This shouldn't last long. Kavelin should be eager to proclaim Bragi by next fall. By then even the Marena Dimura and Nordmen should be sick of the chaos."

"All right. We're in your hands. Be gentle."

The party reached an encampment deep in the mountains of southern Tamerice. It differed little from the one where Credence Abaca died. This one was not Marena Dimura, though. The forest people were scarce in Tamerice. The camp had been created by Royalist refugees from Hammad al Nakir as a base for raids across the Kapenrungs. Refugees had gathered there during the Great Eastern Wars.

Dantice told her, "You and the children should stay out of sight if strangers turn up. Let Dahl and Sherilee deal with them."

Kristen thought Sherilee would attract any man who came within a mile.

Aral said, "I'll give you letters saying you belong here and are under my protection."

...

"Aral is gone," Sherilee said. The suffering of the journey had wakened her resilience. She was now the optimist of the band. "Next time we see him he'll tell us it's time to head home to Vorgreberg."

"I hope so," Dahl said. "I wasn't made for this life."

Kristen snapped, "No one is. It's a life that comes looking for you."

Sherilee said, "This is a nice place. It must have belonged to one of the high muckety mucks."

The structure, partially log, partially stone, was large and had potential for being made comfortable. There were stores in the camp, tools, and even weapons. Dahl said, "Let's don't touch anything we don't need to. We don't want any smugglers upset because we got into their stuff."

"Smugglers?"

"Smugglers. It's what Aral does. Remember? This is a way station on the route into the desert. We'll see plenty of travelers once the weather gets better."

"Then we'd better get the kids educated about what to do when strangers come."

That proved to be no problem. The first travelers were not inclined to socialize, either. Some never showed their faces.

That was both a comfort and discouraging. No discourse meant no news from outside.

...

There had been innumerable dislocations in city life the past ten years. No Vorgreberger knew all his neighbors anymore. The situation suited spies and criminals and anyone else who wanted to go unnoticed.

Espionage was a thriving industry. Crime was less lucrative, other than for smugglers. Smuggling was just commerce where the Crown failed to extort any taxes. Gang crime had fallen on hard times. Some invisible force saved the body politic the added friction.

Dark tales circulated in the underworld. They insisted that dire forces were at work. *Things* came in the night to collect those who preyed on their fellows.

It was true: evil men did disappear.

Crimes of passion remained common. What could be done to curb those?

There was an apothecary shop in Old Registry Lane. It had been there for decades. An elderly fellow had run it till recently. He had been a permanent grouch. When his son took over people noted that the younger chemist was less cranky.

He was about fifty. He may have been a soldier once. He had a bad right knee. He dragged that leg sometimes. He was slow with his customers but was tolerated because he dispensed good advice. He would help those who could not afford a physician. He was more of a talker and gossip and was curious about everything.

His most popular foible was that he sometimes extended credit.

Some said he was the official apothecary to the palace, provided old Wachtel with the specifics he used to keep the Royals hale and hearty—whoever they might be this year.

The popular jest was, Castle Krief had been built around Dr. Wachtel. The ancient physician was a national hero.

The apothecary would not discuss the connection. The favor of the doctor might be charity. A story that gained traction supposed that the chemist was Wachtel's son by a married patient.

No one really cared. The apothecary was not colorful. He was just there.

Strangers visited frequently. They brought medicinal ingredients from far places or wanted concoctions crafted for some distant consumer. None of this attracted any but the most minor notice. It was unremarkable.

...

"I think it's time," Queen Inger told Colonel Gales.

Gales blanched.

"I'm sorry, Josiah. I no longer have a choice. So I insist that you make one of your own."

"Your Majesty?"

"You know. You see the reports. You can add two and two. I won't be able to hold on here without Dane's men. In two months they'll be the only real soldiers left."

The old regiments were dissolving. Whom they had supported before no longer mattered. Kristen had vanished, the gods knew where. The intelligence system was falling apart faster than the army.

Inger continued, "Kristen's friends can't pay soldiers, either. And I won't be able to pay the palace staff much longer."

"I understand." He had seen the estimates. The Queen's friends had stopped making donatives.

"Before long Dane will be able to ride in and take it all, Josiah. I won't be able to stop him. I need to make a move or kiss it all goodbye."

"You could reconcile with your cousin."

"No."

For Dane of Greyfells reconciliation would mean him taking over.

Gales slumped. She was right.

"Josiah, I won't let Fulk become my cousin's puppet."

"Yes, Majesty."

"Any men willing should come now. Admit that I can't pay them right away but that they will eat well." Unlike her native soldiers, the Itaskians did not have families to support. "And I want Babeltausque."

"As you wish." Gales did not doubt that the sorcerer would come. Greyfells would insist.

His moment of choice was, indeed, approaching. It had been inevitable for some time. He could no longer delay the reckoning. Each pole of his loyalty expected him to betray the other. Neither really trusted him. He saw no way to avoid making an enemy. Neither would the friendship of either be enduring.

He ought to desert them both. Let the snakes devour each other.

He could not do that.

His betrayal, however he bestowed it, would not define the future. Neither would rule in Castle Krief by the end of the year.

Gales believed Kavelin's northern neighbors could not resist temptation, however much they had suffered themselves during the Great Eastern Wars.

The horrors had begun to be forgotten the way a woman forgets childbirth's pain.

Josiah Gales had mentioned the threat to Inger and the Duke. Neither wanted to listen.

"I have chores, Majesty, and things to do if I'm going to travel." He was sick of travel. He wished he knew some other way of life. "I'll be back tonight."

"I want you on the road to Damhorst tomorrow."

Gales sighed. "As you command."

Gales was a frugal man. He had been paid well back when soldiers received regular pay. He decided to spend some of his savings getting drunk.

...

The warlords of Anstokin and Volstokin were less tempted than Colonel Gales feared. Both kings did feel the urge. Kavelin lay sprawled like a naked virgin tied to a mattress of silver. But lurking in the shadows above those splayed enticements was a hideous guardian, a monstrous infant inside a transparent pinkish magical excuse for a placenta. A horror renowned for its evil deeds during the Great Eastern Wars.

The Unborn turned up whenever either king's fantasies progressed to the assembling of troops. It needed do no more, so far.

Manifestation of the Unborn was not just a promise of terror. It was a clear announcement that a greater horror still had an interest.

Thus was peace assured amongst the bellicose Lesser Kingdoms. And the absence of war inflicted prosperity.

...

Josiah Gales was out of practice with ardent spirits. Handling large quantities was not a skill much admired in senior military men. Wine with dinner, small beer with breakfast, the occasional brandywine of an evening whilst relaxing with his fellows, those were his norms. Some children imbibed more in a day. His most recent falling-down-sick romance with alcohol happened the day they buried Dane's assassinated granduncle.

People connected to Kavelin had been involved somehow.

Gales was not sure why he ended up at the Twisted Wrench. Probably because the place was a haunt for garrison troops off duty. Even if he was recognized his presence ought not to be resented.

He staked out a shadowy corner and brushed off those who tried to socialize. By not talking he would not betray his accent. Without thinking about it, though, he slipped into a character he once played undercover.

He became the quirky Sergeant Gales. That meant a shift in the set of his shoulders, in the way he held his head, a more expansive set of gestures even while being sullenly unsocial, and a lower class accent when he did have to speak.

The tavern never became crowded. The owner longed for the time when Bragi was king and there were soldiers everywhere.

There was a lot of nostalgia in the Twisted Wrench. And a lot of resentment, too.

Inger had gotten her chance. She had wasted it.

The blame was not all hers, though. The other Itaskian gang enjoyed a fouler reputation. Some folks, in fact, believed the Queen would have done a decent job if her cousin had not been undercutting.

Kristen executed a brilliant strategic maneuver by sliding out of the light when she did. She had taken no blame, only sympathy, with her. The death of Credence Abaca, which had thrilled Inger so back when, now looked like a curse. It, too, conspired to make those still visible look bad.

The Marena Dimura were no longer in a state of insurrection. They had become invisible. They could not now be blamed for all the ills of the kingdom.

Gales was well up the early slope of alcohol consumption. He was pleased to be learning so much. It might be too late to use the information to any advantage but he now had his finger on the pulse of the kingdom.

He should have made expeditions like this before. The knowledge could have kept Inger in much better odor.

It had not occurred to anyone to care what ordinary people thought. Their attitudes did not matter in Itaskia. But this was Kavelin. The monarchs here had been listening for decades. Inger might have, too. She had a mild case of the Kavelin fever.

Josiah Gales had a slight case of that disease himself. He signaled for a refill, then began to brood on that.

Then he began to worry about the time. He should have been back by now. Inger would give him bloody hell when he turned up drunk.

And now he could not leave.

Men he knew had come and gone, none paying him any heed because he timed his piss runs to avoid being noticed. The strategy had worked till an entire squad of archers stumbled in. The Wrench was not their first stop of the evening. Gales wondered how they could afford so much drink. Their pay was in arrears.

The archers settled where Gales would have to pass on his way to the jakes. And they would not move on.

The ache in the Colonel's bladder reached a point where he had to make a decision. He chose to piss on the floor, sitting where he was, not a choice he would have made when sober.

He got urine all over himself. What made it to the floor drained through gaps in the floorboards. The odor did not stand out amongst the other stinks of the Wrench.

Then a shaggy mass of a man materialized. He headed a trio of thoroughly drenched gentlemen. In fluent drunkenese, he bellowed, "Holy fuckin' shit! Will ya lookit! Sarge Gales, you ole cocksucker! How da fuck are you? Hey! You look like shit, man. You been eatin' right? You got pushed out too, huh? Guess you're lookin' good enough for dat. Hey! Tell dese jack-offs 'bout dat time. You know. Durin' da El Murid Wars when you got off a dat ship in Hellin Daimiel or wherever da fuck. Wit' all da women. You guys gotta hear dis. Funniest fuckin' story I ever heard."

Gales began to shake. He did not recognize the man blasting dense wine breath into his face. The story he wanted had been the signature bullshit story that Sergeant Gales of the Queen's own bodyguard had retailed back in the day.

"Come on, man! Nine women in one day!"

The entire tavern had gone quiet, at least to Gales's ears. It seemed everyone wanted to hear the great story. Including the archers, who looked like they were trying to recall where they had heard all this before.

Gales glanced round. If anyone had a bone to pick with Colonel Gales he was well and truly screwed. "It was Libiannin. Yeah. And it was nine women. That's no lie. I was a young man then and we was fourteen days on the transport. We hit the beach with our peckers poking us under our chins. I did nine women. In one day. You know what I mean. In twenty-four hours. Fourteen days on a transport, I never even seen a woman. Yeah. You don't believe me. Nobody ever does. But it's true. Nine women in one day."

Gales did not go through the gestures and antics that had accompanied the tales of the old Sergeant Gales. He had no room and did not want his piss-soaked pants to be seen.

His unrecalled acquaintance asked, "You all right? You don't seem to got so much energy no more. You're 'sposed ta tell it piece by piece, man."

Gales raised his jack. "Too many of these. Yeah." He looked at the other men. "It's true. You ask him. Fourteen days at sea. I was ready. How many women you had in one day? I wasn't showing off. I was working it. Yeah. I'll never forget that seventh one. Yeah. Moaning and clawing. She's going, 'Oh! Oh! Gales! Gales! I can't take no more, Gales! Oh! No! Don't stop! Don't stop!' Yeah. It's true. Every damn word. Nine women in one day. I was a young man then." After a feigned bout of straining to keep everything down, he said, "I ain't so young no more. I maybe better get outta here before somebody takes advantage of me. But one more won't hurt."

He pulled up a small purse. It proved to be empty. "Ah, shit. Somebody done got me already." He faced the man who had recognized him. "You see anybody 'round me back here? Somebody plucked me."

"We just got here, Sarge."

One of the companions asked, "You sure you didn't spend it all already? You didn't get that last jack for free."

Gales frowned as though making a grand effort to retrieve difficult memories. He decided this was the time to take advantage of the mess he had made in his lap.

Another feigned gag. He stood. "I got to go."

The moisture was blatantly obvious. Even the drunkest drunks saw it. He staggered badly. And congratulated himself on how he had disarmed even those who had to know who he really was.

He felt awful, though. He did not have to pretend to be thoroughly soused.

He counted forty steps, leaned against a wall, looked back. Nobody had come after him. He had left them sure that he was not worth robbing, or even worth beating up for being an officer.

He faced forward. He was going to be totally miserable later on. And he had to go to Damhorst tomorrow.

A dark shape blocked his path, a big man in a hooded cassock. He was accompanied by several identically clad friends.

One stepped in behind and pulled a sack over his head. The others dressed him in another cassock. His struggles were ineffective. They had trouble mainly because he was now halfway limp.

Then he puked into the bag.

...

The sun was near the meridian. Inger wrestled a mix of panic and anger. Still no sign of Josiah. His mounts remained stabled. His possessions were in his quarters, including weapons and travel gear. The men tasked to accompany him still awaited his appearance.

Inger paced. She muttered. She cursed. She was certain fate had handed her another cause for despair. Josiah was almost all she had left.

Not many months ago she had been ready to abandon Fulk's claim to Kavelin's crown. Then Bragi got himself killed. Most of the people who wanted rid of her then turned round to support her—except that witch Kristen, whose brat's claim had no legal foundation.

Here she was again, abandoned by another man, ready to shriek, "To hell with it!" and leave Kavelin to anyone who wanted the heartache.

She watched Fulk nap, for once in rare good health. The boy seemed angelic, lying there in a splay of blond curls. Neither she nor Bragi had curly hair but her mother said she had had curls as a toddler. One of her few remaining women came into the nursery. "Yes, Garyline?"

"That unpleasant Wolf person is here, Majesty. He says he has the information you wanted."

Inger rolled up her nose. She avoided Nathan Wolf as much as she could. But when Josiah dropped off the face of the earth she had nowhere else to turn.

"Send him in." She had no choice.

Sometimes she felt sorry for Wolf. The man was never anything but what he ought to be. He never did anything wrong. But he radiated something that made everyone wary and distrustful. Only Dane actually liked him. Inger suspected that Wolf did not like himself much. What others thought reflected back and made him think he deserved the negative responses.

Wolf's manners were perfect. Inger did not face him. She did not want him to see the revulsion his presence sparked. "You found something?" She stroked Fulk's hair, praying his good health would last.

"Colonel Gales spent the evening at a tavern, the Twisted Wrench, which is frequented by the garrison. He drank so much he wet himself. The last anyone saw him, he was going out the door."

"That's it? That's all?"

"It is, Majesty. And I would like to point out that the men and I have done almost miraculous work, coming up with that so fast."

True. Inger reined in her emotions. Wolf had developed that information so fast she wondered if he had not been involved somehow. "You're right, Nathan. That was good work. Can you even guess where he is now?"

"No, Majesty. But these things usually end with a corpse. Or an embarrassed soldier who has been rolled by a prostitute."

Josiah would not have taken up with a prostitute.

Wolf stepped to the door. "I can keep on squeezing the men who were there, but…"

"Almost certainly a waste of time. Nathan, you'll have to do what Colonel Gales was supposed to do today."

"I am at Your Majesty's command."

Exactly the answer she wanted from every man in her service, but from Wolf it seemed somehow both sinister and darkly suggestive.

Poor Nathan could not talk about the weather without making people think he was an oily, wicked pervert.

Inger gave Wolf his instructions, which were exactly those she had given Gales. Though her stomach tightened, she allowed a hint of a suggestion that a substitute who handled the Colonel's work well might expect some of the Colonel's perks.

She felt filthy when Wolf left.

She did wonder why the man seemed so slimy, creepy, and repulsive. He did nothing to validate that.

…

Nathan Wolf, wounded, reached the Breitbarth castle two days later than he should have without having run into trouble. He was afoot. He was the second member of his band to get through, and the last. He arrived to find that the cavalryman who had preceded him had expired before he could explain what had happened.

The Duke himself came to see Wolf. The sorcerer Babeltausque was dressing his wounds. "What the hell happened, Nathan? The other guy thought he was the only survivor."

"An ambush, Your Grace. I didn't get a good look. Marena Dimura bandits, I guess."

Babeltausque said, "He'll be fine if there's no sepsis. Gister Saxton told the same story."

"The Marena Dimura haven't done anything since Abaca died. Why change now?"

Wolf mumbled, "I don't know, Your Grace." He tried to explain why he had come instead of Gales.

"Ah. Possibilities suggest themselves. Gales either stepped out of the equation deliberately, was ordered out by Inger, or was removed by someone else. That seems most likely. So. Why? To get rid of Gales? Or to move Nathan up a notch?"

The sorcerer said, "That is a pathetically long stretch."

"Meaning?"

"I believe in the malicious mischief theory of providence. My hypothesis? Gales went out drinking and got mugged, or killed, by somebody who didn't know who he was."

"A twist on 'It's not conspiracy if it can be explained by stupidity'?"

"Exactly."

Greyfells stared at Wolf. "Nathan has done well, Babeltausque. Remove the curse."

Wolf frowned, confused, as he slid away into sleep.

The sorcerer frowned, too, but his scowl was born of irritation.

Nathan Wolf had offended Babeltausque years ago, without knowing it. He never did figure out why the whole world suddenly found him repugnant.

The sorcerer was not happy but he carried out his Duke's will. He had too grand an idea of his own worth. He would not have survived with the Greyfells family if they had been able to attract a man with more talent and a better character.

Babeltausque schemed, but only in small-minded, personal ways. He did not put his employer at risk.

Dane of Greyfells appreciated that. "Babeltausque, you've served my family long and well. We should show our appreciation more fully. Do you have secret aspirations that we could make come true?"

The sorcerer was startled. He squinted at the Duke. Was he being set up for torment? The man was capable of amusing himself by baiting a dog.

Yet he could not keep from blurting, "I do, Lord. But I dare not state it. Punishment would be swift and harsh."

"Come, now." The Duke assumed his sorcerer had a secret vice. The breed had that reputation. And Dane of Greyfells had vices he dared indulge only rarely. "Go on. I guarantee your safety. And no one else will know."

"Lord, I was obsessed with your half-sister Mayenne before we left Itaskia." He cringed, anticipating a blow.

"Well. You *can* surprise me. I expected something darker. She's a little young, though, isn't she?"

"She's almost fourteen." Too old for the sorcerer's taste, now, but *so* delectable…

Mayenne was one of a dozen children the previous Duke had fathered on the far side of the blanket. He had been fond enough of this one's mother to acknowledge her and her sisters.

The Duke was amused. "Babeltausque, I'm glad you spoke up. This can be arranged." Sudden cruelty edged his voice. "The little bitch needs to learn her place." She had resisted his own advances more than once. She deserved to be thrown to a beast like Babeltausque.

The sorcerer continued to look amazed.

How his fortunes had turned!

…

Nathan Wolf, on crutches, made the rounds of the Duke's soldiers, telling them what Inger wanted them to hear—with the Duke's blessing. A band of three were allowed to slip away. Two days later an eight-man group moved out. Both groups consisted of genuine deserters.

A third band, twenty-six strong, were not the real thing. They included the Duke disguised as an archer and the sorcerer as a muleteer. The archer's guise suited the Duke. He was skilled with the longbow.

Six miles east of Breitbarth an outrider discovered human remains as vultures and ravens made a getaway. Flies were dense despite the season. There had been several days of warm weather. Maggots were at work. The ravens did not go far. They clustered in nearby trees and cursed.

The remains could still be recognized. They were the men who had deserted first. They had been attacked by archers.

"Bandits?" Greyfells asked the air.

"Hard to tell, Your Grace," a soldier replied. "The broken arrows are the Marena Dimura type."

Babeltausque, unhappy about being in the field, said, "It hardly matters now."

"True enough," the Duke admitted. "Sorcerer, here is where you earn your sweet cunny. Make sure it doesn't happen to us."

Babeltausque soon had his chance. "We're being stalked. Four men. In the woods to our left. A dozen more are hiding up ahead, in the brush around that lone chestnut."

Greyfells had been looking forward to this. His troops were all afoot. Each carried a strung bow with an arrow laid across. "The finer you determine where they are the happier I'll be."

"Keep moving like you're ready for trouble but don't really expect it. I'll give you my best." He would. He had a reason to live.

Greyfells halted at the extreme range of the short bow favored by the Marena Dimura. He laid flights of arrows into the ambush area. Shrieks and curses responded.

The frustrated ambushers rose to loose their own shafts. That made the Itaskians' work easier.

Those ambushers still able to do so ran.

The Itaskians found eight wounded men. They recovered their arrows, left seven dead to their more fortunate brothers. They took one youth along for questioning. His wound was not life-threatening. He was not nearly as tough as he imagined.

Watching Babeltausque booby-trap corpses, Greyfells said, "Sorcerer, I'm developing a whole new appreciation of you. I may give you all of my bastard sisters."

"Mayenne will be sufficient, Your Grace." Then greed reared up. "Though Jondelle would make Mayenne a fine companion."

Greyfells laughed. "Wicked man. But be cautious with Jondelle. She is insane."

The party smashed three more ambushes. Babeltausque's stock soared. Years of maltreatment and disdain went by the wayside. Soldiers tended to give respect to those who saved their asses.

Babeltausque was no empire destroyer but he was handy on the killing ground. That carried plenty of weight with the sloggers.

The prisoner was worthless. He had no idea why the forest people were active again. He did what his father told him.

The Itaskians left him alive but in horrible pain. Whoever tried to help would regret his empathy. Babeltausque included a nasty booby trap.

...

Twelve days. Still no sign of Josiah. And no word from Wolf. Things were falling apart. Gales's disappearance had shaken the garrison. He had been more important than Inger had imagined. Once they suspected that the Colonel was not coming back the native garrison began to evaporate. Changes for the worse were evident daily. Those regiments that had remained loyal soon became paper tigers.

The vanishing soldiers were not shifting allegiance. They were just leaving.

Inger had no reliable intelligence about what was going on outside Vorgreberg. It did seem that the pretender's soldiers were deserting, too.

The nobility began abandoning Vorgreberg, finding excuses to return to their holdings. They did not want to get crushed in the coming collapse.

Inger knew she needed to make a show of strength. But she had none to show. Her enemies had brought her to the brink by walking away or by ignoring her.

Then came the six deserters from Damhorst, four of them injured. They had lost one on the way. They had hurt the bandits back.

Bandits. There had been no banditry when Bragi was king.

The lead sergeant informed Inger that, "The Duke and a bigger band are behind us. He means to disguise himself as an archer. The sorcerer will be with him."

"Whitcomb Innsman, isn't it?"

"Your Majesty's memory is excellent. It's been years."

"It is good. This time, though, I was told before you came in. I need to know my cousin's real situation. What did he leave behind? Can he count on help if I ambush him?"

That startled the soldier. Evidently no one had considered the possibility that she would try to turn things around herself.

Excellent.

"Innsman, your situation won't improve much here."

"It'll be better than it was." He described increasingly erratic and ugly behavior by the Duke. Nothing was ever his fault. He was not well, and had become a monster toward those Kaveliners within his power. He abused their younger teen daughters.

"Surely you exaggerate."

She knew that was true, though. It was no secret inside the family.

"Believe what you please, Majesty."

"Forget it. Find yourselves places in the barracks. And ask Dr. Wachtel to treat your injuries. He has plenty of time."

Inger rested her head in her hands. It just got worse. She was doomed. She had only a handful of men, too few to succeed here and not enough to manage an escape. While Dane kept on making sure that Itaskians were hated as much as possible.

This kingdom was insane. It turned good people bad and bad people worse. It ate them all. Then it sucked in more.

General Liakopulos may have demonstrated a burst of genius by escaping. If he was not lying in a shallow grave somewhere.

This was all Michael Trebilcock's fault.

She had no evidence. Not so much as a rumor. But she was ready to bet her soul that Trebilcock was out there tugging strings.

There was some comfort in being able to blame an invisible external devil for all one's woes.

...

A blunted arrow struck Dane of Greyfells' helmet as his purported deserters entered Castle Krief. The soldiers laid down their arms before their Duke finished collapsing. They had no skin in the game.

Babeltausque revealed himself immediately. He had failed to

detect the ambush. Inger's men had not given it away. There would be no sweet Mayenne cunny now.

There might be no getting back home at all.

Babeltausque did not need to indulge in the formal, scientific astrology necessary to predict the future. With Greyfells imprisoned, the man's following would disappear. His fever dream was dead. Once this news escaped Kavelin the Greyfells family would cease to matter in political equations.

Babeltausque, hands bound, feared there would be no live Itaskians in Kavelin come New Years.

Chaos would take complete charge.

...

Inger intercepted the sorcerer before he could be shoved into a cell. "Remove his gag, please."

The soldiers were her last Wesson loyalists. They knew what Babeltausque was. They thought Inger touched for not having him killed right away. But they followed instructions.

Inger looked Babeltausque in the eye. "You know how grim my situation is. *Our* situation, if you include Dane."

The sorcerer nodded.

"Can you abandon him? Can you come over to me?"

Babeltausque nodded repeatedly.

"Unless you're better than I think we're likely to get run out of Kavelin. If we're lucky. If they let us go. You'd have to explain yourself back home."

"As would you."

"I no longer care. I'm not ready to run yet, though. I have a little fight left. I'd have more than a little if I had your help."

The sorcerer nodded some more.

"I'll work you harder than Dane ever did. You'll be a lot more than a pet astrologer."

Babeltausque went slightly grey. "At last. An opportunity to make use of my talents."

The soldiers snickered.

Inger said, "Turn him loose."

They did so with obvious reluctance.

She told them, "If he becomes a problem you can say you told me so while you're roasting him. Sorcerer. Come along. I'll show you where to work." Which would be in the suite Varthlokkur used when he resided in Castle Krief. "You'll get one servant. There'll be no touching. Understand?"

"I gather that fierce temptation will be set so as to test me."

"You don't want to fail."

The sorcerer adopted his most blank expression.

"Let me know when you're ready to start."

"How soon do you need me?"

"Today, if you can."

The sorcerer sighed and strove to keep up.

†

Chapter Six:

YEAR 1017 AFE:

King Without a Throne

The fugitive walked the plain alone, striding purposefully. The caravan job had not lasted. Despite peace looming there was little trade. No caravans were headed this way.

He glanced to his right. The riders still paced him. Occupying his attention while others closed in? The plains tribes were not populous but were the reason caravans needed guards. They would steal anything from anyone. Nobody was too poor not to be robbed.

He sensed no other presence, though. They must be keeping track till they could summon help.

There were two of them. They were cautious. They did not like the odds.

They must suspect that he was more dangerous than he looked.

He strode on, sling in hand in case he kicked up a hare or game bird. If those two tried nothing sooner he would visit them after dark.

He could use a good plains pony.

A grouse flushed. He did not react fast enough. His bullet fell short. He produced another stone and walked on. His homeland was only days away. He should decide where to go first.

He had to arrive as a wanderer, not as himself. He would go where rootless men gathered. There he could discover what he needed to know to cope with today's kingdom.

The land grew more arid, the grass shorter and scruffier, soon revealing patches of dun earth. The grass sea was about to give way to mild desert. Not far ahead, though not yet visible, lay mountains which masked the heart of Hammad al Nakir.

The riders had to make a decision soon. Tomorrow he would reach country where they would not be welcome—though they were not likely to be noticed. He considered what he would do in their position.

He would move in the middle of the night.

He moved as soon as it was dark. There was no moon. Pitfalls seemed to multiply.

Despite all, he found the other camp before the riders left to find him. And rediscovered the quality of mercy.

They were boys, probably brothers, the eldest no more than fifteen. They were trying to work up their courage. Neither really wanted to do anything but neither wanted the other to think he was a coward.

Haroun could not follow their dialect well but did figure out that their main motive was a need to please their father, who was a hetman and wanted them to come home with proof that they had done something brave.

Haroun's own people were nomadic in the main. They enjoyed similar traditions.

The boys finally worked themselves up. They didn't have to take foolish chances. They could tell the truth when the old men asked about their efforts to count coup. For that was what this was. Not really robbery but boys wanting to mark their transition into manhood.

Had an experienced warrior followed them? Probably not. A guardian angel would stand out on the plain.

The essence of the rite of passage was that the candidates had to do for themselves.

He gave them ten minutes, then entered their camp. They were not fastidious. He placed a gold coin in each of their leather jacks, then readied their horses. One gentle spell kept the ponies quiet. He led them to the trace that passed as a road headed into the desert kingdom.

The villain who had given up those coins would not object to them passing on to boys who needed something good to happen.

Haroun wished he could be a fly buzzing round when they, absent their ponies, returned to their people carrying gold enough to buy a herd.

...

Varthlokkur had restrained his darker nature in order to spend an afternoon with the four strange children who constituted his makeshift family. Only Smyrena was his own get. Ethrian was his grandson.

Even to him it seemed odd to have a grandson so much older than his daughter. But it was a bizarre world. He had added a few bricks of strange himself.

Ethrian was a thin, dark youth. In his best moments he had haunted eyes. Madness was his relief from memories of being the Deliverer, a monster managed by a revenant evil that considered itself a god. The Deliverer used its armies of the dead to punish the wrong people for injuries he imagined had been done to him. The revenant had misled him.

Escaping had cost Ethrian love and sanity, a price not yet fully paid.

Some days he did nothing but lie curled in a ball. Others he sat and rocked, eyes vacant, an age and countless miles away. His mind held millennia of memories not his own. He was never sure what was then and what was now.

The wizard did what he could to keep the boy anchored. He had no faith in the boy's chances for recovery, yet did his best for Nepanthe's sake. She would not concede any chance that Ethrian could not be saved

Smyrena could be a spooky little beast, normal one moment, possessed the next. She did not cry. She seemed too alert and attentive for an infant. She enjoyed the presence of the Unborn. Varthlokkur found that dreadfully unnatural. Radeachar was an instrument. It ought not to have friends.

He told himself that Smyrena would grow out of it.

Mist's brats were disturbingly normal. Fathered by Nepanthe's brother Valther back when Mist had entertained no hope of becoming Empress again, they were exotic hybrids, scary in their beauty. The girl was older. The boy was growing faster. Right now they looked like twins. They worked hard to maintain that pretense, though there was no need. There was no survival imperative here.

They did know who they were. Varthlokkur showed them their mother occasionally. He meant the look at their heritage as a caution, not a kindness. He wanted them to know that they could be in danger for no greater cause than being the children of that woman, however much they remained separated from the Dread Empire.

He lied to them, too. He told them their mother had left them with their aunt for their protection. He told them Mist had been dragged into Dread Empire politics unwillingly and had been terrified of the risks to them.

Insofar as he recalled, Mist had left them as hostages she was not concerned about losing.

His cynicism ran deep.

Seldom did he encounter anything that rendered him more sanguine.

Nepanthe joined him. She was cheerful. She went directly to Ethrian, petted and fussed. Varthlokkur and Smyrena both watched with a touch of jealousy.

...

The fugitive entered his homeland. He did not relax. He was a stranger even here. The people of Hammad al Nakir, of whatever political or religious persuasion, distrusted strangers.

He moved slowly, avoiding tribal camps, till he reached the oasis called al-Habor. It was more developed than when he had visited as a boy. More permanent structures had been added and new orchards had been planted, but then disaster had found the town. Most of it had fallen apart since. Today it was dying.

And provided proof that some men did not care about issues that had tormented their people for two generations. Al-Habor had become a haven for rootless men. The forgotten King Without a Throne could begin gathering the strings of his life here.

Haroun was not there when the sun set. When it rose he was seated against an adobe wall, snoring, one of a half-dozen probable miscreants.

...

Yasmid, with Habibullah behind her, an intimidating shade, considered the foreigners Elwas al-Souki had invited to Sebil el Selib. The tall, fat one was a Matayangan swami eager to put distance between himself and his blasted homeland. He was the color of pale mahogany.

His companion, a smaller man of low caste, was darker and less healthy. Nervously, he translated for the bigger man.

Elwas repeated himself. "Swami Phogedatvitsu specializes in overcoming addictions." He wilted under Yasmid's disapproval.

She was angry down to her toenails. The presumption of the man! But she could not just run him off. Not with Habibullah watching. Not after the miracle he had wrought at the salt lake.

Al-Souki's success irked Yasmid. The history of the Faith was speckled with military geniuses who became liabilities after they won their reputations. That started with her uncle Nassef, who had been with her father from the beginning. Nassef, as the Scourge of God, helped build a wide, wild religious empire. And had been a thorough-going bandit when the Disciple was not looking. He had been ambitious, too, systematically eliminating anyone who stood between him and succession to the Peacock Throne. He had wanted Yasmid as his child bride so he could unite Royalists and Faithful under his rule.

Fate had delivered Yasmid to Haroun bin Yousif instead.

The Faithful never lacked brilliant commanders but few were moved more by faith than by ambition and greed.

Yasmid was not ready to believe that Elwas bin Farout al-Souki was something new.

She made a "Get on with it!" gesture.

Al-Souki said, "Phogedatvitsu can conquer an addiction as deep as your father's. I beg you, allow him to try."

She had mixed feelings. And a sense of shame.

She was not sure she wanted her father freed. If he recovered, his daughter would become a simple ornament to his glory. A saint at best.

How shameful. How dare she put herself ahead of God's Chosen Disciple?

Despite all, including her long love for the King Without a Throne, she believed in her father's message. He had a unique relationship with God. Much as she reveled in being God's stand-in hand and voice, directing the Faithful, she did not have that direct relationship herself.

She was a custodian, nothing more.

"Elwas, I will give you the chance you want. The foreigner can try to rescue my father. I will make him wealthy if he succeeds."

"You won't be disappointed, Shining One," the prostitute's son promised. "It may take a year but the world will gain its soul back. El Murid will be a golden beacon once more."

After al-Souki left, Yasmid asked Habibullah, "Is he for real?"

"Totally. And he's not unique. He just doesn't mind letting the world know."

Yasmid looked like she had bitten into something sour.

Habibullah began to frown. Did he wonder what her problem was? Elwas bin Farout al-Souki had offered her a chance to spark new life into the flames of the Faith.

Habibullah was her slave emotionally but he was, as well, one of the oldest of the Believers. He coughed gently to remind her that the One was watching. This might be His mercy at work.

"Call him back."

Habibullah was not gone long.

Yasmid looked al-Souki in the eyes, hard. He was not accustomed to that from a woman. His gaze dropped. She said, "You have one hundred days to show me real progress. If Phogedatvitsu is a con artist his corpse will join thc hundred thousand already fertilizing Sebil el Selib. No more talk. Habibullah, arrange to house and feed those men."

Giving Habibullah that task was meant to put both men in their place. She felt petty doing so.

...

Al-Habor was the well to which social gravity drew the lost souls of the desert. Even the flies and parasites had yielded to despair. Soul-shattered veterans of decades of war haunted al-Habor, shaking, muttering, afraid, or just staring at something only one man could see. They did not talk much. They survived on the charity of Sheyik Hanba al-Medi al-Habor, the local tribal chief. Hanba bore the marks of the wars himself. They had cost him a hand, an eye, and three sons. He could not afford the charity he provided. The wars had seen to that, too.

Still, he did provide.

Al-Habor once was a major crossroads. It was of minor importance still. Trade remained limited because fighting could return any time. The oasis was sweet and reliable and strategically valuable.

Half the mud-brick buildings were abandoned. The best preserved were infested by squatters.

Haroun settled in unremarked. Few would have cared had he announced himself. Al-Habor was the end of the road. No roads led to a future elsewhere. Al-Habor clung to the souls it collected. Haroun found it bleak enough to dampen a brilliant spring day at high noon.

Nobody cared about one more bum fallen into the cauldron. He did not learn much. Lack of care meant a lack of information. Only travelers had any real news. Few of those would waste time on a soul-shattered tramp whose real goal must be to mooch or steal something.

Insidious tendrils of despair shadowed Haroun's own heart. He should move on before he became lost himself.

There were those who preyed on the lost. The most virulent was a big, stupid man called the Bull. The Bull ran with a timid killer known as the Beetle.

It was unusually cold. Haroun had formed an unspoken alliance with two others. Between them they had found enough fuel for a small fire. They sat round that, no man meeting another's gaze.

The Beetle and the Bull appeared. The Bull rumbled, "The Bull is hungry."

Nobody responded. Only Haroun had anything edible. He did not intend to share.

The Bull kicked the little fire apart. "I said..."

Haroun slipped a knife into the back of the Bull's right calf. He sliced down, then sideways. At first the Bull did not feel pain enough to understand. He tried to turn. His leg did not cooperate. Haroun leaned out of the path of his collapse.

The Bull roared, tried to get up. Haroun's blade entered his right eye. "Breathe without leave and I'll take the other, too. Your old friends will have great sport with a blind Bull."

The Beetle tried something stupid. Haroun disarmed him. He settled beside the Bull, nursing partially severed fingers.

"Would you like to spend your remaining days dependent on the good will of the Beetle?" The Bull abused his partner with only slightly less vigor than he did everyone else. "No? You're less stupid than I thought. I'll leave you one eye, then. I'll take it first time you do something to offend me, though."

The Bull looked into Haroun's eyes. He saw no mercy there. He did see a dark future for those who angered the man. He eased back, rose slowly, let the Beetle help him limp away.

One of the others said, "I remember you." He said nothing more. He lowered his head, went to sleep.

The second man acknowledged events with a nod and a shudder. He placed curds of dried camel dung on the resurrected fire, then lay down on his left side.

Haroun noticed changes next morning. Word had spread. His presence was acknowledged subtly everywhere. Had his fireside companion truly recognized him? If so, it was definitely time to leave. Most of the walking dead here had followed El Murid.

Did he dare reclaim his animals and gear? Would the stable keeper even deal with him now that he could not be distinguished from the sort of man he pretended to be?

Nothing developed, though, except the exchange of whispers amongst the lost. Haroun got the news himself three times. No one named a revenant champion from days gone by. The man from the fire had changed his mind or had not been believed. Either was convenient.

...

Haroun wakened suddenly. Someone had come too close. He

sensed no malice, however. He feigned sleep, let the situation develop. He was seated against an adobe wall in a pool of shadow. Moonlight illuminated what could be seen through cracked eyelids. A breeze tumbled the skeleton of a brushy weed.

Someone settled to his right. The man smelled familiar. He would be the companion who never spoke.

Haroun waited.

A long time passed before the man whispered, "A courier came from Al Rhemish." The man had trouble talking. He stammered. "He told the Sheyik's night boy to gather fodder for twenty horses for four days."

Someone would be coming out from the capital. Haroun could not be the reason. Megelin's few incompetent shaghûns would waste no time spying on no-account towns awash in human flotsam. It likely meant only that a Royalist band would pass through on its way somewhere to make someone miserable.

Haroun did not respond. His companion did nothing to suggest that a response was necessary.

Next morning the Sheyik's men came looking for day labor. Haroun joined the volunteers. Some went looking for fodder. Haroun was in the group set to cleaning the Sheyik's stable and corral. He did not see the point, nor did he learn anything useful.

His companions cared not at all. Shifting horse manure or no, it was all the same. The slower they worked the longer they would be employed.

Haroun wandered off, vacant-eyed, as often as he dared. The Sheyik's men would find him and bring him back to the corral. He learned nothing about the layout inside the adobe wall screening the Sheyik's residence, which was a minor fortress built of mud brick.

Back behind his pitchfork, Haroun wondered why he felt compelled to study the place. Because someone had a notion that important things were about to happen? Or because of some unconscious premonition of his own?

He had those infrequently. He had learned to pay attention. But they were not universally trustworthy. A premonition had made him murder an innocent prince and princess.

Someone was coming. Someone with an escort. Who it would

be was secret but it had to be someone firmly convinced of his own importance.

Come sundown Haroun's work party scattered into al-Habor after being fed. Like the others, bin Yousif stuffed himself till his stomach ached and carried away whatever he could hide about his person.

He fell asleep against the same wall behind another tiny fire. The same men shared the warmth. Both had been part of the work party. They were rich tonight, as al-Habor's lost understood that state.

Haroun drifted off wondering if they three would not now offer too much temptation to the Bulls of al-Habor.

†

Chapter Seven:

YEAR 1017 AFE:

Eastern Empire

The Lord Ssu-ma Shih-ka'i, Commander, Western Army, second in the Dread Empire, took some time off work.

Shih-ka'i used a portal known only to himself. He stepped out on an island unimaginably far to the east. Ehelebe might once have been its name. He was not sure. Ehelebe was obscure and might have been something else.

He was not looking forward but he was a man who had attained his station by meticulous attention to detail, to duty, by genius, by an unsullied reputation for being apolitical, and because he once enjoyed some favor from politicals who used him as a showpiece.

Shih-ka'i believed that his character made him uniquely suited to pull Shinsan together following its late, suicidal internal conflicts. The daughter of the Demon Prince was now the fountainhead of empire but Ssu-ma Shih-ka'i, the pig farmer's son, was the symbol, device, and guarantor of the new era. And what he wanted to do now, in service to that guarantee, was make sure that a man he had exiled would be reintegrated into Tervola society. Kuo Wen-chin could be of incalculable value if he would stifle his ambition.

Ssu-ma Shih-ka'i owed Kuo. Wen-chin had plucked him from obscurity, as commander of a training legion, and had loosed him on the revenant god of the east. From that triumph he had gone on to glory in the west.

There was no sign of Kuo. The fortress round the old laboratories was deserted. It was morning but little sunlight reached Shih-ka'i. There was no artificial lighting. Dust lay heavy. It filled the air when he moved. He removed his boar mask so he could sneeze.

He did not call out. Even an apolitical Tervola dared not go round shouting the name of a condemned man he had saved. Who knew who might hear you impeach yourself?

Had Kuo escaped?

Not likely, though the man was a genius. And there was a precedent.

The Deliverer had escaped by swimming to the mainland. Then he had walked on west, allied with forces ancient and terrible.

That route was closed, now. No one would survive it again.

Portals were the only way out.

The dust in the staging chamber made it clear that Lord Kuo had not gotten out that way.

The kitchen was the place to start. Kuo had to eat. Miniature portals delivered foodstuffs there, from sources calculated to raise no questions.

Shih-ka'i strained to remember his way. He had visited only briefly a few times, most recently to stash Kuo. It took a while.

The kitchen did show signs of regular use by someone with few skills and no dedication to order.

A remote clatter caught Ssu-ma's attention.

He found his man down where past tenants had housed their prisoners and monsters. Wen-chin was spoon-feeding a drooling old man.

Shih-ka'i's advent startled Wen-chin, who, nevertheless, continued feeding the invalid. Kuo said, "I didn't expect you so soon. Are you here to end the threat?"

"No. I wanted to make sure of your welfare. Who is this?"

"I don't know. Presumably someone important to the previous

regime. I can't imagine how he survived. He hasn't much mind left. He is a project filled with challenges, the biggest being to overcome his fears so I can draw him back to the world."

"Oh?"

"I would've gone mad without him."

"Then him being here was piece of good fortune." And a grim harbinger, perhaps.

"So. You're not here to kill me. Then tell me what's happened out there."

Shih-ka'i brought him up to date.

Kuo sighed. "The Empire has fared well."

"Better than we had any right to expect, given the foibles of our class."

"I hoped, of course. I'm sad that there's no place for me. But I was resigned to that when I came to you."

Lord Ssu-ma nodded. "It hasn't been a long time but it has been busy. A lot changed. Most importantly, the wars are over. Successfully, thanks to your foresight. But the exhaustion of the state and the legions are such that the surviving Tervola have put aside personal ambitions."

"On the surface, perhaps."

"No doubt temptation will sway some who can't see past the Empress's sex, however sound her leadership and thorough her discipline."

"What do you want from me, Lord Ssu-ma?"

"Right now, truly, only to see that you're well. Later, maybe something more. Assuming your own ambitions are now manageable."

"They were never unmanageable. I did what I did for the Empire."

"A good thing to know." Every fallen Tervola would claim the same. Most would believe themselves. "I'll be back. Probably sooner than this time. Time is less pressing."

Kuo said, "Lord, I will make any adjustment necessary to get out of here." Happily, he was not yet desperate enough to do something stupid.

The attempt would have been fatal.

Lord Ssu-ma Shih-ka'i held a low and cynical opinion of his

fellow Tervola. He viewed all they did through the lens of that cynicism and his own low birth. But he could and did grant kudos to those who rose above their nature. Kuo was one such man.

...

The routine in the prison tower remained unchanged. Only the faces of those who brought the meals were different. They talked no more than had their predecessors.

Ragnarson was tempted to attack somebody to force an interaction.

He did not. The beast inside was cunning enough to understand that he would regret that sort of defiance quickly, deeply.

Mist's remarks during her visit had begun to shape his thinking.

He now spent too much time trying to figure himself out. It was embarrassing. He was glad that his beloved dead could not see him so enfeebled. Haaken, Reskird, Elana, and so many others would never have understood.

He came to fear that his ghosts would understand more and better than he did.

His own philosophy of life had shrunk to a smash-and-grab level.

Once the introspection vice set in nothing was safe from repeated review. Trivial incidents stuck in his head like musical refrains, cycling over and over.

Time flew, then. In sane moments he wondered if this was not just a way to escape the monotony of imprisonment. Then he would recollect an incident or decision that constituted another early brick in his edifice of despair.

Mostly he dwelt on mind-warps that had led him to rush through the Mountains of M'Hand and attack an invincible enemy already determined to exterminate him.

He could not identify the moment when confidence in his own talent and luck had become an irrational conviction that he could never be deprived of good fortune and victory.

He knew the seeds lay in the head butting with Varthlokkur over whether or not to tell Nepanthe what Ethrian was doing in the east.

He concluded, after numerous rehashes, that Varthlokkur was

more culpable than he. That old man's stubbornness, in the face of all evidence, had caused Kavelin's downfall.

Insofar as Ragnarson knew there had been no softening of the wizard's attitude. He would not admit that he was wrong.

Ragnarson could do that. Privately. To himself. He did not know if he could confess the failing publicly.

Days fled. Mist did not return. Ragnarson received no news. He could only imagine what was happening at home. Imaging, he could only picture the worst. The worst he pictured was too optimistic.

He lost track of time. Days became weeks. Weeks became seasons.

It seemed like summer out there.

...

Lord Ssu-ma Shih-ka'i was nervous. He had been called to the Imperial presence. The summons had been there waiting, like an unhappy promise, when he returned from the island in the east.

Reason said it would be Imperial business. Emotion feared that the woman knew what he had done.

And she was scarcely a hundred yards away, now, here in his own army headquarters.

He sent word that he was available and awaiting her convenience.

His messenger brought word that he was to attend her immediately.

Shih-ka'i got no sense of danger but remained uncomfortable.

The guilty flee where none doth pursue.

Shih-ka'i knew the aphorism had a similar form in most all older cultures. It had figured grandly in events leading to the destruction of Ilkazar. The Empire Destroyer had employed that exact formula to frighten the lords men of the old Empire.

The Empress was exhausted and gaunt despite the improvement in Shinsan's fortunes. She beckoned him. She seemed distracted, not angry.

This might not be about Ssu-ma Shih-ka'i after all.

She said, "I know you're no expert but I trust your wisdom."

"To what conundrum shall I bend my wise lack of expertise?"

"I have a secret."

"As do we all. I would like to discuss mine with you someday when you're feeling particularly generous."

"I have two things troubling me," the Empress said. "First, how do I guarantee the safety of my children?" She met his gaze straight on.

Did she imagine him to be a threat? "I may have missed an intermediate step in your thinking. I was only vaguely aware that you have children. Now that you mention them, where are they?"

"That would be the meat of my problem."

Shih-ka'i tried to seem interested. He was seriously off balance. "I don't understand."

"When I returned from exile, during the events that displaced Lord Kuo…" She paused, suddenly remote.

Shih-ka'i took the opportunity to remark, "A good man, at least to me. He allowed me to prove myself against the Deliverer. He was a considerable resource to the Empire."

The Empress looked puzzled. "Everyone tells me you have no interest in politics."

"That would be true most of the time. The politics of the moment have to be acknowledged sometimes because they shape everything else. Kuo Wen-chin was my mentor, friend, and the man who let me grow into what I became. The politics around him meant nothing to me except when they interfered with me trying to do my job. But you want to talk about your children."

She gave him another odd look. "Yes. I do. I have two. Ekaterina and her brother Scalza. Their father gave them those names. No doubt they're comfortable with them and would rather not assume those secretly preferred by their mother. The girl is the oldest."

Lord Ssu-ma smiled. "And you intend to stay vague because you're afraid politics might overtake them."

"I am. I left them behind because I knew they would be safer where they were. They were with people I trusted."

Shih-ka'i enjoyed an intuitive moment. "They weren't people who trusted you."

"So the results would suggest."

"So they're really hostages to fortune. And you have been too busy to do anything about it. But now you have enough free time to feel guilty."

The Empress gave him yet another look. "Pretty much, yes."

"And the pig man fits how?"

"He tells me what he thinks after I admit that I can't figure out where they are."

"The people you trusted?"

"Kavelin has collapsed. People have scattered. Some are dead. The kingdom was stable when I left. But Bragi did what he did and everything came apart."

Lord Ssu-ma held his tongue. He waited.

"The children disappeared early."

Shih-ka'i wondered how near the wind of fact she was sailing. Certainly she was not being one hundred percent forthright—though she herself might head up the file of those she was deceiving.

"Actually, I do have an idea where they are, but I don't *know.* I'm not even sure that they're still alive. If they're where I fear, there'll be no way to reach them."

Shih-ka'i needed no more clues. "You're afraid the Empire Destroyer has them."

"Yes." She said no more. He knew that Varthlokkur's wife was the sister of the man she had been unable to deny.

"Would he try to use them to make you to do something against the interests of the Empire?"

"The fear lurks behind my concern for their welfare. He slipped into a bizarre mental state just before Kavelin began to fall apart."

Frankly puzzled, Shih-ka'i again asked, "And I fit how?"

"You are a marvelous sounding board."

"Really?" Startled.

"Absolutely. Thanks to you, I now know exactly what I'll do."

Shih-ka'i was too lost to say anything, good, bad, indifferent, or wisecrack. "Pleased to be of service. There was something else?"

She frowned, then admitted, "Yes. About the prisoner, Ragnarson. We need to get some use out of him."

That or kill him, in Shih-ka'i's estimation. But he did face the problem of owing Ragnarson a life.

"Be aware that my peasant background marked me with a tendency to rigid views of right, wrong, and the nature of one's honorable obligations."

The Empress looked him directly in the eye. "I know he saved your life at Lioantung. You repaid him after you defeated him."

"I'm not comfortably sure of that. There are no definitive rules of obligation. *Was* mine discharged when I salvaged him and had the healers put him back together? He saved me by brushing a ballista shaft aside—the consequences of which stretch out into time unknown. So must I be his protector forever? How deep is my obligation to others who have done me kindnesses?"

The Empress did not respond right away. Her upbringing had encouraged more flexible attitudes. Then she had spent years amongst westerners whose ideals about honor far surpassed what even Shih-ka'i considered rational.

"Are you suffering some crisis of conscience? It seems you're thinking about more than our guest in the Karkha Tower."

"I cannot hide from your matchless eye, Empress. A crisis of conscience indeed, not concerning the erstwhile king of Kavelin. If you insist that I have discharged my obligation to Ragnarson I'll defer to your judgment. My present moral conundrum is more perilous. For me."

Silent seconds stretched. The Empress stared but showed no abiding interest in his prattle.

Ice crept up Shih-ka'i's spine. Enough! "Pardon me, Empress. My peasant side waxed a little strong for a moment."

"That's worth considering sometime when we're not distracted."

"What?"

"You've been around a long time. You were among the last students taken from outside the senior castes. But in my grandfather's time only talent and merit counted."

"Dedication helped, as did a capacity to remain placid in the face of provocation. But you are correct. The ideals that boosted the early empire have been subverted. The get of Tervola grow up with a sense of entitlement."

"I mean to give that some thought once I'm no longer obsessing about my children."

"Make a big sign."

"What?"

"A joke. The underlying assumption being that Varthlokkur keeps an eye on you. To let him know you're thinking about him and your children. I meant it as silliness but a sign might actually be a way to let him know you'd like to have a conversation."

"That's insanity on the hoof—and might work. It would for sure let me know if the old bastard is looking over my shoulder."

"Yes." Lord Ssu-ma thought this might be a good time to go away. He could niggle around Wen-chin again later.

The Empress said, "Go back to work. I'll do some thinking when there aren't any distractions."

Shih-ka'i bowed himself out, thoughts chaotic. No lifeguards had been present just now. Did that speak to Mist's confidence or to her paranoia?

He stutter-stepped. He had no bodyguards of his own these days. He had not had a friend or close companion since Pan ku died at Lioantung. He had acquaintances. People with whom he worked.

His one shadow of a friend was hiding on an island outside the Empire, his very existence a death sentence for Ssu-ma Shih-ka'i.

...

Varthlokkur spent too much time being Haroun's guardian angel, really. Bin Yousif seldom needed help. When the wizard was not a ghost behind that man's shoulder he tried to keep watch on key players in the Lesser Kingdoms. Sometimes he checked on Bragi Ragnarson or went sneaking around some major personality in today's Dread Empire.

Too often he wasted time trying to scry the future.

Once he had been a master of divination. The future was able to elude him only through ambiguity. He could look ahead for generations. Now he had trouble with days. Weeks were impossible.

He was sure he knew why.

He devoted an hour a day considering how to gain an advantage on the Star Rider.

That had been accomplished a few times but never for long and never with a net positive result.

He let Nepanthe help with some of his less dangerous applications, especially through the Winterstorm. That was simplicity itself. She needed only manipulate a few symbols.

"Varth. You need to see this."

Her tone brought the wizard quickly. "Well. Damn! Isn't that interesting?"

"And clever."

They looked at a blackboard centered inside a transparent globe. Chalked on that board in big block characters, in Kaveliner Wesson, was: **Varthlokkur, where are my babies?**

Board and globe were in Mist's private office. She passed by once while they watched. "Passive message," the wizard mused. "She assumes that I watch her."

"Clever."

"What?"

"She's right."

Varthlokkur grunted, then began to brood on the nature of the magic Mist was using. "Must be a bubble outside the local reality so visitors don't notice. Maybe an offset in time."

"She might just not let people in."

"There's that. But it's so prosaic. That bubble..."

"Foo on the bubble. What are we going to do?"

"About what?"

"About letting Mist know that her children are all right."

He did not get it. Honestly.

"Her children," Nepanthe said, slowly and loudly. "She's concerned about Ekaterina and Scalza."

"Oh. Yes. I don't know if I actually believe that, but..."

"Varth! Stop!"

He stopped. She used that tone frugally, when focused on a single matter. When she was determined to make the universe conform to simple arithmetic terms.

"What do *you* want to do, darling?"

"Just let her know they're fine. How hard is that to figure?"

"There's a high degree of difficulty. It isn't the sort of thing I do."

"You're the ace sorcerer of all time. Make the answer appear on her blackboard."

He chuckled. "I can't do that."

"Why not?"

"Because she wouldn't let me. If I could get in there and do that, that simply, then any Tervola old enough to walk could sneak in and do bad things."

"All right. I understand. But you'll find a way. Hell, invite her to come see them."

That suggestion so flabbergasted Varthlokkur that he was left speechless. But thoughtful.

†

Chapter Eight:

YEAR 1017 AFE:

The Desert Kingdom

There was no wakening touch but Haroun knew one of his companions wanted his attention. A glance at the angle of the moonlight told him it was just after midnight. He heard harness creaks and horses' hooves. There was no need to whisper, "They're here."

Traveling by night.

Interesting.

Might be worth investigating.

Probably not worth the risk of exposure, though.

Haroun moved just enough to let it be known that he had heard.

He *was* curious.

He did nothing for several minutes. The sounds made by the travelers grew louder. They would reach the Sheyik's stronghold without coming near here.

Haroun had a premonition: It would not be wise to go look.

He rose, glided through the moonlight forty yards, slid into a shadow where his companions could not watch. He squatted, carefully extended his shaghûn senses.

The sounds of movement ceased.

Bin Yousif withdrew, cursing softly. Slight as his use of the power had been, it had been detected. A powerful someone accompanied the nightriders.

Up. Stride briskly back to his seat behind the tiny fire. Settle. Relax. Hope his companions did not ask uncomfortable questions.

Both were awake and nervous.

Shouting and order-giving began over yonder. Haroun concentrated on controlling his breathing.

A half-dozen men trotted past. One paused to consider the derelicts. He wasted only a few seconds before moving on.

Haroun caressed the hilt of his favorite knife, gently, and wondered about the sorcerer who had detected his careful probe.

Another group of men rushed Haroun's former shadow from another direction.

Incomprehensible calls indicated that more men were coming.

Silhouettes glided into sight, following the half-dozen who had passed by earlier, three in a loose wedge followed by a man who was nearly a giant.

Haroun did not think. He responded without calculation, lightning striking. He leapt onto the devil's back, left hand seizing his chin and pulling, right hand yanking his knife across the man's throat, slicing deep enough to cut the windpipe before the sorcerer could utter the first syllable of a protective spell. The slash cut all the way to the spine. Carotid and jugular spewed.

Bin Yousif threw himself clear, drove his knife into the belly of Magden Norath's nearest companion, who shrieked as he went down. He slashed another man's raised left arm. The third turned to run. He died from a thrust into his back.

Haroun ran the other direction after taking a moment to drive his knife into the sorcerer's left temple. He considered taking the head away, to destroy it a fragment at a time, but Norath's men had begun to react.

He became another shadow moving through shadows.

He was calm the whole time, from the moment he felt his knife slice Norath's esophagus. This was his life. This was what he had been born to do, till the day he made his lethal mistake. Cut, slash, stab, and walk away before anyone could respond.

Once out of sight he had serious advantages.

Norath's men could not know who they were hunting. He knew that anyone searching must be an enemy.

Magden Norath, though! How could that be? In his way, in his time, Norath had been as terrible as the Empire Destroyer. How could he have fallen so easily?

Norath had gotten sloppy. He had failed to protect himself because he had seen no need. Death had been on him before he knew he was in danger. It was the story of every mouse ever taken by an owl, fox, or snake.

Death was always one inattentive moment away.

Things began to prowl the night, hunting, things created by Magden Norath. Though hardly the *savan dalage* the sorcerer had loosed during the Great Eastern Wars, they were formidable. They were confused. Haroun ambushed one that came within striking distance. It died. He was amazed.

The threat faded.

Norath was dead. The hunt for his murderer went on hiatus while the sorcerer's men surrounded another member of their party. Him they hurried to safety inside the Sheyik's compound.

Amazing, Haroun thought. The course of history might have been changed.

He had to get out of al-Habor. There would be a big, serious hunt once those men got themselves together. They would loose Norath's monsters—unless they just killed the beasts rather than try to manage them without the sorcerer's help.

Haroun sneaked back to his fire. That had been killed and scattered. There was no sign that three men had slept there. The dead had been taken away.

Haroun ripped a strip from the edge of his cloak. He took a packet from a pocket inside his inner shirt, tucked the scrap inside. The herb in the packet had come most of the way from Lioantung. He rubbed it into the cloth, then worked the scrap into a crack in the wall where he had sat to sleep. It should look like something that had gotten caught there.

All set. Time to go.

There was no one in the stable when Haroun arrived. Odd, but his shaghûn senses discovered nothing else unusual. Maybe the night boy was shirking.

Haroun was preparing his animals when a long, hate-filled howl rolled across al-Habor. It was joined by another.

His cloth scrap had been found.

How many monsters had Magden Norath brought?

Bin Yousif thought of them as hellhounds but they better resembled large, stocky cats with hound-like heads.

As Haroun eased into the light of the setting moon he concluded that their number did not matter.

Men screamed. Monsters growled and shrieked in a fight fit for entertaining the gods. Haroun searched the sky, halfway expecting to see a winged horse against the starscape.

Still no stable boy. Surely the uproar should have brought him back. The master was bound to come, to make sure the animals were safe.

Haroun left a generous tip.

The sun would rise before long. Norath's hounds should have to hide from the light. They could be rooted out and destroyed during the day.

If they did not destroy one another. If someone did not delude himself into thinking he could use them the way Norath had.

Haroun hoped his fireside brethren had gotten a good head start. They did not deserve to suffer for his crimes.

...

Megelin's bodyguards were the best surviving Royalist warriors. They moved as quietly as they could, which was not especially so. The horses and camels were nervous. The deathcats had closed in too tight.

Megelin had told the damned sorcerer to leave the deathcats behind. Norath did not listen well. He had brought four monsters anyway.

Someday Norath would cease to be useful. After he made Megelin's enemies die. Then he could join his victims in hell.

Pray this meeting went well. Norath's mystery ally might hasten the opportunity.

Norath's massive bulk rolled in the moonlight just yards ahead. The sorcerer had a distinctive walk because of injuries suffered during the Great Eastern Wars. He was badly bowlegged and had trouble changing course quickly.

Megelin's loathing grew. He was downwind. The man stank.

Norath could stop suddenly, though. Megelin banged into him. "What the hell…?"

Norath ignored him. In a growling whisper, he said. "Someone is trying to spy on us using the Power. We may have been betrayed. We have to catch him. We need to ask why he is here, waiting." The sorcerer husked orders to the men, then to his beasts. Two parties of six men each moved out. Those who stayed began stringing horses and camels together so they could be managed more easily.

Megelin was livid. Not one of his lifeguards had looked to him for approval of the sorcerer's orders.

That reckoning might come soon.

What had happened, anyway? Norath seemed stricken sick. He almost danced in his nervousness.

The sorcerer could not restrain himself. "You. You. Attaq. Come with me. The rest of you stay with the King. Keep the animals together." He said something else in another language. The deathcats rumbled unhappily.

Norath moved off into the moonlight at his best speed.

The deathcats arrayed themselves defensively on Megelin's side of the herd. The remaining lifeguards stationed themselves among the animals, to steady them up. They were one fright short of a stampede.

There were thirty-two horses and four camels. The King of Hammad al Nakir had to help control them as though he was a common soldier. Another mark against Magden Norath.

Megelin tried to talk to the men across the herd. The lifeguards had nothing to say. One unidentifiable voice told him to shut up. They had troubles enough already.

A shriek ripped the night. Megelin jumped. The cry stirred a deep, unreasoning dread.

Expectant silence followed. It lasted only seconds.

Shadows scurried past. Megelin first thought they were his lifeguards fleeing. Then one ragamuffin passed close enough to be recognized as a derelict.

The lifeguards swarmed out of the darkness seconds later. Some grabbed Megelin and hustled him forward. Others helped move the animals.

Magden Norath was not among them.

After Megelin had been herded more than a hundred yards, the nearest lifeguard panted, "The sorcerer is dead. His head was almost all the way off. We need to get you safe."

Norath? Slain? *Magden Norath?* How could that be?

As the band streamed into the Sheyik's compound Megelin heard the distant shriek of an injured deathcat.

Suddenly, Megelin was alone except for three lifeguards. Those three barely restrained their rage. They wanted to go hunt the monster who had murdered their god.

The Sheyik's men took the animals. Others kept pushing Megelin toward safety. They took him to the Sheyik himself, an older, heavily bearded man Megelin knew and did not like. Hanba al-Medi had served both sides: the Disciple when the Faith was in full flood, then the Royalist cause after El Murid began to fade.

The old man was trembling, confused. He kept asking what the excitement was about and got no answers.

At that point there were no answers. The second in command of the lifeguards told Hanba, "There was an ambush. Someone knew we were coming. Four men are dead—including Magden Norath."

The old chief blanched. He faced his king. "That can't be possible. Magden Norath?"

"His head was cut almost all the way off. The men with him were killed, too."

Despite being inside, Megelin heard the shrieks of the deathcats and the screams of men who were too close when they went mad.

Al-Medi was terrified, yet outraged. "I learned of all this two days ago. What it's about was never explained. I could betray nothing if I wanted. What have you brought down on me?"

No doubt he spoke the truth. Norath had arranged to be here. Norath was careful. Only he had known the story. It could be argued that, logically, only he could be the traitor.

Megelin thought his head was going to burst.

Reports came in. They were not good. Two deathcats had gone mad. They had attacked one another and anything living till the bodyguards put them down. Another six men were dead. Four were badly injured. A half-dozen derelicts had been killed as well.

Megelin screamed, “Old man, what am I doing here?”

“You were brought to see me.”

Megelin turned. And was surprised. That strong young voice had come from the oldest man he had ever seen, a bent, shuffling creature thin as starvation itself. But the power round him was so potent Megelin could taste it.

A bony, crooked finger indicted Megelin. “Come with me, boy.”

Time stopped. Everyone became rigidly motionless.

Rage at the ancient’s lack of respect boiled inside Megelin—the more so when he found that he could not resist the command. In a moment he and the living antiquity were inside a small, isolated room, absent all witnesses.

Megelin could not control his flesh but his mind remained independent. He recognized a level of distress in his companion that bordered on terror. The old man was totally rattled—maybe because he understood just how amazing Norath’s fall had been.

The King finally realized who the ancient had to be: that most fabulous of fabulous beings, the Star Rider.

Megelin wished he had the strength and quickness to leave the old devil a sack of dead bones alongside Magden Norath.

The old man’s sneer revealed his confidence of knowing every treacherous thought whisking through Megelin’s brain.

...

Varthlokkur was playing with the children when the unexpected burst. Smyrena lay on his lap, wriggling and giggling, trying to catch a glowing butterfly that kept sneaking past her chubby-fingered grasp to perch for a moment on her pug button nose. Ekaterina and Scalza cheerfully blasted each other in a tag game involving harmless balls of light. And Ethrian…

Ethrian was looking outward tonight. He remained silent, did not interact, did not respond to direct address, but was connected and alert.

Varthlokkur was pleased to see even that much progress.

Nepanthe was thrilled beyond description.

She was downstairs cobbling together refreshments, no doubt including something that had been an especial favorite of Ethrian’s as a child.

The boy did not move much, and then only slowly, mainly just turning his head. He was intrigued by everything, as though seeing it all for the first time. And he was, really, for the first time with any curiosity. His cousins, his sister, the Winterstorm, it all stirred mild expressions of wonder.

The baby was just as intrigued by her brother—when she was not preoccupied with her butterfly.

Nepanthe arrived accompanied by burdened servants. "I decided to bring a whole meal since we didn't have a proper supper."

"Good thinking," Varthlokkur said. "Considering the energy those two goblins are burning off."

Nepanthe started to ask if he had found a way to communicate with Mist but he was not listening.

Ethrian had stiffened. As Varthlokkur turned his way the boy stunned everyone. He pointed at the Winterstorm, said, "Grandfather."

"Nepanthe, take the baby. Now!"

The Winterstorm was stirring but what had triggered Ethrian was not obvious there. That was clear only in a mercury pan seldom used but eye-catchingly alive right now. It had been spelled to trigger only under a few unlikely circumstances.

One would be the sorcerer Magden Norath coming within a mile of the Star Rider's winged horse.

A thousand hours, spanning the years since the Great Eastern Wars, had gone into the mathematics needed to build the spell suite that tripped the alarm. The task had proven intractable till Varthlokkur decided to try tracing the winged horse instead of the Star Rider himself.

After Nepanthe took Smyrena, Varthlokkur told her, "Darling, clear everyone out. The children first."

Which meant something big and possibly dangerously bad was happening. Vaguely, Varthlokkur was aware of Nepanthe fussing over Ethrian as she drove everyone out of the chamber.

In moments the wizard was assessing the situation in al-Habor.

Oh, what an opportunity delivered by Chance! A nudge here, another there, hardly powerful enough to disturb an ant's slumber, and the world changed forever. His part would remain forever unknown to any but he.

Once the nudges had been dealt he settled to observe.

He wished he had the Unborn close enough to do more.

It might be worth revealing himself if he could get the winged horse while the Star Rider was preoccupied.

With any luck he might even have stripped the Star Rider of his principal source of power, the Windmjirnerhorn.

"Let's not get greedy," he muttered, on finding himself searching for the horse using Norath's only surviving deathcat.

It had been a long day before the alarm. Exhaustion took hold. Sweet as harming Old Meddler would be, disaster was certain if he lost control because he was too tired to concentrate. Released, the deathcat would be after Haroun in a heartbeat.

He drove the beast to the Sheyik's compound, over the adobe wall, into the house proper, then released it.

There was a chance it might get the Star Rider.

Varthlokkur let himself collapse, pleased with his day.

...

Life had turned simple. Yasmid was getting plenty of sleep. Too much, she feared sometimes. Was she hiding from her obligations by clinging to her bed? Still, there was little to do but arbitrate personal disputes.

There were no foreign threats. Megelin was back in Al Rhemish, licking his wounds and blaming his failures on everyone but himself. Eventually, he would hatch some new abomination.

The fields of the Faithful promised the richest bounty in years. Flocks and herds were particularly fecund. Mares would foal at a wondrous rate. And because the Faithful need not live off the land, game would make a comeback, too. She had ordered hunts restricted to taking predators.

There would be more game when the future turned evil again.

It would. It always did.

No one was more optimistic than she. Her advisers wanted to work everyone like they were under siege, building new granaries and creating new fields that could be used to raise more grain.

Good soil was not plentiful. It had to be created. But water was in bountiful supply. Snow melt came down from the Jebal. A score of springs, all reliable, lay within a day's walk. All had been cleansed of poisons put in over the years. All had been sanctified anew.

Water that did not get used or did not evaporate eventually found its way to the salt pans. Yasmid thought it sinful that any water got that far—though twice, now, she had had to thank God that it did.

She was half awake, fantasizing ways to bring more water to the desert, when a servant announced, "Habibullah wishes to see you, Mistress."

She felt irritated, then recalled that she had sent for the man. "All right. Let him in."

Social circumstance had compelled Yasmid to create a pseudo-audience in a mess room where she could pretend she was not a woman and it was not necessary to maintain eunuchs, slave women, and cloth screens to conceal her from male visitors. She loathed that kind of formality. She had evaded it most of her life. But success had its price. Since Megelin's defeat the older imams had grown loud demanding observation of fundamental rules. People listened because they saw no more need to be flexible.

If peace persisted those old men would keep isolating her till she lost contact with the world.

She asked herself, "What would Haroun do?"

Haroun would bury them. There were not many of them, they were just loud.

Habibullah joined her. He did not speak. He still limped because of a wound taken in the battle with Megelin.

She let that be. "Do you have anything to report?"

"You have something in mind?"

"What progress is my father making?"

"There is progress. You'd see it if you'd visit. But it isn't as dramatic as Elwas hoped."

"His time is flying away."

"I'd say that he's shown true progress."

"Really?"

"Truly. But I'm not sure that the swami can finish up. Your father would have to do his part."

"He isn't trying?"

"Not much."

Yasmid sighed. “We’ll give them more time. Merim. Come here. You’re dancing like a child with a desperate need to pee. What is it?”

“Elwas al-Souki is in the kitchen. He begs the chance to bring you news. There is a man with him who needs a bath badly.”

“Leave the smelly man there. Bring Elwas. Habibullah, stand as my witness.” She could not become comfortable with al-Souki. It was not a sexual tension thing, either. It was a creepiness thing. There was something wrong about that man, though no one else could see it.

Elwas al-Souki presented himself with his usual rectitude. His pursuit of form and manners only made Yasmid more uncomfortable.

Her mood shone through when she said, “If you’re here to describe the Disciple’s progress Habibullah beat you to it.”

The ghost of a puzzled frown, then an even fainter, more fleeting touch of hurt, crossed al-Souki’s face. “That is something else, Blessed One. There has been a dramatic development amongst the Royalists. The news just came. The man nearly killed himself getting it here fast.”

Blessed One? “Yes?”

“The sorcerer Magden Norath is dead. He was killed in a town called al-Habor, in an attack so sudden that he had no chance to defend himself.”

“I know al-Habor. But, Magden Norath? Dead?”

“Yes, Sacred Voice. Our spy was an eyewitness.”

Not possible. Could not be. Magden Norath had attained near demigod status during the Great Eastern Wars.

“Dead,” she said again, dumbfounded. “But… That’s not… There’s more. Isn’t there?”

“Much more. The rest is not so joyful.”

“No. After that I suppose there would have to be something awful to balance the scale. What is it?”

“The witness believes the assassin was a ghost. Or some revenant, undead thing. He swears the killer was Haroun bin Yousif.”

Her body turned to water. For an instant she got caught up in the ridiculous question of whether or not Elwas knew about her and Haroun. Of course he did. That had been no secret for a long time.

"Impossible!"

Equally stunned, Habibullah said, "We never really knew that, did we? I never heard tell of anyone actually seeing a body. He just stopped being seen alive."

"But..."

"Chances are a million to one against it. This spy just wants to see ghosts."

Al-Souki said, "He doesn't want to believe it, either. He desperately wants the assassin to be something supernatural instead."

Yasmid buried her head in her hands. "This will get exaggerated into total insanity."

Al-Souki said, "I may have overstepped, Lamp of God, but I did move to make sure the mullahs don't whip up the fanatics."

Yasmid stared, astonished.

"Have I overstepped?"

"No. This news could spark a new round of wars. Tribal warlords won't be scared of a Megelin without Magden Norath behind him."

Elwas coughed, looked reluctant, but went on after a pause. "Megelin may have acquired a more powerful protector."

This would be the really bad news, saved for last.

"Light of the Ages, the Faithful have numerous friends in al-Habor. The water remains sweet and reliable. The crossroads needs to be watched. Royalists on secret missions often pass through."

"I've been there. Get to the point."

"Norath and Megelin went there to meet someone."

"Megelin, too?"

"He was not harmed. His bodyguards kept him safe. They moved him into the local Sheyik's stronghold."

Megelin and Norath had gone to al-Habor for a secret meeting? Were the Tervola eying the west again?

Elwas said, "The Faithful in al-Habor say that Megelin came to meet the Star Rider."

Much worse than a visit with Tervola, then.

Yasmid released a long sigh. Somewhere in scripture there was an appropriate verse that ran something like, "And the thing we dread befalls us."

"Stop. Habibullah, clear everyone out. You and Elwas stay."

Habibullah did as he was told, as ever, without understanding. He shut doors then came close so she need not speak loud and be overheard by eavesdroppers.

She asked, "Elwas, how strong is your faith today?"

"Shaken, Shining One. Badly shaken."

"Stop giving me titles. Habibullah? How about you?"

"I am no fanatic but I am a Believer. My faith today is the same as it was yesterday. Why should it change?"

"Elwas. How widely known…"

"Only a handful know now. In a month the world will know."

Habibullah said, "I'm confused. Why is the death of Magden Norath a tragedy for the Faith?"

"It isn't. Him and Megelin having a secret meeting with the Star Rider is."

Habibullah looked no less confused.

"Old Meddler, Habibullah. Behind half the evils of history. He was the angel who saved and educated my father. He wasn't an emissary of God. My father did God's work but he was set on that path by a devil who wanted a world filled with warfare and chaos."

What Yasmid said was nothing new. El Murid's enemies had made those claims for years. She watched Habibullah perform the mental acrobatics needed to avoid angry denial. He converted to sublime acceptance quickly. "God, in His Wisdom, used His Enemy to instigate the Disciple's Great Work."

"Exactly. And that will be dogma from now on. Elwas?"

"The logic is irrefutable. God has Written everything already."

"Good. I want the imams and mullahs gathered for evening prayers with me. I'll also want the Invincibles available to deal with those old men if they give me any grief. We'll establish an official position before the rumors get crazy. Elwas, can I trot my father out?"

"Go see him. Make that judgment yourself."

…

Yasmid was alone, except for Habibullah, whose proximity she seldom shook. Habibullah waited for her to face the most troubling aspect of the news.

Finally, softly, she asked, “Is there a chance that Norath’s killer really was…?”

She could not say the name.

“It must have been. It would have to be. Who else? Dramatic unity.”

“Excuse me?”

“That would be God having a chuckle at our expense. For even more drama He should’ve brought the assassin face to face with the King.”

“Oh. My.” Yes. If that *was* Haroun he must have come within yards of their son, with neither knowing.

“Habibullah, I feel too old and too tired. Find me a place to leave the world behind.”

“I feel that way myself, quite often. Then I remind myself that the only one who ever managed that is your father.”

Yasmid wanted to bark and snarl. But what point? Whatever she said, Habibullah would have an answer. And it would make much too much sense.

†

CHAPTER NINE:

SPRING, YEAR 1017 AFE:

THE LESSER KINGDOMS

Inger stalked into the room where Babeltausque waited. Only a day had passed since his conversion. Already he insisted on seeing her.

She hoped a quick response did not make her seem desperate. "You're ready to go to work?"

"Majesty, first, I want to say that last night I enjoyed my best night of sleep since I came to this wretched kingdom. This morning I enjoyed my finest breakfast since we left Itaskia. I'm in an excellent mood. I'm eager to start work. So let's review what you want me to do."

"I want you to root through shadows. To turn out hidden secrets. To find things. To find people. Can you do all that?"

"Maybe. Tell me what you're looking for."

"All right. First and most critical: find Colonel Gales. Dead or alive. See Nathan Wolf. He's done all the looking so far."

"What else?"

"The treasury money. I'll give you ten percent."

"Most every minute I bless anew the fate that brought me to you."

"Let's hope you feel that way a year from now. Others I want found: General Liakopulos, Michael Trebilcock, and that bitch Kristen Gjerdrumsdottir."

"The Duke had her killed."

"He tried. He might think he was successful. But she's still alive and scheming to make her brat king."

Babeltausque did not argue. Dane of Greyfells had become the tenant of a dungeon cell because of his ineffable ability to believe anything he wanted to be true.

Inger said, "The money is the most important thing. Then Josiah Gales and any looming threats. Especially threats to you. You'll become a target for folks who don't like me. The rest you can deal with when you find time."

Babeltausque said, "As you want it, so shall it be."

"Sweet talk, sorcerer. But these are desperate times. Talk won't help make us the people doing the grinning at the other end."

"You've changed."

"I have. You won't find this Inger nearly as nicc as the one you remember. This Inger can be quite bloodthirsty. What do you need to make what I want happen?"

The sorcerer opened and closed his mouth several times. Nothing came out.

"Tell me, Babeltausque." Her tone suggested pain on the way if he did not buckle down now.

...

Dane, Duke of Greyfells, had a concussion. Its effects were exacerbated by his inability to accept his situation. He was Greyfells, the Duke, senior member of a noble family that, by God, deserved, by God, to rule Itaskia and several neighboring states. Only continuous, relentless evil conspiracy by lesser men kept the Greyfells line from claiming its rights.

He was not one to note what had been done to ease his confinement. He had a cot, topped by a mattress. Fresh straw covered the muck on the floor. He was not chained. He had a stool with a bucket underneath to manage his eliminations. But all he saw was an iron wall with welded straps and rivets that made escape hopeless.

Meals came regularly, through a slot three inches high and sixteen wide. The slops bucket left via its own little door, too small to pass a man.

Reality took days to dawn. He was completely at Inger's mercy, and her mercy would be slight at its most generous.

Those who brought food and removed his wastes would not talk. Maybe they did not understand Itaskian. Maybe they were deaf. It was beyond his capacity to understand that most people hated him. Inger's people thought she was being too soft.

He did see that if he was not heard, if no one listened, if no one understood, he would go nowhere ever again, but while he remained alive the Greyfells fortunes would remain out in the wind.

More than ever he cursed the idiot he had been when he decided that he could steal a crown for his family.

...

Josiah Gales strove ferociously to pull himself together. He could not begin to guess how long he had been like this. He wanted to assess his situation but his head would not clear.

Clever bastards. They did not feed him well. Teetering at the edge of starvation, he attacked whatever food they brought. Which was drugged. Always.

No one interrogated him. No one cared what he knew. No one explained why he was a captive.

He had been removed from the equation by a means less harsh than murder. He no longer signified. He might be turned loose later, or maybe retained as a bargaining chip.

Gales saw few of his captors. They did not talk. They did not acknowledge his existence, except that they fed him.

Drugged, it took Gales a while to fathom the rules of his new life.

If he said nothing and did nothing life proceeded with no inconvenience beyond being imprisoned and drugged. It went smoothest when he just quietly contemplated the stupidity that had brought him to this.

His captors evidently bore him no malice. They just wanted him out of the way.

...

An old man entered the apothecary shop in Old Registry Lane. He seemed almost too frail to manage the door.

A girl of fourteen was minding the shop. She was surprised to see him. He smiled a smile full of fine white teeth, shuffled forward. His body, like his teeth, was in excellent shape. Apparent infirmity was part of his disguise. "You're looking especially nice this morning, Haida. You make me wish I was ten years younger."

Haida flushed, flattered, flustered, but not offended. "I'll see if Chames is in back."

"You don't know?"

"Not always. He comes and goes without telling me. I'm just the help."

The girl was more than that, though not the plaything some suspected. She was the little sister of someone who had been killed, a friend of the man called Chames Marks today.

The old man watched her swish through the hangings in a doorless doorway. He thought Haida would be more than just help if Chames would let her. There was a sparkle in her eye when she said his name.

The old man smiled, turned the sign on the street door to say the chemist was out, then latched the latch.

The wait stretched, five minutes, ten, fifteen. The old man amused himself by studying the pots and jars on the scores of shelves covering all four walls. Large glass jars contained questionable items in liquids of unusual hue. Stage dressing, those, mostly. He was interested in the small phials of imported rarities. Sometimes he paused, nodded. Once he murmured, "Well!"

The hangings in the back doorway stirred. Haida returned. Her gaze flicked round, checking for spaces where something had gone missing. "Turn the sign back. People will wonder. We're always open during the day. Then come with me."

The old man complied. Compliance had been his first layer of camouflage for decades.

The room beyond the doorway was larger than the one out front. It was dry and dusty. It smelled of spices and mystery. The real work of the chemist took place here.

"Wait here. Touch nothing." Haida returned to the front. The bell on the door had announced an arrival. A male voice asked a question the old man could not make out.

Minutes passed. A man came through a narrow door that was disguised as a rack of dusty shelves. The old man held fingers to his lips, pointed behind him. The newcomer nodded, whispered pointless questions about the old man being sure he had not been followed. That did not matter, unlikely though it was. "What brings you out, then?"

"The Queen has recruited the sorcerer Babeltausque. She means to take immediate advantage."

"Really? The Duke never bothered."

"And he's in a cell."

"True enough."

"She has assigned the sorcerer five immediate tasks. Find the missing treasury money. Find Josiah Gales. Find Michael Trebilcock. Find General Liakopulos. Find Kristen and her children."

"Can he accomplish any of that?"

"The Queen thinks so. I trust her judgment. She's known him a long time."

The younger man sighed. "Complications. But it's never easy, is it? We will cope. You'd better get back. Haida will have your order ready when you go out." He gestured toward the front of the shop.

The old man nodded. He began to move. "The sorcerer's most important mission will be to find the money."

"Maybe we should let him succeed."

"You haven't found it, either?"

"No. Those two did a hell of a job of leaving no clues."

The doorbell rang as Haida's customer left.

The old man said, "I'm going now." He had to get back to the castle. He tarried only moments acquiring a package from Haida.

The younger man began to consider how best to respond to the news.

Respond he must, before the sorcerer became a threat.

The matter of the treasury, though. Working that made sense.

Why had those two hidden the money somewhere other than where they were supposed to have?

…

No one challenged Wachtel when he shuffled into Castle Krief. He went straight to the Queen's quarters. He told the maid, "Inform Her Majesty that I've finally gotten the medicine for Prince Fulk."

"That's good news. She'll be thrilled."

Inger appeared while Wachtel was preparing his philter. "You found blue asparagus seed?"

"I did. Everyone watch how this is done. You'll have to do it yourself in an emergency."

"Including the grinding?"

"Including that. The seed needs to remain whole till you have to use it. The oils evaporate."

"How did you find the seed?"

"I went to the chemist myself." His tone was harsh. "I'm getting a little frail for that."

Inger was flustered. "I'm sorry. There just isn't money…"

"Never mind. The deed is done. I got enough to keep you going for three months. And so my fortune grows as feeble as my flesh."

"I'm sorry, Doctor. Truly I am. You'll be the first one rewarded when our fortunes shift."

Wachtel's skeptical expression told Inger all she needed to know about his faith in her promises.

"You'll see."

She had made a too-grand emotional investment in her new wizard.

…

The wizard sat with head in hands, sweating. He was overheated despite the breeze flowing through the open windows. He had made promises. Those had seemed reasonable in the heat of the moment.

Now he had to execute them.

He did not know how to start. There were no threads to pick up. Everyone *knew* that those who had executed the treasury raid had died in the riots. Michael Trebilcock had fallen off the edge of the world and was presumed dead, too.

But, wait! Finding Gales would be a coup! Gales had left some threads. The night of his disappearance was well-documented.

That would be the scab to pick, if only to prove that he was on the job. Whatever he stirred up would lead to something else.

It seemed reasonable to think that those who had taken Gales might be associated with the treasury raiders. And all those people had been associated with Michael Trebilcock.

It could all be connected.

Gales it was, balls to the wall.

Babeltausque grinned, drenched in cool relief. "Toby, I need you." He had been assigned one servant, a boy of twelve, totally reliable according to Inger. Babeltausque was not prepared to bet his life on the boy, whether or not he was a descendant of the apolitical Dr. Wachtel.

"Sir?"

"You know Mr. Wolf?"

"Nathan Wolf, sir? The new Colonel?"

"Yes. Go tell him I need to see him as soon as possible."

Would Wolf respond? He might fear a restoration of that curse.

Toby was waiting for something more.

"Go, boy! Tell him it's important."

"Yes sir." Toby went, fast.

Babeltausque brooded about having the boy underfoot. But Inger would not like it if he ran Toby off. And Toby's family would be offended.

Better to be careful than to make enemies needlessly.

Toby returned with stunning quickness. "Mr. Wolf will be here in a few minutes, sir."

"You found him that fast?"

"I ran into him on my way to the guardroom to ask where to look for him."

"All right. Prepare whatever refreshments we can manage. After you've done that you're free till suppertime."

"Thank you, sir!"

Toby did love his free time.

Wolf arrived as Toby set out weak tea and a few overage biscuits. The soldier was uneasy.

The wizard said, "Forget the past. I have. Thanks for coming so quickly. Speed may be essential. Go on now, Toby. Have fun."

The boy bowed himself out.

Nervously, Wolf asked, "What's going on?"

"I want to pick your brain about Gales's disappearance."

"I'll do my best. I did my best. I'm sure he was killed right away."

"I expect you're right. Unfortunately. Evidently he was a great buttress for Her Majesty."

Wolf leered slightly.

Later, Babeltausque asked, "Anything else questionable happen around this Twisted Wrench?"

"Nothing obvious. But everybody is careful around my people. And now you're wondering how they know which men are mine."

"I am."

"Only men I trust visit the place anymore."

The Twisted Wrench had fallen on hard times.

"Mr. Wolf, why don't you and I visit this place?"

"That could be dangerous."

"Yes. It was for Colonel Gales. A visit could stir up all kinds of excitement. We'll do it tonight. We'll take two men to watch our backs. Don't tell them we're up to something."

"They wouldn't need to be told."

No doubt. Wolf was not a companionable sort even with the curse off. And nobody went drinking with the court wizard. "Which men frequent the place regularly?"

"I put it off limits after Gales disappeared. Only my agents go there. They scare off the regulars. It'll stay off limits till Gales turns up."

"That's good." Easier to grind away at the purses of those who depended on the tavern for a living. "That will have them thinking about how to get the old clientele back."

"Tonight for sure?"

"Yes. The Queen is starved for results."

"I'll be in the forecourt come sundown." Wolf departed looking thoughtful.

Babeltausque had not felt this excited in years.

...

Young Bragi said it for everyone when he observed, "This camp is the most boringest place in the world."

Dahl Haas, seated beside Kristen, holding her right hand, said, "Look at that. The boy is healthy enough to complain about still being alive."

Bragi was too young to understand death in any personal sense.

Kristen worried. Even the adults had begun to share the boy's disdain for danger from Vorgreberg. They were wishful thinking, confident that Inger's regime would collapse soon. It might have done so already. It took ages for news to get here from that far away.

The others thought Inger's triumph over her cousin only made her own fall more certain.

Dahl and Sherilee remained committed to the plan, with the latter not so quietly beginning to waver.

Kristen knew she needed only to cling to her strategy. Inger would build her own funeral pyre. The Estates had abandoned her completely, now. No Nordmen remained in Vorgreberg. It was every man for himself with them now. Nor did even a cadre of most of her army units remain. Not that pro-Bragi regiments had weathered recent months any better.

Kristen was convinced that soon Kavelin's people would beg the grandson of their greatest king to ascend the throne of the blessed Kriefs.

Dahl told her, "Your Bragi makes me uncomfortable, love. He's not ready."

"I know, Dahl. I promise, it will be a long regency. You'll get to show him how to be a man."

Dahl was the kind of man Kristen wanted her son to become.

The shockwave of the news about Magden Norath slammed through the smugglers' pass, astounding the Unbeliever, the Faithful, and the Royalists of Hammad al Nakir alike.

Kristen collected her refugees. "The news about Norath is huge. But does it really mean anything to us?"

Dahl said, "He was in the wickedness with Greyfells."

"Also out of the picture, now."

The others had nothing to say. The children's attitudes made it clear that they did not care. Politics meant little to them.

Sherilee was indifferent, too. She was interested in nothing but the lover who waxed ever more fantastical in her imagination.

Kristen scowled at her. The dim blonde was making the elder

Bragi over into a god, raising her dirty old man a notch higher every day. Even the kids thought Auntie Sherilee was a loony.

Nothing came of Kristen's gathering. The consensus, though, was that they were too isolated to understand the full impact of Norath's death.

Dahl Haas had the last word. "We'll go on sitting tight and stewing till we hear from Aral."

Kristen scowled. She had hoped Dahl would be more optimistic.

She did not enjoy their situation more than any of the others. This camp was the last way station before you stepped off the edge of the world.

She did understand the need to sit still.

...

The man was Louis Strass this time. He was forty-three years old and a veteran of numerous wars. He had begun service as a longbow archer two days before his sixteenth birthday. Today he was a master of the arbalest as well as the long, short, and saddle bows. He could teach the manufacture and operations of bow-based ballistae for use as light artillery.

He was a master. He was a survivor. Twenty-seven years had devoured and turned to shit all illusions of honor or right and wrong that had blinded him as a recruit. He was his world. He was his universe. Nothing else was real. Nothing else had any enduring value.

He had serious doubts about himself.

He entered a camp in the Tamerice Kapenrungs afoot, leading two mules, pursuing the illusion that he could win a new life by executing one simple mission.

He was too cynical to sell himself that for long.

Nothing good could come of this. There was no guarantee that asshole Greyfells would come across with the bounty.

So why go on? Because he did not know what else to do? Because he was no longer just the hunter, he was the hunt as well?

He had been out of touch for months, searching. Now, another sketchy mountain camp. He might learn something here but did not plan to hold his breath. He had come up with nothing at half a dozen others.

He arrived early on a day when the weather was fine and traffic was substantial. He was not welcomed but he was accepted. No one cared who he was. He had money. He bought drink and a meal, then a bath. Some thought him overly chatty but did not find his queries obvious or offensive. Some people just stored it up while they were out there alone.

The smuggling season was in full swing. Caravans were moving through the pass. Those who lived off the men in motion were active, too, operating taverns and brothels in tents.

The traveler found what he wanted among the parasites. But first he discovered that the world had tipped over while he was out of touch.

The death of Magden Norath inspired awe but was of no personal import. The capture of the Duke of Greyfells was critical, though. That bastard was now the habitué of Inger's dungeon. He would pay no debts contracted before disaster swallowed him.

What to do about the changed situation? It was an iron-bound certainty that Inger would welcome the results that Greyfells had wanted, but…

Do it on spec?

It was a conundrum. He had faced few hard choices in a lifetime spent as a life taker. There was no in-between in a choice where he would give death or withhold it.

Ah! Of course. Offer a sample. Kill the mother of the pretender, then visit Vorgreberg. Direct travel would not take long. Greyfells could be exhumed to provide a reference.

He had a course. Now he had to pursue it or abort it.

He relaxed. He drank and ate and recuperated.

Visitors who made extended stays at the camp noticed one another. They were a nervous breed.

Questions began to be asked about Louis Strass.

He made naturally nervous people more nervous. His eyes were like the mouths of graves.

He would have liked more time to recuperate but needs must ever rules.

He and his mules departed, following the uphill trace. He slipped into the forest and doubled back as soon as he could do so without being seen.

He positioned himself between granite boulders overlooking the place where his targets stayed. All preparations had been made. He needed only watch and wait.

He saw several men with the look of professional soldiers. At least one was out prowling all the time. They were more alert than seemed reasonable.

Maybe these were that special breed of men who smelled danger coming.

That changed nothing. He had the requisite skills.

The boulders were as close as he could get without having to sneak. The range was easy for the longbow—if his target did not move after he revealed himself by standing to draw. The crossbow would be more difficult to operate but he could take that shot without having to show himself.

The crossbow it would be. Going unseen meant a better chance at a good head start. And he could fall back without having to hurry. There would be time for an ambush.

So. All choices had been made. Only execution remained.

He slipped away to his hidden camp, assembled his chosen tool, returned to his blind. The wait began.

He could take that for as long as necessary. All impatience had deserted him long ago.

There was no opportunity that day. The occasional child came out but never the right woman. As night fell he withdrew to his camp. It would not do to begin snoring down there.

He prepared food once he was sure the breeze would push smoke up the slope instead of down. He killed the fire as soon as he was done. The air would soon chill and begin to drift back downhill.

He settled to sleep. The ground was not comfortable. He could not drift off. Vaguely, he was aware of the moon rising. A near full moon.

A mule snorted. It must have heard something. He listened.

The laughter of children tinkled on the edge of hearing, way down the mountain.

Could it be? Withdrawal by night would be even better.

They might never see anything. And they had no dogs.

The moon was his friend. His lover. Connected with the goddess of the hunt somewhere, was it not?

He was excited but he was cautious. He was too old to take anything for granted, too old to be anything but careful. He was still alive.

A shadow drifting through shadow, he reached and settled into his chosen blind. There were, indeed, children at play below, frisking by the light of lanterns and the moon.

It was someone's birthday. Not one of the children, although they were harvesting the joy of the day.

He spanned his weapon quietly, rested it atop the shorter of the two boulders. There was no need to crouch or lie prone. Darkness cloaked all but his face. With his hat pulled forward that would not be recognized for what it was.

The children raced around a small, rocky field that might once have been an attempt to create a garden. Their energy kept distracting him.

A woman. There were several choices.

There. That had to be her. No one but Kristen Gjerdrumsdottir would wear her hair in a single fat braid down the center of her back. No one but Kristen Gjerdrumsdottir would have so many children swarm around her, then rush away again.

He took aim carefully, as ever he did. His finger squeezed the trigger.

Someone tapped him on the right shoulder a split instant before the release. He jerked. His aim depressed slightly and drifted right.

His bolt flew.

Never so swift as the sound of his bowstring snapping. The soldier men began to turn while the quarrel was in the air.

That struck the side of a granite post masking the target's left leg. Sparks flashed. The ricochet smashed through the breastbone of a small, beautiful doll of a woman.

The archer was in motion already. He did not see the horrified astonishment on the woman's face.

Blades filled the archer's hands almost magically. But he found no one behind him.

"Oh, shit. It can't be."

He could not muster strength enough to be emphatic.

The thing known as the Unborn hovered over his escape route. The monster infant's eyes fixed on his. And that was Louis Strass's last memory for a very long time.

He did understand who had disturbed his aim. Only Old Meddler had longer fingers than the Empire Destroyer.

...

Dahl and two men stormed the mountainside. They found nothing but an abandoned crossbow and, a few yards on, damp pine needles that smelled of piss.

Below, everyone crowded around Sherilee. Kristen shouted, "All of you, get away from her! Get the children inside!" She dropped to her knees, lifted the blonde's head into her lap. "Hang in there, Sherry. Hang in. We'll get that out and you'll be fine. A couple of weeks of rest and you'll be fine."

It did not occur to her to worry about the sniper, or about Dahl charging into an ambush. Only later would she wonder why the assassin had not taken advantage. That would come after a baffled Dahl wondered aloud why the killer had abandoned two mules and all his gear when he made his getaway.

Tears dribbled from the corners of Sherilee's eyes. She husked, "Tell him I'm sorry. I couldn't… Kristen, I just loved him so much."

Kristen could barely see through her own tears as the light left Sherilee's eyes.

Oblivious to the chance of lethal danger, Kristen held her lifelong friend and wept.

This was Kavelin's fault. No matter who sent the sniper. Kavelin was the reason. Kavelin was the excuse. She screamed, "Kavelin, you cesspit!"

A hundred angry accusations roared through her mind. She articulated none of them. Her throat was too tight. And even in her mad rage she understood that Kavelin was a geographical entity before it was anything else. An artificial feature, colored on a map. What really enraged her was the Kavelin that existed in the minds and hearts of tens of thousands of people who had attachments to an emotional entity.

Kristen wept a long time. No one tried to stop her. Dahl and her children did what they could to comfort her.

She smothered herself in sorrow rather than endless rage and a hunger for revenge.

Vaguely, she hoped she was setting an example for her son, who would be king one day.

†

Chapter Ten:

SUMMER, 1017 AFE:

In the East

Lord Ssu-ma Shih-ka'i, just back from a surreptitious visit to the island in the east, was the first Tervola to hear of the violent demise of the last master of Ehelebe, Magden Norath. He did not shed a tear.

What could it mean?

Initial reports, as always, were confused. Divinations into the past were not instructive. Hours of hard work only left him exhausted and depressed.

The Star Rider was becoming meddlesome again and Norath's killer could only be a man who should have died a long time ago, in prison in Lioantung.

He must have escaped during the final showdown with the Deliverer.

Old Meddler must have had a hand in that.

Ah, there was the villain himself. But...! He was not shaping the plot! He was just another piece on the board where the blood was flying.

Though it was not a critical interest, Shih-ka'i did try to put a tag onto the distracted Star Rider so his movements could be followed.

...

Mist passed the blackboard twice without noticing the added characters below **Varthlokkur: where are my babies?** As always, she was preoccupied. At the moment that was because of the death of Magden Norath. That could shake the foundations of the world.

The third time past her mind registered the message of the new characters: **Mother, we are well, with Aunt Nepanthe. We watch when we can.**

Mist froze, transfixed by the multiple levels of meaning.

Her children were well and evidently happy.

They—and, by extension, Varthlokkur—could look in on her whenever they chose.

Varthlokkur had found a way of reaching into her powerfully protected private quarters to chalk a message on her blackboard.

She had to be afraid.

Not even the Star Rider ought to have that much power.

She collected herself, erased both messages, took up the chalk and, in elegant calligraphy, wrote: **I love you, Scalza and Ekaterina**. And felt just awful when she laid the chalk back down.

She could not be a normal mother while she was Empress of the Dread Empire. It seemed sinful to think she had any real claim on those kids.

She drifted into dark reveries about the horror show that had been her own childhood. She had not had the protection that Scalza and Ekaterina did. It was a miracle that she had survived to become an adult.

A racket drew her to the entrance to her quarters.

Two bodyguards awaited her there. One said, "Lord Ssu-ma has sent a message saying you should join him in the Karkha Tower. He says it's urgent." The other presented a card beautifully calligraphed with that message and Shih-ka'i's sigil.

"Very well. You will accompany me. You have ten minutes to prepare yourselves. Meet me in the transfer chamber."

...

Bragi Ragnarson was sick to the verge of puking of Bragi Ragnarson. Mist should be burned at the stake for wakening this

Wild Hunt of introspection.

But there was nothing else to do.

The more he considered the Bragi Ragnarson of recent years the less he liked the man—despite having been the man. Today's Bragi had serious difficulty understanding choices made by yesterday's Bragi.

Back in what seemed antediluvian times Derel Prataxis had observed that power could warp and damage the most soundly grounded mind. Power was worse than opium. It twisted the mind and soul even more.

A morning spent contemplating his self-debasement, while watching an orange and blood-red sunrise, fell apart around him. Mist appeared.

He had not expected to see her again. Certainly not so soon, though the soon was an emotional age. It would be just a month or two in objective time

He had not kept track. Counting the hours only sparked a dismal melancholy. What he could see from his windows suggested springtime.

Lord Ssu-ma Shih-ka'i followed Mist, then came two behemoths wearing badges identifying them as Imperial lifeguards.

The visitors so startled Ragnarson that, at first, he retreated like a threatened animal. Then, finally, "Mist?"

"Bragi."

He eyed Shih-ka'i and the bodyguards. The general wore his boar mask. Nothing could be read from his body language.

"What's going on? I thought I'd be in solitary forever."

"That was the plan. But things keep happening. I found myself unable to be so cruel as to deny you the news."

Something in Lord Ssu-ma's stance suggested that he thought leaving the prisoner in ignorance would be the kinder cut.

"Tell me what you think I need to know."

The natural observer inside marveled at his pretended calm.

He had not looked into the eyes of another in so long. His heart pounded. His breathing grew heavier.

The lifeguards moved up beside their mistress.

Not a good sign. Why so much muscle? He was one out-of-shape, middle-aged man.

The circumstances guaranteed that the news would be terrible.

Mist said, "Kavelin has fallen further into chaos. Ingrid has imprisoned her cousin, the Duke. In Itaskia vultures are feeding on the Greyfells family corpse. Meantime, Inger has been abandoned by most of her Kaveliner supporters. They haven't turned on her, they've just gone home. If she tried to call up an army it's unlikely that anyone would show."

He did not care. The man who had loved Kavelin had been a fool who lived in an elder age.

"Your daughter-in-law has lost most of her support, too, because she hasn't done anything to help those who stood by her. By autumn it will be every man for himself. There won't be a pretense of authority outside Vorgreberg."

"There is no way you can make me feel any worse or any more responsible. And I'm sure that isn't the news you've brought to torment me. A collapse into a lawless Kavelin has been inevitable since I was dim enough to butt heads with Lord Ssu-ma."

"That was the political update. The real news is that Magden Norath is dead. The man who killed him seems to have been your friend Haroun."

"Haroun is dead."

"Quite probably true. But an eyewitness insists that the man wielding the knife was bin Yousif."

"That *is* a piece of news. If it's true. It will rattle the world. But it's insane. Where has Haroun been? Why? Why show himself now?"

Ragnarson noted a slight adjustment in Lord Ssu-ma's stance. The Tervola knew something. He would volunteer nothing, though.

Mist said, "He didn't announce himself. He was recognized. Maybe. He was one of several dozen derelicts living rough in a remote town. Megelin and Norath went there to meet the Star Rider. Haroun, if it was him, attacked so quickly and violently that the sorcerer had no chance to defend himself."

Ragnarson gaped. This was unbelievable. There had to be some error, most likely by the witness. Maybe he was the killer. Passing the blame to Haroun bin Yousif would make a great distraction. But Haroun was dead.

"That feels like old news. In your world. There's more, isn't there? Something more personal and dark. Right?" He gestured. Four of them. Proof of his contention.

"You're right."

"Out with it, then."

"An assassin employed by Dane of Greyfells found your daughter-in-law's band in the Tamerice Kapenrungs."

The floor seemed to go out from under Ragnarson.

He could not speak. Too much emotion rose up after so many months of nothing but mild disappointments over his meals.

"How bad was it?"

"There was one casualty."

Ragnarson reddened. "Tell me!"

The bodyguards stepped forward. The nearest looked eager. Bragi calmed himself. Explosive emotionalism had gotten him into this fix.

These two would pluck him like a dead chicken.

Mist said, "The assassin was supposed to wipe out the whole party."

Ragnarson's vision began to go red. He growled. He leaned toward Mist.

The blow came quicker than a blink. He sprawled against the side of a divan, head spinning. His left shoulder was dislocated. That side of his face felt as though it had been branded.

Mist observed, "You are a slow study, Bragi. Let me explain this one more time. You prisoner. Me owner of prison."

Ragnarson groaned, worked himself into a sitting position. His head began to hurt. "I'm beginning to catch on. Please tell me what happened to my people."

"The assassin loosed one crossbow bolt, then vanished. We know that thanks to Varthlokkur. He informed us, presumably counting on us to pass it along."

Ragnarson barely suppressed the urge to demand that she tell him, now!

"The initial target was your daughter-in-law but the bolt hit your leman instead."

"Sherilee?"

"Yes. We won't be able to bring her here after all."

"Sherilee." In a hollow, lost child voice.

The lifeguards readied themselves to deal with more bad behavior. But Ragnarson just melted. The concept of Sherilee with no life, going on ahead of him, was so alien that, though long experience had hardened him to the loss of comrades and loved ones, this touched him more deeply than had any but the deaths of his brother Haaken and his lover, Queen Fiana. He had visited Fiana's grave frequently, up till the day he dragged Kavelin's best off to their doom.

After a dozen seconds of silence, Lord Ssu-ma suggested, "Perhaps we should step out for a moment."

"You go," Mist told him. "You three. I'll stay."

Nobody moved.

Mist said, "I want you three up in the parapet. Varthlokkur is going to deliver that assassin here. Only the Darkness knows why. I'm at no risk here. This is a broken man."

No one moved.

"Do execute your instructions before I become angry. And notify me when the captive arrives."

The edge on her voice convinced all three. As they went, though, Mist noted, Shih-ka'i dropped a tiny scroll behind a decorative vase on the small table a step to the right of the doorway. That would be a passive alarm meant to warn him if emotions grew overheated.

Secretly, Mist was pleased.

Bragi did not weep. He just sat there staring into infinity. Had he begun to think he was the philosopher's stone of death for those who got too near him? That those who had died around him had done so only *because* they were near him? A solipsist conceit impossible to refute logically.

Mist and Lord Ssu-ma had arrived soon after Ragnarson's breakfast. The day was fading when the Tervola reported the arrival of the assassin. He found Mist settled on her knees two yards from Ragnarson, apparently watching the westerner sleep but probably meditating. Ragnarson lay on the divan.

"The prisoner has arrived, Illustrious."

"Lord Ssu-ma? Was it the Unborn? Did it unsettle you that much?"

"It was. It did. And that despite the horrors of the war with the Deliverer."

Mist said, "You do recall that the Deliverer was the grandson of the man who created the Unborn?"

"I do."

Maybe he wished that he did not.

Maybe Ssu-ma Shih-ka'i had begun to wish that he had not allowed himself to be seduced away from his quiet life as commander of the Demonstration Legion.

"You would. You're thorough. So, Lord Ssu-ma. What shall we do with this gift? What do you suppose the Deliverer's grandfather had in mind?"

"I couldn't guess his motives, Illustrious. Surely the killer will know nothing useful, and I doubt that the Empire Destroyer would expect us to use his skills."

"Could we be expected to turn him over to Ragnarson?"

"I doubt that."

"Then put him into an empty cell. But let me have a look at him first. Maybe I'm supposed to recognize him."

She did not.

The captive was a gaunt, leathery man of advancing years who did not seem noteworthy at all. He was empty and maybe a little mad after his long flight from Tamerice.

Mist directed that he be cleaned up. She did not want parasites colonizing her tower.

...

In moments when he surfaced from grief Ragnarson realized that something was happening elsewhere in the tower. He heard what sounded like construction racket.

He passed several days in communion with despair. He dwelt, to the point of obsession, on what a different world it would be had he just not led his army through the Savernake Gap.

How many lives lost or ruined because of one fit of pride? And the full toll had yet to be paid. Sherilee was just the latest charge.

"How are you feeling?"

Bragi started. He had not heard Mist come in.

"Better than before. How long have I been feeling sorry for myself?"

"Five days."

"You've been hanging around that long?"

"No. I've been attending my duties outside. Other duties brought me back. I thought I'd look in. You seem changed."

In a voice edged with wonder, Ragnarson said, "I think you're right. I *feel* different. I'm not all boiling inside. It's confusing, but I seem to have been stricken by clarity."

"Interesting."

"It's almost like waking up after a long fever."

Mist considered him critically. "I hope so. You haven't been you for a long time."

Ragnarson paced. This was not his caged animal in a rage pacing. This was slow and thoughtful. "I'm probably not myself now, either. Do people get struck sane by tragedy?"

"Worthy thought. We'll watch for a relapse. But do try to cling to the state you're in now."

"You're leaving?"

"Unfortunately, you aren't the reason for my being here. I just stopped to say hello."

"Well, thank you for that."

...

Mist went to the room that Shih-ka'i had remodeled. She looked around. "It looks good. Is that window big enough?"

Shih-ka'i replied, "It is. You aren't a large woman."

She snorted. A statement of fact, yes, but she was vain enough to take offense. She knew, though, that the pig farmer's son would not understand even if she did explain.

She asked, "Do you suppose he's watching?"

"I would be if I had dropped that man here and right away you started remodeling."

Mist heard an odd inflection there. "You have something on your mind?"

"I do. But it's not germane. We have this project on the table. Shall we begin?"

Mist made another circuit of the room, which resembled Ragnarson's, several levels below. It now had a larger window. She saw nothing to discourage her. "Have we unraveled the mystery of the attack on the tower yet?"

"No. All paths lead to dead ends."

"Michael Trebilcock, then."

"Every prisoner here was high value and most had friends a lot closer than Kavelin."

"Could there be another raid while I'm involved in this?"

"I don't know about that. I do know that an assault will not succeed."

Mist stared at the expanded window. Was she ready emotionally?

"My father and his brother made transfers without a receiving unit. Do you have any idea how they did that?"

The inquiry took Shih-ka'i by surprise. "Illustrious? Is that true? I've never heard of such a thing."

"I don't know why it came to mind. I've never heard anything like that, either. But I just realized, both of them got into Varthlokkur's fortress in the Dragon's Teeth, then got themselves trapped and killed. How did they get there?"

"Is that true?"

Mist paused. *Was* it true? She had the story from several sources, none quite agreeing. Some claimed to have been there. None told her what really happened back when.

"I suppose I'll have to ask. Bring out the board."

…

Varthlokkur chuckled. So. The woman had been playing him with all the hustle and bustle. Though, of course, that had been in support of this.

"Nepanthe. Come look."

Smyrena on her shoulder, Nepanthe came. She peered into the globe Varthlokkur was using. She saw Mist beside a large blackboard, smiling. Mist was dressed in masculine travel clothes. The board proclaimed, **I am ready to come see my children** in bold chalk lettering.

Nepanthe asked, "Are you going to let her?"

"What do you think? Can we trust her not to do something unpleasant?"

Nepanthe considered. "She'll behave as long as the children are with us."

"I imagine you're right. So. Start getting ready but don't tell them. She could change her mind. I don't want their hearts broken."

Nepanthe put her arms around him, from behind, and kissed him on the right cheek.

He blushed. She did not notice.

He had longed for that sort of spontaneous affection across the ages.

Nepanthe went away.

Varthlokkur summoned the Unborn.

...

Ragnarson wakened needing to use the garderobe. He did that more frequently lately. But that was a problem for old men. He was not old. Not yet. No.

There was a moon out tonight. He lined it up so he could see it. It was living proof that there was a reality beyond his prison.

Something the color of freshly watered blood occluded the moon. Ragnarson started. What the hell?

That?

Eyes old in evil stared for several seconds. Then the Unborn left.

Ragnarson's heart hammered. That had been a shock. What did it mean? Was a rescue under way?

Nothing came of it. It was just something to haunt his thoughts. When he wakened next morning he was no longer sure the monster had not been a nightmare.

...

The Unborn could do nothing but execute its orders. Varthlokkur had made sure of that when he bound the monster. But the evil in the beast would express itself.

It tried tormenting the Empress, traveling to Fangdred, by dropping her, then catching her after a thousand feet of freefall. But she was no fun. She did not scream after the first surprise.

Radeachar never felt the magic being woven. It discovered the truth the third time it tried a drop. The woman plunged in silence. There was no pleasure in that.

There was pain aplenty, though. The farther she fell the worse that became.

Radeachar was not capable of complex thought. It did possess a strong drive toward self-preservation. That kicked in fast. Thereafter it concentrated on completing its task as quick as could be.

...

Fangdred boasted a small courtyard behind its gate. In the lowlands the world was easing into summer but winter hung on doggedly in the Dragon's Teeth. Ice rimed Fangdred's grey walls, inside and out. Black ice patched the grey pavements of the court. Mist slipped almost as soon as the Unborn set her down. She cursed. That inelegance was not flattering.

She grumbled about the cold, too. She had not anticipated the difference in weather, nor the impact of the increased altitude.

Varthlokkur, Nepanthe, Scalza, and Ekaterina came out to meet her. The children stared as though she was some fabulous beast. They did not run to her. In fact, Ekaterina retreated behind Nepanthe, peeked around with one eye, as though she was a shy four.

Loss shoved a talon into the gut of the most powerful woman in the world. It ripped.

She could quash an empire of a hundred million souls but could not hold the love of her children.

Heading their way, stepping carefully, she reminded herself that she had not been much of a mother before she went back to the Empire. Not by the standards of workaday folk on whose backs businesses, nations, and empires were built.

The four withdrew into the warmth as Mist joined them. Scalza was the perfect soldier. He bowed deeply and said, "We bid you welcome, Mother." There was no affection in his voice.

Ekaterina stammered something, then hid behind Nepanthe again. Nepanthe and Varthlokkur both seemed surprised, which suggested that Ekaterina was, usually, much more bold.

Nepanthe said, "Dinner is being set. If you need to refresh yourself first..."

"I do."

A servant showed Mist the way to quarters already prepared. The woman pretended to have no languages in common with the Dread Empress.

Nepanthe's own children were with their mother when Mist arrived for dinner. The infant sprawled on her mother's left shoulder, asleep. Ethrian sat to Nepanthe's right. His eyes were vacant.

Hard to believe that he had threatened the existence of the Empire.

Uncomfortably conscious of Varthlokkur, Mist focused on Nepanthe. Her sister-in-law. Valther's little sister. Nepanthe signified most in this domestic drama.

Varthlokkur would be the referee.

Servants brought simple fare, as was to be expected in a dreary castle in the most remote of mountains. Dining proceeded lugubriously, silence broken mainly by Nepanthe as she delivered gentle instruction to Ethrian. "Eat your turnips, Ethrian. They'll help you get better. Good boy, Ethrian. Take your finger out of your nose, Ethrian." And so on, with the boy always mechanically responsive.

He was little more than a skeleton. He showed a fine appetite, yet remained as gaunt as he had been on emerging from the eastern desert.

At one point he met Mist's gaze. He asked a quick question. She did not understand.

Scalza said, "He asked where Sahmaman went. He asks all the time."

Ekaterina, in a voice like a mouse, chirped, "He's getting better, Mother. He can talk now."

Scalza added, "But it's only the same three or four things."

Ethrian asked his question again. This time Mist recognized "Sahmaman" and "go." His inflexion was not appropriate to a question.

"Who is he asking about?"

They all seemed surprised. Varthlokkur replied, "The woman who was in the desert with him."

"The ghost?"

"Yes. But she was more than that. She was a true revenant for a while. She had flesh."

The fine hairs on Mist's forearms began to tingle.

Nepanthe said, "They were lovers. Not physically. I don't think.

She sacrificed herself so that Ethrian could live."

Nepanthe stared down at her dinner. Even so, Mist could see the moisture on her cheeks.

Again, Ethrian asked, "Where Sahmaman go?"

And Nepanthe told him, "She had to go away, Ethrian. She had to go for a long time."

Mist realized that her children were staring, expecting her to say something.

She could not imagine what.

These were not the children she had come to see. She had hoped for sweetlings. But Scalza had become old and cold. Ekaterina appeared to be convinced that she was always just one step from having the world strike her another cruel blow, with cause and effect irrelevant.

How could that be? Varthlokkur was no grand choice as a father figure but Nepanthe was a good mother substitute.

Varthlokkur said, "There are extreme abandonment issues. But things were improving."

Meaning her visit might sabotage the good work Nepanthe had done?

Everything we do, she thought, impacts others, often in ways we do not foresee.

"This is a finer meal than I expected, considering your isolation."

"Thank you," Nepanthe said. "Cook will be pleased."

After that everyone seemed to wait to hear from Mist, except Ethrian, who asked after Sahmaman again, and then said, "On Great One go boom."

...

Silence stretched. Mist became uncomfortable. Her children showed no inclination to interact with her. She did not know what to do. Her own childhood had offered no examples of good parenting.

She asked, "Could I see my father while I'm here?"

Varthlokkur shifted slightly, suddenly wary.

"I know my father and uncle died here, in a trap set by you or the Old Man."

"Actually, by someone a step further up the food chain. They're in the Wind Tower. We don't go there much. But, all right. The risk is minimal. I'd say nonexistent but I did see Sahmaman come back, in all her power." The wizard rose.

Mist did the same. She glanced at Scalza. The boy said, "I'll help clean up. I don't like those creepy old mummies."

Leaving the common room, Varthlokkur said, "It's a long climb. Another reason we don't go up there much. Plus, the Wind Tower contains a lot of bad memories."

Mist finished the climb fighting for breath. "I'm not…used to this…altitude."

"You never get all the way there." He was breathing hard himself, but not fighting for breath the way she was.

Mist looked around at a large chamber that had been cleared out, then vigorously cleaned, quite recently. For her sake?

"Scalza doesn't like me much, does he?"

"Scalza knows his family history, on both sides. He has an exaggerated ideal of what his mother ought to be. The woman inside his head isn't you. And you won't be here long enough to evict her."

"I could take him back with me." Only later did she realize that Ekaterina had not been mentioned. Which was disturbing.

Mist herself had survived childhood mainly because she had had a knack for going overlooked. Ekaterina seemed to have that same capability.

The wizard wasted no breath on the absurdity of her suggestion.

"All right. Wishful thinking. The worst of us want to be thought well of by our children. Where are the Princes? I don't see them."

"Here." The wizard drew aside a curtain identical to those that masked Fangdred's interior walls, keeping the cold at bay and the warmth confined. Moving this curtain showed that the room was bigger than it seemed.

"That's where it all happened?"

"It is. The Old Man should be on the higher seat in the center. I don't know what became of him."

That seat was empty, of course. The remains of the Princes Thaumaturge occupied lower chairs to either hand. Varthlokkur removed the dust sheets covering them.

Mist stared, in silence, for more than a minute.

"Is something wrong?"

"I can't tell which one is which."

Varthlokkur confessed, "That would be beyond me, too. This is where they were when the Star Rider left the Wind Tower. They've been moved several times since."

"How did you get in?"

The question surprised the wizard. "What do you mean?"

"Nepanthe told Valther that the Wind Tower was sealed off after that night and that the sealing was proof against your power."

"Not forever. I chipped at the spells for years."

"Chipped at them. And when you got in the Old Man was gone."

"Yes. Though I'm not sure that the Star Rider didn't take him, back then."

"Yes. You are. You think him coming back for the Old Man was the break you needed to get through."

"You're right. It's probable. With the Old Man gone there might've been no reason to keep the Wind Tower sealed."

"This one was my father. He has a scar on his neck. He took the wound the night he and Nu Li Hsi murdered Tuan Hoa."

"Somewhere, in some hell, your grandfather had a good laugh the night they died."

"I'm sure. You were here."

"I was here."

"That must have been a terrible night."

"More than you can imagine, in ways more dire than you'll ever know."

Mist nodded. Only two living beings knew the full story: this man and Nepanthe. Nepanthe was less likely to share than was Varthlokkur.

Mist asked, "How did they get here?"

Varthlokkur responded with a blank look.

"Transfers are how we humble distance in Shinsan. But a transfer needs a sending and a receiving portal. Two sets for two princes. What I know about what happened is mostly hearsay. I never heard how the Princes got here in the first place."

"I don't remember. There is a lot about that night that no one remembers. We were all dead for a while."

"Some more permanently than others, it seems."

"It was not a pleasant evening. I avoid thinking and talking about it."

"As you will." She considered her father and his brother. "There is no way that they can be brought back?"

"No."

"Ethrian's situation put the thought into my head. You're sure?"

"No one in this…" He paused.

Mist faced him. "The Star Rider did this to them, didn't he?"

"No. I did. He put the remains on the seats."

"Can *he* resurrect them?"

"I don't know. I'm sure he didn't plan to when he sealed the Wind Tower. But he is a clever devil."

"Exactly. Considering the example of the Nawami revenants in the eastern desert."

"You're right. Sahmaman was barely a ghost. I'll make sure he finds nothing to work with here."

"The Star Rider needs to be rendered permanently redundant."

"Have a care with what you say."

"You disagree?"

"Not at all. I'll cheerfully entertain suggestions as to how to arrange that. But thousands before us have shared that ambition. Most likely thousands more will do so after we're gone."

Mist stared at her father. "It will take a bigger, faster, deadlier rat trap." Then, "Let's go back down. This is too depressing. All I really came for was to connect with my children."

"As you wish."

She could tell that he considered her prospects doomed.

…

Mist had gone. Neither Scalza nor Ekaterina ever warmed to her.

Varthlokkur settled into that room in the Wind Tower, the curtain back and the dust covers off the dead. He reviewed the terrible memories and tried to deal with questions that Mist had raised.

How did the Princes get into Fangdred without having portals waiting?

He had the entire fortress searched, years after the fact. The search turned up exactly what he expected: nothing.

They could have ridden winged demons. In fact, that seemed likely. But those things made a lot of noise.

The weather that night had been terrible... Previously dissociated elements clicked into place. Of course. That weather had not been natural.

Nepanthe's brothers must have been involved.

Knowing what to look for let him probe the past and discover that the Storm Kings, and Mist herself, had affected events that night.

Insanity. Mist, and many others, had known that the Princes Thaumaturge would be engaged. Everyone had an interest and each thumbed the situation somewhere, trying to shape the outcome subtly. But there was nothing anywhere to clarify the essential question: How had the brothers gotten into the Wind Tower without receiving portals in place?

There was no choice but to believe either the winged demon hypothesis or that portals, since removed, had been placed for them, in secret, beforehand.

It could be that Old Meddler had made it all happen.

And Varthlokkur was no more comfortable about some other questions Mist had raised.

He had to do something with the dead sorcerers. There was no choice about that.

Nepanthe brought tea. She sat with him, her back to the site of the worst night of a life where most every major memory was a bad one. "Ethrian is having a good day. You should spend more time with him. I think that would help."

"Yes. Certainly. It would be time better spent than sitting here, despairing of yesterday and tomorrow."

Nepanthe leaned forward. She rested a hand on his. "Let's just concern ourselves with what we can do today."

There was a tear in the corner of his left eye when he said, "That should be the way we live." They rose. He slipped an arm around her waist as they walked toward the doorway. He glanced back at the dead, just once, as he waited for her to step out.

That once gave him an idea.

†

Chapter Eleven:

Summer, Year 1017 AFE:

Legendary Confusion

Hammad al Nakir simmered with rumors. Everyone wanted to believe that the King Without a Throne had returned. His very first action had been to kill Magden Norath, ending the terror underpinning bad king Megelin's throne!

The desert awaited anxiously what would happen next.

The man who had caused the ferment had no idea what that should be. Taking Norath down, alerting the world to his survival, had not figured in the fantasies he had indulged during his long trek west.

People would start looking for him. Some would just want to know if it was really him. Others would be frightened. Old Meddler would be upset because his intrigue had been aborted before it could be hatched.

Yasmid and Megelin would want to capture him. The Dread Empire and Varthlokkur had to be considered, too.

He could not hide Haroun bin Yousif from those powers. He had to become someone distinctly not Haroun.

He began immediately. He sold his horses. He bought strange clothing. He acquired a donkey and three goats. He left the desert for the east coast. There he bought a cart for his goats to pull. This and that went into the cart, including all his obvious weapons.

The shore of the Sea of Kotsüm was a region where the people followed the Disciple. Bandits and robbers were few.

He came to al-Asadra wearing gaudy apparel and shaved. He had a red demon tattoo on his left cheek and a big blue teardrop falling from the outside corner of his right eye. His own family would not have recognized him.

He had trouble recognizing him, so thoroughly had he dropped into this new character.

He had no long-term plan.

He was an entertainer, now, a role so alien that no one ought ever to look his way with Haroun bin Yousif in mind. He did puppet shows. He used sleight of hand tricks which, due to his lack of skill, compelled him to employ some true sorcery. Carefully. Everyone enjoyed a magic show—so long as they could be sure they were just seeing conjure tricks. And, finally, he told fortunes using a greasy, worn deck found in pawn in the souk where he put on his first show. Their shabbiness lent them credibility.

Divination in any form was illegal but the authorities turned a blind eye so long as the fortuneteller claimed to be an entertainer only.

Cynics would observe that fortunetellers had been around for millennia before El Murid and they would exist still long after El Murid had been forgotten by even the most esoteric historians. People wanted a glimpse of the future, often desperately.

God had written their fates on their foreheads at birth but that was hard to read in a mirror. It was easy to delude oneself into believing that a mummer might, indeed, reveal the divine plan. And the more so when the future one saw oneself was entirely ugly.

"Hai, peoples. Come see." He performed a conjuring trick that attracted a few urchins. He did the one where he found a dirty green coin behind a six-year-old's ear. The kid sprinted off to turn his riches into food. The news brought a raucous crowd of children.

His confidence did not improve. He was not accustomed to children. He was not social at all. He wrestled ferocious doubts as he strove to hide from the world by borrowing a persona from a man long dead.

...

"All this ferment because of one unreliable witness," Yasmid said. "I don't understand."

"They want it to be true," Habibullah replied. "They're sick of Megelin. He's a weakling tyrant who spawns disasters. But they're equally sick of being preached at. They're hungry for a savior. They are making themselves one out of wishful thinking. The King Without a Throne. The strongman who will bring peace and unity. They forget the facts of the man that was."

Yasmid knew that. She did not like it.

She disliked its religious implications. She disliked its social implications. Selfishly, she disliked it because it suggested that she could lose her privileged life.

"I don't want to talk about it. I don't want to do anything about it. I don't want to be seen as concerned about it. Let the fever run its course."

Habibullah was astonished. "But..."

"We're going to try a new strategy, old friend. This time, instead of roaring around killing people and screaming about God, we're just going to ignore it. We'll leave the world alone so long as the world extends us the same courtesy."

She watched the old soldier begin to marshal his arguments, then lay them down again before he spoke.

He was tired of the struggle, too.

She asked, "Is it time to go see my father?"

"Yes. Elwas wants us to dine with him and the foreigner." His disapproval of that Unbeliever never relented.

"Then let us tend to our garden."

Habibullah frowned, puzzled.

"A sutra from the Book of Reconciliation." Which was not a book at all but a long letter El Murid had written to persecuted converts when he was still young and visionary. It was included in the greater collection of the Disciple's Inspired Writings—cynically assembled by Yasmid to help guide and shape the Faith.

"Oh. Yes. Where he tells us to endure our trials. If we live our lives righteously and tend to our gardens, God will tend to us."

"Very good."

"My father was there, in that camp, when he wrote that letter."

Tangled lives, Yasmid thought, with some entanglements going back decades and generations.

She had her women ready her for the public passage across the mile to her father's tent. Though the hard line imams had been tamed for now she did not want to provoke them. Publicly, she would conform to the standards expected of an important woman.

Those were the unwritten terms of a tacit truce.

It was another in a long parade of fine days. The sky was a brighter blue than in most years. There were clouds up there, stately cumulus caravels like immense, gnarly snowballs edged with silver, numerous enough to be worthy of note. They were uncommon in most summers.

The fakir from Matayanga claimed that the unusual and favorable weather was a consequence of the great war between his homeland and Shinsan.

Yasmid cared only that the weather brought more moisture than usual.

"It's almost cool today."

Habibullah misinterpreted. "Getting cold feet?"

"No. I started thinking about Haroun."

Habibullah sighed.

"I'm sorry. The Evil One has that hold on me. I can't get the man out of my head." She took four steps. "I never could." Several more steps. "He would be away for years. And I would spend most of that time watching the door, waiting for him to come through." She managed another ten steps. "Habibullah, I could have come home any time I wanted. There was no one to stop me. There was just one old woman with me. But I stayed and watched the door."

Habibullah faced the mountains behind them. He thought he might shed a tear. He did not want his goddess to see that.

As they approached El Murid's tent Yasmid halted yet again. "I'm watching the door again. God, have mercy on your weak child."

"He's dead, Yasmid. Accept that. The rumors all result from one fevered imagination."

"I can't accept that."

...

Elwas al-Souki met the Lady Yasmid at the entrance to the Disciple's tent—that being a sprawl of canvas and poles covering several acres.

El Murid had a philosophical resistance to residing in structures built of timber or stone. He would live in tents whenever he could.

This sprawl was a ghost of the canvas palaces he had occupied in his glory days.

Al-Souki said, "Lady, you are punctual. Sadly, we have not been your equal. We have run late all day, getting farther behind by the hour."

"What are you up to, Elwas?"

The man did not dissemble. "I hoped to show you how your father is progressing while we wait."

"Why?" She did not want to be here. Whatever prolonged her torment was sure to irk her.

"Because you need to know. Because your wretch of a father is also the Disciple, a shining star to millions. You need to see what we've done to resurrect the visionary from the ashes of the man."

Habibullah averred, "That's interesting talk, Elwas. Now make it mean something."

Elwas flashed a happy face and beckoned them to follow.

They reached an open area fifty feet by a hundred with the canvas twenty feet above, supported by an orchard of poles. There were few furnishings. The floor was sawdust and wood chips mixed with strained sand and shredded clay in a groomed flat, soft surface. Thin, creamy light coming through the canvas revealed several men engaged in calisthenics. Swami Phogedatvitsu and his smarmy interpreter walked around them. The swami occasionally swatted one with a switch. No one wore anything but a loincloth. None of those bodies were worthy of flaunting.

Yasmid did not recognize her father.

When Habibullah brought her home—subjective ages ago—Micah al Rhami had been a fat slug, half blind, barely aware that he was alive. His caretakers kept him fat, drugged, and out of sight so he would not interfere in what they did in his name.

Most of those parasites abided with the Evil One now. The Invincibles and Harish had helped clean them out.

"Lady? Are you all right?" Elwas asked. He sounded genuinely concerned.

"I'm fine. I was remembering my return from exile, when I first saw what had become of my father. It was beyond belief."

"I have heard tell."

Yasmid glanced his way, unhappy. He was not feeling generous toward her, perhaps because of her profound disgust. That never won favor among men who considered her father the Right Hand of God, however far he had fallen.

Elwas told her, "He is free of the poppy. Heavy exercise is one of Swami Phogedatvitsu's sharpest tools."

"Wouldn't that just aggravate his pain?"

"That is emotion expressed as pain, not actual pain. He feels the loss of your mother physically instead of emotionally."

Yasmid nodded. An odd way of thinking but it did sound plausible.

"The swami also teaches skills for managing both the need for the poppy and the pain that excuses the need."

Yasmid sucked in a deep breath, released it in a long sigh. Her father had suffered chronic pain forever. He had sustained severe injuries during his early ministry. Some never healed right. The pain, and the opium he used to control it, clouded his judgment later. Countless needless deaths resulted.

"I do hope that he conquers the poppy, Elwas. I pray for that regularly. But he has beaten it before, only to backslide when life disappointed him."

"This time will be different. I hope you will let the swami manage your father's health permanently."

Habibullah snorted in disdain but did control his tongue.

Yasmid understood. It would be outrageous to hand the Disciple's health and spiritual well-being over to a heathen mystic. The most coveted treasure a villain could win would be control of the Disciple's person.

Elwas bin Farout al-Souki, though young, was cunning and had grown up in circumstances that made reading people a useful survival skill. "Lady, I have no interest in controlling your father. I am involved because my other duties make slight claim upon my time. We have no wars. We have no threats of war. Only a few young, green men want to train for the next war."

Elwas had more to say. He did not get the chance. Swami Phogedatvitsu finished and sent his patients on to whatever they would do next. He donned a wrap of orange that concealed his flab, approached the observers wearing an agile, gleaming, sweat-shiny smile.

He appeared to be pleased with himself.

That was fine with Yasmid. "I am impressed. You have my father more active than I can ever remember."

Phogedatvitsu's smile turned condescending. "Thank you, Lady." He was making excellent progress with the language. He inclined his head just enough.

Elwas said, "The meal isn't ready. Swami, can you show the lady how you help our lord cope with pain?"

Phogedatvitsu turned to his interpreter. The small man rattled something in a language with odd rhythms. Yasmid believed the swami was buying time to think.

Phogedatvitsu said something. His interpreter then said, "Very well. Please follow."

The swami set a brisk pace for a short distance, along what would have been a hallway in a normal house, then entered an empty, cloth-walled room six feet by ten.

The interpreter said, "These conditions must be met: you will say nothing and do nothing. You will not reveal your presence. Is this clear?"

Yasmid agreed because her father had been engaged in physical exercise.

Phogedatvitsu pulled a cloth wall aside. That exposed three men in loincloths lying face down on padded tables. All three were old and wrinkled and scarred and had not been eating well. Men of Phogedatvitsu's race massaged and stretched the old bodies, asked soft questions, used a small brush to make ink dots on skin.

The swami again made signs abjuring speech, then joined the others. Yasmid drew breath to ask why foreigners were here in her father's tent.

Habibullah grasped her left arm. Elwas moved in front of her. He wore a ferocious "What do you think you're doing?" look.

She could shout and carry on later. Right now she had to stand still and keep quiet.

She shook her left arm. Habibullah's grip was too tight.

She opened her mouth again.

Elwas was in front of her again, this time so close their noses bumped. He turned her around. He made her march. Habibullah did not interfere.

Back down the cloth corridor, voice low but intensely angry, al-Souki demanded, "What is the matter with you? Lady." As an afterthought. "You swore you would…"

"That was before I saw…"

"You had to know you were going to see something unusual. Why would he take so much trouble to strive for silence, otherwise?"

"He was sticking needles into him, Elwas! What did you expect me to do?"

"To be silent and observe. As you promised."

"But he was sticking needles in…"

Al-Souki told Habibullah, "She was right when she chose to stay away. We should not have risked that. She isn't ready."

Habibullah nodded, said, "Perhaps," and stared at the earthen floor.

Yasmid demanded, "Does this mean you're part of some…"

Elwas made an obvious effort to control serious exasperation. "Lady, the swami is using eastern methods to free your father from his opium addiction. Do you know more about that specialized work than you do about building construction? I note that you never inject yourself into the work of carpenters or masons. You will, on occasion, ask why something is being done in a certain way."

Each word arrived under rigid control, reeking of truth. She hated him for that.

Then she started. She might have had an epiphany. A sudden grasp of the mind of the man whose special madness had led to generations of warfare and despair.

"Elwas, take us to where we will sit down with my father. We will wait there. And you will regale me with tales of sticking old men with needles."

...

The meal with the Disciple was not exciting. Yasmid's father went through the motions in a lugubrious, mechanical fashion, like a mildly autistic child. He did not make eye contact. He did not speak. He brightened some at mentions of his wife and daughter but failed to recognize Yasmid as the latter.

Yasmid conceded that Phogedatvitsu had worked a miracle by reclaiming El Murid this much. Perhaps now the Disciple would learn to navigate the quotidian world and begin interacting with people.

But this man was not Papa.

What Yasmid wanted desperately was the man she had known when she was little.

Earthly, practical Yasmid bint Micah knew that the Papa she remembered never really existed outside her head.

The swami thanked her repeatedly for being interested in his efforts but, otherwise, said only, "There is much work to be done yet."

...

Varthlokkur, with a comet tail of youngsters, entered his restored workroom. He was careful to conceal the unlocking gestures. Scalza might be tempted to sneak in. Lately, the boy had shown an inordinate interest in the room. He followed Varthlokkur all over, hoping to learn by watching. Ekaterina tagged along because she was interested in everything that interested Little Brother.

Then Ethrian began following his grandfather. Why? Something had changed. Ethrian was intrigued by the world outside Ethrian now. And his mother was thrilled.

"What are we going to do today, Uncle?" Scalza asked. "Spy on our mother again?"

"That part of 'we' constituted by you will remain out of the way and quiet while the part that is me performs some excruciatingly dull maintenance on the Winterstorm."

"Oh, good! When are you going to start teaching us?"

"Never, and a day."

Scalza primed himself for an argument. Before he started Nepanthe arrived. Smyrena was awake and cooing. The youngsters lost interest in anything but her.

That left Ethrian as a puzzled human island. After brief indecision he drifted toward his mother.

Varthlokkur watched in amazement. Nepanthe had a bottomless store of warmth and love for the children. He never got over that. How did she do it?

The children did not bother him again. Nepanthe was that good a kid wrangler.

It did not hurt that the baby seemed interested in learning to crawl. Everyone found that immensely entertaining.

In time, Nepanthe left Smyrena to the youngsters and came to look over Varthlokkur's shoulder.

He said, "I've been looking for Haroun. I can't find a trace. He must be somewhere on the foreshore east of the Mountains of the Thousand Sorcerers."

"What does he want to do? His whole life changed when he killed Magden Norath. I'm sure he didn't plan to go round stabbing famous sorcerers."

"I hope not. I don't want him headed our way." He grinned.

"If he is on the coast he's not interested in what's going on in Al Rhemish."

"Exactly. Before al-Habor he was heading that way by stages. After al-Habor he headed southeast, for as long as I was able to track him."

"So he has a new interest. What could that possibly be, Mr. Wizard?"

He chuckled. "You're probably right. If he isn't after his throne he must be after the woman he loves."

"Let's hope he doesn't poison himself."

"Haroun bin Yousif won't let old love drag him into mortal peril."

"You take the romance out."

"I try."

"I never liked him much. He was always drama and trouble. But he was one of Mocker's best friends."

That name brought on the silence. Varthlokkur refocused on finding bin Yousif. Nepanthe returned to the children. That nerve was still tender.

Varthlokkur gave up looking. Bin Yousif would surface eventually. He shifted his attention to the west.

It was the time of year for armies to march.

The Lesser Kingdoms were a-simmer with vigorous political disinterest. The weather was the best in a generation. People whose lives revolved round agriculture were taking advantage. Even in chaotic Kavelin most every tillable acre had gotten plowed. The retired soldiers were all at work in forest or field.

The Crown spent no money because it had none and lacked any means of collecting revenue. The Nordmen barons were in little better shape. But commoner Wesson entrepreneurs were digging into their secret caches. They were building things. Varthlokkur discovered new grinding mills and granaries, new sawmills and stone cutting mills. Small caravans moved through the Savernake Gap, both directions. The Marena Dimura, though disinclined to participate in the broader community, had missions out looking for engineers to help reopen mines hidden in the deeps of the Kapenrungs.

"So," the wizard mused. "People inside Kavelin will be too close to this and not understand that things are getting better. But there it is. If the political situation doesn't explode."

As ever, what Kavelin needed most was freedom from the ambitions of those convinced that they ought to be in charge.

"Varth?"

He did not acknowledge her. Nepanthe touched his shoulder lightly. He started. "What?"

"You've been staring into that for two hours. It's time to eat."

"Oh."

"You didn't find Haroun?"

"I gave up. I went looking at Kavelin." He needed help getting up. He had remained seated too long. "Good things are starting to happen in the Lesser Kingdoms. How good will depend on Inger and Kristen. They could ruin everything with a civil war."

There was another potential source of despair. Michael Trebilcock.

Varthlokkur had had no success finding Michael, either.

Most people thought Trebilcock was dead. Varthlokkur was not convinced. He thought Michael had pulled his hole in on himself but was out there somewhere, watching and waiting.

Trebilcock was no sorcerer but had a personal magic unique to himself. He might be the most important man in the Lesser Kingdoms now. If he was alive.

Varthlokkur wished he knew how to get in touch.

He could find Michael. He could find Haroun. By a means as subtle as a thunderstorm. By sending Radeachar to look. The Unborn could be stealthy when the target was fixed and known but in a search it tended to attract attention.

Varthlokkur wanted to remain forgotten.

Nepanthe asked, "Why is that? Have Radeachar tow a banner across the sky warning Michael." She had a soft spot for Trebilcock. He had spent months of his life, risking a cruel death, in order to effect her rescue, once upon a time. "Or whoever took over for Michael if he's dead."

"Aral Dantice." The response was instantaneous. "Dantice is protecting Kristen and her children. That's worth a closer look." Then he asked, "What do you think about my putting risers under the legs of my chairs so I don't have to work so hard to get up?"

...

The conjure man moved to Souk el Arba but did not stay there long. He established his existence in a few hundred memories. He did not render himself notorious. He seemed too honest to succeed.

Soon he began to drift westward, spending a few days in each foothill town, moving ever deeper into the mountains. He came to al-Khafra. That village marked the limit where the law prevailed. It would not be reasonable to proceed into the higher mountains alone.

Rootless men waited around al-Khafra, hoping for work as drovers or guards on caravans crossing the mountains. Master caravaneers did their hiring there so they did not have to pay men not needed in the peaceful country farther east.

Haroun found the youngest fellow he could, one Muma al-Iki, hired him to look out for his goats and donkey. Then he shed his tattoos and got himself work as a caravan guard. The master was happy to acquire what looked to be a skilled sword arm. He was escorting someone or something of high value. Haroun made a point of showing no curiosity.

He made himself accepted amongst the guards and drovers through his entertainment value instead of his skills with sharp steel. He had no opportunity to demonstrate those. No wickedness rolled down out of a shadowed side canyon intent on taking plunder and slaves.

The caravan master bemoaned his wasted protection expenses.

An Invincible called al-Souki had been teaching harsh lessons to the little tribes scrabbling for survival in the high range.

The traveler recalled having seen a few high-range people when he was a boy. They were small and wiry and darker than the peoples of the desert and the coast. Their languages, related to one another, were linked to none outside the mountains—unless, remotely, to those of the Marena Dimura in the Kapenrung Mountains.

The conjurer's first view of Sebil el Selib, from a crotch between tall, round-backed foothills still a day away, struck him dumb.

A camel drover asked, "First time here?"

"No. I came once when I was a boy," he lied. "It was different then." There had been no sprawl of farmland, no eye-searing green miles of pasture. No flocks so vast they looked like gulls on their nesting islands. In those days there had been little more than a couple of ugly stone fortresses that he had not seen with his own eyes. He had been too young to join in the raids.

"It's changed a lot in my lifetime. And I'm way younger than you."

"I'm not older than you, I'm just married."

Which made the drover laugh so hard his comrades came to investigate.

"He said it so deadpan!" The others were amused but nothing more. "I guess you had to be there."

"It's all about the timing," the traveler said. "And the unexpected. I caught Isak by surprise. You all came to find out what was so funny. You had expectations."

Isak was impressed. "Man, you got some kind of brain in your head."

"When you have a wife like mine you get a lot of time to think."

Someone asked, "If you're married what're you doing out here?"

"Taking time off to do some thinking."

That amused the drovers. One observed, "I know. You married your cousin. Now you can't get out." A reasonable explanation. The desert peoples typically married closely. But none of these men really believed that. They knew about his sketchy career before he joined the caravan. Muma liked to talk.

No one cared.

The traveler might be a rogue but he was a rogue who did his share. He had undertaken dangerous assignments without quibble. He had helped the injured when the hazards of travel overtook someone. He had a way with animals. Horses, in particular, were nervous in the thin, electric air of the high Jebal but they calmed down when he was around.

Oddly, not once did he hear anyone wonder if he was a spy. That would have been his own first suspicion of someone like himself.

Maybe that was because, in some way he did not recognize, he made it clear that he was something else.

"We need to get back to work," one of the drovers said. "The Pig has noticed us lollygagging."

The Pig was the lead drover, a partner in the enterprise. He was neither a bad man nor a harsh boss but he did have expectations. And was cursed with a face reminiscent of a porker.

Haroun looked for his own boss, the partner in charge of defense. He did not see the man. In any case, guards were free to wander and dilly-dally so long as they did not collect in one place.

Still, it was time to start doing things in a way that would leave no outstanding memories once the caravan broke up.

The enterprise would reform in a new shape, leaving some behind and gathering others, before it moved on into the desert. Haroun told some folks he meant to stay at Sebil el Selib. Others he told he would move on after he visited the holy places.

He hoped for confusion—or that no one would care.

There was no reason anyone should. He was just another traveler.

Muma accepted the balance of his pay. "What will you do now, Aza?" Aza being the name Haroun had worn while crossing the mountains.

"I don't know. All I ever thought about, till now, was how to get here. This is the place where things begin. This is God's home. This is the goal. I never thought about what to do next."

The boy was surprised. "I always thought you knew exactly what you were doing. You seem like you're more than just you."

"That makes me a good actor, I guess. What about you?"

"I'll stay with the caravan. Pig liked how I handled animals and stuff."

"Good luck, then. I need to find a place to camp. I have some money, now. I can lay around a few days." Telling fortunes and selling charms might not work here. Hardliners took literally El Murid's declaration that such things were the handiwork of the Evil One.

Muma said, "The field below the New Castle is where pilgrims camp. Just ask for directions. And good luck, Aza."

The boy left with a parting wave.

They had been close for weeks but Haroun had learned nothing about Muma, other than that he was dishonest about himself, too.

No matter. He was no threat.

Haroun found the ground reserved for pilgrims. The field was vast. Thousands had camped there in the past. Today there were only a few hundred. There was grazing for animals, water, and little of the stench common when too many people crowded into too small an area.

He got his tent up, used sticks from his cart to make a pen for his animals, then got busy making himself into a new man.

Travel had left him looking too much like the fellow who had murdered a wizard in al-Habor.

He discovered that he lacked sufficient firewood to build a cook fire.

Then the Invincibles arrived.

There were two. They were old. One lacked part of his right hand. The other had had the left side of his face ruined by a sword or ax. He was absent an ear and an eye. An island of bone shone where his left cheek ought to be. No doubt he and pain were long time brothers.

There was a specific form of address due these veterans but Haroun could not remember it. When they asked what he was doing here, he tapped his ears and shook his head. He pressed his tongue against the roof of his mouth and did not move it when he said, "I am a children entertainer. I came here hoping to see the Disciple for his blessing. Maybe God will see me here and restore my hearing."

The Invincibles had him repeat himself several times. His story sparked neither commentary nor sympathy. They heard its like too often. They were going through the motions, bothering at all only because they were bored.

One of them probed Haroun's possessions with little interest. The cards did not trouble him, nor did the dicing paraphernalia. He was apologetic. This was the only work he was fit for anymore. Haroun found nothing to offend him. The Invincible shrugged and turned away. The other man gestured at the empty fire pit.

"The wood seller is down where the banners are. He's reasonable. If you want to collect your own he'll tell you where that's permitted."

Haroun bowed and slurred, "A thousand thanks, Gracious One."

The man frowned, then. "You look familiar. From a long time ago. Were you at Wadi el Kuf?"

Haroun could honestly answer, "No. But my father was."

"Maybe that's it."

"Possibly. He's gone now." Thinking the man must have been a boy at the time if he was a survivor of that disaster.

The Invincible was inclined to visit further. His companion was not, though. He waved the ruined hand and strode away.

There was daylight left when Haroun got back from seeing the wood seller. His situation intimidated him. He would have to deal with a lot of people here. His time on the eastern littoral had not been preparation enough. He had spent too much of his life alone.

He would meet the challenge.

He would befriend other pilgrims, visit the shrines and the former monasteries now housing religious offices, and even go see the Malachite Throne.

His father had seen the Malachite Throne once. He had come within moments of killing the Disciple in front of it.

He would ask questions, as a pilgrim might, hoping to run into people who could not help showing off how much they knew.

He took a last look round in the twilight.

The only woman he ever loved was just half a mile away.

He wrestled the temptation to use the Power to spy. He knew better. Someone would be watching for a wakening of the Power where it was curst and condemned.

He had no need to hurry. He was safe. He was in the last place where anyone would expect to find the King Without a Throne.

Chapter Twelve:

YEAR 1017 AFE:

Kavelin: Shadow Dancing

Nathan Wolf and two Wesson men-at-arms awaited Babeltausque. Wolf introduced the soldiers as Erik and Purlef. Neither appeared to be especially bright. They would execute their assignments without wasted soul-searching.

Any man smart enough to look ahead had left the soldiering trade already.

They pushed into the Twisted Wrench. The place was moribund. It boasted three customers where sixty could crowd in. One had passed out at a table in back, amidst a copse of pitchers. The other two occupied a table for six between the bar and the doorway. They were awake but beyond being understood by one another or anyone sober.

There was no wait staff. The publican, a man about fifty, who had no outstanding physical characteristics, eyed the newcomers with both hunger and trepidation. He was desperate for business but recognized Nathan Wolf.

"What can I get you gents?"

"On me tonight," Babeltausque told his companions. "Order up."

Erik and Purlef were not slow to respond. Wolf was scarcely a beat behind.

"And for you, sir?"

"Tell me my choices while you draw for them." The others had asked for dark ale.

"We're not so fancy here as you're probably accustomed to, sir. Especially in these times. We have the dark ale, small beer for the kiddies, and a piss pale barley beer mostly drunk by the women. We don't get many of them or the kiddies. They mostly call theirs out."

As though to underscore his statement a girl, maybe a young fourteen, shoved through the street door carrying a tin pail. She frowned as she looked around.

Babeltausque laid a crown on the bar. "I'll try the barley beer." He was not much of a drinker, which he found surprising himself, considering how he had been treated over the years. "Keep my friends topped up." He watched the girl. She was small. He imagined the sweet nubbins beneath her rags, wondered if she had given it up yet.

She handed her pail to the barkeep along with some coins. The barkeep handed Babeltausque his tankard, then filled the pail with dark ale.

Babeltausque turned for a better look. The girl flinched away. She was frightened now. She took the pail and left as fast as she could go without spilling precious cargo.

Wolf set his mug down. "That was strange."

The publican said, "That girl ain't never been right."

Erik said, "I figure she'll be fine, she ripens up."

Babeltausque faced the bartender. "Show me your hands."

"Sir?" The man wanted to argue but recognized the sudden intensity of Babeltausque's companions. "Customer is always right."

Babeltausque considered the hands, saw nothing to suggest that the man was anything but a publican. "Reach over here. Both hands."

The wizard took hold. Startled, the barkeep tried to pull away. He could not. Babeltausque smiled an ugly little smile. "Tell me about Colonel Gales."

The publican's gaze darted, possibly looking for help that would not come.

Wolf surveyed the bar. He said, "Erik, take the front door. Don't let anybody in. Purlef, you make sure we get no surprises from the back."

Babeltausque said, "Excellent, Mr. Wolf. Should there be an actual rescue attempt, take one villain for questioning. Barkeep. You must know more about the disappearance of the Queen's man Gales than you admitted to Mr. Wolf earlier. I want to hear the rest now."

The publican kept shaking his head, never making clear what he was denying. But Babeltausque did reach a disappointed conclusion.

The man truly knew nothing useful and lacked interesting suspicions as well.

Babeltausque let go. "That first crown is for your trouble and discomfort." He produced another. "The drinks will be on this. Top us all off. Mr. Wolf, I was wrong. This gentleman knows less than we do."

"Shit!"

"Include me in that sentiment."

"Still a dead end."

"Perhaps." Babeltausque turned back to the bartender, who had filled all the mugs and now stood there shaking. "You recall the night in question? The drunk put on a show."

"He pissed himself."

"He did. Were any of your current clientele in here that night?"

The bartender started to shrug, flexed the fingers of his right hand, thought better of playing dumb. "The one in the back, there, I don't think I ever seen before tonight. He was drowned drunk when he got here. His whole crew was. They ordered up all them pitchers and was working them hard when, all of a sudden, like a flock of pigeons, they up and swooped out. I guess they couldn't get him woke up to go."

Babeltausque had a feeling. "That would have been when?"

"Maybe ten minutes before you showed."

About the time they exited Castle Krief. Interesting. "I see. How many were there?"

The barkeep looked back at the sleeping man's table. "I see six pitchers. Each one ordered one. So five of them left."

"How about these two?"

"They was probably here that night. They're here every night. I don't know where they get the money."

"Mr. Wolf, please investigate the gentleman back there. I'll talk to these two. Erik, Purlef, please remain alert. I'm sure we're being watched. Someone else would have tried to come buy a drink by now, otherwise."

Babeltausque had just planted himself with the drunks when Wolf said, "Sorcerer, I need you here."

Though irked, Babeltausque got up and went. "What?"

Wolf got a fist full of hair, tilted the drunk's head back.

"I see."

"Looks like death on a stick."

"Let me ask a few more questions."

Babeltausque returned to the publican. "Did you recognize any of the men who came in with that fellow?"

Headshake. "I'm pretty sure they was from out of town. Maybe from Sedlmayr, out that way, the way they rolled their Rs."

"I see. Thank you. Fill me up, please. This is actually rather a pleasant brew. You add just a pinch of ground rail bark, yes? Mr. Wolf? Erik? Purlef? Do you need topped up? No? And I thought I would be the lightweight. Sir. Tell me. Did yon fellow's friends do any drinking themselves?"

"Like they wanted to float their kidneys. Like they wanted to get every pitcher empty in record time."

"Excellent. You have been most helpful. Another crown for your trouble."

As he settled down with the drunks Babeltausque realized he was enjoying himself. He could not recall the last time life was just plain fun.

He collected himself, grasped the near hand of the man to his right. The drunk started as though shocked. His eyes opened. He sat up straight. He gulped air, took a long drink, began muttering a prayer. He had been present the night of the kidnapping. He remembered the show. He was unaware that anything had happened to the drunk after he left the Twisted Wrench, nor did he know that Gales was anything but what he had pretended.

He had to labor through a half minute of grueling thought before he could name the current monarch—and then fell short by one.

The second man was the brother-in-law of the first. His wife had forced him to take that night off. He knew nothing at all.

The sorcerer announced, "We won't get anything more here. Lead the way home, Mr. Wolf. Purlef, you and Erik support our new friend, there. I'll follow along with a few spells readied."

He watched Wolf calculate and conclude that those instructions made sense for a passage through potentially hostile territory.

Babeltausque turned to the publican. "In a few minutes someone will come in asking about us." He produced a bronze medal with turquoise inlays. It weighed a good six ounces. "Give this to the man who appears to be in charge. And this paper should go to a companion who seems dim and doesn't say much. And this crown is me buying them drinks, however much they want." He rubbed the crown over the medallion and paper. "Don't touch these again except to hand them over."

Wolf asked, "You're going to pull their noses?"

"I am going to grab hold and yank till they squeal." He told the publican, "Expect the men of the garrison to come back, soon. Mr. Wolf. After you."

The bartender watched them go, unsure if he should be pleased or terrified.

It was not every day that a wizard tramped through an ordinary man's life. When one did excitement usually followed.

...

Flustered, hastily dressed, Inger rushed into Babeltausque's quarters. She found Dr. Wachtel examining Josiah Gales. The wizard and Nathan Wolf watched, murmuring. The old doctor had been dragged out of bed. He was sleepwalking through his task.

Wolf told her, "They left him at the place where they kidnapped him. That makes no sense to me but I'm sure they had a reason."

Babeltausque said, "I hope this doesn't sound self-important, Majesty, but I believe that reason was me. They thought I might trace Gales, even if they killed him, so they just gave him up. I expect they had no more use for him, anyway."

"*Could* you have traced him?"

"I could have. I had his belongings to give me a scent."

"Doctor, what's his situation?"

"He's dirty, dried out, and weak from lack of exercise. He wasn't tortured or starved, though good nutrition was neglected. I see no reason why he shouldn't recover completely, physically. Mentally, we'll have to wait and see."

"Could there be problems?"

"I don't know. At the moment he is drunk and drugged. He tries to talk but makes no sense. He may be hallucinating."

Inger stared at Gales. He was filthy but did not look bad otherwise. "Nathan, Babeltausque, thank you. You've made an excellent start. Come with me. Let's talk about what comes next. Doctor, my apologies for your having been dragged out of bed."

"It comes with the calling, dear." He did not look up from cleansing a wrist abrasion.

Inger went to a small room no longer in use. She looked for eavesdroppers, checking the passageway behind one wall. "There must be more to this than you said."

Babeltausque responded, "They knew we were coming. They knew who was coming. That should be instructive. They know what we're going to do as soon as we decide to do it."

"Nathan?"

"I'm impressed with the wizard now that he's out of the shadow of your cousin. There's a lot more to him than I imagined."

Babeltausque puffed up a little. "Thank you, Mr. Wolf. Your Majesty, I left those people with messages of my own. I'm hoping they're stupid. If you will indulge me, then, I need to get back to work."

"Doing?"

"Following up. This isn't over because we recovered Colonel Gales. Unless you want those people free to go on about their mischief."

"No! Get on with it. And I'll pray that your luck continues."

...

Chames Marks dipped a cup into the pail of beer. The girl followed suit. He said, "You're too young for that, Haida."

"I need it. The way that man looked at me! Wearing that sweet smile..."

"There might be a monster behind the merry eyes?"

"I really wanted to bring him here so Arnulf could work on him."

They were in the back of a butcher shop. Arnulf Black was the proprietor. Haida was under the mistaken notion that Black disposed of people Chames did not like.

"I'll see to it that you don't run into him again."

"I don't think he was looking at me. I think he saw a fantasy girl."

"Probably true. Get the chessboard. We'll play while we wait for Brom." Chames smiled. It was not hard to distract Haida if he engaged her intellect.

She played him tough. He could not shut his mind down.

The back door rattled suddenly, frantically. Chames rose. "Something's gone wrong. Slide out the other way. Go to the shop. Wait there. No lights."

Rattle again, accompanied by hoarse, worried whispers.

Marks opened the door. Three men tumbled in, one bleeding from wounds on his face and hands. "Shut that, Edam. All of you, take a deep breath. Calm down. Then somebody tell me where Madden is and what went wrong."

Edam locked the door. "It went just like you said till we went inside the Wrench. We never got a chance to ask questions. The barkeep saw us and said, 'You would be the ones.' He started filling mugs. 'On the gents that just left,' he says."

"I see. Well. I didn't expect them to taunt me back. Go on. Then what?"

"So we drinks our beers. Minter says how Hartaway was gonna be browned off on account of he was following them others and gonna miss out. So then the barkeep asks do we want to top up, the guy from the castle paid for plenty. We says, yes sir, thank you very much, sir, since it's on somebody else. The barkeep tops us up, then he hands Madden this big-ass bronze medal with some kind of blue stones set in it. Then he gives Minter a folded piece of paper. Madden goes, 'What's all this, then?' The bartender goes, 'I don't know. The guy running that bunch said give it to the guy running your bunch. He said give the note to the guy that looked the stupidest.'"

"And?"

"So Madden is looking at that medal and we're looking over each other's shoulders. The barkeep is on the other side of the bar, trying to see, too. Madden touches one of them blue stones. And, *Bang!* The medallion explodes."

"It tore him all up," said the man who was bleeding. "Took both of his eyes, blew off the hand he was holding it in, and ripped out the side of his throat. He had it in his left hand, like this, maybe a foot from his face. I had to pick pieces of his fingers off'n me."

Edam said, "The blast got the barkeep, too. His face was messed up."

"I get the picture." Better than did they. The barkeep was not part of the plot. "You still have that note, Minter?"

"I sure do, boss. I never even looked at it."

Where would be the point? The man could not read. "Lucky you."

Minter went pale behind his shrapnel wounds. "You think…?"

"Unless that note is just a bit of mockery we may have only minutes to live. Give it here. And hope some 'Neener neener!' is all it is." Marks took the note. "All right. Everybody out. Find Hartaway, then get out of town. Right now if they didn't shut the gates tonight."

The gates did get left open more often than not, depending on how far the guards' pay was in arrears.

"What about my face and hands?" Minter asked.

"The wounds aren't dangerous. Clean them up once you're twenty miles out of town."

"Oh. Yeah. Shit. Let's get the flock out of here, troops."

Marks shut the door behind the three. It was a shame about Madden. But he could do nothing about that, now.

Madden being the victim might actually have been good luck. The others were good men, but stupid. Madden would have carried nothing to connect him with anyone else.

He pushed the folded paper over beside the chess set, stared at it. He felt no obvious danger but had little feel for sorcery. He used his belt knife to prod the paper.

Nothing happened.

He sniffed.

Nothing.

He used two butcher knives to unfold the sheet. How long did he have? A while, probably. With Gales in hand those men would report to the Queen first. After that they would try to track the tracer spell sure to be attached to the note.

Clever, evil bastards. Kill the only man smart enough to be in charge and the stupid ones would run straight to their control carrying a tracker spell.

Never touching the paper with his fingers, Chames spread the note. Which was blank. Presumably the tracer was inscribed in invisible ink.

He held the sheet with one knife and smoothed it out with the back of the other. The note convulsed suddenly and said, "Boo!"

Time to go.

...

"I doubt that we'll catch anyone," said Babeltausque, watching soldiers load the dead man into a cart. Poor old Wachtel would have to get out of bed again.

"We need to try," Wolf replied.

"Of course we do. For our own sakes as well as the Queen's. If we fail her we fail ourselves."

Wolf grunted, unhappy with that truth.

Rumor had an angry Kristen ready to come out of hiding, hell-bent on revenge for the murders of her best-loved companions.

The sorcerer told the soldiers managing the corpse, "Take him to my workroom after Wachtel says he's really dead. I'll see what he can tell me."

The soldiers looked uncomfortable.

Let them think he could conjure the shades of the dead. Let that notion gain currency. There were spies in Castle Krief. Fear might make them reveal themselves.

Wolf asked, "Can you still detect that charm?"

"I can. It's down that way, probably less than three blocks."

"Think they figured out what it is?"

"I hope so."

Wolf said, "You puzzle me, man. Maybe even scare me a little."

Babeltausque whispered, "I'm starting to scare myself."

Wolf laughed but only from nerves.

Babeltausque said, "Let's go find our operative."

Five minutes later he, Wolf, and a half-dozen Itaskian soldiers arrived outside a butcher shop. Babeltausque said, "There's no one in there now but this is where the tracer ended up."

"Should we go in?" the Itaskian noncom asked.

"Sure. Front and back, with someone watching the windows. Be careful. Something clever may be going on."

The sorcerer was confident that he would not find anything useful. The butcher himself would, surely, be clueless. Still, the effort had to be made. There was no excuse for not seeing if the villains had not left some trivial clue that might lead to their downfall.

Babeltausque asked Wolf, "What do you know about the night the treasury monies vanished?"

"Nothing new. The movements of the principals are common knowledge, subject to hearsay distortion."

Babeltausque grumbled, "Common knowledge. They were supposed to hide the treasure in a preplanned place but didn't because events got in the way. Then they died in the riots."

"All apparently true. Prataxis and Mundwiller showed up for their own funerals."

"Nathan. A joke. How unlike you. Tell me, do you have any sense that we're being watched?"

"Somebody must be keeping track. I would be."

"So would I." Babeltausque wished he owned the skills needed to fix the villains.

The senior noncom called, "We're in, sirs. The place is empty except for one unhappy pig."

Babeltausque muttered, "We're all comics tonight." He went to meet the pig. "Stinks in here."

Wolf said, "Rotten meat and blood. Even the cleanest butcher shop smells. And this one isn't the cleanest. Hello, pig. Wasn't your lucky day, was it?"

The noncom called, "Somebody was here in back not so long ago."

Babeltausque joined him. "Everyone freeze. I may be able to… Well!" His ugly face split in a huge grin. The noncom was pointing. "I should be able to guess the movements of anyone who was here during the last two hours."

He shut his eyes and tried to slip into the state that would let him read the memories of the air. He could not push past the excitement caused by the presence of that partial pail of beer.

He hoped to see that girl again. She was a tad ripe, but beggars can't be… He had not indulged in a long time.

Oh, the potential he had seen in those big, beautiful eyes!

Oh, the wonder—after she gave up the villains for whom she had bought the beer!

Sigh. "Mr. Wolf, we need to leave this place. We'll touch it no more than we have already. We'll go back and concentrate on the missing treasury." Babeltausque winked when only Wolf could see.

Nathan Wolf showed him a raised eyebrow but said nothing.

The sorcerer got heads together with the noncom managing the soldiers. He wished he could throw an arm across the man's shoulders in comradely fashion. He did not, not because the man would be repelled but because he was too tall. Babeltausque murmured instructions behind his hand so a clever spy could not read his lips.

The noncom nodded, indicated two men, took off.

Wolf asked, "What was that?"

"Royal charity." He scanned the surrounding night but could not find the watcher.

…

Chames Marks eased back from the dormer vent in the attic over the apothecary shop. That man knew he was being watched. Best not tempt fate. He had shown unexpected abilities already, as a thinker and a magic user.

The sorcerer had not been distracted by the return of Colonel Gales and he had left the butcher shop looking like he had gotten a concrete lead.

Marks could not imagine what had gone wrong. He had done this his whole adult life. He did not make mistakes. That was why he was still alive. Minter had brought the tracker spell but he had been ready for that.

Black should be squarely in the center of the frame.

Marks took a careful look.

The party was breaking up down there.

He could hear some of their talk. They were not going to go after the butcher.

Damn! The man deserved the intimate attention of the Queen's interrogators.

Chames backed up again. "I suppose that's true justice. I shouldn't be so petty."

Forward again, to get the best last look he could. In a similar situation he might hide a man or two to see what happened after it looked like the nosies had cleared away.

No one had stayed behind.

He went downstairs. Haida was in the back room, looking shaken. She husked, "That man was looking for me, wasn't he?"

"No. He had no reason to connect you…" His eyes widened. "What happened to the beer? What did we do with that?"

"I don't know. I gave it to you." Then, "It's probably still over in the cutting room."

"And the sorcerer saw you buy it." Chames sighed. "He wasn't after you before but he will be now. We need to get you on the road west."

"But…"

"You knew what he was thinking when he looked at you?"

"Yes. Uncle Paget used to get that look when…"

"This one might be worse than any of your uncles. Which means you need to be somewhere that he isn't."

"Yes, sir." Wearily. Resigned. "I'll get my stuff. Who should I be?"

"Bertram Blodgett. He's your best character. Go to Errol enThal in Sedlmayr. While you turn into Bert I'll write letters of introduction in case you can't get to Errol or someone else you know."

Carrying a small pack, looking like just another vagabond, the newly minted Bert slipped out the back of the apothecary shop half an hour later.

Chames Marks sat alone, contemplating a candle nearing the end of its life. Everyone else was covered. Now to cover himself.

He had tempted fate by tugging the royal beard. The stunt had snapped back in a big way.

...

Babeltausque chatted with the injured publican while tired old Dr. Wachtel tried to repair the man's face. The sorcerer convinced the bartender, Rhys Benedit, that the explosion had not been meant to happen inside the Wrench. Those men should have taken the medallion to their boss.

"Doctor Wachtel is the best doc in Kavelin. He'll make you right. There'll be an annuity, too, while Inger is Queen. Mr. Wolf has already told the troops that the Wrench is the official watering hole of the garrison again."

Babeltausque inscribed strings of characters and symbols in precise calligraphy on strips of the same heavy paper he had used to carry his tracer spell. He used five pens and five inks, sometimes including several colors in a single glyph. In addition to black he employed an intense scarlet, a dark green, a fierce yellow, and an ink that could not be seen at all, thus leaving spaces that looked like blanks.

Dr. Wachtel said, "I've done everything I can for Master Benedit. From now on he'll have to depend on luck and clean healing. He'll probably lose sight in his right eye. Unless you can do something."

"Other than reducing the risk of infection all I can contribute is moral support. My healing skills are limited. Although I do have the ability to find the best medical man available."

Wachtel gave him a brief, inscrutable look, as though unsure he had just heard that.

Babeltausque said, "Mr. Wolf, I have something for you." He folded a paper strip. "I'm creating protective spells to surround my space here. I expect to hear from Kristen's gang before long. I want to be protected but I don't want to have to drop everything whenever somebody trustworthy needs to get in. That script will get you through the barrier spells. Come. I need to prick your thumb and draw a drop of blood. Once that's in the paper it won't do anybody any good to steal your pass. It won't work for anybody but you. Doctor, I have one for you, too. I'll see Toby, the Queen, and some others tomorrow. But right now I'm ready to collapse."

Wolf was not happy about having to wound himself, however trivially, but did what needed doing. As did Dr. Wachtel.

Babeltausque then said, "Friend Benedit is miserable. He's in pain, he's scared, and he's exhausted. Doctor, do you want to take him with you? Or should he stay here? I have the spare cot Toby uses sometimes." Which was, right now, occupied by the man killed in the explosion at the Wrench.

The barkeep mumbled.

Babeltausque said, "He says he'd be more comfortable staying with you."

"As you wish. Come along, then, sir. There is an infirmary off my quarters. We'll keep you there till you're fit to go home."

Wolf stayed. Once the others were out of earshot, he asked, "You got what you wanted?"

"I did. But I can't do anything about it now. I *am* exhausted. We'll deal with it tomorrow."

"Let me know when you're ready. I'm enjoying this." Wolf slipped his pass into a pocket as he departed.

Babeltausque went to bed right away. He stared at the ceiling, wondering how best to enjoy himself once they captured the girl.

The prospects were delicious.

†

Chapter Thirteen:

1017 AFE:

Eyes of Night

Nepanthe deposited Varthlokkur's dinner on the table designated for the purpose, close by where he was working. "Hey. You. Wake up. Time to eat."

He did awaken, displeased with himself for having fallen asleep.

Not good.

Sorcerers who fell asleep at work became known as late lamented sorcerers.

"I was resting my eyes."

"Right. Why are you taking chances? What are you doing?"

"Looking to build a better rat trap based on the latest research."

It was too damned cold for rats in Fangdred. "Ethrian tried to talk this afternoon. He couldn't put a sentence together right but he tried hard."

The wizard moved to the food. Nepanthe settled opposite him. She had brought something for herself. She could pretend to share a meal.

"That sounds good. Why not let him help with Smyrena? Teach him to change diapers."

"Oh! I don't know. He's really clumsy. And he gets frustrated."

"Sometimes I think he must have had a stroke. Sometimes it feels like he's completely aware but is trapped behind a wall he can't break through."

"You told me…"

"I know. But I'm no life-magic specialist. If the Old Man was here…"

"He's gone. Wishes and fishes." She noticed a change. "What happened to the mummies?"

"I got worried that the Star Rider might find a use for them. I put them where he'll never get to them." Each now resided inside a block of concrete distressed to look like an old aggregate boulder in the shadowed bottom of a distant canyon. And that was temporary. He wanted to reduce mummies and concrete to dust that Radeachar could scatter across a thousand miles of wilderness.

"Part of your strategy of denying him his resources?"

"Exactly."

"Any plan for the Place of the Iron Statues?"

Varthlokkur's spoon halted inches from his mouth. His eyes went vague.

"You didn't think about that."

"I didn't." That stronghold of the Star Rider had not intruded on his consciousness for decades. "I'm amazed that you did." With her memory problems of late. "I don't even recall where it is."

"Somebody went there during the wars. Maybe Michael. Maybe one of my brothers. I don't remember."

She had had memory problems since the night they died together. He had some himself. Even concentrating he could come up with only the vaguest recollection of someone ever having gone looking for the Place. He could not recall who, when, why, or what the result had been.

Nepanthe said, "The night we all died…" And quit. The pain was too intense.

"You're right. Iron statues were there. They tamed the Princes Thaumaturge."

"You had something to do with that place, too, once, didn't you?"

"Maybe when I was Eldred the Wanderer. I don't remember it now."

That troubled him. He was having ever more trouble remembering details of his earliest years. It would be awful to lose those memories altogether. Things he had done, bargains he had made, impacted the world every day, even now. And his mother lived on nowhere else but inside the reaches of his mind.

Ekaterina and Scalza bustled in. They wore heavy clothing so must have been playing outdoors. Scalza hollered, "We're going to see what Mother is doing, all right?"

"Don't touch anything but your scrying bowl."

He had set them up with their own means of farseeing. They could use the bowl any time, though he insisted on being told first. He wanted to be aware that he needed to keep an eye turned their way.

Neither child ever thought much before acting. A reminder to take care might be resented but was never wasted.

Nepanthe said, "I wish I had a tenth of their energy." She sighed. "I'd better go. Smyrena will wake up soon. She'll be hungry. Have the wild animals bring the tray down."

The sorcerer touched her hand lightly, then resumed eating. Mention of the Place of the Iron Statues reminded him that he had not paid much attention to the outside world lately.

Things happened where he was not looking. A lot, in Kavelin, during those intervals.

Scalza bellowed, "We found her, Uncle Varth! She's in that tower place again."

He pushed back from the table. This might be interesting.

...

Ragnarson thought he had the emotional instability whipped. He had to. Total control was now necessary. He had no time to waste on self-indulgence.

He had a chance to get out. Mist had something in mind. It was a razor-slash of light at the end of a ten-mile tunnel but it was there.

He had no idea what they were thinking. He meant to give no excuse to stop that thinking. This prison came close to his idea of hell.

The only way to make it worse would be to reduce the size of the cage.

"I'm living pretty damned high on the hog here, aren't I? When you get right down to it."

"Excuse me?" Mist stepped in. "Who are you talking to?"

"The smartest man in the room. A fat tangle of superlatives, he is."

"I see. Lord Ssu-ma thought you might be interested in seeing the assassin before we release him."

Ragnarson aced the test. His heart hammered and his vision reddened but he kept his composure. "You're going to turn him loose, why?"

"Our interest was purely curiosity. He broke none of our laws and harmed none of our subjects. He was forthright when questioned. He's a sad case. He has been alone and enclosed so long he doesn't know any way but the way he's followed forever."

"We're all like that anymore."

"You could be right without actually recognizing why."

"And without understanding what you mean."

"This assassin isn't quite a real man. He's more like a devil manufactured by the darkness inside us all. Though that isn't what I'm really trying to say." She clapped her hands in frustration. "I saw elements of all of us in him. He's hollow inside."

Ragnarson was baffled. Mist did not get philosophical.

Mist said, "One reason I call him supernatural is, he doesn't remember his own name."

"How can you not know your own name?"

"I think because he's used so many. I found him intriguing. Lord Ssu-ma was taken by him, too."

"You've lost me."

"Come along. You'll see."

Mist left. The door did not close behind her.

Ragnarson moved that way like a mouse intent on sneaking past a cobra. This could not be what it seemed. It had to be a cruel prank. Something awful would happen. He was safe as long as he did nothing. He should climb into bed and shut his eyes. There would be no pain in sleep.

Sherilee crossed his mind, then Elana, who had given him so many children, all of whom he had outlived. Then Fiana, so remarkable in her passion. She had given him a child he never got to know. And Inger, who had given hope and love in a time of deep despair, and a beautiful son, but who could not overcome her blood.

He stood before the door but did not consider it. He fixated on Inger. His wife had done little that was wicked before hubris drove him to destruction by Ssu-ma Shih-ka'i.

He bore Shih-ka'i no ill will. The Tervola had done his duty, defending his empire. The man had gone out of his way to repay a debt once his duty had been satisfied.

"Are you coming?"

Ragnarson could not see Mist. Her voice came from above. He stepped into the gloom beyond the doorway, spied steps leading upward, to his right. He managed twenty-eight of those before he stopped to fight for breath.

Mist called down, "One more story."

She lied. It was two. He managed eight steps, took a break, then did six more. After that he took the steps one by one. He caught up unable to talk and unsure if he would get his breath back before he collapsed.

"You are leading too sedentary a life."

He gasped, "Nor am I an eighteen-year-old stud anymore."

"Get your breath. We still have twenty steps to go."

It took Ragnarson ten minutes to clear those. He developed a cramp in his right thigh and an uncontrollable twitch in his left calf. He could not stand up straight. It seemed he would never stop panting. And he was much too aware of every overexcited thump of his hammering heart.

Mist said, "Go lean on the rampart. Don't sit down. I'm not big enough to shift you if your muscles lock up."

She was teasing. He hurt too much to care. "Just get on with it."

"As you wish." Mist moved several steps away. "Shin-jei. Bring the prisoner."

Ragnarson paid no attention. He feasted his eyes on the cityscape. He enjoyed the breeze. He absorbed sounds he never heard in his apartment. He drew in alien smells, especially the rich, spicy odors of eastern cooking.

The Empress had known deprivation in her time. She was patient. But minutes were all she could afford. "Look at this man,

Bragi. Tell me if you know him."

Ragnarson looked at a westerner about six feet tall, well-weathered, and gaunt. His eyes were a changeable blue. He appeared to be totally resigned. "Have we ever met?"

"I doubt it." In a feeble monotone, not avoiding Ragnarson's eyes. He was not afraid.

"The Guild. With Hawkwind. Before the El Murid Wars."

That startled the man but his face closed down immediately.

Ragnarson said, "We may have been in the same regiment when we were young. There would be nothing else to connect us. Except Sherilee."

"I am disappointed. I'd hoped there was some drama of deep time coming to a head."

"He might not be the man I'm remembering. He would have been just another recruit who went into the desert with Hawkwind."

Mist gestured. Her bodyguards took the assassin into the tower.

"Did I pass the test?"

"You controlled your temper admirably. Though I do hope you can tell us more about that man."

Ragnarson said, "No such luck. An arrow from a broken bow."

Mist looked to Lord Ssu-ma, who had done his best to remain invisible. He had nothing to contribute now.

Mist said, "We will take time to enjoy the sunset. I'm told the wondrous colors are by grace of the wars with Matayanga and the Deliverer."

"A sky painted with the dust of souls," Ragnarson observed. "Don't attribute that to me. Derel Prataxis said it."

Mist did not believe him, but why argue? "Those wars are over. Their horrors have been sucked down into the quicksand of time. If gaudy sunsets are their memorial, let the survivors enjoy them."

Ragnarson grumbled, "Aren't we deep into a philosophical pocket of night."

Mist said, "Time to go back to your quarters. The trip should be easier this time."

"Harsh."

"And I have to get back to being mistress of this mad empire."

...

Ragnarson settled for the night feeling renewed and too excited to sleep. He obsessed over the wonderful trivia he had seen. His happiest recollection was of lightning bugs in their courtship dances.

He was amazed that they had fireflies in the east, too.

...

Shih-ka'i asked, "Did we gain anything tonight?"

"Nothing knowledgewise. He did demonstrate a renewed ability to master his emotions."

"For what that is worth."

"You are a sour one lately."

"That I cannot deny, Illustrious."

"What do you need? A new war in which to shine? I can't give you one for a generation."

"Illustrious, I prefer the struggle for peace. Sadly, we don't live in a world where such thinking is practical."

"What do you want, Shih-ka'i?"

Lord Ssu-ma marshaled his courage. "A suite here. In this tower."

"For your own hideaway? Or for an enemy you want bound without hope?"

"There is someone I want to install in a place that respects his standing while assuring an absence of contact with the world."

"You make it sound deliciously mysterious."

Shih-ka'i shrugged. "The reality is quite banal."

"Make it happen quickly. We have the final peace terms to dictate to Matayanga."

"I'll be there when you need me."

...

Shih-ka'i transferred to the island, he hoped for the last time. Though Ehelebe never much impacted his life he traversed the installation as though it had been the scene of significant childhood events. As though he wanted to reinforce memories of places he would never see again. He did little things as he wandered about.

He found Kuo Wen-chin and the crazy man making breakfast. The island was that far east. Kuo was pleased to see him.

"I know it hasn't been but it seems like a long time since you visited." Kuo eyed Shih-ka'i expectantly.

"I haven't yet dropped your name into conversation but I have been given permission to use a particular piece of property as I see fit." He explained.

"I would be a prisoner in that tower instead of here."

"It's the best you can expect."

Kuo smiled a tired smile.

"Somewhat less than optimal for you," Shih-ka'i said. "The food will be better."

"And what would be the attitude of the Empress toward Kuo Wen-chin these days?"

"She has none. She never mentions you."

Both Tervola glanced at the old man. Though he moved slowly he did his share. He hummed as he began clearing away. The tune was catchy but unfamiliar.

Kuo said, "I can't abandon him."

"Uhm?"

"He's better than he was but he's not ready to take care of himself."

"I wouldn't leave him. He may be a link to the history of this place." Shih-ka'i paused briefly. "Magden Norath is dead. A serendipitous thing. This was his headquarters, once."

The old man ceased humming. "Ehelebe," he said, then got lost in his own mind again.

"I can't divine the past," Kuo said. "I'm sure there is interesting historical stuff to be found here. If I could. Unfortunately, a clever man might use the same tools to manage long distance communications."

Shih-ka'i replied, "You would know better than I. I'm not the technical sort."

"I'll move if my friend comes, too."

"Definitely not a problem."

"On the other hand, permitted the tools, I could make a career of exploring this island's yesterdays."

"We might consider that after the Empire relaxes and persons of stature have become less paranoid about what ancient sorceries potential rivals might be unearthing."

Kuo Wen-chin sighed. "I understand. I don't like it, but my likes are irrelevant. It isn't just Norath and Ehelebe, either. This place is ages older than that. This may have been the Star Rider's base before the Pracchia betrayed it and the Deliverer drew attention to it."

The old man, moving glacially, twitched or winced each time Kuo said a name. Neither Tervola missed that. And neither believed the old guy understood why he responded that way.

Shih-ka'i said, "I do think it's a good idea to keep him close."

"Yes. I'm ready to leave when you are."

"We should disguise you. The transfer operators might recognize you."

Kuo said, "I'll be a bodyguard. The old man can be a prize we're moving for safekeeping."

...

The timing was coincidental but the Star Rider visited the eastern island shortly after its evacuation. He had not been there since the flight of the prisoner Ethrian, who had become the Deliverer. He expected the place to have been abandoned. The evidence argued otherwise.

Use by the Dread Empire was clear. The fortress reeked of Tervola. It was an excellent place to operate quietly. They would be back.

Old Meddler's nerves had not yet recovered from the shock of Norath's murder. Inimical anarchy lurked in every shadow, lately. Experience left him confident that his jumpiness was justified. Ahead lay an age where all the survivors would hammer their imaginations for inventive ways to kill him.

He rested briefly, then cleared out before he stumbled into any of the booby traps certain to be cleverly disguised.

...

Mist reviewed the current status of the portals installed inside Kavelin over the decades. Technicians tended to be apolitical and kept good records. But search results were not encouraging.

The chief of technical research told her, "Those people were quite skilled at finding and destroying portals once you left."

"I know that, Lord Yuan. Portals that aren't there now don't interest me. How many survived? Must I have new ones smuggled in?"

"Several remain but we've only just started trying to reconnect with them. I have my cleverest man, Tang Shan, doing the work."

"Where would they be?"

"One is in the caverns behind Maisak. One is in the attic of the house you occupied in exile."

"I can't see them not finding that."

"It was a bolt hole type carefully disguised."

"And the others?"

"One more, in the mausoleum of Queen Fiana. It was a sleeper, never activated."

"How grotesque. I want the exact status of each by the end of the day."

"As you will, Illustrious."

...

Varthlokkur had spent several interesting hours with Ethrian. He did so most mornings, now. This particular morning the boy had sustained his half of a simple conversation. He had asked about Sahmaman no more than a dozen times and appeared to get it when Varthlokkur explained.

But he did not retain the information.

The wizard had gotten the boy to practice writing lists of nouns using a charcoal pencil.

Impatient Scalza demanded, "How soon can we go to the Wind Tower? I want to use my scrying bowl."

The boy had blood power. It would be amazing if he did not, with his antecedents. He had learned to manage the scrying bowl in two lessons. With it he did more than spy on his mother. Varthlokkur had given him a watch list of interesting operators to follow.

Scalza was of an age where peeping tom efforts were an attraction, too.

Varthlokkur hoped the boy never caught his mother sporting, though he suspected that Mist had lost interest after Valther's demise.

"Patience is the first skill the young wizard must master," Varthlokkur said. "We'll go after lunch."

Scalza headed for the kitchen to find out how long he had to remain patient. Ekaterina trailed him, saying, "Told you so." Loftily, from the eminence of her superior years.

"Be quiet, brat."

"Ha ha!"

Varthlokkur watched. The children squabbled constantly, yet remained inseparable. He could not recall one ever being more than ten feet from the other. They would not sleep in separate rooms. When nightmares moved in they ended up in the same bed.

Varthlokkur worried more than did Nepanthe. She had grown up with a tribe of brothers, younger and older, none of whom treated her different from one another.

"Varth? Is something wrong?"

"Nepanthe? No. I got caught up in the old nightmare about what happened to my mother. Again."

Nepanthe massaged his shoulders. "Lunch is ready. The children are in a hurry to go upstairs."

"Of course. I'm coming. But I… I wonder why I still have trouble with what happened. Only a lunatic would believe that a boy as young as I was could have done anything to keep them from burning a woman who frightened them."

"But still you obsess."

"I do. Obsession drove me to avenge her. Obsession drove me to win you. And now, despite time-won wisdom, I suffer an intermittent obsession focused on the past."

"Come have lunch. It will improve your spirits. Then you can focus on better rat traps."

Varthlokkur did as she suggested. A half hour later, in the Wind Tower, he could not remember what he had eaten. Mist's rascals were too distracting.

His efforts with Ethrian were paying off but he preferred time spent in the Wind Tower. There he felt like he was getting somewhere in his quest to create that better rat trap.

He surrounded himself with notes reminding himself that he was not the first. A mobile hung above his work table. Its strings bore twelve cards, each recording known details of a failed effort to rid the universe of the Star Rider. He would find more as he developed more tools to mine truth from the deep past.

He wanted to dive all the way down to the beginning of the world. To do that his first great task would be to find a means of breaking through barriers set to prevent that, without being noticed. He believed he was making headway. The research, so far, had not been as difficult as expected. The magic of the Winterstorm, and of the Unborn, were key. The grand challenge was to remain undetected.

Others had believed that the answers could be found hidden in deep time. Several master sorcerers of yesteryear had tried mining the secret histories of the world. They had failed. Their digging had hit a tripwire at some point.

How? Wizards delved the past regularly without drawing fire.

He began by investigating the investigators. He was a loner. They had been loners. He knew how his mind worked. Their mental processes would have been similar. And he had a big advantage over them.

He had time. Centuries, if he needed them.

"Hey, Uncle Varth! Something's going on in that tower of Mother's."

"What?"

"They're bringing in new prisoners."

Which likely meant nothing. But he owed Scalza the courtesy.

Ekaterina leaned on her brother's left shoulder, enthralled by the quicksilver surface. Scalza, seated, elbows on the table and chin in his hands, was completely engrossed, too.

Varthlokkur saw nothing remarkable initially. Then he recognized the tallest man: "Kuo Wen-chin! He's supposed to be dead. I'd better study this. Thank you, Scalza."

The boy's bowl offered visual access only. He could not eavesdrop. That was intentional, so Scalza would not be eavesdropping on his elders.

Most far-scryers, though, suffered from that handicap. Sound was difficult to capture.

The device Varthlokkur activated presented a three-dimensional image and did transmit sound, unreliably. As it came to life it revealed something more amazing and exciting than an unexpectedly healthy Kuo Wen-chin.

Varthlokkur laughed softly, wickedly. This was priceless. More than priceless if Old Meddler did not know.

That old man might be just what he needed.

And Ethrian might be the key to that old man.

Ethrian would be getting a lot more attention now.

Chapter Fourteen:

1017 AFE:

Ghosts of Tangled Destiny

Yasmid had gone to her father's tent again. Elwas had claimed a serious breakthrough. She had been excited. He made it sound like El Murid was back.

Her father disappointed her again. He disappointed Elwas and swami Phogedatvitsu, too. Both really believed that the victory was at hand. El Murid proved them wrong. Yasmid was confident that the sabotage was deliberate.

"I know what you're doing, Habibullah. It won't work. I was there. I saw what I saw. He may be my father. His seed may have quickened my life. His early ministry may have given that life meaning. But the soul inside the man we saw tonight is not that of God's True Messenger."

Habibullah shrank into himself. "More than you do, now, I believe in the foreigner. He will lure the Disciple away from the insidious sway of the Evil One, I am confident."

It had grown dark while they were inside her father's tent. They were returning home now. Light from fires on the field below the New Castle, to their right, and from torches born by Invincible bodyguards, illuminated them. A chip of moon somctimes shone briefly through the grand flocks of clouds cantering westward over the Jebal. Somewhere out there, once the temperature dropped, they would dump their moisture.

Passing the pilgrim camp, Yasmid observed, "Not much interest in shrines anymore, is there? Pilgrims came by the thousands when I was young."

"They tire. The world tires. Many of those pilgrims there now live off the charity of the Believers."

A voice from the waste called, "Hai! Is truth unknown to…"

Whatever followed got snatched away by a gust that promised rain, but those words, in that rhythm, seized the imaginations of Yasmid and Habibullah, both. They stared at one another. Then Yasmid ordered, "Find that man. Whoever he is."

Minutes later Invincibles descended on the pilgrim camp.

…

Haroun bin Yousif had not survived so long by being slow to recognize his own mistakes. Somehow, suddenly, he had become interesting to some passing Invincibles.

He faded away immediately, resurfaced in a different guise, amongst people he had believing that they had known him longer than the few days that was the truth.

Scowling Invincibles with bad scars and parts missing took turns interrogating pilgrims. They were looking for someone but had no idea who. They hoped their quarry would give himself away. Haroun had to relate his life's story all the way back to his great-grandfather.

"Of course," he said. "Anything you want to know, God be praised. My father was Yousef the shoemaker of es Souanna. His father was… But wait! I remember you. We did this just a few days ago."

"Hell, he's right," said another Invincible. "We did. He's some kind of mummer. Weren't you going to head on west with one of the caravans?"

Haroun recalled having had a hearing problem before. "Yes. But al-Mesali would not let me because of my infected ears. Which started healing as soon as it was too late. I am hoping for better luck next time. Meantime, I am surviving on wild greens salads.

What's up, anyway?"

"Nobody knows. The Lady and her eunuch heard something while they were passing by here. They went weird. We're supposed to find somebody without knowing who we're looking for."

"Did you say lady? Your lips are hard to read because of your beard."

"The Lady Yasmid, blessings be upon her. Daughter of the Disciple."

Haroun tried to look awe-stricken. He had been that close to greatness!

He had been that close to disaster. He understood that, for the moment, he had eluded an arrow that he had not known was in the air.

The eunuch mentioned must be Habibullah, who had served Yasmid since she was a child.

It must be the banter that had betrayed him.

He asked, "Do you want to look through my things again?"

How stupid could one man be? And how lucky?

"No."

"This is amazing," Haroun said. "To think that I was that close. I wish I had known so I could have gotten a glimpse."

"You wouldn't have seen much," the talkative Invincible said, moving away.

"Muftaq!" his remaining companion snapped.

"What? It's no secret that she's as homely as the back end of a camel."

"You have no right to say such things in front of perfect strangers."

Haroun muttered, "I'm definitely not perfect. I wouldn't be in this fix if I was."

The Invincibles moved on, leaving the traveler in furious thought.

...

"Could it have been?" Yasmid demanded. "He would have to be mad to be here. Wouldn't he?"

Habibullah agreed, in private and aloud. "He would. But his madness has never been in question."

Yasmid struggled to shed a maelstrom of conflicting feelings. "You did hear what I heard?"

"It was the exact singsong the fat man used when we were young. Minus the accent."

"Can there be an explanation other than the one our foolish hearts want it to be?"

"In God's eyes all things are possible. We'll know for sure soon enough. The Invincibles will question everyone who isn't one of them. Anyone suspicious will wind up at your feet."

Yasmid said, "Uh-oh."

Habibullah said, "I'll put out a warning not to operate alone. If it is him he won't scruple to kill a man for his robes."

Yasmid said, "I don't want him slain outright, Habibullah. I want to see him first."

"I understand."

Watching the door again. Habibullah knowing that. Her knowing that Habibullah had told her what she wanted to hear. She was a woman. She was weak. She would not do what needed to be done. If Habibullah got there first Haroun would die resisting capture.

Habibullah's foolish heart did not share the hungers of her foolish heart. Habibullah nurtured an abiding and deadly grudge.

...

Haroun indulged in wishful thinking but did not waste time sitting still. Aza was compromised. Aza would be very popular soon. Aza had to evaporate off the desert like dew in the morning sun.

Haroun pawned his cart and contents, and his animals, with a one-eyed rogue known as Barking Snake, a parasite grown fat off desperate travelers. He smelled desperation when Haroun arrived in the night. He took every advantage. Haroun did not argue. He did make a point of remembering the fat face and greasy beard filled with a vulpine smile.

Haroun had just departed when a dozen Invincibles descended on Barking Snake's establishment. He listened. The Invincibles were out rousting the usual suspects. Barking Snake lied smoothly, unctuously, while his underlings were still moving reluctant goats in the background.

Haroun allowed himself a grim smile. Unless he was slicker than he looked Barking Snake would soon be answering questions for which he could offer no satisfactory replies.

Haroun wore shabby clothing he had acquired from Barking Snake, still smelling of its previous owner, who may have died in it. As a disguise it would be useless soon. Once the hunters knew that Barking Snake had bought Aza's things they would make him tell them what to look for.

He considered becoming one of the hunters. But that would be impractical except as a momentary expedient. The old warriors here all knew each other and were working in groups.

He could not return to being a pilgrim. No Believer would hide him.

Patrols came close. They failed to catch him mainly because they had no real idea of what they were supposed to find.

Haroun considered fleeing Sebil el Selib. It was the logical course. But he could not reach the pass back to the east and he was not equipped to survive the desert. With a couple of water bags he could make it to el Aswad.

They would think of that right away.

It might be a useful false trail to lay down sometime.

The need for constant evasion pushed him toward the Disciple's tent.

He rested in a shadowed dip fifty feet from that absurd sprawl of canvas. There was activity at its entrance, but only out of curiosity. The guards and staff refused to get caught up in the broader excitement.

The idea seemed obvious enough. If he could get inside... Rumor said that the interior mostly went unused. A company of horsemen could hide in there.

Out of adversity, opportunity?

Why had the place not been picked clean by thieves?

If you were a Believer, perhaps, the Disciple's presence made it holy and immune.

Haroun did not see the man as a god descended to earth, but was willing to profit from such thinking.

He used shaghûn skills several times, always at the weakest intensity. Still, that should have attracted attention. Did they not have anyone watching for sorcery? Was the Disciple's ban on witchcraft and wizardry actually observed at Sebil el Selib?

Excellent. He could be more bold. But not now. For now he had to remain a ghost.

He reached the tent unchallenged. This sector was quiet. These people were their own worst enemies.

Shadows embraced him as he explored.

He never saw a patrol, though there was a path beaten alongside the tent, maybe laid down by those who made sure pegs and ropes remained properly set and taut. The bottom edge of the tent was secured by iron spikes at two foot intervals. Haroun oozed along for a hundred feet without finding even one of those missing.

That was a lot of iron. He could not imagine why some villain had not taken every other one and sold them to Barking Snake, who could have a blacksmith hammer them into a slightly different shape before he sold them back as replacements.

He had to pull this off without leaving evidence. He had to penetrate a space he could explore only with a shaghûn's senses. His skills were not infallible when he had to keep watch in a dozen directions at once.

Maybe there *was* a sorcerer out there. The excitement was collapsing slowly toward him rather than expanding.

...

Yasmid and Habibullah had just taken the latest confused reports from several baffled and weary Invincibles captains. Some of the elderly, hard-line imams had come to poke their noses in. They could not be denied.

Yasmid murmured, "Please, God, make this a false alarm. Better, make these old coots keep their mouths shut and their ears the same."

Habibullah broke her heart by whispering, "The man in the pilgrim camp is the one we want. And he sounds like the man we don't want."

She understood. "Yes. He's the one." The fact that he had become a ghost was evidence enough. "But he isn't Haroun bin Yousif."

Habibullah surprised her. "I concur. This is someone who wants us to believe he might be a dangerous dead man. But he hasn't affirmed it with the patterns of death that are the signature of the King Without a Throne."

Yasmid considered Habibullah. What nonsense was this? Haroun never tried to leave the survivors thinking what a clever murderer he was.

Elwas reported, "He must have fled into the desert. There is no sign of him."

Yasmid sighed. She could not conquer mixed feelings. She yearned for the door to spring open and those powerful arms to sweep her up… Waiting for that villain to miss a step and fall foul of men who had hungered for his life for two generations.

She loved him hopelessly.

She hated him with a deep and abiding fervor.

The coldly calculating eyes of the imams were hungry, too, since rumor had it that the invisible pilgrim might be the King Without a Throne. Yasmid met the gaze of Ibn Adim ed-Din al-Dimishqi, her most virulent detractor. She put into her gaze her absolute willingness to snuff his irksome candle.

Elwas went. Other Invincibles came. They had nothing good to report. "If you could give us a better idea of what you want us to find," one said. "That would be an immense help."

Another suggested, "Dawn isn't far off. We should rest until we can see what we're doing."

That did sound sensible. Rushing around in the dark, someone was sure to get hurt.

There had been no contact with the pilgrim since two Invincibles interviewed him during the first few minutes of excitement.

"Ah. Jirbash is here. This could be interesting."

Jirbash al-'Azariyah was a protégé of Elwas bin Farout al-Souki. His background was equally dubious. His brains and ferocity made him a terror to enemies of the Believers. He ran a contemptuous eye over the three old men and the slightly younger Ibn Adim. Only al-Dimishqi did not sway back.

Jirbash had been the architect of their humbling. He remained openly unhappy because he had been denied permission to bury them.

He stepped up to Yasmid and Habibullah, offering each a precisely calculated bow. He did not go to his knees. Yasmid had forbidden the practice. Only God Himself rated that level of obeisance.

"Report," she said.

"We have been examining the effects of the criminal Farukh Barsbey al-Fadl, called Barking Snake. We are solving a great many criminal mysteries. Al-Fadl did take the pilgrim's livestock and property in pawn, at a discount violating the usury laws. He claims to know nothing about the man, who called himself Aza. I believe him. Tonight's events have shaken him. He never thought he would attract the attention of the religious authorities. He thought he was protected."

Habibullah asked, "This news helps us how?"

Jirbash showed no impatience. "Even a void says something. It says there is nothing here. Go look somewhere else."

A slight pinking appeared in Habibullah's cheeks. "I see."

"The villain Farukh al-Fadl says the pilgrim asked for water bags, which al-Fadl could not provide. He asked if there had been reports of dangers along the road to el Aswad. Al-Fadl says he advised the pilgrim not to go that way because the road is haunted by ghosts from the battle on the salt pan."

Yasmid said, "El Aswad. The springs still flow there."

Habibullah said, "There were early reports of disappearing water bags."

"Jirbash. Catch Elwas. Tell him you two will catch the pilgrim on the road to el Aswad. Subdue him and bring him back alive."

Behind her Habibullah offered subtle expressions assuring Jirbash that the alive part was not critical.

It was a boys' conspiracy, entered into because the girl was too soft.

...

Haroun found himself in a part of the tent that appeared not to have been visited in years. His weak spirit light revealed that it was storage for plunder. The leather goods were dried out and starting to crumble. There was mold all over one heap of camel saddles, despite the bone-dry air. No one had cleaned the blood off.

The plunder "rooms" were vast and unorganized. Those who had stored the goods had not cared. Worthless stuff had been thrown everywhere. It took Haroun only minutes to create a hiding hole and disguise its entrance.

...

Elwas told Yasmid, "Lady, mentioning el Aswad was a diversion. Had he meant to run that way he would have done so straight from the criminal's place. And he would have kept his mule."

"You're sure?"

"We looked. He didn't go that way. Not even scavengers travel that road anymore."

"Then he did what he does so well, again." She vacillated between convictions. Right now she was convinced that she had passed within yards of her own Haroun before fate made it impossible for them to meet. No one had any idea where he had gone. El Aswad? Into the desert? Back across the Jebal? Some other direction? Or had he used sorcery to disguise himself as someone she saw every day?

Haroun bin Yousif. Her husband. The father of her only child. Her beloved. The man she hated so much.

Habibullah's conviction of the moment was the opposite. Each report left him more certain that they had become entangled in a popular fantasy that would never wither completely. Too many people wanted it to be true.

"I am not pleased," Yasmid said. "This pilgrim made fools of us all." Who but her husband had the will and the skill?

"Back to the beginning. The man was here for days, camped where he should be, visiting shrines and memorials like any pilgrim. Evenings, he put on puppet shows for the children. Right?"

No one disagreed.

She asked, "Why wasn't he doing anything? Wouldn't a man with a sinister purpose make an effort to forward it?"

Jirbash suggested, "He was waiting for the right time."

Yasmid wanted to believe that moment was one where he could see her alone. "Indeed? Could he have been just some Royalist spy?"

Jirbash said, "We can't answer that without knowing who he was."

Always the fantasy of a revenant Haroun returned to one pair of eyes.

Yet again, Yasmid demanded, "Why was he here?"

Ibn Adim suggested, "The demon came here because this is where he would find his mate."

Deadly emotion crossed Jirbash al-'Azariyah's face. The imam might have won a death sentence with one malicious remark.

Yasmid did not chide Jirbash.

Elwas suggested, "Why not assume that his goals are evolving? I agree that who he is would be useful in predicting what he might do, might want to do, and is capable of doing. But everything we do, perforce, shapes what he will be able to do."

Ibn Adim recognized the death glow in Jirbash's eyes. His voice was tight. "We're chasing specters. Which will be what he wants."

"Explain," Yasmid said.

"He's long gone, laughing. Whatever kind of rogue he was, he wasn't the infernal genius you all want to make him."

"Do go on," Yasmid said. Honestly. The man might be making a point that had evaded everyone else.

"I propose that he was a common crook. A confidence man. He ran to al-Fadl when the Invincibles started digging. He got money and got out. He's halfway to Al Rhemish or back in Souk el Arba, congratulating himself for being quick and clever."

A couple of Invincible captains muttered agreement.

Yasmid looked to Habibullah. He shrugged. Elwas did the same. "So. We could be making mountains out of termite hills. So. We'll search for two more days. Ask every question again. Re-turn every stone. Try to think of something that hasn't been suggested before. If nothing new surfaces we'll bow to Ibn Adim's wisdom and congratulate the pilgrim for being quick and clever."

...

Haroun was suffering from imposter syndrome. He could not believe his own success. He was inside the tent of the Disciple, his deadly enemy since childhood. He was within striking distance. Nobody knew. Nobody was alarmed.

He studied the geography of the tent and the routines of life inside the fraction that saw use. He learned that most staff lived outside. They did almost nothing when out of sight of their supervisors, who did not themselves much care if the staff kept busy.

Much of the complex was in worse shape than the trash space where Haroun hid. Several vixens had denned up in one eastern area. They and their kits squabbled constantly. The staff knew about them all. They knew about the rats and mice and camel spiders, too, and ignored them. All they did was keep the rouge on the old woman's cheeks by maintaining what could be seen from outside.

These people had abandoned El Murid's dream.

They stole from him, too. Mostly food, now. Traffic in salable trinkets had dried up because there was so little worthwhile plunder left. Haroun suspected that the staff payrolls included some family ghosts, too.

The court of the Disciple was swamped in corruption.

Come nightfall Haroun was free to do as he willed. He ran into no one even when he pilfered food. He eavesdropped when he could. He had nothing else to do but wait.

In time he would feel safe going out again, as someone new.

He could kill the Disciple. That would be easy. But it would put him on the run again, with nowhere to hide. And the result might not be positive. El Murid's religion had become locked into an inward-facing stasis. His latest genius war captains defeated all external threats but no longer insisted on converting the world.

The movement was old and tired and befuddled, like its founder.

Kill him and someone competent might step in.

Assassination could wait until God Himself could be framed for it.

He wished he could slip the old madman some opium. One fat dose would undo all the good so many had achieved.

Even by day the people who worked in the tent never left the small occupied stain behind the entrance.

Haroun enjoyed himself the first week. During the second he grew more active because he felt more driven. During the third he began crafting schemes.

...

Yasmid greeted Elwas unhappily. "You have brought me nothing again."

"True. The ghost has not returned from the spirit world. And we did agree that we would leave him there, some time ago."

"Yet you kept looking."

"I did. For your sake."

"And?"

"No one has seen him since that night. People remember him on the coast. People remember him coming through the pass. He came here, then he vanished."

"I really do have to let go." Talking to herself, not Elwas.

"I want to talk about al-Fadl. He has given up the names of the people who sold him some of the more unusual properties we found at his place."

"You're about to tell me something I'd rather not hear?"

"I am. About bad people in places where we want only the best to abide. Barking Snake was rich. He got that way selling stolen goods. Most of those came from your father's tent or from the shrines. Barking Snake's business has been bad lately. Your father had been robbed of everything small enough to smuggle out of his tent. I talked to the guards. They check everyone going in but no one coming out. The need never occurred to them. I don't think they were involved."

"My father's servants stole from him?"

"It wasn't organized. It was individuals seizing opportunities."

"Elwas, I despair of humankind. The best man in our world, chosen by God Himself, has been surrounded by rogues and thieves, like flies around dung, since the first day he preached. I wish God would put patience aside and destroy the evildoers."

"That wouldn't leave many of us to deal with the corpses, Lady."

"No doubt. Any suggestions about how to deal with the thieves?"

"Let them know that they've been found out. Punish the most egregious. Let the rest be, but with a never another chance warning."

"Accept their villainy?"

"Your father doesn't tolerate change well. The swami worked a miracle, getting accepted as quickly as he did."

True. Meals with her father were a regular event, now. He did not recognize her or speak to her yet but the Matayangan insisted they would get there soon.

She saw some improvement herself.

Phogedatvitsu said most of the indifference was stubbornness donned for the occasion.

"Can we recover any of the stolen goods?"

"Some, but, unfortunately, what the criminal still had is of little value."

"Find out who was the most flagrant villain. Have his right hand cut off. Then have someone who knows how look at their accounts."

"Very well. Will you cancel the next dinner?"

"No. Where is Habibullah? It is a beautiful morning. I'd like to go walking."

"It is a fine day, indeed. Unfortunately, Habibullah is sick. He has whatever has been going around among the old men. He'll be back in a few days."

It was a fierce sickness—if it was not poison. One ancient imam and several elderly Invincibles had expired. Several other imams were not expected to recover.

Could someone be eliminating them?

Two more imams and another Invincible died. Habibullah recovered. Still so weak he needed help walking, he took his place opposite Yasmid next time she dined with her father.

Just they two were there. Elwas was outside removing a thief's stealing hand.

It said much about El Murid's attendants that none had fled despite al-Fadl's arrest.

Elwas came late to his seat beside Habibullah but the Disciple was later still. Phogedatvitsu showed up long enough to say, "There will be a delay. This is the anniversary of an encounter from which he barely escaped death at the hand of a Wahlig of el Aswad. He thinks he saw the man's ghost this morning." He did not use his interpreter.

Habibullah told Elwas, "There was a raid soon after Nassef captured Sebil el-Selib. Yousif and his brother Fuad caught the Disciple near the Malachite Throne. Only Nassef's timely arrival saved him."

"That was a long time ago."

Yasmid asked, "Is this a good sign? That he can get excited about something? Or is it bad?"

Elwas said, "It's a step forward. He has engaged the external world."

Yasmid said, "An imaginary world."

Habibullah said, "He could start seeing real people next."

And Elwas, "Lady, when I brought the swami here your father saw legions of imaginary beings, mostly ghosts. And not the ones you would expect. Not your mother. Never your brother. He doesn't remember that you had a brother anymore. He did see Nassef a lot. Nassef was always here. They engaged in spirited debates about everything imaginable. I heard only your father's side and I'm too young to have seen the Scourge of God himself but I think I know him pretty well, now. He was a remarkable man."

"Yes. And a bizarre mix." Yasmid did not want to talk about the dead. Hammad al Nakir was inhabited more by ghosts than live actors. The people were tired of war but all looked back to the glory days of war, when captains like Nassef, Karim, el-Kader, and el Nadim had made the earth shake.

Yasmid had seen those days from the inside. She knew that the golden age was a delusion. The look-backers had forgotten the cost: women without husbands and sons, children without fathers, works public and private destroyed and, even now, not restored, and all the fertile lands laid waste. All in the Name of God the Compassionate.

Recollections of evil were fading. They would go extinct once the last folk who had survived those times went to their rewards. Then the Believers would grow infatuated with tales of glory till some young Nassef or el-Kader, some half-bandit, half-charismatic holy warrior, began the cycle anew.

"Lady?" Habibullah sounded concerned. "Is something wrong?"

"Yes. But we can't do anything about it. We must be what God wills."

Silence came. No one wanted a religious discussion. Habibullah did say, "Submission is God's Law. You think about it too much."

Yasmid lowered her gaze. "I do, don't I? I always admired my father's conviction. He never knew doubt." She looked up. "How much longer…? Ah!"

She screamed and collapsed.

"Lady? What is it?" Elwas demanded.

Habibullah asked the air, "Did she faint?" He looked around frantically. "Why did she scream? Look for a snake. Maybe it was a viper."

Yasmid had fallen onto her right side, then had curled into a ball. She seemed to be suffering severe stomach pain. No snake Habibullah knew could cause that.

"Maybe a spider."

Yasmid mumbled something about ghosts.

The men were on their knees around her when Phogedatvitsu arrived with her father.

†

Chapter Fifteen:

SUMMER, YEAR 1017 AFE:

Sedlmayr

Dahl Haas and Aral Dantice rode ahead to make the arrangements.

Kristen slipped into Sedlmayr soon afterward. Her party followed, a few people at a time. They all vanished into the home of Cham Mundwiller and his brothers.

Cham was a long time dead but his kin shared his vision. They would support the lost king's grandson while the younger Bragi continued policies parented by Queen Fiana and the first King Bragi.

Kristen was a believer. Her father had been a Wesson soldier who had risen to become King's Champion.

Kristen's party assembled in a banquet room in the Mundwiller compound, which was a minor fortress. From without the public saw a square, three-story structure a hundred forty feet to the side, without windows at ground level. Light entered the second level through archers' slits. There were regular, shuttered windows on the third floor. Stepping back, the outsider would see the stone tower that stood in the yard inside. That final refuge could be entered only by climbing a ladder.

All important Sedlmayrese families lived in some sort of urban fortress. Business and political disputes could become quite animated.

The Mundwiller compound stood out because its architecture had been adopted from cities farther west.

During the reigns of Fiana and Bragi, Sedlmayr had become a semi-autonomous city-state acknowledging the Crown while disdaining the nobility and any feudal obligations.

There were other, similar charter towns. All were rich. Sedlmayr was weathering the current chaos with less hardship than any Nordmen demesne.

There was jealousy and resentment. Naturally. But prevailing economic conditions made it impossible for the Nordmen to impose themselves.

All of which Kristen learned within minutes of her arrival.

She and hers were in a room so crowded with Sedlmayrese that the heat was becoming intolerable. Many of those bodies had gone too long unwashed, as well.

Body odor was not something most people noticed. Kristen did so because the Sedlmayrese diet was heavy on pork. Sedlmayrese smelled different.

Bight Mundwiller was the youngest of the surviving Mundwiller brothers. His family had assigned him to Kristen. He stuck like a jealous lover, left hand always on the hilt of a long knife. Kristen suspected that he had not been pleased with the assignment before he met her. Now she feared she would not be able to get shut of him.

Dahl and Aral Dantice were amused.

Bight was seventeen.

The grand dame of the clan, Ozora Mundwiller, called for silence.

Silence rained down immediately.

A raised eyebrow from Ozora Mundwiller could alter the destiny of the clan.

The old woman said nothing after the silence fell.

Aral stepped up to address the crowd. He told everyone that Queen Inger's writ no longer had any force outside Vorgreberg's wall. Kristen whispered to Dahl, "What is he doing?"

"I'm not sure. How about we listen and find out?" He slipped an arm around her waist.

Dantice went into detail about the situation in Vorgreberg. Kristen found his report depressing.

Inger had a staff sorcerer. He appeared to be competent. His main assignment was to find the missing treasury money.

Those who thought young Bragi should be king had little more influence in the countryside. The Nordmen nobility were content to operate without any strong central authority. Kristen thought they were being short-sighted. In time they would realize that life was better when there was a strong king in Vorgreberg.

She whispered her thoughts to Dahl. He said, "Tell these people."

She understood. They wanted to know if she could think. So she spoke up.

Ozora Mundwiller nodded. "That's true, child. But I think you see the flaw in your argument as well. Periods of prosperity and peace were few and brief because we were so often at war, if not with El Murid or Shinsan, then with one of our neighbors. And if not with any of those, then with ourselves for whatever reason seemed fashionable. Those who ponder such things believe Old Meddler caused most of the turmoil."

Ozora Mundwiller had to be ninety, yet was neither stooped nor frail. She had no trouble making herself heard. "The remarkable truth is that, given any window of peace, even as briefly as a few months, Kavelin produces wealth and makes life better for its peoples."

The woman surveyed her audience. "We have entered upon such a period of peace, if only because every faction is exhausted. Things are getting better. Those who look backward do not see that. They see wanderers on the road, looking for work. They do not see that work found everywhere, in field and forest. They see castles falling into disrepair because the nobility have squandered their fortunes on aggression. They do not see the new mills and mines. They do not notice the caravans beginning to move through the Savernake Gap. Where they are particularly constipated of outlook they have failed to see the remarkable explosion in agricultural confidence brought on by what has been the most benign and propitious climate to bless us in a generation."

Ozora paused. Tentative applause tickled the silence. Kristen realized she knew nothing about what the woman was saying. She did, in fact, have very little idea what was going on anywhere in the kingdom. Which might be the old woman's point.

One theme had run through the reigns of the old Krief, his child-bride Fiana, and her lover King Bragi. Each had been determined to do what was best for Kavelin, not for themselves. Each had made huge mistakes and had committed dreadful sins but none of them ever forgot that they were part of something bigger than themselves. Each, in his or her way, had been married to Kavelin, forsaking all others.

Kristen looked up at the old woman. She understood where this was going.

Sedlmayr would support Bragi II—provisionally. Sedlmayr would not spend lives or treasure to put him on the throne. He would be protected till time decided between him and Fulk.

Ozora Mundwiller suffered from the disease that had afflicted Kavelin's last three monarchs. She would not support anyone who would not keep the peace and who would not keep the state hard on the course those monarchs had plotted.

Inger wanted to shift course. Her support had collapsed. She could make no changes. She was a fever that had to run its course.

The only guarantee that Kristen and Bragi would follow the desired course was the girl's word.

Ozora Mundwiller painted her into a corner. Her only exit was to publicly swear to pursue the ideals of her father-in-law.

She glared at Aral Dantice. Had he shaped this situation deliberately, perhaps with the connivance of Michael Trebilcock?

...

Babeltausque joined Queen Inger for breakfast, at her request. "Tell me you have something positive for me," she said.

"You will have to judge."

"About what happened to Colonel Gales?"

"Those who held him have scattered like startled mice. We did identify a girl known as Haida Heltkler. Miss Heltkler hasn't been seen since she left the Twisted Wrench with a pail of beer."

Nathan Wolf had told Inger all that already. "And the butcher was cleared?"

"Mr. Black claims he was framed. He might actually have been."

"Who would do that? And why?"

"The girl. She's his niece. Busybodies in the neighborhood think she might have been getting back for him having taken indecent liberties."

The sorcerer was alert for any nuance of response. He was sure Inger's male relatives had taken liberties with her when she was young.

He needed to know how much she would tolerate.

He was safely free of the Duke now. He was in a good place to indulge his own secret needs.

Those had begun to surface the night he looked into the eyes of that girl Haida.

The Queen shrugged. "Is that important?"

"Only in the sense that someone may have wanted the butcher to suffer."

"It's an odd thing to be distressed about. But I'll take your word."

"Most gracious of you. Majesty, we will continue to look at that, hoping the villains give themselves away. Meantime, I must deliver some unhappy news. Mr. Wolf and I have identified the spy."

"And?"

"The spy is the doctor. He uses Toby as his runner."

"That can't be. That old man has never been anything but the castle doctor. He was the castle doctor even while Shinsan occupied Kavelin."

"I share your disappointment. I didn't want to believe it myself. I like Wachtel. But there is no doubt. Something must have changed."

"What could that be?"

"I don't know. I suggest we ignore it. We gain nothing by arresting him. Let's keep treating him as a national treasure but don't let him near anything interesting."

"Make sure of that and I'll go along."

"With Toby, too. The boy may actually be the lead conspirator."

Inger shook her head, mumbled. Babeltausque suspected that

she was hurt by Wachtel's treason. He wondered, too, why she never had the boy king close by. Fulk was little, sure, and sickly, but he should be suckling the ways of kingship along with mother's milk. Though he never got near his true mommy's teat.

Inger asked, "What about the money?"

"Still missing. Mr. Wolf and I have exhausted every idea we could generate. We're reduced to doing what everyone else has. Trying to re-create the itinerary of the thieves and search everywhere along the way."

"Others are looking?"

"It's supposed to be a lot of money." Careful to sound neutral, he added, "We may have to accept the possibility that the money has been taken already. Perhaps by General Liakopulos. Or maybe Michael Trebilcock has had it all along."

Inger snapped, "Keep looking! Never stop looking. That money is our only hope of hanging on here."

A servant brought word that Nathan Wolf wanted to see his Queen right away.

Inger looked at the sorcerer. He shrugged. "Send him in."

Babeltausque was irked. Wolf's timing was awful. He had been about to nibble around the edges of his need.

Wolf wasted no time. "Kristen has moved into Sedlmayr. The Mundwillers have been taken her in. Sedlmayr's elders have declared for Bragi. Again."

"When can we expect trouble?" Inger glanced at Babeltausque. Her look said find that treasure fast.

Wolf said, "We won't have to, apparently."

"Nathan?"

"Their strategy, that they mean to preach everywhere, will be to ignore us."

Babeltausque observed, "That's an odd way of doing business."

"I report what was reported to me. They intend to take a business approach. They will consolidate the kingdom from Sedlmayr, avoiding any fighting. Looks to me like they'll end up in control of the economy. The Estates will accommodate themselves to the reality."

Inger said, "There is something you don't want to tell me, Nathan. What would that be?"

"I don't want to upset you more than you already are."

The sorcerer forced a bland face.

"Spit it out."

"Majesty, the people backing Kristen are making no military preparations. They don't consider them necessary. They expect us to collapse under the weight of our own incompetence."

Nathan tried to soften the sting. Likely the people he mentioned themselves named no name but Inger's.

The Queen said, "We shall disappoint them." Her look told Babeltausque he was the man to make or break the future.

He left with Wolf, disappointed. He had not managed to lay any groundwork.

Wolf stayed with Babeltausque all the way to the latter's apartment. "Do not despair, Mr. Wolf. We aren't yet out of options."

"Did you get anything from that corpse?"

"No. That was a head game with our enemies. Cunning will have to make up for what we lack in money and numbers."

Wolf was not reassured.

Babeltausque wondered how long Nathan would endure. The rest of the Itaskians would follow if he deserted .

...

Babeltausque slipped a silver groat to the warder. The man wandered off, probably to the Twisted Wrench. He forgot his keys.

For a month, now, there had been only one prisoner. The man whimpered when he heard keys jingle.

Babeltausque peered in at Dane of Greyfells. The Duke's situation was no longer so grim. He had been moved to a better cell. He had lamps. He ate the same as the garrison. He had his own chamber pot, cycled daily. He had a small table, a chair, pen, ink, and inexpensive paper, though he was permitted no communication with anyone outside. There was fresh straw for the floor each five days.

He had a cot, a pillow, and a soldier's rough blanket.

"Doing good for an unpopular prisoner," the sorcerer observed.

Greyfells cowered in a corner. He made a mewling sound when Babeltausque rattled the keys.

The sorcerer stared for half a minute, then grumbled, "Evidently the balance has been rectified. This doesn't interest me anymore. Be at peace, My Lord." He returned the way he had come, leaving the keys where he had found them. Soon afterward he left the castle. He did not care who noticed his departure.

...

Chames Marks, known also as Chames Felt, Ghaiman Felt, Marcus Michaels, and a half-dozen others, had returned to his apothecary shop after a brief hiatus. The castle folk were not interested in him by any name despite his known connection to Haida Heltkler.

He did not trust that indifference despite assurances that Nathan Wolf and the sorcerer had given him only the briefest look. They seemed confident that he had no interests outside his apothecary business.

Chames thought those people might be smart enough to see that his business made a good cover for traffic generated by espionage. Maybe they based their thinking on the fact that he had a broad, solid business, not just a storefront. Maybe his best character witness, Dr. Wachtel, had been found out and was being played. He decided to go about his business as though every breath was scrutinized.

He replaced Haida Heltkler with Seline Shalot, a younger, more flamboyant girl the castle folks ought to be able to suborn. She could deliver regular reports on how boring he was.

He grinned. The game was getting dangerous. He savored the heady risk.

...

Summer was on the wane. Early crops were being harvested. Across Kavelin anyone not committed otherwise became involved in the harvest; reaping, winnowing, slaughtering, preserving, storing. A thousand tasks had to be managed. Crops were good everywhere. Piglets grown into hogs and lambs grown into sheep were spared the killing knife because their sacrifice would not be needed. There was forage enough to bring them through the winter so they could be bred to expand the herds and flocks.

Prosperity threatened not just Kavelin but all of the Lesser Kingdoms.

There was but one evil omen.

That monster harbinger, that angel of evil, the Unborn, had become a fixture of the nighttime sky, haunting Kavelin, its presence blatant. Wicked old Varthlokkur wanted it known that he was watching.

That hideous lich caused a hundred schemes to miscarry.

Even those who thought Varthlokkur ought to see them favorably tried to avoid being noticed by the Unborn.

...

Dahl Haas said, "I don't understand why you feel so negative, love. It's all going good. Even the Estates are coming around."

"But they don't mean it in their hearts. Bragi looks like the coming thing so they're covering their asses."

"Yeah. But you're thinking too much. Most people don't look past the end of next week. Have faith in the stupidity of your friends and of your enemies."

"Dahl, I'd rather not think at all."

They were alone. The soldier leaned in and planted an ardent kiss on the king's mother. The king's mother responded enthusiastically.

Haas pulled back. "Ozora is brilliant. It's going exactly how she predicted. Time is our champion now. Inger won't last much longer."

"Aral says she's trying hard to find the missing treasury money. If she does…"

"She'll be disappointed. Assuming Aral told the truth."

"Uhm?"

"He claimed Michael said there wasn't much treasury left."

"It grows in the telling?"

"Because of wishful thinking."

"Does Varthlokkur know? There have been so many Unborn sightings. That makes me nervous."

"Which would be the point. Varthlokkur and Bragi had a falling out but that didn't end the wizard's interest in Kavelin."

Kristen was sure Kavelin would hear directly from the wizard soon.

...

Babeltausque slipped into the abandoned house, quivering with anticipation. He paused in the darkness, looked back into the moonlight. Eager though he was, he did not move for minutes. He dared not be tracked by Inger's enemies.

He sensed watchers every time he left the castle. He did nothing to confound them by day but for these nocturnal ventures he used every trick available.

Satisfied that he had arrived unnoticed, he drifted into the interior. Ghost fire revealed the damage done by treasure hunters.

For a long time every hunter started with the house, but no longer. A hundred visitations had produced only a few random copper coins from beneath furniture or, in one case, wedged between floorboards.

There was an intimidation factor, too. The owner had left numerous booby traps. Men had died. No trap had yet been found actually guarding anything. They were not based on western magic so they antedated the night the treasury disappeared.

Once he became the Queen's own sorcerer Babeltausque spawned rumors that bigger and more deadly traps had yet to be sprung. He then installed a few of those himself.

At first he wanted the house shunned because he suspected the treasury might actually be there, despite repeated failures to find it. Then he had come to appreciate the place for its more arcane possibilities.

He had yet to explore it all. There were areas where the residual sorcery was so brawny it frightened him, left him feeling like he was sliding through a canebrake of spells. He never stopped turning up new facets of the most magically active site in Kavelin. Still, he had yet to make an effort to chart its defenses or uncover what it was hiding.

Because it was shunned it was now the place he went when he wanted to be alone, to relax, to enjoy.

He had been conquered by his need. He had begun to indulge it. Here.

He could wait no longer. He must run to his beloved.

†

Chapter Sixteen:

YEAR 1017 AFE:

The East

Mist took every precaution testing the portals into Kavelin. Tang Shan's skills had been sufficient to establish connections with each, but there was no way to know what lay beyond without going to look.

She chose to go herself, despite the protests of her lifeguards.

She did indulge in one old-time, non-magical safety technique. She tied a rope around her waist before she stepped through. Her bodyguards could drag her back.

They could have overruled her. They had that right. But to do so could mean loss of place or even exile should the Empress be sufficiently irked.

Her first crossing took her into the caverns behind Maisak. She stepped into utter darkness. The air was still, dry, and carried a taint of old death. She withdrew immediately. "I need a lantern."

The lantern helped only a little.

She was in a large, empty space once used to receive transferring troops. Dead portals stretched away to either hand.

Lifting her lantern overhead, Mist could just make out a sprawled skeleton.

Those bones were not human.

Something moved behind her. She gave up a startled squeak.

A lifeguard joined her, bringing another lantern. He said nothing. He followed when she moved toward the bones.

The Captal of Savernake, once master of Maisak, had enjoyed the friendship of many nonhuman creatures, mostly products of his own sorcery. Mist had met some in those dark old days. They had been gentle, timid creatures who loved their creator too well. They were all gone now. The world was poorer for it.

From her vantage over the bones Mist could see three more skeletons, all human.

Her bodyguard said, "We are not alone. Return to the portal."

She felt it, too. Somehow. She neither saw, heard, nor smelled anything, but something was watching. This was a moment when she was not the paramount will of Shinsan. She moved.

The lifeguard's sword sang as it cleared its scabbard.

From the darkness came a long, sad sigh that turned into a desperate moan.

Mist stepped across to safety. Her bodyguard followed. She asked, "What was it?"

He snapped, "Seal it! Shut it down!" at the operators.

Something as pale as a grub began to emerge from the portal.

The operators ended the session.

Three quarters of a man fell to the floor. He left behind parts of his right leg and right arm. He did not bleed. He did not speak. His eyes blazed with a desperate, hungry madness. He was a wild, nasty mass of filth, unkempt hair, and rags.

Mist said, "He's wearing Imperial… He's been trapped there since…"

Despite his injuries, the man crawled forward, toward humanity.

The enormity of what he must have suffered hit Mist like a fist in the gut. She threw up.

"I'm all right. Get me something to rinse my mouth with. Let me get cleaned up. Tang Shan. Send a task group to find out if more of our people are trapped in there."

"Any who are will be quite insane."

"Even so. They're ours."

"As you will, so shall it be."

"Good. Where to next?"

Her bodyguards and the portal specialists alike looked at her askance.

"I'm fine. Just bring me some water. Let's get on with it."

Tang Shan said, "I would recommend the mausoleum of the Kaveliner queen. Lord Yuan is not yet entirely confident of the connection with the other portal. Nor am I."

Mist frowned. Tang Shan remained cautiously neutral always but she suspected him of traditional convictions. The Imperial throne should not be occupied by a girl.

She said, "I'm ready."

A lifeguard said, "This time I go first."

"Of course." Though what danger was likely to be lurking in a mausoleum?

Ghouls? Hungry ghosts?

All right. Danger might be sleeping with the dead.

She got squatters.

They were a Siluro family of six who had not emigrated. They belonged to the smallest and least loved ethnic group in Kavelin.

Mist did not ask for their sad story.

Any couple with four sprats under six, driven to take refuge with the revered dead, would tell a sad tale indeed.

Her charity went only so far as to flush them out rather than compel them to join the occupant of the mausoleum.

The lifeguard did not approve. They might carry tales.

"Ghost stories, perhaps."

She paused to consider the dead queen. "The wizard did wonders with this one."

Fiana looked like a girl asleep, awaiting the wakening kiss of her prince. She remained as colorful and fresh as she had in life.

Her glass-topped casket was filled with a gentle light that remained active after all these years. It made her look younger and more beautiful than she had at her passing. The long agony of birthing Radeachar had been massaged out of face and body.

Bragi's last gift to his love, begged from Varthlokkur.

"Extreme caution is necessary," the lifeguard said. "This place hasn't been plundered or vandalized."

"The homeless lived here unharmed."

The beauty in the box had been the best loved of Kavelin's recent monarchs. That was why no evil had taken place.

"Let's go outside." It had been a long time since she had looked into Kavelin's skies. She had fond memories of a less harried life here. Her children had been conceived and born here. The only man she ever loved was buried here.

It was nighttime. No clouds masked the shoals of stars. There was no moon. Only a few tiny lights marked the location of Vorgreberg.

The bodyguards said, "To the north. The woods."

"I see it. Let's go."

A pinkish dot had risen. It quested briefly, then headed their way, fast.

Back in the staging room, Mist said, "The Unborn sensed us."

Tang Shan suggested, "Or it sensed the portal's use."

"Whatever, I won't test the other one yet. It's only a few miles from that one."

Tang Shan seemed relieved.

Mist asked, "Is that a good thing?"

"I said, Lord Yuan isn't comfortable with the..."

"You told me all three were sound."

"And so they are, Lady. In the sense that we trust them enough to send me through them. But the escape portal in your old house has a bitter flavor. We are less willing to risk you going through."

Should she be flattered or frustrated? "I want it usable by this time tomorrow." Flattered, because Tang Shan disdained female leaders.

"As you will."

...

The door to the world creaked behind Ragnarson. He looked over his shoulder, saw Mist and her right hand, Lord Ssu-ma. But who else would it be? It was not mealtime

Mist looked puzzled. "What are you doing?"

It was unusual to find him reading or writing, though he could manage both without much skill.

"Derel Prataxis once suggested that I would find it useful to make tally sheets if I was contemplating actions that might impact a lot of lives. I didn't listen then."

"And this is what you got." Her gesture included his surroundings.

"This is what I got."

"So what are you planning?"

"Nothing. I'm working the sums for what I lost because I didn't think before I acted and then was too stubborn to change once it was obvious that I'd done something stupid."

Ragnarson considered the Tervola. Lord Ssu-ma seldom said much. His opinion, though, carried considerable weight with Mist.

She asked, "How are you managing emotionally?"

"I'm operating under the conviction that losing Sherilee shocked me sane. That could be a delusion, though."

Lord Ssu-ma said, "You have failed to take advantage of the new liberties you have been granted."

Ragnarson was free to go to the tower top. He had done so only once. It had taken immense will to abandon the safety of his prison, though he knew he should be challenging the stairs regularly, building himself back up. He shrugged, reported the truth. "I don't feel comfortable up there."

Mist asked, "Have you lost your taste for freedom?"

"No. What are you up to?"

Lord Ssu-ma wore his mask. This visit was not informal.

Mist said, "What would you do if I sent you back to Kavelin?"

"I've played that what-if a thousand times. Till last month I wanted to show the world what the poet meant when he said don't inflame the wrath of kings. I was set to burn Kavelin to the ground. I was pitifully selfish. Now I understand who did the real betraying. So I'm just pitiful."

"That response surprises us only in that you were able to articulate it," Mist said.

"Is that why you're here? To see if you dare cut me loose?"

"What would you do if you woke up in Kavelin tomorrow morning?"

"Go looking for my family. Kristen and my grandkids, not Inger and Fulk. I wouldn't make war on Inger. I'd try to get her to go home to Itaskia."

"She might not be able. The Greyfells fortunes collapsed after she locked up the Duke."

He could not restrain himself. "Excellent!" Greyfells villains had caused him misery since he was a boy.

Mist said, "Sending you to tame the chaos is under consideration. Steps are being taken. But nothing has been decided. My councilors will argue that the chaos is benign. Why risk loosing such a stubborn enemy?"

Ragnarson smiled. "Nor would I want the world to think I was beholden to you."

Mist actually chuckled. "You wouldn't, would you?"

...

The door shut behind them. Shih-ka'i asked, "Was that true?"

"He could pull Kavelin together. A strong central authority there would be to our advantage, commercially."

"I see."

"We're here. You said you want me to see something."

"I have captives of my own. One, as Ragnarson is for you, is an old friend and recent enemy, now entirely harmless."

"Ooh. Mysterious."

Shih-ka'i's nerves tautened.

"You want to show me your prizes, then?"

"In a manner of speaking."

"Do it. I don't have much free time."

No one would ever call Shih-ka'i a coward. Not after his war with the Deliverer. But the pig farmer's son was not confident. His hands trembled as he entered the apartment where Kuo Wen-chin and the sad old man were caged.

Kuo was nowhere to be seen. The old man was a few feet from the entrance, looking vague.

Mist halted as though met by some savage weapon. "Lord Ssu-ma. Can this be?"

"Illustrious?"

"This ancient…?"

"He is the companion of my friend, who is my prisoner."

"You don't realize who he is?"

Shih-ka'i stopped. Her intensity alarmed him. "I do not, Illustrious. He is here because my friend insisted on bringing him. He's feeble-minded. He can manage only simple tasks."

"Really?" The Empress sounded disappointed.

Shih-ka'i studied her briefly before asking, "Who is he, then? Or, who was he?"

"One of the eyewitnesses to my father's demise. That night probably left him like this. I suppose nobody in the whole world knows he's still alive."

Ssu-ma Shih-ka'i had not been a witness. He said so, tartly.

"I'm sorry. He's the legend. The Old Man of the Mountain. He occupied Fangdred before Varthlokkur."

Shih-ka'i was so moved he took off his mask. This man might be as old as the Star Rider. He stood witness to thousands of years.

Kuo Wen-chin stepped into view. "The Old Man? Truly?" His voice was soft but rich, vibrant with awe.

Shih-ka'i failed to catch the Empress's response to Kuo's continued existence. He was enthralled by the moment, too. That grinning idiot was half as old as time?

That brain must hold incalculable knowledge. The magics of the ages, perhaps. All inaccessible, now? Sad beyond comprehension if true.

Shih-ka'i asked Kuo, "You didn't know?"

"I had no idea. Of myriad possibilities that particular one never occurred to me. I thought him a tool abandoned by Magden Norath." Kuo bowed to the Empress. He did not speak to her.

Lord Ssu-ma asked her, "You're sure he is who you say?"

"I've done dozens of past divinations involving that night. This man was there. He hasn't changed in appearance, except to become more gaunt and frail."

Mist considered Shih-ka'i and Kuo, unshaken by Kuo's survival. She asked Kuo, "You consider him your friend?"

"Not exactly. I felt responsible for him after I found him. He's better now than he was."

She considered the apartment. It resembled the one where King Bragi was confined, two floors below. She instructed the Tervola to arrange cushions around a low table. The three settled there, leaving a space for the idiot opposite the Empress.

She considered Kuo, then looked Shih-ka'i in the eye and said, "I understand." She told Kuo, "Don't make me regret my trust in Lord Ssu-ma's judgment."

"I am at thy mercy, Illustrious. Blessed be, I am bereft of ambition. Not that I was ever driven. I honor those who were friends in the harsh times as well as the sweet."

Shih-ka'i frowned. Kuo might golden-tongue himself into a tight spot.

The Empress said, "I hope that we have entered into a new age. The Tervola have begun to demonstrate a more traditional attitude toward the values underpinning our empire."

...

Scalza asked, "Do you understand any of that, Uncle Varth?"

"I'd say that I understand without fully comprehending."

The boy told his sister, "He's about to unload a bucket of mystic wizard crap."

The prophecy was harsh but essentially accurate. Varthlokkur had been about to say something vague meant to protect children.

From what? he wondered. Maybe Scalza could use an unadulterated, full-flavored dose of grownup reality.

"Lord Ssu-ma is your mother's most important ally. The other Tervola is Lord Kuo Wen-chin, the man she deposed. Evidently, he and Lord Ssu-ma were close. Lord Ssu-ma saved his life and hid him. Lord Ssu-ma has revealed himself. Your mother has chosen to honor his decisions."

Ekaterina asked, "Where does the old man fit? How come he worries you?"

That was a grownup question. "Because he was who he was. The Old Man."

"The one who was missing here when you went to find him?"

"Yes. I thought he was dead."

Nepanthe arrived, bringing lunch. Ethrian accompanied her, carrying Smyrena and a pail of small beer. The glow in front of Varthlokkur drew him.

He became quite animated. He pointed at the Old Man and chattered.

Varthlokkur said, "See that he doesn't drop the baby."

Unnecessarily. Both children did so automatically. Ekaterina said, "He says that's the man who helped him get away when he was a prisoner, before he got turned into the Deliverer."

"You understand him?"

"Sometimes. Not always."

Varthlokkur was amazed. He had not realized that children often understood one another when adults heard only baby talk and half-formed word sounds.

He did not turn the moment into an interrogation. These kids would turn stubborn on principal. "That old man may be the key to the future. He's in a bad place mentally but he could recover and help break the tyranny of the Star Rider."

Nepanthe had come to look. "I thought he died."

"We all did. We all thought wrong. Eka says Ethrian says he was the one who saved him on that island."

"Does the Star Rider know he's still alive?"

The wizard chuckled. "You all need to clear out so I can work without distractions."

"Can it wait till after lunch?"

It could, of course, having waited so long. But Varthlokkur rushed, making no comment on Nepanthe's effort. He had banged headlong into one of those rare moments when he could get excited again.

First thing, he had to recall the Unborn. The monster's transit would take hours. So he went looking elsewhere while he waited.

There was fading excitement at Sebil el Selib, at the extreme range of what he could see. He missed some details. Some people thought they had been visited by the King Without a Throne but Varthlokkur found no sign of Haroun. Clearly, the incident had grown outsized because of deep fears and wishful thinking.

At Al Rhemish Megelin remained paralyzed by indecision. His advisers were content to let inaction prevail. Megelin had dragged the Royalist cause from one disaster to another. Enough. The chance that Haroun bin Yousif might return inspired a thousand hopes.

A sweep round Kavelin left Varthlokkur thinking that Mist's plan to send Ragnarson home was pointless. Agricultural prospects had everyone outside Vorgreberg warmly optimistic. Inger's influence continued to dwindle. Kristen's was waxing. She and the younger Bragi, as custodians of the ideological flame, were attractive right now. The doyen Ozora made arguments the artisan and mercantile classes found irresistible.

Important men visited her by the score. Some had been regulars at Inger's court as little as six months earlier.

Varthlokkur was tempted to ask Mist to keep Ragnarson locked up. But that might be residual animosity.

The wizard did not yet understand what had gotten into him, back when. His behavior had been irrational. He had done stupid things. So had Ragnarson. Had Old Meddler managed to twist their minds somehow?

Unlikely. Powerful though the Star Rider was, nothing suggested that he could do that. This was one of those cases where ascribing to malice or conspiracy was silly when plain old stupidity explained everything.

The looking consumed six hours. The Unborn was approaching the Dragon's Teeth but would be two more hours in transit. Varthlokkur ate supper with Nepanthe, then returned to his long-range espionage.

He had time to take only a cursory survey but found peace and prosperity everywhere excepting for one family in Itaskia, whose properties were being seized and sold to satisfy debts undertaken to finance an adventure in Kavelin.

No new Greyfells strongman had emerged.

The Unborn arrived. Varthlokkur brought it into his Wind Tower workroom. Nepanthe would be upset when she heard. She loathed Radeachar. She was sure it would turn on them someday. She believed Radeachar's nature would compel it to do so.

Varthlokkur knew the Unborn was a monster, but it was his monster. Every atom of evil in it was directed elsewhere. Wicked as Radeachar was, it remained an extension of the Empire Destroyer.

He overlooked its behavior while transporting Mist. He failed to acknowledge that his wife, wards, and children were not the Empire Destroyer himself.

He communed with Radeachar till well after midnight, then sent it out with a message for Mist.

He reflected on Radeachar's reports. Something interesting might be moving under the surface in Kavelin. Folks had begun taking the Unborn into account.

...

The Empress was not visiting the Karkha Tower when the Unborn arrived. Candidate Lein She found the courage to deal with it once he understood that its behavior was not aggressive. It delivered a small wooden box addressed to the Empress. The identity of the courier declared the source of the box.

Lein She sent a man to the Empress's headquarters. He carried a note suggesting that the Empire Destroyer could not follow her movements as closely as feared.

...

The lifeguards were too enthusiastic in their efforts to protect their Empress. They damaged the box, which had been handcrafted by Scalza. She was surprised that the boy's effort moved her so.

The message from the wizard was important. So was that from Lein She.

Yes, it was important to keep the Old Man's survival secret. And, yes, the Star Rider's awareness, or lack thereof, could be tested.

Every means must be employed to help the Old Man reclaim his memory if he was so truly in revolt that the era of the Deliverer had been sparked by an act of defiance of his.

The Matayangan treaty was about to be finalized. There were no threats on any horizon. There was time for this and time for building something with her children.

†

Chapter Seventeen:

YEAR 1017 AFE:

Ghosts

"What a stupid thing to do," Haroun muttered again as he inventoried his travel gear. He had to move fast. They would surround the tent before they began the search. His only hope was to be gone before the cordon closed.

Why did he take that chance? Hearing her should have been enough.

He eased out into the evening via a prepared emergency exit. No one saw him. His destination was Barking Snake's establishment, which was abandoned if the Disciple's criminal servants were to be believed. He would hide there.

Why in God's Name did she have to look up just then? And, for the hundredth time, what madness had brought him to Sebil el Selib?

It was dark now. He had encountered only one man, so far, who had offered only an indifferent, surly greeting in passing.

Where was all the excitement?

Yasmid must not have reported him.

Why not? Because he was her husband? Because she thought he was imaginary?

The Disciple had reported seeing a similar ghost.

A challenge. "Who is there?"

Damn!

They had left a watchman.

...

Yasmid glared at Ibn Adim ed-Din al-Dimishqi, who was frightened but refused to let her see that a woman could scare him.

She did see and savored it. The deaths among the elderly were God's gift, without assistance. But let Ibn Adim fear the worst.

"I have a task for you, son of Adim," Yasmid said. "It is well-suited to your detail-oriented nature."

"As ever, I am here to serve."

"Good. You have heard about the thievery in my father's tent?"

"You were most compassionate, punishing only the one criminal."

"Too much so. The corruption runs deeper than I thought. Some whom we believed to be righteous actually skimmed the take of lesser thieves." Let him think she meant the men of action he so despised. "Go into my father's tent. Examine the records. Find out where the money came from. Find out where it went. Create an exact and detailed inventory of everything stored there."

"Lady? Could you be more specific?"

Yasmid thought she had been clear. "Over the years my father received thousands of gifts and untold treasure as his portion of booty. It all ended up in that moldering atrocity of a tent. There is no reliable inventory. Therefore, there is no way to know what was stolen."

"I understand, Lady. That is something I can sink my teeth into. How much help will I have? How much leeway in questioning recalcitrant witnesses?"

"Consult me on a case by case basis. For assistance feel free to conscript any cleric not already handling an assigned task." That would get the old men out of her hair.

"When shall I begin?"

"Up to you. Habibullah has warrants prepared. Inform me of any exceptional discoveries or outstanding efforts to obstruct you."

The imam took his leave, accompanied by Habibullah.

Yasmid permitted herself a smug smile.

Ibn Adim would do her work. He would suffer the odium of the investigated while finding out if someone had been hiding in her father's tent.

Even Habibullah thought she had suffered a seizure that night.

She was convinced that she had suffered a hallucination brought on by the swami's talk about her father having seen the ghost of Haroun's father.

It was all power of suggestion, rooted in what she thought she had heard from the pilgrim camp.

...

Being King of Hammad al Nakir meant suffering frustrations and indignities and things always going wrong. Megelin suspected that a diabolical force was thwarting him. It made his life uglier even when he did nothing.

The disaster on the salt lake should not have happened. He had failed through no fault of his own. The antiques who commanded his battalions did not carry out their orders. Those saboteurs. They undermined him all the time. He would be rid of them if he could.

Sadly, he dared do nothing obvious. Some had been around since his father was a pup. They were fixtures. The soldiers—the few who remained—considered them tutelary spirits.

Patience was his only tool. They must surrender to the inevitable soon enough.

But patience was not in Megelin's nature.

And these rumors, prevalent since Magden Norath had been so stupid as to get himself killed, about his father's return…? What to do? How to respond? True or false, they impacted everything, every day. The possibility that Haroun bin Yousif was out there touched every decision anyone made.

Megelin was not sure what he would do if his father did reappear. He understood that the Royalist faithful would let the man to do as he pleased and would support him. Haroun bin Yousif, despite his faults and failures, was now a demigod.

The question nagging Megelin, and anyone else who cared, was, where *was* the revenant king? Why did he not show himself?

As ever, Megelin obsessed about Norath's death. He had

witnessed nothing. He had been too thoroughly protected. But that creature he and Norath had been there to meet…

The Star Rider. The oldest villain of all. Possibly the Evil One incarnate. What had become of that wicked old troublemaker? Was he the one making everything go wrong? Was he still feeding the insanity of the Disciple? Why, then, meet Norath and himself? And why stay away now?

Megelin had expected to see the man again after the excitement of the murder subsided. Nothing ever happened.

Impotent in his own capital, amongst his own subjects, Megelin did nothing but brood. Alone. Always alone.

People were rigidly proper in his presence and accepted his every directive. But once they left his presence something happened. Even simple orders would not be executed properly. Because he would not go see for himself it was impossible to tell if insubordination was responsible.

The nearer people were to him the more pathetic Megelin seemed.

Thousands hoped the murder of Magden Norath was a good omen.

…

Haroun answered the challenge, "Mowfaq al-Tiriki. Tell Snake I'm back from Al Rhemish."

The guard unshuttered a small lantern. He thought on his feet, too. "I'm new. Does Barking Snake know you?"

Haroun put suspicion into his voice. "Everyone knows al-Tiriki. Who are you? What's going on?" He drew a knife, making sure the sound could be heard.

The guard responded by drawing a sword. "You are under arrest. In the name of the Disciple, drop the knife."

"I don't think so, pup." Haroun backed away. A suitable clot of darkness presented itself. He stepped inside, released two small, prepared spells. One interfered with the guard's eyesight. The other made it hard for any eye to fix on Haroun bin Yousif.

The guard became frustrated. He muttered. What should he do? Stick to his post? Run to his superiors?

Either choice could be wrong. He would be the goat whatever might go badly.

Haroun flitted from shadow to shadow, circling. He would not go to ground here, now, but might find something he could use. Not so, however. Just minutes proved that the Invincibles had cleaned the place out.

The sentry decided to report. Haroun retraced his approach. As midnight loomed he slipped back inside the Disciple's tent. He went to his best hide and buried himself.

He fell asleep telling himself it was time to hatch a real plan. A passive life was not his style.

What a fool. He had endured so much to get here but had no fixed purpose now.

...

Elwas brought the man in, though he was a man mostly by reason of having done a man's job. He was about fifteen. "Tell the Lady Yasmid."

Sometimes mumbling, often stumbling, the boy told his story.

"Mowfaq al-Tiriki?" Yasmid asked Elwas.

"A senior lieutenant of Farukh al-Fadl. One of the criminals we haven't yet caught."

"You wanted me to know about it because?"

"Because al-Tiriki vanished as thoroughly as the pilgrim did."

"The same man?"

"Probably not. Boy. You did say he was clean-shaven?"

"Almost. He had been shaved recently. I couldn't tell much else in the dark."

Yasmid thought the lad confident beyond his years. He had faced up to danger in the night. He was standing steadfast here. She would commend him to Elwas later.

"Anything else? About the man?"

"He smelled bad, Lady. He had not bathed in a long time."

That was not unusual. She raised an eyebrow.

The boy said, "I prefer to keep myself clean. In accordance with the early teachings."

Yasmid looked to Elwas. He shrugged. "Some young men are extremely fastidious. Al-Tiriki would have sweat a lot during a journey from Al Rhemish."

"I won't turn the world upside down again but I do want the

Invincibles to keep a sharp watch. Al-Tiriki could give us some insight on what's happening in Al Rhemish." She made a small gesture indicating that the interview was over. Then, "Elwas, when next you run into Ibn Adim tell him I want to see him when he has a moment free."

Yasmid bint Micah was no despot in the time-honored mode but Elwas executed her wishes as though she was. Ibn Adim was on his knees in front of her within the hour.

"Up. I hear you're starting the audit today."

"I was assigning tasks when al-Souki came."

"As you inventory I want you watchful for signs of squatters."

"You think...?"

"Nothing. See if those thieves didn't move their families in where my father never goes."

"I see. Of course. I'll keep my eyes open."

"My father says his tent is haunted. Ask about ghosts."

"As you will, so shall it be."

...

Haroun found it more difficult to steal food. Outsiders roamed the empty reaches of the tent. They did not find him. They did discover the vixens and kits. The latter were nearly grown. They caused a great deal of excitement. Haroun hid elsewhere and waited out the scramble.

They found no evidence of his presence.

He learned that he could slip out nights with little risk.

...

Yasmid was exhausted. Trivia that would never have come near her during wartime inundated her now. Nobody wanted to be remembered for having made a decision should blame ever be assessed.

"Elwas, in six months these people will expect me to change their babies. Let's start a war."

Elwas started to say something serious.

Yasmid burst out laughing.

"Lady?"

"I'm sorry. Your expression. When I was eight I saw that look on my father's face when Nassef asked if he couldn't start a war so he wouldn't have to waste time listening to people with the brains of chickpeas whine about trivia."

"Makes you wonder."

"Elwas?"

"How many wars happen because somebody with the power to start them was bored or sick of listening to nitwits?"

"So pass on the bit of tedium you've brought me now."

"There has been an increase in petty theft and vandalism."

"Oh?"

"I think bored kids are stealing things and destroying property. There is no pattern. There are no witnesses. Nothing taken has much value."

"Then let parents and sons know that the parties responsible will be exposed to public humiliation when we catch them."

"Excellent. That's all I had."

"Then I'm calling it a day. You do the same."

"Thank you, Lady. Perhaps we should consider mandating shorter days and longer nights."

Elwas was a good man, she reflected as she withdrew into her private quarters. He left her wearing a smile when he could.

It never occurred to her that Elwas bin Farout al-Souki, Jirbash al-'Azariyah, or any of several others young enough to be her sons, might be infatuated.

It did not occur to those young men that they were besotted by the daughter of the Disciple because it was not the mad fascination brought on by the proximity of a beautiful young woman.

Habibullah saw it. Habibullah understood. He remembered the young Yasmid and never missed a chance to see today's Yasmid. He had been besotted for generations.

Despite the stresses and irritations of her day Yasmid went to her rest happy and almost content.

...

A chill took Yasmid in her sleep.

Fright clamped talons round her heart.

She was a maiden again, wakening to terror in the night. The feeble mutton tallow lamp did not help. It set wicked shadows fluttering all round.

Something terrible was near by, watching, slavering in its hunger to defile her.

Seconds passed before she recalled that she was a grown woman, old enough to be a grandmother but cursed with a son who would not give her grandchildren.

Reflection tamed her fright. Amused, she began to slide back down into the sink of sleep, wondering why Megelin did not wed. It was not that he preferred men. His worst enemies had found no evidence to suggest that.

The boy just did not relate.

Something pricked her senses again. She jerked involuntarily. She squeaked. She was wide awake, shaking, chilled to the core. She rolled and sat up, seized an unconsecrated Harish kill dagger that had been a gift from the last master of that cult. It needed only to enforce the slightest cut to cause an excruciating death.

The lamplight did not reassure her. There was a man-shaped shadow fading in and out. Someone *was* there. How had he gotten in? Only Habibullah had access at night. He would never dare.

Yasmid rose slowly, ready to fight. She fixed the intruder with a hard stare. He remained a pattern of shadow inside a dancing shadow. It was hard to stay focused.

How long would it take for help to arrive once she yelled?

"Show yourself."

The shadows coalesced.

"It *was* you!"

Haroun stepped out of the shaghûn cloak of darkness. "It was me. And after waiting so long I decided to take a chance." He advanced another step. He was almost close enough to cut. Almost.

He would come no nearer. Not even when his own wife held the knife. No telling where her heart lay after so long.

Yasmid put the kill dagger aside, carefully. It could bite her as easily as him. "Come talk to me. It's been a long time. You must have a grand tale." Tomorrow was soon enough to decide what to do.

"Not so much. I spent most of it in prison."

"Sit."

That boy Invincible was right. Haroun smelled perfectly awful. The smell might lead to difficult questions tomorrow.

†

Chapter Eighteen:

YEAR 1017 AFE:

Distracting Darkness

Inger told Nathan Wolf, "This is ugly beyond anything I can grasp." She reread the brief report. Eleven years old. Tortured. Raped repeatedly. Discarded in an alleyway near the Western Gate, probably still breathing at the time. She had not been found for days. No one had been looking.

Wolf said, "I nearly puked, Majesty. I will spare you the full ugliness. I won't spare you a demand that we do everything we can to find the monster who did that to her."

"Do you have a personal interest, Nathan?"

"No, Majesty. What we know comes courtesy of the sorcerer's lame efforts. Her name was Phyletia Plens. She was the adopted daughter of Herald and Janna Bors. They identified the body. They say that her real parents had a chance encounter during the excitement back when. Phyletia was not a happy child. She ran away sometimes. This time she didn't come back."

Inger made a growling sound. This was more information than she wanted. "Nathan!"

"Majesty, more than anything else… We could reap the whirlwind if we don't protect the children."

"Yes." Inger had a child of her own.

What she did not understand was why Nathan Wolf, unmarried and childless, was emotionally engaged. She asked.

"Majesty, I can't explain. I don't have the words. I just know that whoever did that to Phyletia Plens was a soul uglier than a *savan dalage*."

His intensity pleased Inger, though its foundation remained obscure. She asked again.

"I doesn't matter. All we can do for her, now, is mourn her. But another girl is missing. Hanna Isodor. She disappeared just before Plens turned up. She's the same age, similar background, same physical description."

Inger started to speak. Nathan gave her no room. "Also missing is a Carrie Depar, almost thirteen, different physical description. She's been gone five days. She told friends she was going to run away with her boyfriend. They didn't know who the boyfriend was."

"This could change everything even though it has no strategic significance."

Nobody in the provinces gave a rat's ass whether the Queen protected Vorgreberg's children but Vorgrebergers certainly did. Protection was the reason kings and nobles existed. The protected worked hard to produce surpluses in kind and coin to support a warrior class meant to defend them from predators external and internal.

In most kingdoms, much of the time, that mutual obligation was under stress, humans being the despicable beasts they became given any opportunity. But what was happening here was the nightmare that lurked in every parent's heart.

There was no denying it. The Boogerman walked among them.

Angered, Inger summoned Josiah Gales, Babeltausque, and Doctor Wachtel to join her and Wolf. She seated them and Wolf at a table her husband had used when he wanted his henchmen to brainstorm. "We have to handle this fast. I don't know how but we have got to find the man who tortured the Plens girl. If we don't we'll lose Vorgreberg, too. I've had an inventory run. It revealed two things. First, the servants have been stealing from us. Second, we should begin eating the horses to save their grain for a possible siege. Which we might withstand for as much as six days."

Colonel Gales coughed, meant as a signal. It was heavy, liquid, and disturbing. He remained far from recovered.

The Queen stopped jabbering. "Josiah?"

"Cleave to the problem at hand. Don't look into the gloom just yet."

"Of course. Gentlemen. We have a monster among us. How do we find him? Babeltausque?"

The sorcerer shifted uneasily. Gales and Wolf looked at him like they dared him to open his mouth. Both had been in Greyfells service a long time.

Inger had heard rumors, too. "Well? Wouldn't you understand this kind of mind better than anybody?"

Babeltausque asked, "Is there the remotest chance that your cousin has been getting out at night?"

That was well-played. Inger would relive her experiences as a comely lass in a household where wickedness was routine and Dane of Greyfells was one of the more wicked players.

Gales and Wolf kept on eyeing him darkly.

He tapped into his courage. "Torture isn't what moves me. I never harmed anyone. I only love them till they break my heart."

Gales and Wolf donned contemptuous smiles.

Inger seemed appalled.

What a screw up. He had used the present tense.

What mad, self-destructive force compelled him to indict himself that way? Was he so conflicted that he would set himself up to be convicted of another's monstrous behavior?

Wachtel looked eager to get that word out. He might betray himself in his haste.

"All of you, listen. I did not harm Phyletia Plens. I didn't know her. She is nothing to me. Was nothing, in that way. Look for someone else. As Her Majesty noted, there may be no hunter better than I. Doctor, sit. Relax. We'll be here a while. Tell us, has this happened before?"

The old man took his time. Finally, he nodded. "Sadly, you are correct. There have been similar incidents, the most recent before your arrival. Things were more confused back then. No one had attention to spare for an anonymous child who probably brought it on herself."

"Anonymous?" Babeltausque asked.

"She turned out to be Ellie Wood, a runaway, in flight from an abusive father. There was another one, seven or eight years ago, named Tefe Black, thirteen and pregnant by her father or one of her brothers. It would have been a marvelous scandal if there hadn't been a war on."

Babeltausque nodded. "Their deaths touched you."

"They were children. Nobody loved them. They were tormented by their own kin first, then a monster consumed them. No one cared. No one but me. And I was powerless. Not even Michael would take it on."

Tears filled the old man's eyes. The others were amazed.

Babeltausque said, "Black isn't a common surname, is it? It sounds Itaskian. Right? Mr. Wolf, didn't we run into that surname somewhere recently?"

Wolf looked blank. "I don't think so."

"The butcher. In the shop where the Heltkler girl left the beer."

"His name was Black? I don't recall that."

"Maybe I didn't mention it. Neighborhood gossip says Haida Heltkler was an abuse victim."

"The butcher?"

"Maybe too obvious. He wouldn't destroy the girl physically. He would be feeding a different need. He would be the unwanted lover. Someone else would be the punisher. Someone close to the butcher. Let's find out if Tefe Black was related. If so, we'll look for the man Black's girls ran to… Doctor?"

Wachtel seemed to be choking.

...

"That isn't particularly subtle," Nepanthe observed, watching over Varthlokkur's shoulder. "You said you don't want people remembering you."

The Unborn was making a night progress over Sedlmayr. "This is the time when little plots will come to life. Radeachar will discourage them."

"What will you do about what's happening in Vorgreberg?" She meant the girl-killer.

He sighed. He did care. He was appalled. But there were only so many hours and no way everyone could be saved. There were bigger issues. And those people were not idiots. They could manage if they wanted.

"And tell me this, husband. How can you eavesdrop in Castle Krief but not on Haroun or Mist?"

"We lived in Castle Krief. I know every inch. Every inch remembers me. And I bespelled the place before we left." And he could eavesdrop on Mist, when conditions were right. But Mist insisted on making it difficult now that she knew it could be done.

The truth was more technical but that was the gist.

"The baby-killer."

Exasperated, "What would you have me do?"

"Something. Good men do nothing."

He counted silently.

Nepanthe said, "The Star Rider will be there till the end of time. Meantime, the monster has hold of another girl."

"I understand." Surrendering to the will of the wife.

The villain should not be hard to find. A divination at the body dump... "I'd have to go there. I can't manage the time dives from here."

Fright flashed across Nepanthe's face. "Really? You're not just saying that so I'll ask you to back off?"

"No. I have to be there to catch the necessary personal resonances."

Nepanthe freed one of her classic sighs. "What must be, must be. Go."

"You insist?"

"I do."

"I'll set Scalza's scrying bowl so you can watch." That lacked any facility for listening in. He did some this and that while mumbling about it being a good thing that Radeachar did not have much character. The monster had gotten flung all over creation lately, with little respite.

He had the Unknown show itself blatantly, then called it back to Fangdred.

...

Ozora Mundwiller glared at Kristen. She scowled at Dahl Haas. "That thing is going house to house, staring in windows!"

Dahl said, "The wizard wants it understood that he's watching."

The old woman seemed inclined to lay the blame at their feet.

"We've always known that. Why the sudden close-ups?"

Kristen said, "Neither of us knows Varthlokkur well enough to fathom his thinking. If I was to guess, though, the intent is to panic somebody into thinking that the wizard is onto them."

"Somebody in Sedlmayr."

Dahl nodded. "Would that be a first?"

"No. But it would be someone skilled at not getting noticed."

Aral Dantice came to all three minds. And Aral had disappeared.

Ozora announced, "I have regained my composure. I will assume the Unborn's behavior to be a message. I'll ask questions. If there is anything going on I will expose it. Bight? Where is that boy?"

Haas said, "He's got a new crush."

"That Blodgett chit? He's not supposed to let Kristen out of his sight."

"She would be the one," Kristen said, amused. "She may be just a wee bit more pliable than I am."

"I'll ply…"

Haas added, "She seems like a nice kid. Down to earth. For her age."

"But an orphan," Ozora grumbled. Styling. It was no secret she actually liked Bertie Blodgett. The girl made her laugh. "Living on the charity of the enThal family. Where did she come from, anyway? Those people…!"

Old family animosities were at work there. Ozora was too old and set to let them slide. She was, surprisingly, still flexible enough not to issue anti-fraternization decrees on that basis alone.

Later, Dahl teased Kristen, "You got too old for Bight."

"What you mean is, too sophisticated."

"And too taken."

"That could be changed. I see the way you look at that Bertie."

"Can I help it if I'm not dead yet? A man is a man. I never do anything but look."

Kristen did not take that in the spirit in which it was offered.

…

"I don't have the skills to divine the past!" Babeltausque declared, not for the first time. "I'm not really a necromancer. The spirits I command can't look back, either. We need to find something of the villain's and trace that. Or just keep on working the neighborhood where the girls grew up. We'll find something eventually."

Nathan Wolf asked, "Does it have to be something that belonged to the villain? We do have the dead girl."

"That might work," Babeltausque conceded, irked that it had taken a layman to suggest what should have been obvious to him.

So far working the neighborhood had produced only rumors, ugly stories, and malicious finger-pointing. Few local girls reached their wedding days untouched by family or neighbors. People considered it part of growing up.

But nobody sanctioned what had been done to Phyletia Plens. They pretended to cooperate, speculated freely, and strained muscles in their eagerness to point fingers.

The butcher was a magnet. Neighbors wondered if he had not killed Haida Heltkler and blended her into his sausages.

Still fighting that cough, Josiah Gales said, "We could put Black to the question. That would get to the facts."

Inger said, "Do arrest him. What is all that noise?"

A grand racket had developed elsewhere in the castle.

"A mob?" Babeltausque asked, suddenly frightened. Wasn't it too soon for that kind of trouble?

Inger said, "Nathan, find out what's happening. And bring the doctor when you come back."

As the door closed, Babeltausque said, "Black isn't our killer but he does know something about the girls who lived in his house."

Possibly. One girl later murdered and another now missing. Significantly, though, the other victims and missing girls had lived within a short distance of Black's shop.

Inger said, "I want the doctor because I have a notion worse than running girls through a meat grinder. Which, you'll recall, did not happen to Phyletia Plens. What we do have is the monster's seed that he spilled into Phyletia. Babeltausque, you and the doctor will..."

The door opened. A man stepped inside.

Inger finally exhaled. "Varthlokkur!"

"I am not happy to be here. My wife insists that I help stop what's been happening."

Babeltausque withstood the wizard's stare. "It isn't me."

"True. But you do know what became of one missing girl."

Babeltausque inclined his head. "She isn't missing. She's hiding."

Oh, he hated to confess. He did not want to suffer the disapprobation he would face now. But he would not grant the wizard a blackmail hold.

"I see. Consensual."

"Entirely."

The wizard surveyed the others. "One disappearance solved already. Tell me about the others."

Wolf and Wachtel arrived while Babeltausque was confessing. The doctor looked older than his incredible age. He was pale and grim. His hands trembled.

Wolf said, "I sent men to fetch Black. Meantime, we have a small mystery, brought to my attention while I was out. There, by the way, is the cause of the excitement." He nodded at Varthlokkur.

"What is the mystery?"

"We have ghosts in the cemetery."

"That seems the most likely place to find them."

"Absolutely, but for the fact that nobody ever saw any until, a while back, a Siluro family squatting in Fiana's mausoleum were evicted by ghosts who then vanished when the Unborn appeared."

Everyone looked at Varthlokkur, who said, "I have no idea. Maybe I should go see. Now. I've heard from Her Majesty and my fellow wizard. Suppose you speak next, Colonel Gales?"

"Not much to tell. I was a prisoner. They turned me loose. I've been trying to regain my health. My experience doesn't connect with the matter at hand."

"The Heltkler girl was associated with your captors."

Gales shrugged. "I never saw a girl. I saw one man. He brought food and made sure I didn't try to get away. I was drugged most of the time. Those times when my head did clear I was too sick to act."

"Nathan Wolf. I know little about you."

Wolf shivered, told what he could. The wizard did not interrupt. He tolerated repetition of information already given. He was sniffing for previously undetected connections.

"Excellent. You are a skilled observer. Is it possible that the Heltkler girl disappeared into the same fog as the men who kidnapped Colonel Gales?"

Babeltausque opened his mouth, then shut it. That possibility had not occurred to him. His hungers, fears, and preconceptions, fueled by the hysteria stirred by Phyletia's dark fate, had shoved political possibilities right out of his head.

He was not alone.

Josiah Gales gave up a cough that was a small confession of embarrassment.

Babeltausque said, "So. A plausible explanation for what happened to another girl. Does that take the load off Arnulf Black? She might have run to escape him instead of us."

Varthlokkur faced Wachtel. "Doctor? You have something?"

The old man shook. "I won't be doing surgery much longer."

Varthlokkur told him, "These people all know your secret. For my part, I don't care what made you become political."

"My physician's oath. These invaders only mean to use the people of Kavelin like farm animals."

"As may be, we have children to save. We have a monster to identify. Can you contribute to that cause?"

Wachtel talked about girls found dead in the past.

"Might there have been others?"

"Almost certainly."

Nathan Wolf suggested, "There could have been dozens. Girls go missing all the time. Most run away. The ones we know about are the ones whose bodies were found."

Varthlokkur said, "Youth sells. There are those who exploit that. With Her Majesty's permission I'd like to interview people who operate houses of prostitution. Those who get stubborn can answer to Radeachar. Doctor. You still have Phyletia Plens?"

"I do. Preserved in collaboration with the sorcerer. I was sure we would get back to her eventually."

"Excellent. You and I will examine her now. Babeltausque, please join us. I'll need to see where she was found after I examine her remains."

...

Word swept the city. Varthlokkur had returned. He was hunting a child-killer. Once he interviewed them Vorgreberg's pimps and procurers stopped employing talents under fourteen. It took only one visit from the Unborn to drive the message home.

That monster became a permanent aerial phenomenon.

Vorgrebergers were six parts terrified and the rest of a dozen thrilled. Every vanished daughter for thirty years past was one villain's fault, suddenly. Tavern speculation concentrated on what might be the ugliest possible means of dealing with the beast.

There were no votes for quick or kind.

Inger told Josiah Gales, "We're riding high today. If we found that money now we could really cash in."

Gales was tired of hearing about a treasure he no longer believed existed. "Ask Varthlokkur to find it."

"I did. He chuckled and said it will be no help if we do find it."

...

A sense of unease descended on Sedlmayr, fed by the news that Varthlokkur had returned to Vorgreberg. The truth, that he had come to hunt a foul murderer, was disbelieved by many.

The road east filled with agents determined to learn the real story.

...

Babeltausque shuffled slowly along to see his Carrie Depar. No special hunger drove him. Something was wrong with him. He ought not to be tired of Carrie so soon, yet his infatuation had begun to fade. Because everyone disapproved? Why? She was damned near legal. Certainly older than he preferred.

Could it be fear? The mob would not stop to listen if he tried to explain that Carrie was with him by choice.

He knew that no one really listened even at the best of times. No one wanted to be reminded that they had failings of their own.

It was dark. A sliver of autumn moon drifted toward the western horizon. The air was brisk but not yet outright cold.

Something burred past Babeltausque. He thought it must be a big bug, yet experience made him dive into the ditch beside the road. That bug had to be a sling bullet.

There was water in the ditch. It was cold and rank.

A voice grumbled. Another, closer, said, "Nah. I think I missed."

Babeltausque slithered forward, quietly as he could. The ditch would debouch into a wet weather creek just ahead. That passed through a culvert under the road. He should fit. Holed up, he could plan his counterattack.

He listened to them grumble as they searched. He did not

recognize their voices. They did not know the terrain. They did not have a light by which to find his obvious trail.

This must be political. They must want to strip Inger of her most dangerous ally.

Babeltausque's heartbeat settled some. He plied his sorcerer's skills. He did not counterattack but, rather, marked the men with little spells that would betray them later, hoping they could be traced back to whoever sent them.

He waited for them to give up. That took another miserable half hour. He had time to reflect. He had become so predictable that enemies were able to set an ambush. That had to change. Then he thought about the geography between Castle Krief and Mist's old mansion. There were other culverts. There was an abandoned well. There were several cesspools, including a dried up pit behind Mist's mansion. There were improved springs, cisterns, and fish ponds. Few of those had been examined by treasure hunters. People figured that a Rebsamen don like Derel Prataxis would not hide anything in unpleasant places.

Babeltausque suspected that he and Nathan would be getting wet and filthy soon.

Tonight, though… Tonight was for Carrie.

The fire had returned.

...

Babeltausque inched toward the stairway down to his beloved. How bored was she? How much would she whine about being cooped up here with nothing to do but wait till he felt the need?

He had only a moment to realize that he was not alone. An exotic beauty emerged from broken wainscoting and rose in front of him, bits of broken wood sliding off her.

She was more surprised than he. That allowed him a running start.

He hit the night with arms and legs flailing.

This was the first time he had seen that woman but he knew who she was.

He was too focused on covering ground to notice the Unborn descending behind him.

†

Chapter Nineteen:

YEAR 1017 AFE:

Chaos in Peace

Mist shoved the broken woodwork aside, duck-walked a step, rose to find herself face to face with a chubby man in black. He smelled like swamp water. He squeaked and ran. She followed, hoping to keep him from reporting her presence. That hope died when she stepped outside.

The Unborn came down from the night as though it had been waiting just for her.

Reason suggested that it must have been tracking the man now in such enthusiastic flight.

The Unborn settled at eye level, a dozen feet away. It was unafraid.

Mist wondered if it was capable of fear.

It shot upward, then whipped away toward Vorgreberg.

Mist's lifeguard stepped out in time to watch it dwindle. "Is there a problem, Illustrious?"

"I don't think so. Though there was a man here when I left the portal. He ran away. We should have time to poke around."

Wait! Here that man came, a pale witch light burning over his left shoulder.

"Illustrious?"

"He doesn't seem belligerent."

The pudgy fellow approached till he was three yards away. His light grew stronger. Mist's bodyguard stepped out to her left, watching the man's right hand.

Mist asked, "What are you doing?"

"Waiting."

"For what?"

He faced Vorgreberg. "It won't be long." The Unborn reappeared. "Not long at all." He turned back. "I am Babeltausque, a wizard. Mouse size, relatively speaking."

The Unborn closed fast. It was not alone. Varthlokkur dangled beneath it.

"Illustrious! Get behind me."

"There is no point. Either we are in no danger or it is too late to protect ourselves. You. Sorcerer. What is he doing here?"

"Helping find an ugly and elusive child-killer."

"Tell me."

He was still talking when the Unborn deposited the Empire Destroyer beside him. Mist felt tension rise in her companion.

Varthlokkur smiled. "You were the ghost in the graveyard, too."

So. The squatters had talked. And so had the Unborn. "I'm told you're hunting an especially horrible villain."

"A clever or lucky one. My skills at divining the past have been inadequate, though he made no deliberate effort to hide from my sort."

An outsider might have suspected that there was more than verbal communication going on. Both were deceitful in appearance. Both were ages older than they looked, though not necessarily wiser.

"I'm willing to contribute," Mist said. "This young man told me a great deal. He lied a lot, too, but I'll forgive him. He was protecting his principal."

"Oh?"

"I have a daughter."

Mist wondered what she was doing.

Both wizards were calculating, too.

She had to buy time. Varthlokkur had identified her only other entrance into Kavelin. She needed to get more set up quickly. Just in case.

She repeated herself. “I have children, too. I might be able to help.”

That knocked Varthlokkur off balance.

Her lifeguard had sense enough to keep his mouth shut.

The chubby man was horrified, though.

Varthlokkur said, “My colleague believes that you must be the darkness distilled. His attitude will improve if you give us a means to prove that the child-killer isn’t him.”

Mist eyed the pudgy man. He had a creepy quality. Most western sorcerers did. They were all twisted somehow.

A chill touched her. She had lost friends who were weird western wizards. Another chill. No one she knew ever died a natural death.

Varthlokkur asked, “Are you all right?”

“I think too much. Comes of having too much time on my hands. Tell me about your killer.”

The wizard did so, adding, “I came up empty when I tried to divine the dump. The killer kept his features hidden. And he was lucky.”

“How so?”

“Ley lines intersect near the site. Their resonances interfere with the scrying.”

“You can get around that.”

Her bodyguard made a sound that was not a word.

“Of course. I have an empire to manage. I have the Old Man to reclaim. There’s no time for hobbies.”

“Your suggestion?”

“Track the girl, not the killer. You know who she was. You know where she lived. Go back to when she was safe. Follow her forward.”

Varthlokkur offered a nod of respect. “That’s sure to travel some ugly road.”

“No doubt. You westerners tolerate…” She stopped. She did not *know* that her own people were less wicked. “I should go.”

“Any luck with the Old Man?”

“No. How about you with the Deliverer?”

“Ethrian. His mother’s optimism seems justified but the process will take longer than she hopes.”

“Let me know what works.”

“Does Old Meddler know?”

"I don't know. What do you think?"

"I think not. Not yet. Will you free Ragnarson?"

"I haven't decided."

"Kavelin has begun to recover. Him being here might do more harm than good."

"I *must* go." She dared not say that they had made a huge mistake.

Inger would know that Bragi lived before sunrise. All Kavelin would know within days. It might no longer matter if she sent him home. The possibility would alter the political climate anyway.

The chubby man looked bland and indifferent and small. He understood what he had overheard.

Almost idly, he told Varthlokkur, "Two men tried to kill me on my way out here. I didn't recognize them. They were Wessons. They didn't have unusual accents and they didn't say anything that explained why. I marked them with tracer spells."

Varthlokkur said, "You're good at that, aren't you."

"Everybody has to be good at something."

Mist retreated into the house. That was the last she heard.

...

"The Vorgreberg portals have to be considered compromised," Mist told her technicians. "I expect them to be destroyed. Get replacements into place before that happens."

She dismissed her bodyguard. He needed rest and family time, unlike his Empress. She relaxed a few hours herself, then chose another lifeguard to accompany her to the Karkha Tower. She was not surprised to find Lord Ssu-ma visiting. He had a lot of free time. He spent much of it with Kuo. She invited herself to join him, Wen-chin, and the Old Man.

They were surprised to see her so early in the day.

She said, "They don't see it themselves but things are coming to a head in Kavelin. And Varthlokkur is in the middle of it." She explained.

Shih-ka'i asked, "Might his slips have been deliberate?"

"No. He's lost the habit of caution. He doesn't need to watch himself at home. The news should cause fundamental shifts but I can't guess what those might be."

Shih-ka'i suggested, "Ask Ragnarson."

"He's farther removed from today's reality than I am."

Wen-chin and Shih-ka'i were playing shogi. Each had made one move since the Empress arrived. It was Wen-chin's turn. He spoke for the first time. "Ask anyway. You know him well. You judge his response."

"I'll be back in a few minutes."

...

"There is a shift underway," Wen-chin observed.

"Uhm?" Shih-ka'i focused on the board. He was the superior player but was in a bad position this time around.

"Just years ago we were all playing games of empire. That ends tomorrow, when you execute the treaty with Matayanga. The whole world will be at peace."

"You think?"

"Consider. In Kavelin one pretender's ambition is to catch a criminal. The other waits like an ambush predator, showing no ambition whatsoever. Rather the same situation prevails in Hammad al Nakir."

"True. As far as we know. The west is caught up in the doldrums of peace. North and south, they're interested only in harvests and their burgeoning mercantile ventures."

"Peace?"

That came from the Old Man, who drowsed in a western-style chair while disinterestedly watching the game. He began to shake. He made a brief whimpering sound, then slipped away to hide inside himself.

Shih-ka'i said, "His fear could be justified. Old Meddler must be livid. But even he can't chivy an exhausted world into another round of butchery. Generations have to pass."

"Let that be true. Will you yield?"

...

Ragnarson was at his little desk when Mist arrived. He did not look up. "I can't remember the color of my mother's eyes."

"Blue, I expect. They're all blue up there, aren't they?"

"You'd think. But my mother wasn't Trolledyngjan. My father brought her back from a raid on Hellin Daimiel."

"Then they were brown, or darker. Does it matter?"

"Not in the history of empires. I wanted to capture what I remember about the people I've lost. The memories have begun to get away. Those people shouldn't be forgotten. So. To what do I owe the honor?"

"I visited Kavelin last night. When I came back I rested till people would be awake here."

"Did something happen?"

"A lot of nothing. But Varthlokkur was there, helping Inger hunt somebody who tortured and raped a little girl. Kristen's faction is sitting in Sedlmayr, waiting for Inger to eliminate herself. Nobody is talking politics anymore."

"Same here. I don't like being locked up but the lack of pressure is nice. They've stopped killing each other, haven't they?"

"Yes. Do you want to spend the rest of your life here?"

"No. But I don't want to be the man you locked up, either."

"I'll see you soon."

Once she was gone, he added, "I won't be your tool, either."

...

Mist found Shih-ka'i tearing his hair, figuratively. He and Wen-chin were involved in the same game. He would not yield.

Mist said, "Ragnarson seems indifferent to what's going on in Kavelin, evidently because everything has collapsed into peace. He seems inclined to stay away."

Shih-ka'i said, "Amazing, the impact a good harvest can have."

Mist nodded. The world was drifting into pacifist indifference.

She would not complain. She was fond of peace herself.

Something was happening, down below the level of consciousness. The world and all its warlords were putting their swords aside.

That contradicted human nature.

Mist left the Tervola to their game and the attention of the now unnaturally alert Old Man. She went to an empty apartment, told her lifeguard, "Wake me in three hours."

She had to rest before meeting with the Matayangans.

...

Mist wakened with the future fixed in her mind.

†

Chapter Twenty:

YEAR 1017 AFE:

Peaceable Kingdoms

Varthlokkur had gone to bed, supposedly exhausted. Babeltausque dragged the Queen out of Josiah Gales's arms to report.

Inger looked old and tired when she came out. Nathan Wolf arrived moments later. Colonel Gales pretended to arrive from his own quarters less than a minute behind Wolf.

Babeltausque said what he had to say concisely. "I did my best to remain invisible."

Never mind somebody tried to murder her sorcerer, Inger fixed on the critical point. "Bragi is alive?"

"And they're thinking about dropping him on us."

"Should I cheer or cry?"

"Your Grace?"

Inger said, "Tell me your new ideas for finding the treasury."

He told her. And began to grow mildly disaffected because she showed no concern about the assassination attempt.

She was a Greyfells for sure.

The meeting did not last long. Bed called out to everyone.

Babeltausque did not fall asleep immediately. He ought to be hunting those killers. And caring for Carrie. He had to get her out of there. He should move her in here. She was no secret, now. Why should he hide her?

They would talk but nobody would do anything. Inger needed him too much.

...

Josiah Gales perched on the edge of a chair beside Inger's bed. He had not yet recovered enough to do much but hold her. He did not recall being beaten while captive but he had a testicle that would not stop hurting. There were occasional blood spots on his small clothes. His urine sometimes had an odd brown color to start. When he sat to defecate, dark, dense blood leaked from his penis. He was frightened.

Inger asked, "What do you think about what Babeltausque said?"

"About the King? We should keep that quiet. About new places to look for the treasure? Some of those have been checked already, the well several times. Throwing money down a well was the kind of thing Derel Prataxis would have considered funny."

"Derel wasn't by himself. You always ignore Cham Mundwiller. He had a bizarre sense of humor, too."

"Which is why we'll drain the sewage deposits."

"Nobody has done that yet. Right?"

"Not yet. I need to go. I'm feeling weak."

"If you must. I so miss you. But I don't want to lose you. Take care of yourself, Josiah."

...

Only five people were supposed to know what had happened between Varthlokkur and Mist. The wizard was one. He discussed it with no one. The others would claim that they had told no one. They would not be lying.

There were, as ever, those who lurked within the castle walls, eavesdropping. Word that the old king was alive got out via a maid whose politics were those of indifference.

King Bragi's survival was not all she reported. Treasure hunting enjoyed a surge in popularity. That ended when the Queen's men began harassing the hunters. One stubborn band gave up only after the Queen's sorcerer demonstrated a willingness to boil them inside their own skins.

...

Varthlokkur followed Mist's suggestion.

Phyletia Plens had lived a life of constant sorrow. Little good ever happened to her. Because he had suffered the childhood that he had, Varthlokkur felt all of her pain.

Sad Phyletia had not been strong. Not like the son of the woman burned in Ilkazar. Phyletia did not fight back. The one time she found the will to take charge of her destiny she ran off with the man who became her death.

Varthlokkur's new line of investigation did not take him where he expected. It exonerated the butcher Arnulf Black, in part. Again. He had used Phyletia but had not been involved in what happened to her later. Likewise, the apothecary Chames, whose behavior was so odd and shrouded and deceptive that he needed interrogation out of sheer curiosity.

The true villain was known to the neighborhood as a good man. He was a priest at the only church. Phyletia Plens was one of dozens of children who had found refuge in his rectory. Most had survived. Many remained in the neighborhood. Interviewed, most refused to talk.

Varthlokkur followed the Plens story minute by minute till he found the night when the priest lost control, hurt her badly, and had to be rid of her in a hurry. Other children might wonder about the noise.

Varthlokkur had Radeachar collect the priest, then let Inger know what he had learned.

Father Ather Kendo confessed to fourteen murders. Thirteen involved the torture deaths of girls between eleven and thirteen. The other had been a boy who stuck his nose in, wrong place, wrong time, and saw something he should not have. Of surviving victims there were scores.

Father Kendo died forty hours after his capture, in fire, screaming, by popular demand. But first they nailed him to a sign blessing those victims whose names he remembered.

The interrogations of the priest and his surviving victims produced the names of a dozen adults whose crimes against children were only slightly less obscene.

...

Dahl Haas said, "Something has changed in Vorgreberg…"

A Mundwiller youth interrupted. "Remarkable news! King Bragi is alive! He's a prisoner in Shinsan. But they're going to send him back."

The first part was not news. The rest? Neither Dahl nor Kristen knew how to take that.

Dahl said, "Sounds like they want us to think he'll be their puppet."

"They wouldn't send him back if they didn't see an advantage."

Their nipping at the news did not last. Ozora summoned them.

The old woman said, "Fortune has played a prank. Just when we're headed toward the end of the harvest, with the weather turning, when neither we nor the Queen can do much, we get this news."

Ozora paused. Neither Kristen nor Dahl had any response.

"All right. Tell me what's going to happen."

Kristen said, "I couldn't guess. Bragi being alive will touch every Kaveliner—and our neighbors, as well. The response is beyond me. I'm out of touch."

Dahl nodded. "I expect nostalgia. People longing for the good old days. But these days are pretty good, despite us and Inger. Yeah, we have a civil war going. Technically. But nobody has killed anybody since…" He stopped. The last known casualty had been Sherilee.

Ozora agreed. "All true. How will the news affect Inger? And Varthlokkur?"

Dahl said, "I couldn't guess about Inger. She's unpredictable."

Kristen said, "Let's just sit tight. Somebody could be blowing smoke."

Dahl added, "Maybe the news will get Inger to do something dumb."

Ozora said, "Then passivity remains our strategy. You two try to stay invisible."

Later, in private, Kristen said, "Ozora has begun to regret having taken us in."

"She's afraid your father-in-law will come back all blood and thunder and slavering after revenge."

They made love for a long time.

Afterward, Kristen asked, "Revenge on who?"

"Interesting question. Once upon a time the answer might have been Kavelin, for having failed him. But, assuming Mist wouldn't send a crazy man back, nobody, now. Anybody he'd have a real beef with is out of play. By now, he must realize that he failed Kavelin, not the other way around."

...

It was raining, a late autumn drizzle that seemed colder than it was. Inger sat in her coach, shivering despite being buried in a mound of comforters. Josiah Gales, sharing, shook constantly. She raised a window cover, leaned out to see if any progress had been made. She saw only the droopy misery of her driver and team. "I should have waited in the castle."

Gales nodded. "It waited this long. A few days more means nothing."

Inger ground her teeth. Josiah was like this all the time now. Always with the sharp word. Wachtel said he was in constant pain. She thought that he had had plenty of time to get better.

She would not tolerate this much longer.

A lie to herself. Josiah was all she had. Sickly Josiah and sickly Fulk. And maybe Nathan Wolf. So pathetic.

Babeltausque opened the door. "I was right! We found it! Uh… I *think* we found it. We're dragging it out now."

"I want to see this. Umbrella, Colonel."

Gales dug one out of the stuff piled on the seat opposite. He handed it to the sorcerer. He would not leave the coach himself.

Babeltausque was too short and too wide to keep Inger sheltered. She took the umbrella. Out of earshot of Gales, Babeltausque murmured, "I think the Colonel is sicker than he pretends."

Startled, she said, "Oh?"

"He picked up something ugly while he was a captive. Wachtel doesn't know how to fight it."

"Do you?"

"No. I don't do serious healing."

They neared a half-acre farm pond that had not featured on the sorcerer's original list. It lay a mile from the nearest city gate.

Though not a cesspool it was nasty enough. Cattle and hogs watered there. Neither species was shy about evacuating while drinking. The pond had been in place for decades. Its bottom consisted of several feet of noisome mud.

"Is he dying?" Inger asked.

"I don't know. He is getting weaker. Varthlokkur might be able to turn that around."

The wizard had not returned to the Dragon's Teeth. That made everyone nervous.

"Would he help?"

"I don't know. You'll have to ask. He is the one who can. Try making a deal. Ah! Here it comes."

Nathan and several soldiers had been dragging the pond by casting grappling hooks. Now they were working something that kept getting away. Inger expected their optimism to be wasted. That could be anything.

Nathan went into the cold water, retrieved something. He swished the mud off, headed for his sovereign.

"It's a chest." He held up a plain box four inches high, six wide, and sixteen long. It stank. So did Wolf. "It might be teak."

It was. Inger said, "We're in the right place. There should be a little ceremonial scepter in there."

Wolf fumbled the simple latch. "Sorry. My fingers are so cold they won't work right."

He got the box open.

"Damn!" Inger swore. "Damn it all to hell! What the…?"

The prophesied scepter was there but in an ugly state of decay.

Babeltausque said, "It was a fake."

"It wasn't when Fiana was queen."

"Then Bragi was a crook."

Wolf said, "Someone was."

Inger snapped, "Drain the pond, Nathan. Muck it out. Find the rest of the treasure." She had a feeling that this would not turn out well.

Feet wet and freezing, the rest of her damp, Inger clambered back into the coach. Josiah asked, "Bad news?"

"So it seems." She explained. "The jewels were junk. They'd partly melted. And now I'm remembering that only two men, one very old, carried the treasure away. How much could they lug, real or fake?"

"I hoped they'd taken mostly gold."

"I'm expecting fool's gold now."

Varthlokkur had warned her that she would be disappointed.

...

Members of the castle garrison tagged along wherever Varthlokkur went. He shook them off when so inclined. They expected that and did not resent it.

Why had he come out in this cold rain? Whatever he did was sure to come a disappointment.

He let his tails see him enter Arnulf Black's butcher shop. That pathetic villain had been questioned by Babeltausque, who declared him a bleak pervert whose need was to humiliate the weak and build himself up by tormenting the helpless. He abused his girls but did not murder them. Even the weakest eventually ran away.

In that impoverished quarter Black had no trouble finding replacements.

Varthlokkur left the shop. His shadows did not see him go. They had other things on their minds.

He headed for a nearby apothecary shop.

Arnulf Black said his girls usually ran to the druggist, whoever the druggist was.

The shop had been there forever but had changed hands a year ago. The new druggist was the son, grandson, or nephew of the man who had retired.

The wizard expected it to be closed and those associated with it to be gone. Chames Marks had to know he was being watched. But the door opened when Varthlokkur tried it. The overhead bell jingled.

A girl came through the curtains filling the doorway to the rear. Varthlokkur guessed her to be eleven or twelve. She was drying her hands on an old grey rag. She started to make an apology.

She looked straight at him.

She blanched. Her mouth worked but nothing came out. She had trouble breathing.

What was this? The child ought to have no idea who he was.

He made a quick gesture with his left hand. Her gaze followed. He said, "Stay where you are."

She froze. Varthlokkur considered his surroundings. This was a serious apothecary shop, whatever else it might be—assuming the contents of those containers matched their labels.

Here was a fortune in medicine.

"What is your name?"

"Seline, sir. Seline Shalot."

"Where is your master?"

"Making a delivery in Eatherton Close. Belladonna. Dr. Jaspars uses it. He should be back soon."

"Why didn't you make the delivery?"

"Chames thought it might not be safe. What's been happening to girls around here has him worried."

Varthlokkur put her under deeper so she would not resist more personal questions.

Chames had not touched her. It was all right if he wanted to. He was good to her. He might have been intimate with Haida. Haida had bragged that he was. It was no big thing.

Someone came in the back way. Varthlokkur heard a clunk and clatter and muttering, then the tread of shod feet headed their way. "Seline, I need you to pull jars while I formulate. We have a big wholesale order…"

Varthlokkur grinned wickedly. "Well! Hello. This puts a new spin onto everything."

…

"I fooled myself," Babeltausque complained to Nathan Wolf. It was dark. A fire, shielded from wind and rain by a tent under the constant assault of the elements, did not yield enough light to continue work.

Wolf agreed. "You should've thought about the weather before you told her. You knew she'd go nuts." There were bits of ice in the rain. They stung.

The pond was empty. The dam side had been broken. Rainwater was flushing the muck. Babeltausque, Wolf, and several miserable soldiers took turns keeping the outflow burdened.

They had recovered six coins. Two were silver. None were gold.

"You're right. But that's not what I mean. Nobody will know if we just get in and hunker down by the fire."

"She can't fire us. What were you talking about, then?"

"Those men who attacked me. I marked them with tracer spells."

"So you could see where they ran. So?"

"So I lost them. They left town. I should've grabbed them."

Wolf grunted, disinterested. He was busy quitting work. He kept his back to Babeltausque so the wizard could not read his expression. "This will at least clean the pond out."

Babeltausque glanced that direction, was content to let the darkness have the pool. "I hope we have enough firewood."

...

Ozora Mundwiller told Kristen, "Inger found the missing treasury."

Kristen slumped.

"Take heart. They didn't find much. Not enough for Inger to clear her debts. She won't be hiring any troops."

"That's good news, then."

"The wizard may have gone home, too. He hasn't been seen lately."

"More good news."

"To old news. Did you try to kill Inger's sorcerer?"

"No." Kristen had heard about that but had given it no thought.

"Nor did I. Who, then? The sorcerer said they were Wessons."

"Which would rule out the Marena Dimura. But they aren't heard from much anymore, anyway."

"So who, then?"

"Does it matter?"

"In the sense that it may affect us, of course it does. The enemy of our enemy isn't necessarily our friend."

"The eastern empress could have hired them." But that was silly. Mist would be more direct. "No. Of course not. Maybe some Nordmen."

"But the Estates, nominally, support Inger and Fulk."

"How about Aral Dantice?"

"Or Michael Trebilcock? Is he still alive?"

Kristen said, "I think so. How about you, Dahl?"

"Word would have gotten around if he really died."

Kristen said, "Maybe if we knew why he was attacked?"

Haas said, "I'll go try to find out."

"Or you could stay here and keep me happy."

"I could do that, too." Haas chose that course. But he did poke around in the shadows of Sedlmayr when he could get out of the Mundwiller complex unnoticed. He did not learn anything useful.

...

"I see three possibilities," Babeltausque told the usual gathering. "What we found is a red herring. The King took the treasury with him and Shinsan has it now, which is what I think happened. Or, what we dredged up really is the whole treasure and Kavelin was broke before we took over."

Inger scowled at the "we" but let it slide. "Or somebody got to it before we did."

Gales asked, "Somebody who could keep from bragging or spending a farthing?"

Wolf agreed. "Nobody could keep that secret. Even if they took the money out of the kingdom. We would've heard."

Babeltausque nodded agreement.

So. They all thought she had been chasing a fantasy, making wishful thinking over into policy. "Then we have to rely on ourselves after all. How much goodwill have we gained by rooting out those abusers?"

Wolf remarked, "The perverts aren't happy." He glanced at the sorcerer. Babeltausque scowled back.

Vigilante justice had caught up with several bad men. An especially vile bordello had burned. The mob responsible also laid into several known thieves, a moneylender, and his collectors.

Inger said, "We should clamp down. How do we do that if we can't pay our soldiers?"

Gales suggested, "There's always the old-fashioned way. Steal from them who do have money."

Inger growled, "Cynicism noted. That would require soldiers, too."

Gales observed, "Nothing should happen before the world sees what happens with the old king."

Inger asked, "Has anyone seen Varthlokkur?"

Headshakes. Wolf said, "I've heard that he went back to the mountains. I don't believe it. He'd want to know what Shinsan is up to here, first."

Inger suggested, "Maybe he hasn't been seen because he doesn't want to be seen."

"That sounds right to me."

"So what might he be up to while he's keeping his head down?"

"Maybe trying to find the portals Shinsan has here," Babeltausque said. "That's what I'd be doing if I wasn't trying to find treasury money that probably doesn't exist. Those portals might be a lot more important than the money."

Inger glared. "Meaning?"

"Meaning we're here and in charge because the Empress Mist hasn't yet developed a taste for Kavelin."

Inger's glare intensified. She was severely displeased. But Babeltausque had not said an untrue word. Kavelin could no more defend itself than could a naked virgin in a coma.

She admitted, "Facts are facts. We're dead meat if that's what Shinsan wants."

Josiah said, "The Nordmen and Wessons would resist."

Nathan Wolf nodded. "But not on our behalf. And, probably, not very effectively."

Inger shuddered. "All right. It's true. We're in the stew. There are no obvious or easy ways out. Basically, we spent a year getting ourselves into a place where we either have to run away or throw ourselves on the mercies of our subjects."

Wolf said, "That could end up ruining the monarchy."

He did not need to explain. Exactly that had happened in Ruderin only two years ago. The crown there never recovered from the Great Eastern Wars. The nobility so weakened the central authority that King Byar became nothing but a national symbol. Ruderin was in worse chaos than Kavelin. As in Kavelin, a bountiful harvest had contributed heavily to a root level economic resurgence. That, in turn, had enfeebled the normal human inclination toward bad behavior.

One poor harvest and both kingdoms would descend into banditry, plagued by petty warlords.

Inger saw that future plainly. Anyone with half a brain could see it. But no one would yield anything of their own to prevent it.

"Call a parliament," Inger blurted.

"Your Majesty?"

"Send out word, Josiah. I'm calling the Thing, made up the same as last time." She raised a hand to forestall comment. "I know. Some of them are dead. People know who the heirs should be. Just get the word out. We have to pull everyone together."

Wolf said, "That's begging for trouble. *Begging* for it."

"And I'll give it back if they ask for it." Pure bluster, that. "A Thingmeet should be good for Vorgreberg. All those people will be here spending money."

The men eyed her curiously, wondering whence that notion had sprung.

It had begun as a fantasy about gathering all the troublemakers in one place so she could massacre them. Her thoughts had trickled on to possibilities less bloodthirsty.

She said, "Babeltausque, you can drop the treasure search. Find Mist's transfer portals instead. And any other evidence that Shinsan is still interested in Kavelin. Assuming Varthlokkur hasn't found the stuff already."

"Your Majesty?" Then, "Of course. As you will." He got it. Inger had found an enemy everyone could hate.

A Thingmeet must, inevitably, devolve into incessant squabbling. Meantime, though, everyone would forget about fighting one another. Every grownup remembered the occupation by Shinsan…

And everyone attending the Thingmeet would have to spend money. So Vorgreberg would fall in love with Inger all over again for the first time.

For the first time in months hope surfaced. Too much, really. But… Hope!

Inger said, "Once the summons goes out we issue new regulations for innkeepers, taverners, merchants, and so on. They will allow no credit. They will demand cash in advance, of which a tithe will be ours. They won't do business with who already owes them, either. A Thing member who dodged his obligations before will make good beforehand or not be seated. And we will take a tithe."

Her mind raced. Ideas came faster than she could articulate them. "Debtors won't even be allowed through the gates while their obligations remain unpaid. How does that sound?"

"Populist," Gales said. "The kind of man who welcomes dishonor by ignoring his debts isn't likely to care enough about his seat to settle them."

"Possibly. But if we make this sound like we're really putting the design of the future on the table… I think they'll all want to have their say."

Babeltausque said, "There will be a great deal of animosity from our enemies, Your Majesty."

"How so?"

"They'll assume that you mean to chunk them into the dungeon with Dane if they actually show up."

Inger nodded. She had not considered that. Her natural inclination was to say, "So what?" and declare anyone dim enough to disagree with her to be outside the equation. But that would only worsen the strains amongst the factions. If a Thingmeet was to happen there had to be a potent sense that it was real.

Josiah said, "You'd be taking a huge risk, Majesty. If you call a Thingmeet to decide the future you'd better be ready to live in a future that you'll find less than condign. Whatever happens, we won't be able to impose your will."

"That's true. All true. Hang on." After a moment, she asked, "How about safe-conducts for all Thing members? Whoever they are, say, beginning three days before the first meeting date through three days after adjournment."

"That would stun the kingdom, Majesty," Nathan Wolf said. "It stuns me. I like it. If nothing else, it will buy us time."

"Thank you, Nathan. You and Josiah get it rolling. Babeltausque, I need evidence that Shinsan is lurking behind our hedges."

The sorcerer nodded. Here was a chance to show off. Carrie would be impressed by his royal connection.

Inger would give Kavelin a common foe. The gimmick was older than prostitution. It remained in play because it worked.

He had to produce evidence that was not obviously manufactured.

He should start where he had run into the woman, being a little more careful to avoid an ambush. A visit to the cemetery would be in order, too. He would do that first, and try to find those squatters. They should make useful witnesses.

Mist's people had her mansion cleaned out already, he imagined.

This might be too big a task. He was a bit player, not the Empire Destroyer. He could not do much more than keep water from boiling.

How to get Varthlokkur involved?

He *was* involved, just not politically. Would he appear as a witness?

He explained it all to Carrie before taking a nap, after which he meant to change into clothing suitable for knocking around the countryside. She listened, interested. Carrie was a changed girl now that she lived in the castle. She took her role as his companion seriously. She mentioned that her grandmother had been married at her age. She no longer whined about everything.

Her family thought she had scored a coup by connecting with a palace wizard. Her age was not an issue.

He figured Carrie would move on if she had a chance to move up.

That was good enough.

Carrie was mercenary but she gave good value. These days she laid into her work with nurturing enthusiasm and was a good resource for understanding what ordinary Vorgrebergers thought.

Carrie said, "You shouldn't fuss about the wizard. Just acknowledge what you know."

Wow. This was a far cry from constant whining for new shoes and clothes.

She was more confident now, maybe because he treated her like a real, thinking companion when not using her to satisfy the consuming need that had driven him to find her.

"Hmm?"

"You probably shouldn't waste time taking a nap. That wizard has more resources than you do."

"Time with you is never wasted." He meant that so sincerely that it did not sound corny.

"You are a devil man." She began to shed her clothing.

Babeltausque became uncomfortable when she did that in the light, which too plainly revealed how much she had ripened.

She would be fully a woman soon.

He was useless with grown-up women.

†

Chapter Twenty-One:

WINTER, YEAR 1017 AFE:

An Era Ended

Seasons were not extreme at Sebil el Selib. Winters were cooler but seldom really cold. Most years it was damper but not remarkably so. Those who grew up there and did not travel could not conceive of the fury of a thunderstorm.

Some knew sandstorms but even those had to be experienced elsewhere.

On rare occasions the wind did shift enough to bring a taste of alkali off the salt pans.

Rains, even in this year's notably wet seasons, seldom amounted to more than sustained heavy drizzles.

Haroun eased his head through a slit in the exterior wall of El Murid's tent. Rain was still falling in what locals considered torrents. It was cold. The wadi boiled with raging brown water. He muttered, "Twenty years of this and the ancient seas will be back."

Megelin Radetic, Haroun's boyhood teacher, had insisted that salt pans were the bones of ancient seas. In the heyday of Ilkazar today's pans had been vast lakes. The scars of old shorelines remained visible on the flanks of mountains.

The swift drying of those lakes had been part of the vengeance of the Empire Destroyer.

All Hammad al Nakir had been more lush in those times.

But this was now. This was remarkable. This could become dangerous. Rushing waters tore away tons of hard soil. The wadi bank had crept five yards nearer the Disciple's tent.

Suppose a truly violent downpour came along?

Bin Yousif pulled back inside. He settled to think.

This weather could be used to cover his getaway. And go he must. Yasmid could not cover up much longer. Her henchmen were suspicious. They wanted to know why she kept disappearing inside her father's tent.

So far they thought it had something to do with him, possibly involving the foreigner. They thought she might be trying to consolidate her position as the old man's successor.

Luckily, Phogedatvitsu never went out where he could be isolated and interrogated. He would not hide the fact that Yasmid spent little time with her father. Instead, she vanished into the empty quarters for hours, then returned disheveled but in a better temper.

This was insanity.

This was what had kept him going during his captivity and long journey home. He was back with the woman who was the other half of his soul.

The circumstances were insane, not the relationship.

But he had to go. This had persisted far too long. Fate had been tempted in the extreme. Elwas al-Souki talked about searching the tent again.

Al-Souki smelled something not the stench of vixens' dens.

He should have moved on months ago. Al Rhemish called. Megelin had made a muddle of everything.

Haroun realized that he was not alone.

He had let himself drowse where he was not secure.

His gaze found that of El Murid. The Disciple looked vague but not caught up in a poppy dream. The man extended his left hand, pointed. "You are the one. Why do you haunt me?" He spoke slowly, voice dreamy.

Haroun rose slowly, so as not to spook the man. His keepers should be looking for him. They would rush toward any excitement.

Bin Yousif spoke softly, turning the question. "Why do you torment the world so, Tongue of Darkness?"

The Disciple stared. His mouth moved but nothing came forth. He had only a passing acquaintance with reality still. It took him some seconds to analyze what he had heard.

Haroun took a quick look round. He had left no sign of his presence. When the Disciple's eyes shifted away Haroun stepped through a gap in canvas wall, disappearing.

Those looking for the Disciple could be heard, now, moving closer. It was for sure time to get gone.

Haroun was within earshot when they found their man, who announced, "I wrestled the Evil One again. And once again I banished him."

"Outstanding, Lord. I apologize for everyone. Some dared doubt you. Come. We must have the doctor make sure the demon did you no harm. Then we will celebrate your triumph."

That fellow was skilled at playing to the Disciple's manias. No doubt he had a lifetime of practice and habitually ignored El Murid's delusions.

Would Elwas al-Souki be more inclined to investigate?

Yasmid visited him as he sorted through treasures he might want to take along. During his stay, killing time, he had winkled out dozens of small items overlooked by earlier, hastier thieves.

Thoughts of her sapped his will to do what had to be done.

...

Yasmid congratulated her father on his latest triumph over the Evil One. He would not stop going on about it. She dearly wished he would shut the hell up. Elwas was sure to get interested.

How could Haroun have let the old fool slip up on him?

She brushed the irritation aside. Stuff happened. Magden Norath had been inattentive. He had died for his lapse.

She slipped away from dinner, as had become her custom, leaving her father to his attendants. They never questioned her anymore.

The effort to wean the old man off opiates was successful. Sadly, the man reclaimed was not the man the poppy had conquered. El Murid restored was a spectral reminder of the firebrand of yore.

Today's El Murid was old and tired and slow.

Old was to be expected. He *was* old. And tired made sense. But the slow, especially on the mental side, was deeply disappointing.

This Disciple would make no impassioned speeches to the Believers. His delivery would be so tedious as to put them to sleep before he finished.

His mind, however, did not appear to have burned out entirely. Given time, he thought quite well. Yasmid had read two recent letters to the Faithful dictated after ponderous reflection. They were as closely argued as those of forty years earlier.

He did have some idea of what was going on in the world. Swami Phogedatvitsu did not feed him pabulum news.

In the more recent letter he hinted at doubts about the divinity of he who had brought him to God. It was just a whiff that suggested rational processes stirring somewhere deep under the surface of his mind.

Yasmid found Haroun quickly. She had had regular practice. They embraced. He said, "The rain won't stop."

"That's good. I can leave Habibullah behind for the sake of his aching bones."

Time passed. Neither spoke. Finally, he did tell her what she was expecting but did not want to hear. "I have to go."

"But…"

"I know. I don't want to. But our luck won't last. Al-Souki is suspicious already. What happened today will set him digging."

"I know. They all wonder. I tell them I'm looking for something."

"Some may think you're finding it. The Matayangan isn't stupid."

"But… Still… In all these years… We've had so little time."

She expected nonsense about Fate and obligations to Destiny. He said only, "Yes. It's cruel." And held her tighter.

"Father thinks he bumped into the Evil One this morning."

"I dozed off in the wrong place. I woke up and he was there."

"Where will you go? No. Don't say it. If I don't know I can't give it away."

He played along, though they both knew there could be only one next destination.

Yasmid mentioned her father's developing disenchantment with his angel. Haroun asked, "Have you asked him about that? At all?"

"No. He would tell me that, even though his angel might only be the Star Rider, he did do God's Work. How often has he told us that God drives the wicked to advance His own Plan?"

"It's an old argument, impossible to refute. And if you do come up with one the True Believer just reshapes the Will of God to fit."

"So?"

"I'm wondering if your father is disillusioned enough to act against the false messenger."

Yasmid stiffened. His embrace tightened. "I'm just thinking. Looking for ways and means."

"Out loud? I've never heard that the old devil accused of being able to read minds."

"Silence it is. But think about it." He released her, picked through a last dozen items, stuffed a few into a battered black sack. It's contents appeared to consist of food and souvenirs.

She said, "They say the rain may stop later tonight."

"If I go now it will wash away my trail."

One last embrace.

She rejoined the others before anyone came looking, though the swami scrutinized her closely. She brought several items Haroun had given her to provide evidence that she was indeed looking for something that ought still to be hidden in the tent because no thief had yet confessed to having taken it away.

Elwas turned up shortly, wet and unhappy. She was glad she had returned before he did.

Relief made her overlook his mood.

...

Nepanthe called out, "Scalza, do you have any idea how to get hold of your uncle?" She had none. Varthlokkur had foreseen no need for making emergency contact.

"No, ma'am. What's up?"

Ma'am? Being polite? He was up to something. "It's probably not important. I was fiddling with the scrying bowl. I found that man he's been hunting for months."

Fiddling indeed, getting the hang of shifting point of view, she had stumbled across the ragged traveler at the limit of the bowl's range. The long-missing Haroun wore uncharacteristic clothing, lacked a beard, and was afoot in the desert.

Ekaterina and Scalza joined her, one to either hand. The boy said, "I do wish I could get hold of him. He'd definitely want to know. Lock the point of view so we don't lose him again."

"I don't know how."

"I think I do. Let me try."

Scalza took her seat. He did some things she did not understand. Ekaterina made little sounds behind him. Each time she sucked spit or clicked her tongue Scalza paused, reflected, then took a different approach.

The vision locked up with Haroun fixed in its center. He stayed there no matter which direction he moved.

Scalza pulled the magical eye back. "So we can maybe tell where he is from his surroundings. Well, so maybe somebody can. I've never been anywhere so I can't really recognize anything."

"Not even your grandfather has visited that part of the world."

Ekaterina seldom said anything. Though the brighter of Mist's children she usually deferred to her brother. She acted like his little sister instead of being two years older, on the precipice of menarche. She startled Nepanthe. "*Uncle* was born there. He created that desert. He has been back a million times. He knows every rock, bush, viper, and grain of sand."

Finished making the longest speech Nepanthe ever heard from her, Ekaterina moved to where Ethrian sat staring into the Winterstorm. Something about the boy's body language troubled his mother. He looked ready to pounce. But she was too engaged in trying to fathom Ekaterina's remarks, and with Haroun, to give her son devoted thought.

Watching Haroun sneak through a desert could be interesting only if you were a dedicated fan of stealth techniques.

Something passed between Ethrian and Ekaterina. Nepanthe did not notice. Scalza caught a hint. His eyebrows bounced but he said nothing.

Scalza was, deliberately, the mask Mist's children offered. Ekaterina was in stealth mode always. Scalza was a little frightened by her.

He enjoyed this wizard stuff. He tried to learn anything his uncle would teach. Ekaterina, though, had no need to study.

She watched and caught on intuitively. She could be spooky and nerve-straining because she was determined to keep her real self hidden.

One of the Council of Tervola might observe that Ekaterina was her mother's daughter, descended from the Demon Prince and Tuan Hoa, and those who had come before them.

Despite all that, Ekaterina had a first blush of womanhood crush on her cousin, Ethrian.

Scalza was furiously jealous but never considered acting upon that bleak emotion.

And Nepanthe, typical of adults in such circumstances, remained oblivious. Her perception of the children's development ran well behind the actuality, especially there in the splendid isolation of Fangdred.

Ekaterina was quiet but not a dark soul, and she was wise enough already to understand that, romantic as the notion might be, she would not be the one to liberate her cousin from his prisons of grief and guilt.

"Aunt."

Startled, Nepanthe blurted, "What?"

"Ethrian is remembering."

Nepanthe shot to her feet. She found Ekaterina positioned to keep her from charging Ethrian, to interrupt the process at work.

Nepanthe was having a day where emotion did not rule her completely. "Oh. Yes. I shouldn't disturb him."

Scalza kicked in, "He'll heal faster if you let him alone." He shot his sister a look.

Ekaterina acknowledged the help with poor grace. She foresaw sabotage later.

She was complex. She did not understand that her brother was not. What he showed his small world was ninety percent of Scalza.

Ekaterina suggested, "Aunt, why don't you just keep an eye on that man while Scalza thinks of a way to contact Uncle?"

She made a "Get busy, Worm!" face and body gesture once Nepanthe turned back to Haroun. Nepanthe concentrated only a moment before she turned again. Ethrian was, clearly, going through something unpleasant.

Though it hurt, Nepanthe stayed put. Ekaterina was right.

Interrupting *would* break the train.

For a moment she understood why Varthlokkur had shielded her when her son was the Deliverer. She could have done nothing but make things worse. And she would have done so. She had managed that even while ignorant of the facts. And she would not have heard any caution offered her.

Ethrian was her baby.

Startling notion. Could she be making Ethrian's recovery more difficult because she would not let him stop being her baby?

The possibility left her thinking poorly of herself.

She began watching Ekaterina as closely as she watched Ethrian.

The girl did not intrude upon his space. She did not distract him by trying to make him acknowledge her presence. She was just there, able to lend a hand, touching him gently when he needed calming.

Not his mother's approach at all. Nepanthe was determined to swamp him with love.

"To smother him," she murmured. Then, too softly to be understood by the children, she wondered, "What is he remembering?"

At that moment Smyrena announced the end of her nap, with considerable gusto, adding that, surely, it must be feeding time.

A glance showed Haroun crossing more desert.

There was plenty of that. It never did get very interesting.

†

Chapter Twenty-Two:

WINTER, YEAR 1017 AFE:

Throyes

The portal technicians requested the presence of their Empress at their headquarters. Mist put aside nonsense that was a consequence of having too much time, made her way to the home space of the Imperial Interstitial Communications and Transport Corps. If they had completed their assignment she would use their self-aggrandizing designation cheerfully.

Lord Yuan Tin Yuan welcomed her personally. Lord Yuan seemed even more elderly. And, true, he had been a boy at the same time as her departed grandfather. Like Lord Ssu-ma Shih-ka'i, Lord Yuan survived shifting political winds by remaining indifferent to the source of his orders. Lord Yuan was interested only in his own narrow realm. Existence itself was all about communication. He provided the best, most efficient tools.

Mist supposed the end of the several wars had left Lord Yuan's corps with a lot of free time. Mischief time, Lord Ssu-ma would call it. Mischief prevention was one reason that the trainees of the Demonstration Legion were given so much make-work.

The legions themselves were, already, beginning to transition to a public works orientation. They would begin by building border fortifications to defend new borders.

"Lord Yuan, your presence graces us," Mist said.

"I have no other diversions right now, Illustrious, so I choose to steal the glory of the clever young men who do the real work."

"May I assume that my western adjustments have been completed?"

"You may, Illustrious. And in the most laudable fashion, I must say."

Lord Yuan could be a talker. She ought not to offend him by hurrying him. Time was not pressing, nowadays.

"I know you have a thousand tasks, Illustrious, so, difficult as it may be for an old man with a wandering mind, I will try to be concise."

Mist's lifeguards stirred but did not allow their amusement any more obvious demonstration.

"Thank you, Lord Yuan."

"The functioning portals remain in place, there to be sacrificed. To those venues we added dead portals to be discovered, too. We also positioned reconditioned damaged portals that will function without benefit of cosmetic upgrades. Those remain inert. We hope the westerners will ignore them because they look dead. We can activate them at will later.

"At the cemetery we installed portals in another two mausoleums, then a third portal, better disguised, in the rear of the tomb of the dead Queen. There are new units concealed in the ruins of your former home, too. And, finally, there is a new unit in a ruined temple in the forest southwest…"

Repetitious mention of ruins penetrated. "What do you mean, ruins? My house was damaged when I saw it but it wasn't a ruin."

"I speak figuratively. The natives tore it up while looking for treasure and portals. Then a girl who was living in the basement set a fire. No one knows what that was about. The place is empty, now, though."

"They didn't find any treasure."

Lord Yuan added, "Nor did they find the new portals. They've only just begun searching the cemetery."

"I can use the portals if I want, then?"

"Exercising utmost caution, Illustrious. Those are unpredictable people out there."

"Yes. And the Empire Destroyer is still there with them."

"We believe so, Illustrious. He has become invisible himself but his familiar haunts the nighttime sky."

"Let me think about this. Oh. Good work, everyone. Thank you."

Lord Yuan said, "I will see that you get the designator, alert, and activation codes as soon as we finalize them, Illustrious."

...

Mist joined Wen-chin and the Old Man without warning. There were playing shogi and drinking tea. The Old Man's color had improved. He had gained weight. There were black speckles at the roots of his hair and a twinkle in his eye when he considered her.

The man within had come back a long way if he could now appreciate what he was seeing.

She asked, "Have we been making progress?"

Wen-chin said, "I'm losing games, now. At this rate the advantage will be all his soon."

"Any recollections?"

"Some, but it's like the dementia of old folks. He has crystalline memories of things that happened so long ago that they don't even echo in our mythologies today. He seems especially focused on something called the Nawami Crusades. Heard of that?"

"Obliquely, during the skirmish with the Deliverer." She considered the Old Man, who did not seem to mind being discussed. "How is his attitude toward the Star Rider?" She enunciated carefully, testing the Old Man's hearing.

He heard her just fine. He started. Then his shoulders slumped. He shrank into himself.

"I see." Then, "Could his dawn-time memories be more useful than anything recent? What say you?"

"An argument could be made, I'm sure."

"Only a few of us know he's alive. I'm sure the Star Rider isn't one. Starting tomorrow you'll be dogged by scribes. They will record everything, especially recovered memories. Copies will be made, distributed, and scattered as fast as possible. More copies will be made elsewhere, with some being hidden. If we suffer the fate of all of Old Meddler's previous enemies we will, at least, leave a legacy too vast and in too many forms to eradicate. One that might be used by a future generation."

Wen-chin rose, stretched, bowed. "So shall it be." Then, "Make sure your scribes know how to keep out of the way."

"They will."

Scribes were always unobtrusive when they served those at high levels. That was a skill as critical as excellent penmanship.

Wen-chin seated himself. He made a move that pleased the Old Man. He grumbled, "Stupid! Stupid! Stupid!"

...

Ragnarson was in a good temper. He thought he had his inner conflicts worked out. He had been exercising, too. He supposed he could walk a mile without collapsing now. He asked Mist, "Has something happened?"

"Mostly not, really. It's more like we're winding down everywhere."

"Calm before the storm?"

"Possibly, in my head. And maybe in Varthlokkur's. Probably hoping that it is, the Star Rider. The rest of the world is sitting back and putting its feet up."

"Sounds like a good thing."

"I wouldn't disagree. But I do know that Old Meddler is out there and he hasn't given up his wicked ways."

Ragnarson grunted. That was not meant to communicate anything.

Mist asked, "You have any thoughts on that subject?"

Ragnarson grunted again. "None charitable toward him. But I don't have any toward the wind or rain, either. Weather is a fact of life. So is Old Meddler." Then, "I saw him once, you know."

Mist frowned. "And? A lot of people have."

"They hadn't, back then. Some of Nepanthe's brothers and El Murid were about all. It was during one of the fights in the Savernake Gap. The time the Power went away. He was way up high overhead. I only picked him out for a second, I'm pretty sure because he screwed up. Nobody was supposed to know he was interfering."

He guessed his confession meant nothing here. Mist had gone away inside her head while he was talking.

She came back a new woman, full of energy and excitement. "I've had an epiphany. And I've made up my mind. You're going back to Kavelin even if you are still crazy. I'll put a leash on you so I can calm you down if you need it. We have to end the chaos. We need stability and strength. Some things can't be allowed to relax. Some things have to be kept together."

Ragnarson confessed, "You've lost me completely."

She was not listening.

...

The Empress ran her lifeguards ragged. She was manic. She darted round the empire till she found Lord Ssu-ma. She spent an intense hour with the pig farmer's son, then scampered back to the Karkha Tower for a slightly less intense sit-down with Kuo Wen-chin. It would have been more efficient to do that before she looked for Lord Ssu-ma but she had been excited and just had to see Shih-ka'i first. He was now the man she most trusted in this world—despite his deceit in the matter of Kuo Wen-chin. And that had begun to look like an inspired bit of insubordination.

From the Karkha Tower she raced off to see Lord Yuan Tin Yuan, rousing that ancient from the bed that was the one luxury he allowed himself. Following a long chat she plunged into the night in a Kaveliner graveyard.

Nothing had changed there. Nothing had been done to keep Shinsan from walking the transfer streams into Kavelin.

However…

The mausoleum portal had been sabotaged so that it could not be used to make a getaway. "Which might not demonstrate clarity of reasoning by whoever did the damage," Mist told portal technician Tang Shan, who had accompanied her. "Snap this trap on the wrong prey, you could end up wishing you'd left them a half-dozen holes to get back out."

The technician was not smitten by her brilliance. He nodded vacantly and focused on finding the problem. Mist led her lifeguards out into the night.

A pink dot appeared in the direction of Vorgreberg seconds later. She remarked, "That didn't take long."

The dot headed their way.

Closer, something stirred amongst the tombstones, hurried away. It was something sizable but left too fast to be identified. It might have been a deer. Deer did graze among the tombstones. The grasses were sweet and some flowers left by the living made tasty treats.

An owl said something suitably mournful not far away. A bat swooshed within grabbing distance.

A lifeguard drove a short infantry thrusting spear into the ground. Another tied a courier case to its butt using the cord the infantryman would keep tied to his wrist so his weapon would not get lost if his grip failed.

"Good enough." Mist led the way back into the mausoleum as the Unborn drew close enough to be seen as something less pleasant than a pink light.

One added level of clever lay behind the sabotage. If she got away that indicated the existence of another portal.

Unless…

Genius Tang Shan reported, "Somebody drove a sliver the size of a toothpick in beside the access modal. The catch was jammed. We're all set now."

"Great work, Tang Shan," Mist said. "So, let's get the hell gone. That thing turned up faster than I expected."

…

Varthlokkur approached Throyes cautiously. It was nighttime, of course, and there was no moon out. No need to let people down there get a good look at what the Unborn was hauling. Troubling enough that they would see the monster itself.

Radeachar deposited him atop the Karkha Tower. He waited while the lookout went for the man in charge. The Candidate took his time. Varthlokkur did not recall his name. He arrived moving slowly and with considerable care. He had not yet recovered fully from wounds suffered earlier in the year. He talked slowly, too, enunciating carefully, apparently unaware that Varthlokkur had spent his youth in Shinsan and spoke the principal dialect quite well.

The wizard did not set the Candidate straight. Little advantages must be hoarded.

The Candidate said, "The Illustrious is not here right now. I am to make you comfortable in one of our apartments till she can grace us with her presence."

Was he out of touch with the language after all? "Are you being sarcastic, Candidate?"

The very suggestion appalled the young man. "Sir? No! Why would you even consider that?"

"I withdraw the question. I forgot the impact she can have. Indulge me, if you will. I have chosen to bring an associate. I would like to wait here till Radeachar brings him in."

"But… I wasn't informed…"

"It won't take long. He's just across the river. We leap-frogged getting here." He spied Radeachar in the distance, approaching slowly, at a considerable altitude.

…

Ragnarson was tired and not feeling particularly patient. It was past his customary bedtime. He had nothing to say, either, though he suspected he had no languages in common with his companions.

Though not dressed it, the younger man was Tervola and had to be in disgrace to be locked up here. The other, who never spoke and did nothing but study a shogi board, seemed vaguely familiar.

Neither introduced himself. Fine by him. He stood by a window, vainly hoping to see something of the city. He saw only the same nothing from a more acute angle.

A strong pink light waxing and waning told him the Unborn was active out there.

Why? What was going on?

He would find out when that suited someone's whim.

The door opened. People entered. The first two were legionnaires armed and armored for the sorcerous battlefield. Behind came two tall men in western dress, then the Candidate who managed the tower, then three more armed men. The soldiers spread out. The Candidate said, "The Illustrious will be here shortly. Scribes. Your presence will not be required."

Two nearly invisible little men, not of the ruling race of Shinsan, gathered their writing materials and exited.

Ragnarson paid no attention. He stared—glared—at the westerners. First was Varthlokkur, looking distinctly uncomfortable. A step behind him came Michael Trebilcock, looking far older than his actual age. He had gained weight, gone grey, developed a limp, and acquired a sense of style suited to the common man.

Both gravitated toward Ragnarson, though the wizard had fixed on the old man hunched over the shogi board.

Trebilcock extended a hand. Varthlokkur did not. Ragnarson shook. Trebilcock said, "Reports said you might have survived but I never quite believed them. It didn't make sense." Which made it clear that the raid on the tower had not been initiated by Michael Trebilcock.

"Not much that goes on here does." Ragnarson and the wizard went on staring one another down.

Trebilcock said, "The stupidest thing you can do is hang onto stupidity already committed. Particularly when even congenitally stupid folks see that you *were* stupid and you're going right on being stupid."

Ragnarson broke eye contact. Neither he nor the wizard addressed their conflict nor responded to Trebilcock. They had, silently and tacitly, agreed to put all that in the past, for now.

Ragnarson asked the wizard, "How is the boy?"

"Coming back, but slowly. His mother is more optimistic than I am." The wizard stared at the old man.

Ragnarson asked, "You know him? He seems familiar, somehow."

"He should be. From Fangdred. You probably didn't see much of him at the time, though."

"That was a long time ago. Michael, I heard you were dead, too, but your name always came up whenever anything happened that nobody could explain."

"The world is supposed to think I'm dead." Trebilcock turned to look at the new arrivals.

Ragnarson recognized Lord Ssu-ma but not his companion, a Tervola of extreme age. Varthlokkur, though, did. He headed for the man as though excited.

Ragnarson glanced at Trebilcock. Michael shrugged. "Any idea what we're doing here?"

"Nary a clue, though this is where they keep me. How come you're with him?"

"I'm not sure. He's been freeloading and getting underfoot since he walked into my shop looking for something else. He doesn't explain himself. No clue at all?"

"None. This is new. But there is one odd note. Other than

Varthlokkur and the two who just walked out, everybody here is supposed to be dead."

Trebilcock frowned. "I don't know anyone but you and him. Most people do think you and I are dead. There was a hot rumor about you a while back but it blew over when you never turned up."

"How come you're dead? Why aren't you helping Inger?"

"Truth? You may not like it."

"Try me."

"She didn't deserve help. I tried. I cut her miles of slack. She couldn't stop being a Greyfells. So now the only people she has left are ones who didn't have the balls to run away."

Wistfully, Ragnarson said, "She was so fine when I met her."

Michael responded with a conspiratorial smile. "That would be back when she was just another woman amongst women you hadn't yet had."

"Yeah. Before the world made her over. Before I opened the gate to hell."

He watched Lord Ssu-ma introduce the ancient Tervola to the Tervola in civilian dress. The former, plainly, was astonished to find the other in good health.

Varthlokkur returned. "That old man was one of my teachers. He was a youngster then, though. We were as nearly friends as could be where one was a fast-rising technical genius and the other an emotional cripple with extreme potential. I'm amazed that he's still with us. He claims they won't let him die because he knows more about the transfer streams than any dozen of his staffers combined."

Ragnarson showed Trebilcock a set of raised eyebrows. This excited wizard was not the Varthlokkur either of them knew.

Trebilcock asked, "He say anything about why we're here?"

The wizard shook his head.

Trebilcock said, "As usual, he knows more than he's telling."

Ragnarson said, "Whatever, they're taking it to the highest level. The other Tervola is Ssu-ma Shih-ka'i. He's Mist's number one military guy."

"She's up to something."

Varthlokkur said, "Her father was the Demon Prince. Imperial founder Tuan Hoa was her grandfather. She has made herself empress twice. She was born, 'Up to something.' She'll die when something she's up to bites her head off."

The legionnaires along the far wall, beside the entrance, snapped to attention. They had not done so before, even for Lord Ssu-ma.

The Candidate bellowed, "The Most Illustrious..."

Mist patted his left cheek. "They know who I am, Lein She." She told her chief lifeguard, "You may leave, now."

Neither he nor his men moved.

"Daring," Ragnarson said. "They do have the right but, man, will they pay later!"

Mist was irked in the extreme. Obviously, she thought the safety of her secrets trumped that of her person. And it was plain that she did not want to press the issue. That would require compulsion and, likely, lead to a dearth of volunteers for the lifeguard company.

Michael Trebilcock observed, "That wasn't smart. She must be under a lot of stress."

Ragnarson grunted agreement.

Varthlokkur asked, "What do you mean?"

"She should have anticipated the problem. She should have worked it out ahead of time."

"Maybe she did. Maybe it's supposed to show us how determined her lifeguards are."

Ragnarson did not think so. What it might mean down the road would depend on the characters of the men gathered here—and might depend on the purpose of the gathering, as well.

Mist chose to pretend that she had provoked her lifeguards deliberately. She said, "We're here to talk about the entity who rides the flying horse. Don't use any of his customary names. He may have placed spells that will alert him if he's mentioned directly by someone he thinks might cause him grief."

Silence followed.

"I want to destroy him. I know it's been tried before. Failing destruction, I mean to disarm or to weaken him. Failing that, I mean to gather a body of information so large and spread out so widely that it will survive any effort to extirpate it. The information will be hidden in a thousand places, to be found by some fool who can build on it, toward a more successful outcome."

The man opposite the Old Man moved a piece on the shogi

board. "Were I himself and inclined to spy, this tower would be a favorite target."

"You would need to know it exists."

Ragnarson noted the subtlest of changes in Lord Ssu-ma. The man had regained respect for his empress, but something disturbing had occurred to him. He beckoned the Candidate, Lein She, to him, breathed into the man's ear. Lein She turned pale, nodded, limped out.

Mist continued, "Until today no one came here except by transfer." She watched Lord Ssu-ma and the Candidate, constrained a frown. "Most of you prisoners are dead to the world outside. Unless he cares about a handful of local criminals left over from before we took over… Lord Ssu-ma, what?"

"That may, in fact, be true, Illustrious. I asked Lein She to consult the records, to see if any of those men were involved in the Pracchia conspiracy."

Ragnarson saw the red flags. The Star Rider might know about the tower already. He might have initiated that attack. The Unborn's several visits would not have gone unnoticed either.

Mist said, "That possibility hadn't occurred to me. It's certainly plausible. The raiders' true purpose might have been to plant spying talismans." She began to think out loud. "That would be something small and easily overlooked. So he wouldn't be watching directly, himself. He would get reports from someone here in the city. Those would be slow, infrequent, and unreliable. Magden Norath may have been the last dependable friend he had."

Lord Yuan invited himself to leave without asking permission.

No one said anything. Ragnarson thought the slapped-together character of the gathering was about to assert itself. Chaos might be afoot, particularly if Old Meddler was watching.

He considered Varthlokkur. The wizard would have been the most difficult to locate and get to attend—had ridden the Unborn into a half-ass conspiracy in full view of thousands.

Old Meddler might still be several steps ahead.

Questions, questions. The wizard had come from Kavelin. Mist must still have transfer access there. Why, then, would Varthlokkur show himself getting here? He could have made a transfer and remained invisible.

Mist said, "We here share a treasure house of knowledge. Especially…" She indicated the Old Man, who flinched, for the first time demonstrating any awareness of his situation. "There are others I wish could be here. The Disciple and the Deliverer would be especially valuable."

That caused a stir. It surprised Ragnarson, for sure. But neither of those two had more than a couple toes anchored in this world. Right?

Lord Yuan returned. "Lord Ssu-ma's intuition was correct. Monitors are parasited onto the transfer portals, presumably about the time of that raid, but only big enough to report usages, not who is coming and going. They're not sophisticated. It will take time to wring out the details. Illustrious, you should consider how best to profit from the opportunity."

Might Varthlokkur have suspected and so have avoided using the portals? Probably not.

Once there had been talk of a dread monster that lurked inside the transfer streams, preying on travelers. But that had been dealt with during the war with the Deliverer. Had it not?

Maybe there was something else.

Everything seemed to have an underground, secret side.

Ragnarson enjoyed an intuitive moment.

Mist wanted to pull the relevant secrets into a single pot so she could cook up something unique. Though chaotic at this moment, this was no spur of the moment gathering.

She asked, "Are any of you opposed to what I'm proposing? On any grounds but degree of difficulty?"

…

The Old Man turned, peered at Mist directly, entirely present and fully engaged. A remarkable change, if real.

He did not speak.

"No one? It's a good thing I mean to do? It could risk this entire empire."

Wen-chin said, "It may be too altruistic for most, Illustrious."

Was there a caution buried there? A subtle admonition that this was not a path her ancestors would have chosen to walk without first having seen a major chance to aggrandize themselves?

She shrugged. Whatever she did, some Tervola would suspect a darker intent. That was the nature of the beast. Such men viewed the world through the lenses of their own characters.

"I see no objections. Gentlemen, I do mean this." Despite the terrible fright Lords Yuan and Ssu-ma had just delivered. "I will take the Empire to war against that wicked entity. There'll be no getting out after this."

She proposed an adventure that had begun a thousand times before.

She looked round. She had, indirectly, polled each one earlier. Lords Yuan and Shih-ka'i would be reluctant. They had no skin in the game—though Lord Yuan could be captivated by the technical challenge of implications that had emerged during the contest with the Deliverer.

He had remained invisible throughout that struggle, behind the scenes, fixated on maximizing the carrying capacity of the transfer portals. The success of the eastern legions had depended entirely on transfer logistics. Tactical and operational stresses had been extreme, too. Lord Yuan had not had time to examine all of the temporal anomalies and philosophical conundrums that had arisen. But he was getting excited now.

The pig farmer's son, then. She needed his stabilizing support. But how to make him a believer?

That would be a challenge. She was no fanatic herself.

She wanted to do this. She saw it as worthy work that could change the world. But she did not want to become a martyr to her cause.

"Still no one?" She looked at Shih-ka'i directly. He did not respond. "Very well. Some questions, then."

She meant that not as a call for questions but as a prelude to presenting several topics. But Michael Trebilcock spoke quickly. "Here's one. Why am I here?"

"The question intrigues me as well. Consult the wizard. I didn't invite you. Of this gathering you're the man I know the least and trust the least, but it's too late to evict you. I won't rail against what I can't change, though I suppose I could always kill you. I would caution you but I do know you well enough to understand that that would be pointless. You thrive on danger. You seek it the way the Disciple seeks opium."

Varthlokkur volunteered, "I brought Michael because he has

unique intelligence resources and can provide priceless support if you do return the King to Kavelin. I thought it would be useful if Michael understood what is going on and why."

Mist nodded. That exposed a problem sure to rear up again. Some of these men were used to thinking for themselves. They would do what they thought needed doing without asking.

This would be the hardest thing she had done yet. She might be doomed to fail simply for having made the choice to try.

Old Meddler had survived forever. No doubt he smelled this taking shape. Given his oft-demonstrated talent for suborning even those with everything to lose by assisting him, she would not be amazed to discover that someone here was his agent already.

The Old Man? He and the Old Meddler had worked together for ages. Their falling out might be more apparent than real.

Or it could be Michael Trebilcock, just for the thrill? Michael loved complex conspiracies.

Someone said, "Illustrious?"

Varthlokkur said, "Gentlemen, our leader just underwent a severe paranoia spasm."

Mist glared as he continued, "That's his most insidious strength. He makes you waste time looking over your shoulder. Your own class relies heavily on the same power."

She forced a smile. "Well. You haven't declared yourselves out. So. All right. Are any of you prepared to declare yourselves in?"

Lords Ssu-ma and Yuan did not lift their hands. Lord Yuan she understood. This was political. He was not a political person. He would do as he was told once the political choices had been made. He would go baying after the research possibilities.

The only way Old Meddler could suborn Lord Yuan would be to promise him all the secrets of the transfer streams, which was beyond his power to do. Every historical indicator suggested that those streams were divine artifacts not only alien to the Star Rider but possibly even actively inimical.

Her researches had been limited but she had found no reference to any interaction between the Star Rider and the transfer streams, yet that digging had her thinking that the Windmjirnerhorn had to operate on a related principal. The riches that thing spilled had to come from somewhere.

She said, "During our wars with the west the entity we will not name once thwarted everyone by using the Poles of Power to kill all sorcery for a brief time. Do any of you know anything about them?"

No one volunteered anything. She peered at Varthlokkur, sure he must know more than she did. He said nothing.

"All right. The thinking used to be that the Windmjirnerhorn was one of the Poles. That's probably not true. I can find no reason to believe it. It is certain though, that one is something called the Tear of Mimizan." She surveyed both attentive and marginally bored faces.

"My late husband and his brothers served the Monitor of Escalon during Escalon's war with Shinsan. Once it became obvious that defeat was inevitable the Monitor slipped the Tear to my brother-in-law Turran. There is nothing on record to explain how or why the Tear came into the possession of the Monitor. My suspicion is, he got it from a certain old villain who thereby created false hope that extended the struggle and guaranteed a good deal more destruction. Turran had the Tear smuggled west to Bragi Ragnarson's first wife, Elana." It would not be politick to mention that Turran had had a considerable affection for Elana. Bragi would not be pleased by any public reminder that she had been murdered while in bed with Mist's brother-in-law "She didn't know what she had. Others suspected, though not how important the trinket might actually be. But never mind all that. I want to know what became of the Tear."

Lord Yuan lifted a hand tentatively.

"Lord Yuan?"

"You proffer an essentially traditional view of the Poles. It may not be correct."

"Lord?"

"A strong case can be made for the transfer streams being one of the Poles. Possibly the more important Pole. Leakage may be what all sorcerers feed on. Leakage could be the Power itself."

Mist was not about to debate Lord Yuan. He knew this subject better than the rest of the room combined. "Will you explain that in words fit for a simpleton? I don't follow." Near as she could tell, neither did anyone else, excepting possibly the Old Man. And his nod might be due to sleepiness.

"As you wish, Illustrious. I believe the Power we use in our sorcery is actually leakage from transfer streams that have become old and inefficient through lack of care, just as irrigation or navigation canals will become porous and leaky if not adequately maintained. Mathematically, we shouldn't be able to access the Power at all, nor even the transfer streams. Those are, I am convinced, far more complicated than commonly assumed. We see them only in the workaday dimensions, like a network of creeks and canals we use to row our boats from place to place. They may, in fact, be the bones of the universe. Or something beyond anything the human mind can imagine. The Tear of Mimizan and, possibly, the Windmjirnerhorn, may be keys or control devices."

The ancient may have suffered an epiphany. Or a stroke. He did go still and silent. It was plain that he did not plan to say anything more right now.

Mist said, "Excuse Lord Yuan. He does this. Anyone else care to contribute? Lord Ssu-ma? You've been particularly subdued. Would you like to explain?"

"I have no thoughts of consequence, Illustrious. I am a pig farmer's son. It is beyond my capacity to encompass how this proposition can benefit the Empire if we pursue it with a vigor actually necessary to bring us to confrontation with him so terrible we dare not name his name."

He had a point. "I see. You so fear the potential cost to the Empire that you concede defeat beforehand."

"Considering the historical evidence, that temptation is there."

"Would you have felt the same about the Deliverer had you not been ordered to take charge of a campaign already begun?"

She waited while he gave the unfair question honest consideration.

"I might have had I known the full story of the monster behind the Deliverer while not knowing that we had no choice but to fight."

Mist said nothing. She wanted more. She thought he could not help but fill a vacuum now. And so he did.

"I spent my life teaching the Empire's most promising youngsters, knowing that nine of ten would die badly. I did not think that it had to be that way. The Empire did not need to be at war every day, all the time. Our unreasoning passion for conquest drove us to where we are today, exhausted and on the brink of collapse."

Mist nodded. Shih-ka'i exaggerated but she did not disagree with his sentiments. The Empire had paid an awful price for its recent successes. But it was true that now there were no longer any enemies who could do the Empire serious harm, other than the Star Rider.

Old Meddler always acted through proxies. The collapse of the Pracchia conspiracy had left him with few of those. Magden Norath had been the last of any significance.

Today's most terrible danger might still be ambition in the Tervola class. The respected old men said they were reining the madness in, because it had cost Shinsan so dearly, but the treachery disease would continue in a certain kind of heart. And Old Meddler might pluck those strings to compose some nocturne where the empire once again turned upon itself.

Mist grimaced. She would have to be as harsh as her father and grandfather had been. Nothing less would serve.

Some people just asked to be killed.

She said, "You took up the struggle against the Deliverer because you were directed to do so. I understand. I'll rely on a similar formula in the matter of him who toys with the world."

She paused. She had begun to improvise. And that had hatched an interesting notion. "Lord Kuo. You will assume responsibility for the staff side. Plan. Coordinate. Find resources. You know the staff role. Lord Ssu-ma will be responsible for execution."

None of the Tervola missed the significance of her calling Wen-chin "Lord." Good.

Lord Ssu-ma bowed, resigned. "As you command, so shall it be, Illustrious. That settled, may I ask about the others gathered here?"

"I hope to employ their skills, genius, and knowledge. I am counting on Lord Yuan to improve our arsenal substantially." Did that sound too rehearsed?

She had had little to do with Lord Yuan till recently. Lately, though, he had begged frequently to be freed from workaday responsibilities so he could concentrate on ferreting out secrets of the transfer streams. Which inevitably preceded an appeal for more funds.

In that he was not unusual.

Mist said, "I will step aside and let you brainstorm now. Or complain, or argue, according to your nature."

She paid little attention. There was not much to hear. No one wanted to say anything. Mist began to contemplate Lein She and her lifeguards.

Michael Trebilcock told her, "Don't give in."

"Excuse me?"

"Ignore that temptation. They're good men."

Had he been reading her mind?

"You don't need to trust them. Watch them. If they fail you they may lead you somewhere interesting."

Or not. They had been selected randomly, excepting Lein She, and the tower raid would have weaned him from any service to an outside agency—assuming Old Meddler was the ultimate cause of all that blood.

It would cost little to follow Michael's advice.

...

Varthlokkur told Mist, "I should take the Old Man to Fangdred and put him together with Ethrian."

Ragnarson glanced from the wizard to the Empress. Was something going on in the shadows, there? Both seemed guarded.

Mist responded, "No. Because I think he'll be safer here."

Though the wizard looked inclined to argue, he said only, "You may be right. The only way in here is by transfer. He never... Oh! Stupid."

Ragnarson swallowed a temptation to mention winged horses and flying evil familiars. He needed to stay small, his ears not taken into account.

Anyway, Varthlokkur had remembered without having to be prompted.

Mist said, "I can keep him from coming in from above. The horse is immortal but not invulnerable. Bring the boy here."

Varthlokkur sighed. "I don't see Nepanthe letting us do that. She did a stint as a guest in these parts."

"That wasn't me or mine. Remind her that we have the world's best healers, including those who heal damaged minds. I will put together a team to work with the Old Man."

Ragnarson thought Mist's project insane and doomed. The allies would have to make sudden decisions and act quickly to keep up with an enthusiastic Star Rider. They did not trust one another enough not to waste time looking for hidden agendas any time anyone made a suggestion.

Another edge Old Meddler had.

Varthlokkur said, "Nepanthe might listen if you argued convincingly. Expect her to insist on staying with him, though."

Mist nodded, then beckoned. "Lord Yuan."

Varthlokkur gave Ragnarson a searching look, then Michael Trebilcock, who was eavesdropping, too.

Yuan arrived. "How may I be of service, Illustrious?"

"I asked you to dig into the past of your shop to see if it played any part in the incident that claimed the lives of the Princes Thaumaturge."

"I did that."

Ragnarson and Varthlokkur were puzzled. What could that signify now?

Lord Yuan said, "As I told you before, Illustrious, I played no part personally. Neither your father nor his brother would have approached me about participating in such crimes. That stipulated, there is no doubt that someone younger and politically more ambitious might have seen an opportunity. I searched the records exhaustively. It would appear that transfer portals were not used to put the Princes into Fangdred that night. I hope you aren't disappointed."

Mist sighed. "I'm not. That's what I suspected." She glanced at Varthlokkur, who shrugged, and at the Old Man, who was focused on the shogi board. "Demons, I suppose."

Lord Yuan said, "Almost certainly, Illustrious. Though I found notes indicating that the Windmjirnerhorn may have been active at the time."

His remark was a big, "So what?" to Ragnarson but obviously meant something to Varthlokkur, who seemed almost excited.

Mist was having original thoughts of her own, though Ragnarson doubted that they matched the wizard's. She said, "I see a solution to the problem..."

Varthlokkur started to ask Lord Yuan something at the same moment. He stopped, deferring.

Mist said, "If we placed a portal in Fangdred, positioned so you could be comfortable about controlling it, Nepanthe and Ethrian could move back and forth to suit themselves. Scalza and Eka, too, if they wanted. The Old Man could go there and still be able to duck out if danger threatened."

She spoke tentatively, evidently intent on going easy on Varthlokkur's paranoia. The wizard just nodded. "That might be useful. Lord Yuan, can you detect the Horn in use?" Not using its full name for the same reason no one named the Star Rider.

"Not it, *per se,* but the power echo when it's in use."

The wizard's excitement dwindled.

Lord Yuan went on, "The device has a unique signature. It reverberates in the transfer stream rather like water dancing in a tumbler when a tuning fork is struck close by."

Even Varthlokkur frowned, not following.

Mist interceded. "You two talk that out later. It sounds like something we can use."

Lord Yuan shook his head. "I haven't found a way. It's not even directional. It's on or it's off, in use or not in use, the latter so infrequently that there is no point wasting man-hours watching for it."

Varthlokkur said, "Even so…"

Ragnarson had begun to feel like the man whose job it would be to watch for the Windmjirnerhorn to announce itself. He could not focus. Michael listened intently, memorizing every word without understanding a one, in case it proved useful later, but his eyes had glazed over. Mist observed with benevolent exasperation. Elsewhere, a raging game of shogi roared along with distressed commentary from Lord Kuo Wen-chin.

Ragnarson met Mist's eyes. She said, "I have sown the seeds."

"They appear to have quickened, too. Where do we go now?"

"I have a master plan. If I say one word more than I have already, though, the Fates will rip it apart like jackals devouring a week-old carcass."

†

Chapter Twenty-Three:

AUTUMN, YEAR 1018 AFE:

Weather Developing

Josiah Gales and Queen Inger, with toddler-king Fulk between them, entered the converted warehouse where the Thing had indulged in rowdy deliberations since its inception. The Crown never had possessed wealth enough to raise a purpose-built structure. Josiah's health had not improved. He limped. He carried a cane. He leaned on it heavily when no one was watching. The little king was doing better.

Inger said, "This place is a sty. Pray the weather has the grace to let us air it out."

Preparations for the Thingmeet had raised obstacles entirely unforeseen, as, here, where enterprising livestock dealers had used a vacant building as an indoor feed lot, thinking it a sin that so much sheltered space should go unused—especially when the inattentive administration at the castle never visited the property.

People had squatted there, too. Many had been the sort who could not grasp such basic concepts as taking it outside when they need to vacate their bladders or bowels.

Three ragged soldiers trailed Inger and Josiah. Two had helped Babeltausque and Nathan Wolf at thc Twisted Wrench. They constituted a significant percentage of the remaining castle garrison.

Still, optimism was in the air. The Thingmeet was a stroke of genius, so far, though neither Kavelin nor Vorgreberg yet understood that. The classes and factions just saw an opportunity to air grievances and defy chaos.

Gales saw it. A respect for order *had* been hammered into the people during the last three reigns despite a tradition of immaturity and factionalism. The King had been lost. Kavelin had followed up with a prolonged tantrum. Old scores had been settled—till chaos came calling another time. But peace and prosperity had been murmuring seductively all summer. People were ready.

Fickle, fickle people. How long before some self-starter felt comfortable enough to resume being unpleasant?

Vorgreberg's folk were pleased, if reports could be trusted—though some frugal early Thingmeet arrivals had found a loophole and were tenting on fallow ground outside the wall.

Even they had to buy food and services.

Inger's popularity was rising, locally.

Scanning the progress volunteer cleaners had made, she declared, "We may yet pull this off. If we do, we may yet survive."

"If Kristen remains passive." There had been little news from Sedlmayr. The Mundwiller strategy appeared to be losing its popular appeal. Inger, at least, was doing *something*.

"They will send a delegation."

"Of course. You guaranteed universal safe conduct. We'll see a lot of old friends who abandoned us earlier this year: Sir Arnhelm, Sir Rengild, Quirre of Bolt, lots of others. They'll drool and fawn and spin tale tales about how they had no recourse."

"You give them too much credit. They won't care what we think. They'll be safe."

"Yes. I'm surprised so many took you at your word." She was, after all, a Greyfells.

It irked Inger that even Josiah could not get past his expectations.

Fulk vigorously proclaimed something in toddler. She did not understand. Josiah hoisted the boy onto his hip, wincing. "That better, Short Stuff?"

Fulk burbled happily. He leaned against Gales's shoulder, shut his eyes. He was ready to nap. Gales said, "He needs to get out more.

He tires too easily. He needs exercise and exposure to people, too."

Inger stepped into the box whence she would deliver a brief speech declaring the Thingmeet convened. "We should all be doing lots of things. But I've pretty much lost the drive."

"And here comes Nathan looking determined to lead us deeper into the slough of despond."

Not quite true. Wolf announced, "We've found a transfer gate. Babeltausque says he can clear the booby traps in time."

Inger asked Josiah, "That's good news, isn't it? So why so glum? You too, Nathan."

Wolf said, "The sorcerer never gave up hope of finding that missing treasury money, Majesty. He really wanted to please you. He kept digging—when he wasn't playing with his girl toy or looking for a replacement who isn't as overdeveloped."

"That was unkind, Nathan."

"Apologies, Majesty. It was, though probably not untrue."

Gales observed, "We might all be less uncomfortable if we spent less time judging Babeltausque."

Wolf nodded. "Of course. We do have to work with him. And we can't fault his work. Or his effort. But, still, what I wanted to say is, Babeltausque says he found the exact place where Mundwiller and Prataxis hid the stuff that night."

Inger felt hope explode—and then fade. Nathan would hardly be so dour if the news was positive. "And?"

"And we got the best part already. They unloaded it into the creek twenty yards upstream from that farm pond. Babeltausque found just about as much more as two old men could have carried. The Crown Jewels were there. They were all crappy reproductions that melted. I'd bet that Mundwiller and Prataxis didn't know. They wouldn't have gone to all the trouble if they had. Maybe nobody knew. Maybe some crook swapped everything out ages ago."

Inger sighed, already resigned. Dredging the pond had left her without hope. Still, she did slump some. "There went a rare good day. So what's the deal? Was there any money at all?"

"It was under the mud in the creek feeding the pond. Babeltausque says the mud probably built up after the stuff was dumped. The boxes we found in the pond probably got washed down during a storm. After we cleaned the pond that mud had somewhere to go again…"

"Money, Nathan?"

"Copper and bronze. Less than twenty pounds by weight, all corroded. The jewelry boxes might be worth more if we get them restored. They're antiques."

Inger borrowed some lower class invective and explored it creatively. Then she beckoned a soldier. "Hassel, take Fulk before the Colonel collapses."

"Yes, Majesty."

"Nathan, tell Babeltausque I appreciate his efforts, and yours, too. I need you both here, now, though. We need to set this up."

…

The commission from Sedlmayr formed an entire caravan. Ozora Mundwiller was in charge and was less discomfited by the rigors of the road than sons and grandsons half or even a quarter her age. She proudly said it herself: she was one tough old buzzard.

If she could do something, youngsters ought to be able to follow suit while hopping on one foot and playing the panpipes.

Kristen, Dahl, and young Bragi were there, tempting fate. Haas remained steadfastly opposed to Kristen taking the risk. He was sure Inger would not refuse such a fine chance to respond ignominiously, safe-conduct be damned.

She was a Greyfells and there were ample precedents. Dahl did, however, understand that trying to change Kristen's mind was a waste of air.

He and she settled down to a cold lunch, beside the road, with Bragi napping and most of the caravan bustling around taking the animals to water, preparing food, doing all the things that had to be done during a rest stop.

Kristen mentioned the heavy traffic, moving both directions on the road. Lone drummers, tinkers, and caravans great and small, kept the air laden with dust.

Haas grunted. He had little to say. He was hanging in there, sullenly awaiting his chance to declare, "I told you so!" Or so Kristen teased.

Bight Mundwiller and the Blodgett girl settled close enough to be overheard. Bight carped, "I just don't get what her problem is."

"She doesn't like me anymore."

"Well, duh! But I don't get why. She thought you were great before."

"It's because of who I was staying with. Something happened between her and some enThal when she was our age."

"That's stupid."

"Sure it is. But old people just hold grudges."

"She doesn't know you."

"Hey, neither do you. Not really. I could be some kind of monster. Right? But it doesn't matter. She don't want me getting my paws on the Mundwiller fortune. She can't believe that I'm not interested. She thinks she sees Ozora in Haida. Be patient, Bight. It'll all work out. Think about Vorgreberg. We're almost there. Aren't you excited?"

"Some. But mostly because you are. I've been there. It isn't any big deal. Sedlmayr is nicer."

"Cleaner and friendlier, anyway."

"What?"

"That's what you all keep telling me, anyway. So it must be true. Right? Or will we find out something different when we see the real thing? Only…"

"Only what?"

"Only, it is the capital! Right? Come on, Bight!" She scooted closer, leaned against young Mundwiller lightly. "Come on! You *know*…"

Ozora Mundwiller shouted for Bight.

Kristen whispered, "That old raven does have it in for the girl now. What changed? What did she mean, Ozora sees a lot of herself…?"

"Ozora wormed her way into the clan by seducing Aram Mundwiller when he was younger than Bight is now. Then along came Cham. They couldn't run her off, then."

"It worked out good for the tribe. In the long run."

"You know Ozora can't think that way." Then Dahl shrugged. He did not much care. He watched a caravan trudge past, westbound. It included a dozen camels, which excited the Blodgett girl tremendously. She ran off to pester the drovers. Haas grumbled, "Girl, don't give those men the wrong idea. I'm feeling too lazy to rescue you." Then he grunted and hastily turned his back on the road.

"What?" Kristen asked.

"I know some of those guards. I don't want them to recognize me."

He need not have worried. The Blodgett girl was not unattractive. Without stirring any deep fantasies she captured the attention of the caravan men, then was clever enough to leave them all smiling when she walked away.

Kristen whispered, "Check the old woman. She was hoping they would carry her off."

"Really, Kristen? You're not being fair to her now."

Ozora finished ragging Bight. She barked orders meant to get the party moving again.

"Oh, my," Kristen murmured. "Dahl. Look there." She indicated a solitary traveler headed east. He was ragged. He shuffled dispiritedly. He looked like the last of the displaced persons who had trudged every road just a year ago. "Isn't that Aral?"

"Him or his handsome twin. You get stuff ready here. I'll catch the little sh… bugger." He bounced up and trotted after the traveler, who appeared not to have noticed the resting Sedlmayrese. Being that far gone in thought was begging Fortune to poke you in the eye.

So. Inger's Thingmeet was drawing a broader-based crowd than the Queen anticipated.

This could turn interesting.

…

Bragi settled on a weathered block of limestone, exhausted after clambering out of the ruined temple—or whatever it was in its time.

"Damn! I'm still out of shape! I thought I was getting it back. I was so wrong!"

"It's not just that," Michael Trebilcock said, settling nearby. "The transfer had something to do with it. Look at this guy. And he does it every day." He indicated the Tervola Tang Shan, who was just oozing through the gap in tumbled stone masking the stairway down to the hidden portal. "He's about twelve and he's woofing for air."

The Tervola was, likely, older than either of them but had not suffered the wear and tear. He said, "The drain was caused by a filter Lord Yuan installed. It keeps the unnamed from tracking who is going where. Lord Yuan will ameliorate that effect when he has time." Tang went to assist two bodyguards having trouble getting through the gap because of their size.

Bragi surveyed the world into which they had emerged. It seemed comfortably Kavelin come autumn, after the leaves began to fall, yet he recognized nothing. "Where are we? This don't look right." By which he meant that everything was too clean and tame to have been abandoned long. The surrounding fields had yet to return to nature. The forest, more than two hundred yards downhill in every direction, had not yet begun to encroach on the cleared land. The fields boasted tangles of wild grasses and late wildflowers but none of the scrub and thorny brush that invaded abandoned fields almost instantly elsewhere. Insects buzzed even though the season was late and the nights had to be chilly.

Tang Shan, laboring to make himself understood in a language he did not know well, explained, "This ruin is eight…miles?… south-southeast of your Vorgreberg." He extended an arm to point. Ragnarson could just make out smudgy air in that direction. The Tervola continued, "Our instructions are to accompany you partway. We should reach a main road in an hour or two. We will leave you there, hoping that Destiny has no more cruel tricks in her sack."

Ragnarson frowned at Trebilcock. Trebilcock shrugged. "Some idioms don't translate."

Tang Shan said, "This was once a temple, important to its cult. It has been abandoned for a century but the consecrating power has not yet faded. It is a good place."

Ragnarson felt that. "I didn't know it was here." Something this close to Vorgreberg ought to be common knowledge and part of the local folklore.

Tang said, "You will have a hard time finding it from outside. Protective glamours turn you aside gently beginning so far away that you wouldn't notice except to think you were getting confused the way people can in the forest. Our troops found it while hunting partisans during the occupation. The partisans were unaware of it despite exploiting the surrounding forest for cover."

Ragnarson grunted acknowledgement. He had encountered similar "outside" islands when he was young and living by his wits and blade. Those, though, had not been sweetly benign. He said, "We should get moving. These places are never as tame as they try to make you think."

One eastern soldier smiled thinly. Bragi assumed that meant that arrangements were in place already.

Tang Shan and the lifeguards wore what, at a hundred yards, might pass for local clothing. Any nearer, though, and one would have to be afflicted with terrible eyesight not to see that they were no local peasants. Even Tang was big for Kavelin.

Shan said, "You are correct. We should. Lord Yuan has work waiting for me. I'm looking forward to it."

"I'm not so sure I still love you, either." Ragnarson groaned as he got his legs underneath him.

Trebilcock remarked, "You'd better not need carrying. You do, you'll be having supper with the wolves."

"I'll manage. It's all downhill from here."

And up. And sideways. With no road. With no path. Without even a decent game trail trending the proper direction through the autumn-painted tangle of palisade for the ruins. After two hours Ragnarson gasped, "Shan, how will you ever find your way back?"

The Tervola grinned. "We're clever. We have secret skills."

Trebilcock said, "They've been dropping bread crumbs."

Tang agreed. "After a fashion. Worry not. We saw to our needs before we gave any attention to yours."

"That fills me with confidence."

"I am pleased by your praise."

Ragnarson realized, to his surprise, that he was in better spirits than he had been for an age, though fighting the undergrowth up and down gully banks was murderously exhausting.

In time, Michael said, "Shan, we've been at this for three hours. You said two. Are you leading us around in circles?"

Tang Shan, worn out himself, gasped, "I am currently providing the rearguard. If we meander please blame the man out front."

The man breaking trail was best known as Michael Trebilcock. He did not stop grumbling. But, just minutes later, he flung up a hand for a halt, then used it to cup an ear.

Faint road traffic noise leaked into the woods. The five oozed toward it.

Twenty feet further on the tangle became the usual vaguely groomed Kaveliner woodland where the deadwood stayed harvested and the brush did not get much chance to flourish. It looked exactly the same as far as the eye could see in every direction.

Ragnarson muttered, "There's some witchcraft stuff going on here."

"Can't get anything past you," Trebilcock countered.

"I'd forgotten what a wiseass you can be."

"Look there." Something moved from right to left up ahead. "Are those camels?"

The shapes were vague through the trees but, yes, those big lumps of ugly were camels. Ragnarson turned to ask the Tervola if he was sure they had come through the right portal.

There were no easterners to be seen.

While Ragnarson gawked at their absence Trebilcock drifted forward, sniffing. "No doubt about it. Those are camels. And I know where we are."

"They're gone. Those three. Vanished."

"They stepped back inside the illusion. Ask Varthlokkur to look for the place next time you see him. We're just south of the southern road west. Sedlmayr is off that way maybe forty miles. Two or three miles that way is your old house. Two more miles and we'll be knocking on the castle gate."

Ragnarson snorted. "I can imagine the party my wife will throw if she finds out I'm back."

"She might surprise you. So. Let's stroll on over there and take a gander at a world that has camels in it."

Bragi was reluctant. He no longer had the inclination to play politics. He was a blunted sword, possibly bent, maybe even broken.

Michael misread him. "Who would recognize us? I look fifteen years older. You've lost weight, you got no beard, you're turning grey, and you're dragging…"

"I get your point, thank you very much. Young girls won't throw themselves at me anymore." Sherilee was back in his head, like a nagging toothache.

"And you're crabby. Not to mention, you're dressed weird." Trebilcock flashed a huge grin.

"Lead on, boy wonder."

Now Michael flashed a grimace. "Would it be smart for me to leave you out of sight behind me?"

"Why don't we find out?" Then, muttering, "Camels? How come there are camels on the Sedlmayr road?" He did not like camels. In his youth, while with Hawkwind in the desert, he had had camels close by constantly. He associated their stench with that of misfortune, still.

...

Dahl Haas finished hitching the donkey to the cart. He helped Kristen board, hoisted Bragi up. He would lead. They looked like prosperous peasants. Haas hoped no one wondered why there was nothing in the cart but a child and an apparently pregnant woman.

Nearby, Bight Mundwiller and the Blodgett girl played at clumsy courtship rituals, Bight by far the more maladroit, mainly to irritate Ozora. The matriarch was suitably irked but refused to be baited by children.

Dahl murmured, "At some point Ozora will make that boy sorry he withdrew his affections from you."

"Not funny, Dahl! And is there suddenly something wrong with the girl?"

"Like what? She's a girl being a girl figuring out that she has the power to fog men's minds. She'll only get more wicked as she hones her skills."

"Somebody is going to get honed if he don't watch his attitude."

"My thesis proven. What's his problem?"

Bight was staring in the direction the camels had gone. Nothing unusual there. A couple of shabby old travelers were approaching lazily. They might be brothers. They were tall and graying but both still had their own hair.

Haas approached the youngsters. "Is there a problem? You know those men? Are they trouble?"

The girl said, "No, Mr. Haas. The one on the right reminded me of my Uncle Bridewell. That startled me because he died last year. Then Bight said that they were too far away to recognize, anyway, even if we did know them."

Bight said, "I got upset because I thought she was upset."

She said, "Anyway, I can't see through him so he can't be a ghost. And, now that they're closer, I can see that he's taller than Uncle Bridewell was. But I wish they would look up so I could see their faces."

Haas caught an odd note there but could not imagine why. He drifted back to his cart, watching the travelers as he went.

Aral Dantice came out of the woods, where he had gone to consult the famous horse trader. He grumbled, "I don't remember eating anything that would do that to me. The flies are going to be in heaven. Well. Speaking of some remarkable shit. Look at this." He ogled the tall old men with far more surprise than Bight or the girl had.

They were just twenty paces away and focused on the dust in front of their feet, shoulders hunched against the attention they had attracted.

Ozora barked, "What are you people doing? If you don't move we'll have to spend another night camped out with the bugs and mosquitoes."

Something clicked. Dahl recognized the man on the left. The one on his own right. Not the one who had Aral's attention, that the girl had mistaken for her uncle.

He did not shout. He said nothing to anyone. He just oozed over to the road to intercept the pair. "Excuse me, sirs. A moment, I beg."

Both men kept searching the road immediately in front of their feet, shuffling dispiritedly, which willful focus made managing full awareness of their surroundings problematic. It was an ostrich approach to personal camouflage.

The nearer man responded with a dramatic start. He looked up.

Dahl lurched back. "Gods damn me!" He retreated several steps before good sense took over.

Both travelers shifted hands to the hilts of daggers and considered their surroundings.

Haas moved to Kristen, placed himself between her and the road, hoping to control her reaction.

At which point the Blodgett girl blurted, "Uncle Chames?"

Chames? What happened to Bridewell?

The girl galloped to the roadside. She was not at all shy about throwing herself onto one of the men.

Dahl heard him murmur, "Haida, we're really trying to avoid attracting attention."

"Oh. Hell! I'm sorry. I got excited."

Haas moved back toward the travelers, as did Bight Mundwiller, the latter uncertainly. The other Sedlmayrese stopped to gawk.

"Too late, now. The cat has dumped the cream."

Though she was not interested Michael introduced Ragnarson to the girl as his cousin Leopard Marks. "I forget why we call him that. His real name is Flynn."

"Because I changed my spots."

Trebilcock offered no name for the girl, Dahl supposed because he did not know what name she was using. He had not missed him calling her Haida.

The girl retreated into resounding silence.

Haas glared at both men, willing them to do nothing to turn the moment more treacherous than it was. He looked back at Kristen. "Flynn" did the same, having recognized her. And she had recognized him, now. She lacked all color.

They had talked about what this would mean, for her, for them, for the younger Bragi. Though the King's return was only a theoretical possibility it never seemed vaguely likely outside popular fantasy. Unless…

Dahl looked back up the road. No. They were alone. But…

Shinsan would not arrive in full kit with bands playing if the King was back as their man.

But!

These two had been missing and presumed dead for a year. Now they were sneaking back. Together. That could have immense meaning, perhaps going all the way back to before the King's dumb eastern adventure.

Dahl turned to Aral Dantice. Aral was Michael's best friend.

Aral was helping the Sedlmayrese get ready to move out. His moment of surprise past, Aral was making like he had recognized no one.

Had he been running point for the others when Kristen spotted him?

Ozora commanded, "Blodgett girl! Come here! Now!"

She did as directed. Bight followed. He would bark back if the old woman was excessively unreasonable.

The old king said, "Chames, we need to move along. A pleasure to meet you, young man." He inclined his head toward Kristen. "And your missus. Blessings be upon the babe to come."

He did not sound sincere.

Dahl suppressed an impulse to explain that there was no need for anger. Only, the Queen Mother *could* have become pregnant. The displeasure directed her way was not entirely misplaced. They were not always as careful as they should be.

The old king added, "Keep up the good work, son. Maybe we'll meet again in more comfortable circumstances." Meaning he saw no reason to trust anyone behind Haas. Longing shown when he looked at the younger Bragi.

"I shall look forward. Good fortune dog your journey, sir."

"And yours as well."

The tall old men shuffled on, watched by the Sedlmayrese. Only Ozora said anything, though.

The Blodgett girl answered every question with an elaborate and plausible lie about distant uncles, one of whom she had never met before. The ease with which she dissembled amazed Dahl. She convinced Ozora of nothing, but the old woman did pretend to believe her. She had recognized neither uncle herself.

Dahl wondered what tall tales the girl had spun already and would continue to spin. Clearly, she was one of Michael Trebilcock's gang.

The Sedlmayrese clattered into the courtyard of their city's commercial factor station as twilight assembled in Vorgreberg, whereupon the Blodgett girl vanished quicker than a puff of mist. One moment she was playing maiden games with Bight, the next she was not and no one had seen her fade into the gathering shadows.

Definitely one of Michael Trebilcock's phantoms.

...

Babeltausque ambled into the Twisted Wrench. He visited frequently, evenings. His implied motive was concern over what had happened to Rhys Benedit. Benedit was not convinced. He believed that the wizard wanted an excuse to drink while fishing for the skinny on anything happening amongst the ticks infesting

Vorgreberg's underbelly.

Both men were right.

Benedit was doing better now that the garrison was back but he was not prospering. The soldiers had no money while some potential customers would not share space with the Queen's men.

"I'll try the new dark tonight, Rhys. You were right. It is an acquired taste. And I'm acquiring it."

Benedit produced a pint. Babeltausque kept the man in front of him briefly, considering his eye and damaged face. "Any sight coming back?"

"A little, sir. More than I expected. Better than being all the way blind."

"I'll help if I can find a way. This is much better than the last batch."

"Thank you, sir."

"So what's on your mind, Rhys?"

"Sir?"

"You're shuffling like you're trying to make up your mind if you should tell me something." Babeltausque strained to produce a smile.

"Uh… Yeah. I guess I am."

"And?"

Benedit needed a few seconds more. Then he sucked in a deep breath, took the plunge. "That Haida Heltkler. I seen her maybe a hour ago, going past in a big hurry. I made like I never recognized her."

It took Babeltausque a moment to recall why he ought to know the name. Then, "That's interesting. Very interesting. Thank you, Rhys."

"Don't tell nobody I told you."

"Told me what? I hardly know you. Top me up." He pushed an extra groat across the counter, then nursed his beer and eavesdropped. Bar talk focused on the Thingmeet, which would start doing whatever Thingmeets did soon after sunrise tomorrow. The sorcerer was amazed at the popular level of ignorance. The soldiers only cared because extra work would be expected of them.

While Babeltausque lent an ear to that he bent the other to Rhys Benedit.

The publican had gotten into the habit of muttering to himself after his injury. It made everyone uncomfortable. The tick became markedly worse when Babeltausque was around. But folks failed to listen, failed to see that communication was going on.

...

Nathan Wolf joined Babeltausque as soon as he could escape from Inger and Thingmeet preparation. "You have news?"

"The Heltkler girl is back. She was seen outside the Twisted Wrench three hours ago. I want to see her."

"Carrie won't like that." Wolf dreaded the wizard's lover. The child could deploy a sharper tongue than the Queen herself and was more skilled at using it to get what she wanted.

"Carrie isn't involved. Heltkler has information we want. Round her up."

"Any suggestions as to where?"

"Start with that butcher shop. Then try the apothecary. Do whatever you need to do."

...

Toby eased away from where he had been eavesdropping, careful to make no noise. Then he raced to his grandfather.

...

A tired-looking Wesson soldier in drooping, frayed livery pounded on the door of the apothecary shop. He was amazed when a man actually responded. He had been here several times lately, to purchase medicines for the doctor, and had never gotten an answer.

"What is it, Fletcher?"

The soldier handed over a letter, made it clear by his stance that he wanted an answer. The apothecary nodded, broke the seal, read.

The soldier thought the man seemed disheartened. After a moment, he said, "I'll get started right away. It will take time. Have him send you back tomorrow evening for what I can get ready. Blue asparagus seed will be a problem. He should still have some of that, though. It will be cash on delivery from now on. No more credit for the castle."

"I understand, sir." The castle owed everybody, including him. "I will relay your message exactly."

...

Ragnarson raised an eyebrow when Michael Trebilcock returned.

Trebilcock said, "They're onto us already. Well, onto Haida."

The girl lay with face on her arms on the table. The three had been sharing a rough meal.

"She passed out after you left. Must of was tireder than me."

"Playing a role can be exhausting. The stuff she dug up will be useful but I don't see why she thought she had to get it."

"She wanted to please you."

Trebilcock stared at Ragnarson.

"It's pretty obvious, Michael."

"Yes. Well. As may be." He gripped the girl's right shoulder, shook gently. "Haida. Girl. Wake up. We have to go. Castle soldiers are on their way."

She got up, groggy, eyes half open, crossed. "Uh?"

"Did you visit somebody on your way here? Or see somebody that you knew?"

"Huh? Nobody. I came straight. Why?"

"Somebody saw you. They knew the Queen's sorcerer wants to get to know you better. Wolf is coming to get you."

She was wide awake now. "We need to get out of here!"

"Yes. We do. But don't panic. Where should we go? After we watch the raid?"

Nobody had an answer. Ragnarson said, "I've been gone longer than either of you. I don't have anywhere left." The only place that came to mind, Fiana's crypt, would work only till Inger looked there.

Thinking about Fiana was unproductive. If he started he would not be able to stop. Fiana had been an obsession in her time, as Sherilee had become more recently. He could not shake either woman out of his head. He saw no reason to try.

...

"Well?" Babeltausque asked. The key fact was obvious. Nathan had no cute young cunny in hand.

"There was nobody at the butcher shop. Somebody was in the apothecary shop earlier but not when we got there. Candle smoke was in the air. The doors were unlocked. I think we were expected and they left us no excuses to break stuff. They weren't generous with clues this time."

"They got the warning fast. Real fast. Let's do some checking."

"It's late, wizard."

"As they say, we can sleep all we want after we're dead."

There were fewer than forty people resident in, or even part of the commuting staff of, Castle Krief. It took only minutes to determine that neither Toby nor Dr. Wachtel had left. Only three people had gone since Babeltausque's initial discussion with Nathan Wolf. Colonel Gales, under orders from Her Majesty, had gone for yet another visit to the Thing hall. Inger's attendant Garyline had gone home to her mother for the night. The mother was dying. Garyline helped two married sisters care for the woman. Finally, there was Freider Fletcher, a Wesson soldier so dim he had trouble remembering how to tie his bootlaces, had gone off duty and had, presumably, pursued his habit of visiting the Twisted Wrench. He was there now, soaking up ale he could afford because small arrears payments had been given the men out of early tax returns coming in because of the Thingmeet.

"Must be sorcery," Wolf said.

"You might think. Or maybe somebody is lying."

"You think? We'll find out. *You* will find out. I'm sure you will."

"Right. Though I'm beginning to wonder why we bother."

"Because we don't have anything else. We can't go home. The family enemies in Itaskia have fixed it so we can't."

"There is that. Well. Our devoted associate Rhys passed along one more interesting nugget. We should look at that since we can't catch my favorite girl."

The sorcerer shivered. He had seen Haida Heltkler just that once, for just a few seconds. She was too old. But still she could get into his head for hours, haunting every thought, like a snatch of song getting stuck in his mind.

"And what would that be?" Nathan interrupted the developing train of obsession.

"Aral Dantice is back, too. He came in with the delegates from Sedlmayr."

"The gangster."

"Purported. And smuggler, and probably a lot more besides, including being a known associate of Michael Trebilcock and, probably, Trebilcock's designated successor."

"Shall I arrest him?"

"For what? Not to mention, he'll have ten friends handy for every one we do. And ours are friends only because everyone else is their enemy."

"Just checking." Wolf made the slightest head gesture toward the doorway.

More attentive than he had been, Babeltausque knew about the eavesdropper. He felt Toby's fluttering heartbeat. He said, "I've had all the adventure I can stand today. I'm going to turn in."

Wolf winked. "Good idea. The villains will still be there tomorrow. And we should be fresh for the Queen's business."

There was a faint, hasty scurry outside as Wolf headed for the door. Toby was getting sloppy. He had to be used up before he did something so blatant that Babeltausque would no longer be able not to take notice.

Toby and the old doctor had their share of guts, keeping up their espionage after being told outright that their treason was no secret.

...

Like the Blodgett girl, Aral Dantice vanished with no one seeing him go. He reappeared around midnight, Blodgett in tow. He was so exhausted he could barely argue rationally with the gatekeeper. He had several friends. He was smooth enough to get the gateman to show him to quarters set aside for him. He was a resource Ozora Mundwiller wanted kept close to hand. Friends could crowd in with him—and the girl could find herself a place on the floor in the servants' quarters. Ozora had made no arrangements for her.

She got that much consideration because Bight had a special interest and he was a kid folks could not help but like, including that gateman.

The girl chose to stick with the old men. Made no difference to her that the gateman considered that unseemly.

The gateman never reported their arrival. It was just another event late in a bust day. They went unnoticed till the crowd gathered for breakfast.

†

Chapter Twenty-Four:

AUTUMN, YEAR 1018 AFE:

Strange Attractors

Varthlokkur hugged Nepanthe long and hard and whispered a suggestion that she be prepared for a busy night. Then he hugged the children, one and all. Ethrian seemed surprised. He sounded honestly puzzled when he asked, "Where Sahmaman?"

"What is with you, Varth?" Nepanthe asked. "What happened?"

"Yeah," Scalza and Ekaterina chorused as though they had practiced to sync their timing. The girl startled everyone by demanding, "What did you do with that old sourpuss we sent off a couple months ago?"

Varthlokkur smiled broadly. "Presents are on the way. And treats. And fresh fruits and vegetables." Then he frowned. "Months?"

Yes. Months. She was right. Autumn was well along. "Oh, my!"

"Time and having fun?" Nepanthe proposed. "We'll do our own catching up while you're telling us about the mischief you've been into."

The Unborn had gone after delivering Varthlokkur. Ekaterina was visibly disappointed. The wizard scowled, then told her, "It had to go get the presents." And a quarter ton of fresh foodstuffs that would be appreciated by everyone. "I'll rest him after that." Though there was much more work that needed doing, quickly. "Beloved, we need to talk about a new hope that I've found for Ethrian."

On hearing his name, the boy asked, "Where is Sahmaman?" He made the question sound like an ordinary expression of curiosity.

Varthlokkur experimented. "She got lost, Ethrian, and we can't find her."

Ethrian's moment did not last long enough to let him process the wizard's response.

"What was that?" Nepanthe demanded.

"Me testing a hypothesis. I didn't get the response I hoped for. But any response is an outcome. As I said, some good did come from my absence. Mist is willing to have her mind experts help bring Ethrian back."

Nepanthe waited for the other shoe to drop.

"Of course. She's no altruist. She wants whatever Ethrian knows about… She is determined to go to war with…" He made swooping gestures.

Scalza got it instantly. He started to name the Star Rider, thinking it was a game. His sister snapped, "Quiet, Worm. We don't name that name anymore. Right, Uncle Varth?"

"Exactly right. How clever you are to grasp that so quickly, on so little evidence, Eka."

The girl was not embarrassed. Rather, the wizard got the impression that she was irked because she had let too much of her real self show.

That left him a little uncomfortable. It reminded him of a boy of long ago, who had seen his mother burned for having talents legally reserved to men.

There was one critical, dramatic difference. There was no trauma in Ekaterina's background to twist her into becoming a tormentor of the world.

Varthlokkur's life proceeded domestically, quietly, for an hour. He enjoyed a family meal. He wound down from the stresses of the world outside. He listened to the relatively minor concerns that stood in the stead of life and death issues here, proving that human beings would get worked up about something and that could be a runny nose if nothing of more consequence could be unearthed.

The children, Scalza in particular, had self-limited patience for obligations familial. The boy broke the rhythm to report, "Aunt Nepanthe found that Haroun man you were looking for. A while ago, actually. We wanted to let you know but you didn't leave instructions on how to get hold of you."

Varthlokkur set his teacup down, surveyed faces. Only Smyrena, who had grown dramatically and was walking, in his lap and sleeping right now, showed no degree of accusation. "Proof we never get too old to learn."

Several things had left him unable to think of something so basic, the greater being a centuries-deep habit of living alone. Add his determination to protect Nepanthe from the cruel eyes of reality, and there you went. The home folks could not contact him, whatever their need.

He said, "That won't happen again."

Ekaterina considered him with right eyebrow raised. His gaze slipped aside as he admitted, "No doubt I will find some other, more creative way to fail you all." He could not help noticing that the girl had begun to mature. She would not have the advantages her mother had but would be a stunner, even so. He thought of Babeltausque, which stirred a *frisson* of horror. That girl of the sorcerer's, Carrie Depar, was only slightly older than Eka—though, because she was who she was, Ekaterina might just ambush the beast.

Or, maybe not. Eka had no true concept of the ugliness prowling the broader world.

"Uncle?"

"Never mind. My head is on sideways today. I keep thinking about the awful things that can happen instead of the good. Which just makes me a sad old pessimist who doesn't deserve such wonderful people around him."

A younger pessimist grumbled, "Better put our old shoes on, sis. It smells like it's going to get deep."

Varthlokkur gawked. That kid was too damned young to be cynical or scatological. What was he doing when his aunt was not there to observe? The staff were not all refined people.

The wizard said, "Enough, then. Let's go spy on bin Yousif."

...

Radeachar brought a purpose-built transfer portal to Fangdred on Mist's behalf. Later, the monster delivered a sobbing Tang Shan, soaked in urine and feces. The Tervola suffered from a bone-deep terror of heights. He got passing out drunk right away. Twelve hours later, bathed, calmed by the lady of the castle, hung over, he began the work he had been sent to do. By then Varthlokkur and the Unborn had gone away on a secret journey.

The portal delivered was designed to put two people through in quick succession before it lay fallow for several minutes. That effect was the result of Lord Yuan's efforts to prevent outside tampering or espionage.

First to come through were Mist and a massive bodyguard. The man was painfully uncomfortable in the cold, thin air.

Nepanthe saw the remoteness of Mist's children nearly break the woman's heart, though she did a grand job of hiding her disappointment. In a private moment, though, she asked Nepanthe, "What can I do to kindle the affections of those two?"

Nepanthe was snuggling Smyrena. Scalza was hunched over his scrying bowl. Ekaterina had isolated Ethrian near the Winterstorm and was talking a mile a minute, yet shyly, probably saying nothing at great length. The women watched, Mist puzzled, Nepanthe pleased and hopeful. Ethrian sometimes talked back when no one was close enough to hear. Eka claimed he said nothing of substance even on good days. Mostly he asked what had become of Sahmaman.

Nepanthe thought there was more. Eka was guarding a special relationship jealously.

Nepanthe had become a devotee of the stroke theory. Stroke was in the family. It had claimed some elder relatives and an aunt. She was terrified for Ethrian. What if he was still a fully functional, thinking being imprisoned inside a brain and body that would not let him interact with the outside world?

The horror.

When she dwelt on that possibility she became dreadfully claustrophobic. If not soon distracted she became physically ill.

She answered Mist's question. "Your best tools are patience and perseverance, plus rigorous devotion—when your Imperial role allows you the time."

Nepanthe thought the recent outbreak of peace ought to free Mist for occasional personal moments.

Mist sighed. "Nepanthe, I miss Valther. Gods, I miss that man."

"As do I." Amazed because there were actual tears in the eyes of the most powerful woman in the world.

A bell clunked. The transfer portal hummed, then groaned. The Old Man stepped out, took two steps, froze, looked round in wonder. He remembered. He had come home.

The ancient's companion came through right behind him, stumbled into him, held him up, gawked himself. He turned slowly.

Nepanthe muttered, "Maybe we shouldn't have put that transfer thing in here with Varth's other stuff."

The most recent arrival focused on the Winterstorm, awed. Nepanthe thought he might start drooling.

Mist reassured her. "Be confident that he made sure surrendering to temptation can't possibly turn out well."

"Oh. Of course."

Ethrian finally looked past Ekaterina to see what the activity was all about. His face went blank and pale. Several seconds later it revealed signs of intense internal stress followed by an explosion of inner light.

Nepanthe gaped when Ethrian seized Eka's left hand, as though needing an anchor, and headed for the Old Man.

The Old Man sensed his approach, rounded toward the Winterstorm. Ethrian stared down into his eyes from scarcely two feet away.

The same light exploded inside the Old Man.

His companion joined the women. "This appears to have been the perfect strategy, Illustrious."

"It has begun well, Lord Kuo. Nepanthe? What do you think?"

Nepanthe's focus was on Ethrian's right hand. He had grasped Ekaterina's left so firmly that the girl was grimacing. She did not protest, however, and did not try to shake loose. If anything, she moved closer, possibly so she would be in the same visual frame as Ethrian, insofar as the newcomer could see.

Ethrian said something to the Old Man. Nepanthe was too far away to make it out but believed that he had expressed a complete and coherent thought.

Man and boy stared at one another. A slow smile formed on the Old Man's lips. He said something, too. Nepanthe thought he looked like a man who had just won a great victory, against impossible odds.

The joy in both soon faded. Neither was in a sound enough state to go on interacting at any more complex level.

Nepanthe's long sorrow burst through in a trickle of tears.

Mist told her, "Don't be sad. That was a huge success. It was proof that neither one of them has lost his past. Bringing them back may just require perseverance."

"I know. I understand. But the mother in me was hoping for more." And maybe something less, too.

Ekaterina had her hand back, now, and was rubbing life into still pale flesh.

Was Mist blind? She had not noticed the hands part at all.

The portal bell clunked. That had been a longer delay, that time, Nepanthe suspected.

The portal hummed like a big, happy beehive. Two men came through, disoriented and frightened. Nepanthe found both unfamiliar. Neither was Tervola. Both were frightened.

Mist explained, "These are the mind specialists. Let me go tell them how Ethrian and the Old Man reacted when they first saw one another."

Now they seemed to have forgotten one another. Lord Kuo had produced a shogi set. He and the Old Man were looking for a place to set up.

Nepanthe beckoned Ekaterina. "Did Ethrian hurt you? Let me see your hand."

The girl extended it. "It'll be all right. Maybe a bruise. It was worth it to see him light up like that, even if it was just for a minute."

"Yes." Not so sure. Wondering how she could be jealous of this child. "What did he say? It looked like he actually expressed a thought."

Ekaterina nodded, eyes a tad remote. "It was almost a conversation. He said, 'I swam. All the way. The dolphins helped. Sahmaman was waiting. Where did she go?' Then the Old Man smiled like he just got the most wonderful gift. He said, 'I'm so glad.' And then he said, 'I don't think she was ever more than a happy dream, even when I loved her.' Then the light went out and he was just confused till his friend came and said they should go play shogi."

"My," Nepanthe said. "Oh, my. I didn't know it was that big a breakthrough." She let go of Ekaterina's hand. "Ice will help keep the swelling down." And, "Your mother was right about bringing them together."

Warmth and shared happiness left the girl. She shoved her hand behind her, retreated to where Ethrian watched the drifting, glowing symbols in the Winterstorm.

"What just happened?" Nepanthe asked in a whisper, lost.

The bell on the portal clunked. Lord Yuan came through. His companion was several hundred pounds of equipment instead of another human being. Only his Empress seemed inclined to greet him.

Scalza let out a yelp. "Hey! Some excitement is about to start."

Nepanthe went to watch over the boy's shoulder.

...

The King Without a Throne had been within visual range of Al Rhemish for weeks, lurking, eavesdropping, staying out of sight as resolutely as he had while coming out of the Dread Empire. He knew he was being cautious at a level explicable only by raging paranoia.

He reminded himself that he was alive because he trusted nothing.

He was not pleased by what he saw.

When the Disciple was master there Al Rhemish had enjoyed a renaissance. Aqueducts had been built to bring water down from the southern hips of the Kapenrungs, into the great crater where the city sat. A lake, which became a broad moat—and, unfortunately, a cesspool—came to life in the deepest part of the basin. The crater walls had been terraced for crops or planted in orchards. The entirety had become green and gardenlike. Haroun had seen that at its peak.

Megelin bin Haroun had not seen fit to maintain what his enemy had created. The young king lacked all foresight.

Some orchards and farms had not yet gone to waste but that would happen considering the inadequate care shown the land and the aqueduct system. Given the rains and snows of the past year there was no excuse for Al Rhemish not being amply wet.

Haroun, looking nothing like any king Royalists would remember, grew increasingly bold. Cleanly shaven, facial tattoos restored, wearing a tiny glamour meant to make him look older, he made brief appearances in places outsiders would be expected to visit, such as the Most Holy Mrazkim Shrines. He listened attentively.

He stayed away from places where he could run into someone who knew him. He failed at that but did avoid recognition and confrontation. He heard himself mentioned once in a while, nostalgically, not in any "The king walks among us" context. In the main the commentary denigrated the fool who insisted that Haroun bin Yousif had murdered Magden Norath.

Haroun bin Yousif had to be dead. If Haroun bin Yousif was alive he would not be missing. He would be in the middle of everything, imposing his will. He would be breathing life into the Royalist cause. He would have ended Megelin's feckless reign. He would not have wasted a moment once he took the wicked Norath down.

Haroun did not run into it himself but there were veteran minds less fixed in attitude, a few old men who had been around for ages who recognized the possibilities of deeper concerns.

The amateur yammer smiths never plugged the Star Rider into their calculations. Nor did they consider the fact that the King Without a Throne had a wife who actually meant something to him.

No one expected to see Haroun in Al Rhemish so no one saw him.

An old hero named Beloul lived in Al Rhemish, amongst other retired heroes. Once a general, Beloul's pitiful pension and the bile of the current king forced him to live in an adobe hovel shared with an equally decrepit former aide and that man's middle-aged illegitimate daughter. Beloul had been one of Haroun's most devoted and brilliant commanders. He had been the same for Haroun's father before him. Haroun was amazed to see how poorly Beloul was treated but more amazed to find him still alive. He suppressed the urge to contact Beloul immediately.

There were few rootless men around Al Rhemish. The current regime discouraged the presence of the crippled of mind, body, or soul. Megelin found those people distasteful. Those who pandered to the king drove off anyone so dim or ill-starred as to have become disfigured in service to his cause.

Haroun liked his offspring less every day but not once did it ever occur to him to put the boy aside.

He made quite sure that neither Megelin nor his henchmen were watching before he went to visit Beloul.

Trouble was, he could not shake the fear that he was being watched himself. He suffered this constant, creepy paranoid certainty that never discovered a fleck of sustenance. It went way back. Random and seldom during his flight from Lioantung, lately it had become a fixture, and much more aggressive. It had to be a product of his insecurities, grown fatter after the Norath incident and his wastrel spending of good luck during the sojourn at Sebil el Selib. Not once, even employing all his shaghûn skills in the privacy of the erg, had he apprehended any genuine observer.

In bleak humor he wondered if God Himself was not the watcher.

Reason suggested that a genuine observer would have to be Old Meddler but the sense of being watched antedated that point—the encounter with Magden Norath—when the revenant would have garnered the interest of that old devil. Before that Haroun bin Yousif was dead to the world.

One cool evening, while street traffic was heavy, bin Yousif went to the general's door. A woman answered, which rattled him totally. Women did not do such things. They did not show themselves to strangers. Their men folk did not allow it. But… Here she was just another fellow in the household?

Beloul and El Mehduari must have been poisoned by outside ways while they were in exile.

The woman looked him straight in the eye, bold as any warrior confident of his prowess. She intimidated him. He was amazed.

"Well? Can you speak? No?" She began to close the door.

"Wait. I've come to consult the general."

"The general is retired. He doesn't contribute anymore. He isn't allowed to contribute. In return for his silence we are provided a stipend sufficient to hold starvation at bay. I will not jeopardize that. Go away. Consult someone else."

"Beloul ed-Adirl! Present yourself!"

She had rattled him that much. And now she was about to make him hurt.

"Admit him, Lalla," came from the gloom beyond the woman, in a voice like dead insects being rubbed across one another.

The woman did as instructed, eyes locked with Haroun's, assuring him that he faced plenty of pain if he gave her an excuse.

Wow. Never had he encountered anyone whom he *knew*, instantly, was as hard as this woman. She might be as hard as him.

The setting sun had been in Haroun's eyes. He entered the house as good as blind, but eventually did make out an amorphous shape amongst cushions against a far wall, too small to be Beloul or El Mehduari—though, at this remove, he surely remembered them larger than life.

That shape extended a pseudopod, gestured, suggesting he take a seat. "I have heard your voice before. Who are you?"

Beloul became more clear as Haroun's eye adapted. He did not like what he saw. Beloul in his mind was Beloul thirty years ago, powerful, confident, a champion fit to contend with the Scourge of God. This Beloul…

"You do not know me?"

"I cannot see you. These eyes betray me."

That might explain the darkness, some, though not for the fierce woman.

"You rode with my father. You were too indulgent with me and my brothers when we were boys. You're still too indulgent toward my son."

"Do you have a name?" There was an edge to the general's voice, now, as the old steel surfaced.

The woman rested a hand on the hilt of the curved dagger at her left hip. Haroun was sure she knew how to use it.

"I do. I won't say it here, in this city."

"Now I know you. Come closer. I have never conversed with a ghost."

That did not reassure Haroun. Did Beloul want him inside grabbing range? It would take but an instant for the woman to… He stepped forward. The old man swept a hand at him, hard, sure it would meet no resistance. "Ouch!" He began massaging his wrist.

"Damned solid for a spook," the woman observed. "He must be a demon instead."

Beloul chuckled, a dry old man's laugh. "You aren't far wrong."

"Would this be who I think it must be, then, Uncle?"

"Yes, Lalla. The revenant who untangled the curse of Magden Norath. Be seated, youngster. Tell me tales of the years. Tell me what brings you here in my end times."

The woman asked, "Is there anyone I should inform? Someone I should summon here?"

"That will wait. Let's hear his story first."

Haroun settled onto a ragged reed mat. Nothing lay beneath that but dirt, which would become mud during any persistent rain. He faced Beloul. The man had been a personal hero when Haroun was a boy. He was saddened by the way time and Megelin had treated Beloul.

Haroun did note that Beloul offered him no honor as king.

He was just another man, possibly not in good odor—though Beloul was not one to be seduced away from the grand Royalist strategy by side issues. Beloul owned a conscience that was unique.

Had Beloul been making ultimate decisions back when, today's world might wear a different face—though that would in no way resemble the world that Beloul had hoped to see. Old Meddler, the Pracchia, and Shinsan would have sucked the blood out of Hammad al Nakir and the West despite Beloul. The Disciple had been just another torment.

That water had sunk into the sands. The world that existed now was the world in which everyone had to struggle, including every survivor on the other side.

After some silence the general asked, "Well? Why are you here?"

"Honestly? I don't know. It was a destination. I was looking for something that I can't name. I have these grand ideas, but…" He paused to collect himself. "I vanished when I did because the Dread Empire imprisoned me. They got caught up in a huge war with a revenant devil and forgot me. I escaped. I made my way across the entirety of Shinsan. Getting back drove me obsessively. But once I got through I had no idea what to do. All that time buried alive changed me. I am no longer the man that I was."

"It *has* been a while since Norath went down."

"Yes. And that just happened. It was an unexpected opportunity. I didn't think. I acted. Afterward, I still had no plan, for a long time, till I thought that I might find what I needed in Al Rhemish. I'm here, now, and now I wonder, what next?"

"Uhm."

"I'm a lost soul, Beloul. I'm alive. I'm very good at staying alive. Barring Old Meddler, I'm maybe the best there ever was at that. But what do I do with the life I've so devoutly preserved? Choices I made, that led to my becoming an unwilling guest of the Tervola, cost me my claims on most everything else. I can't be king again. Megelin is king. I made him king so I could run off on my own."

"You're right. Megelin is king. And he is a bad king. Only those parasites getting fat because of his incompetence would argue if you demanded your crown back."

"I don't want to do that. Are you saying I should?"

The door opened, apparently on its own. Night had collected outside, but a pinkish glow backlighted those few buildings that could be discerned through the unexpected opening. Looking over his shoulder, Haroun thought there must be a fireworks show happening on the far side of Al Rhemish.

Catlike, the woman Lalla glided in that direction armed with a massive tulwar that Haroun had missed completely.

She was, for sure, one dangerous being. Yet, though the old man mentioned it, Haroun never quite got her name.

There was a powerful flash in the doorway. The deadly woman yelped and threw the tulwar down. It shone an angry scarlet.

The wizard Varthlokkur stepped inside, across the overheated blade. His hands were up, palms forward, shoulder high. "I intend no harm." He spoke with an odd rhythm, inflexion, and pronunciation.

Of course. He was speaking his own boyhood dialect.

The dialects of Hammad al Nakir all descended from the language spoken in Ilkazar. The written form remained unchanged.

Beloul recognized the wizard. He kept his hands in sight. "To what do I owe the honor of this unsolicited home invasion?"

"This one is needed elsewhere. He has a critical matter to attend. I came to move him before one whose name is no longer mentioned flies in to end the threat."

What might have been a fireworks erupted outside, in the distance. The wizard glanced back. "A diversion. Rumor will blame the master shaghûn who destroyed the wicked Magden Norath. He is here and he has the righting of wrongs in mind. That will distract everyone."

Haroun declared, "But I was responsible…"

"I watched. General. Let it be no secret that this man was here. You sent him away. Let the fear of him rage amongst the wicked. Encourage those inclined to do so to waste time and treasure hunting the ghost."

Beloul responded, "He will be beyond discovery?"

"He will abide with the living dead."

Haroun observed, "That doesn't sound encouraging."

Varthlokkur said, "You will meet outsiders like yourself. Most will be friendly."

Haroun realized that he had begun to drift mentally. The wizard had done something to weaken his will and relax him. He even lacked much curiosity about why this was happening—though he did wonder how his will and curiosity had been suborned so easily.

The woman eased her dagger into her left hand, fluid as a panther preparing for a kill rush. The skin on her right palm had begun to blister. She crouched slightly, to get more spring into her legs. The general shook his head almost imperceptibly.

Haroun caught the exchange. Varthlokkur did not. The wizard had come within a heartbeat of sharing the fate of Magden Norath and missed it entirely.

…

The Unborn made it as far as the high Kapenrungs in Tamerice, carrying two men. Fatigue claimed the monster there. It set them down barely in time to avoid disaster.

Catastrophe in a different mask began to gather almost immediately.

Varthlokkur and bin Yousif grumbled and created a camp while the Unborn, a sickly mix of bloody orange and rotten fruit brown, hovered and shivered as though freezing. The thing inside closed its eyes for the first time in the wizard's recollection. He was immensely irked by the delay. Old Meddler would miss the excitement at Al Rhemish only if he had gone into hibernation. Its purpose had been to catch that villain's attention and fire his curiosity, to get him to expose himself, hopefully rendering himself more traceable, while sparking his interest in discovering what was going on inside a Fangdred gone rigorously opaque to spying eyes. There was so much more that Varthlokkur needed to do to convert the fortress into the ideal death trap.

But he was stranded out here in a different wilderness, nearly as cold as that at home, with a companion who remained unconvinced that he had an obligation to participate in the coming struggle.

Haroun might slide away if Varthlokkur's attention lapsed. He might even try to eliminate the threat implicit in the wizard's knowledge of what had happened to Prince Gaia-Lange and Princess Carolan, before he did his slide.

Or maybe neither of them would escape the tribesmen slowly surrounding them. They were not the friendly sort of Marena Dimura common in Kavelin's mountains.

These people were, for all their determined isolation, not wholly ignorant of the modern century. They knew what a pink globe in the sky meant. They knew those concerned about survival exercised extreme care around the Empire Destroyer. They failed to be sufficiently intimidated, though, to select the more sensible course and just stay away. Young warriors had to show their courage. Being young, naturally, they disdained the obvious exaggerations about the Empire Destroyer.

There were sorcerers in their tribe, seen every day. Those old frauds were not scary. They could barely make milk curdle, and that took time when it was cold out.

So half a dozen youngsters lost their hair, including beards and eyebrows, as they prepared to rush the outlanders. Lucky boys. They ran into Varthlokkur's wards before Haroun's. The latter would have granted an opportunity to participate in a mass funeral.

The elders ordered everyone back. The outsiders ignored the tribesmen, then, while they extended the same courtesy in return.

The Unborn needed two days to recover. Thereafter it leapfrogged them, fifty miles to a man, wilderness site to wilderness site, but making a common camp during times of rest. Varthlokkur tried to sell Haroun on a scheme that he would not explain in concrete form, saying only that there was an evil as old and foul as smallpox that needed extirpation. He would not name that evil's name.

His own non-plans aborted, bin Yousif did agree to withhold any refusal till he had spoken with other members of the cabal.

He determined the identity of the unnamed target quickly enough. "This sounds like a mirror image of that old devil's schemes."

"That's true."

"But his plots reach inside institutions. The Pracchia was everywhere, inside everything, like a plague. To be a real reflection you'd have to create reliable turncoats amongst his associates."

The wizard nodded. "Also true, and unlikely to happen—with one exception. But there *are* some living men we know he's touched. Your son and your father-in-law, for example. Neither may signify anymore. Neither seems to be anything but a pawn. Neither amounts to a mile marker on the road to the heart of darkness anymore."

"Let me think about them."

"You will participate?"

"You have the best answer I can give. I'll cooperate provisionally. Where are you taking me? Somewhere way up north, obviously. You haven't told me who you want me to see, either. Why should I take you on faith?"

"What I don't tell you, you can't tell anyone else."

Bin Yousif nodded. "I see."

"I hope so."

"Or maybe I don't."

The wizard knew he had to give up something. "Our destination is the Wind Tower at Fangdred."

"I remember the fortress. I remember the Candareen. I was a festering young fool, then."

Varthlokkur smiled.

"But that fool was blessed by Fortune. He survived to become this old fool of today. I look forward to seeing what changes time has scribbled on that monument to my youthful indiscretion."

"You're going to be disappointed. You're remembering another mountain and another fortress, Ravenkrak. Which was on top of the Candareen. I don't believe you've ever seen Fangdred, which balances precariously on top of El Kabar."

Bin Yousif's recollections were confused. He saw nothing even remotely familiar when the Unborn brought him to Fangdred, and that was not just because of the aerial perspective. The wizard was right. He had not been here before.

Unlike most of Radeachar's clients, bin Yousif enjoyed the aerial view. He was less comfortable inside Fangdred, with all those people, few of whom he knew and some of whom had put the hell into the last few years of his life.

Wandering through the castle, followed by the whelp of the grand she-king of the east, barked at if he thought about touching something, Haroun decided that he really wanted to get on to the next phase of this scheme. Unless he was clever enough to slip out and vanish.

Even after having been briefed he did not completely understand. These crazies wanted to eliminate the perpetual world plague sometimes called the Old Meddler. Laudable ambition, but one that stood no chance of attainment. Might as well aspire to resurrect Ilkazar in all its cruel glory, or to throw a saddle on a whirlwind.

The wizard had let fall the fact that it was hard to track Haroun inside Hammad al Nakir. He just might make sure that was even harder once he got back there.

He thought he would be headed there soon. These people did not show much of their hands but he had no need to see much to penetrate their thinking. He knew how such minds worked. He had one himself.

He might even see Yasmid again.

He looked forward to that.

...

Inger indulged in a quick final consultation with Josiah, Nathan, and Babeltausque. That morning, early, the news was uniformly bright. Virulent factions had yet to develop. Delegates were paying for what they wanted. Taxes were being collected. The locals yielded theirs up with smiles. Prosperity threatened. Indications were, most of those gathered for the Thingmeet really did want to abort any return of the chaos that had prevailed after the disappearance of the King.

"Stop fussing," Josiah told her. "You'll do fine. Just step out and tell them what you told me. They'll give you your say."

She eyed Fulk, half-asleep in his little chair, dressed in clothes that had been fashionable when Gaia-Lange wore them long ago. There had been no money for anything new.

Josiah went on being reassuring. "I'll be with him. He doesn't have to do anything but show himself. If nobody makes a fuss he won't get distressed and suffer an attack. How is he now?" The Colonel looked hard at Doctor Wachtel.

"You are correct, Colonel. I gave him his medication."

The old man kept answering his calling despite the stress of being a known foe lurking near Fulk and Inger. Inger firmly believed him incapable of violence. She was correct. Wachtel would do no physical harm to forward his politics.

Gales dropped to a knee before Fulk, made tiny adjustments to the boy's ruff. "Remember what to do?"

The boy nodded. He was a little scared and a lot nervous, but serious and determined as only a small child can be.

"Good. So. People. Let's do it."

Babeltausque went first, as an intimidator. The rumble of a hundred conversations began to diminish.

Nathan slipped away to circulate and eavesdrop.

Out Fulk went, followed by Gales, then by Inger. The boy took his position, in view of everyone. He did not show the distress that Josiah had feared—in part because his eyes were not good. He could not make out most of the faces turned his way.

Inger stepped to the rostrum, released a small, near-whimper. Her vision was excellent. She saw every face just fine. Many belonged to men who wished her ill fortune. She began her speech disconnected from its content and intent as she tried to execute Babeltausque's advice about meeting the eyes of every audience member at least once.

She did fine till she came to the delegation from Sedlmayr.

Her jaw locked.

Her body froze.

She could get out nothing but an inarticulate sort of squeak. That went on and on and on.

A grumble began, delegates asking what had happened.

Gales needed half a minute to get it. His eyes were not prepared to see the impossible.

Ozora Mundwiller donned a hard, cold, smug smile. She held two pair, kings and knaves. Two Bragis, plus Michael Trebilcock and Aral Dantice. Not to mention a selection of queens.

Babeltausque could not tear his gaze away from the Heltkler girl.

How had those people gotten in unnoticed? Though there were few guards, none of them instructed to look out for dead kings, somebody should have noticed something.

The noise kept growing because Inger kept staring, ashen, a mouse frozen by the stare of a viper. Fulk began to get scared. Gales oozed a step nearer Babeltausque. "We're in the deep shit now but don't do anything unless we're attacked."

Babeltausque recognized only that one face. He felt the tension of the moment, though. Things were not going according to plan. Perilously not. "Got you. But we need to do something."

A tall man left the Sedlmayrese. He shed a massive travel duster and the limp and slouch that had helped conceal his identity. Eyes on Inger, he came forward. Others began to recognize him. By the time he joined his wife pandemonium shook the Thing hall.

†

Chapter Twenty-Five:

LATE AUTUMN, YEAR 1018 AFE:

Desert of Despair

Megelin's favored henchmen were the twin functionaries Mizr and Misr the Fatherless, which they preferred to abd-Megelin, or servant-of-Megelin. Lesser Royalist lights had begun to distance themselves, softly and cautiously. Rumor said the twins were older than Al Rhemish itself. They had changed names and faith as often as the city had. They were archetypically venal, with a knack for charming anyone close by. For no rational reason Megelin trusted them above all the other blackhearts around him.

Megelin's current favor was, largely, extorted. Mizr had bumbled in while the king was conferring with a being commonly considered mythical. The twins were not harsh in their demands, though, because Megelin's friend was without pity or remorse. There was no escaping his farseeing eye or far-reaching wrath.

It took only a few words from that entity to convince the twins that they ought to become extensions of the will of King Megelin. Naturally, both kept their fingers crossed while their oaths were being extorted.

Misr and Mizr were there again when the entity came demanding details of events the night the monster Radeachar visited.

What little Megelin had to report he had gathered only because he feared that he might be asked. He did not himself care what happened on the old men side of town.

Even the stupid understood that the monster had wanted to be noticed. Even the dim knew which puppeteer dangled the Unborn. What even the brilliant could not fathom was, why Al Rhemish?

Megelin suggested, "It was all about confusion. Meant to cause exactly the disorders we're beginning to see now."

"Layers," the ancient mused. "There will be layers, more and deeper, some planned minutely, some improvised, some coming to life despite never having been foreseen. What else happened that night?"

Megelin's seekers had found nothing more solid than a thin rumor that his father had been seen over where the antique soldiers still hung on, consuming resources and informing the world of all the better ways they would do things if they were still in charge.

This rumor meant no more than scores just like it heard almost every day. Hammad al Nakir was nostalgic. Hammad al Nakir had forgotten the bad times. Hammad al Nakir wanted its old king back. Hammad al Nakir was trying to conjure him back from the realm of the dead.

"Fantasy or not, pursue that," the Star Rider ordered. "We need to know what that sorcerer was doing while his familiar was entertaining idiots."

The world shifted into an instant of total disorientation. Megelin and the twins were unsure why. The Star Rider's admonition became a driving, throbbing obsession. They began to torment already touchy subjects more vigorously, trying to ferret out facts they might not recognize if they found them. They made plenty of new enemies.

The Empire Destroyer's diversion not only fulfilled its design, it sparked ferocious resentments that had fermented quietly for years beneath the despair blanketing Al Rhemish.

...

Yasmid let Habibullah lead her to the meeting place. He had collected not only Elwas al-Souki and her favorites but Ibn Adim al-Dimishqi and his cronies. Al-Dimishqi was less obnoxious now that he was consumed by his audit but he remained a storm on the horizon. Inclusion in her conspiracy had not changed his ground state attitude.

The men seemed grim today. The news must be awful.

She was not well. Every morning was miserable anymore.

She rejected the obvious explanation fiercely but each day made that a grander challenge at self-delusion.

Al-Souki's stony visage collapsed into frightened concern. "Shining One! You're so pale! You should have refused us."

"Habibullah tells me I have no choice. I'm breathing. I have my obligations. Let's get to it. What is the bad news?"

Elwas scowled at Habibullah. His anger failed to intimidate the old man, who said, "If our Lady's health concerns you so much I suggest that you waste no time."

Yasmid considered Habibullah's rigid back. He was distressed. He had begun to suspect, she feared. He was too close. He must have asked the right questions in the right places. A stone tossed into a pond might vanish but surface ripples would still report its existence and passage.

Habibullah might not work out exactly who, when, or where, but ripples aplenty remained to tell him how.

Elwas said, "Habibullah gathered us because exciting things are happening in Al Rhemish. The sorcerer Varthlokkur sent his familiar to prance across the night sky there. Everyone believes the prodigy was a diversion. From what remains obscure. Nobody died. Nobody vanished. Nothing disappeared. If spells were cast or charms were laid on, that was done too subtly to be detected."

"All interesting but important to me now, how? And why?"

Habibullah stated the obvious first. "Because Varthlokkur was behind it. Boldly. Yanking Megelin's beard in public. It has to mean something serious. Varthlokkur never involves himself with Hammad al Nakir."

"True enough."

Imam al-Dimishqi said, "It signifies only because a grand minion of evil hopes we will waste time and energy worrying about what he is up to. While we sift shadows he will be up to something else. He has done whatever he set out to do that night."

Elwas said, "Odd though it might sound coming from me, I agree with Ibn Adim."

Yasmid demanded, "Because?" Elwas never agreed with al-Dimishqi. She suppressed the misery in her gut.

"We have friends in Al Rhemish. They report a brief-lived, soft rumor that Haroun bin Yousif visited Beloul ed-Adirl that night. The rumor didn't last. Nothing else happened. But our friends promise that a mystery man did visit the old general, then another stranger came and took him away. The second visitor might have been the Empire Destroyer."

Al-Dimishqi chuckled. "No doubt he had exactly the right number of eyes, ears, arms, and legs."

Elwas made a two-handed gesture of accession. "The evidence is indeed that slim, Shining One. It is equally thin for a suggestion that Old Meddler turned up for a confab with Megelin right after. There are supposed eyewitnesses who won't talk."

Yasmid chose not to speak until she had had time to think. Then, "He visited Megelin directly?"

"Probably, but not for sure. It could be a rumor planted by somebody who doesn't like him. But there's definitely evidence that there were other visits. Megelin may be in the villain's thrall."

Al-Dimishqi agreed.

So even the fanatics now doubted El Murid's angel.

How she wished that monster, the Star Rider, could be extinguished. There could be no truth more powerful than a reappearance of the angel while Old Meddler lay dead in the dust.

"Intriguing news, all of this," she conceded. "But is it really the sea change Habibullah predicted when he dragged me from my sickbed?"

Al-Souki said, "We need you as the One Who Speaks for God."

Suddenly, it felt like they were looking inside her, tapping into her thoughts and fears. Her stomach refused to let her be. She had a hard time giving a damn what anyone thought right now.

Past everything, and all the impossible morning misery—she was too damned old!—she was terrified. She could not hide this much longer. The world would then get very ugly indeed.

She rose. "If that is all..."

"That's not everything," Habibullah said. "We could have saved that till you felt better. The truth is… Only Elwas has heard this. The news came after I sent the call to assemble."

Yasmid settled again, with a sigh. "This is the part that I won't like. Right?"

Habibullah nodded. "This is that part. In trying to catch the ghost of Haroun bin Yousif, and to find out what Varthlokkur was up to, Megelin pushed a little too hard."

Yasmid said, "There was an uprising."

"Yes. It's still going on."

"What happened to Megelin?" Whatever else, he was her only child.

"I don't know. The storm had only just begun when the news left Al Rhemish. It didn't look good for those in charge, though. I should know more soon."

Yasmid looked around. Each man showed mixed feelings, on her behalf and his own.

Megelin being pulled down should be good for everyone but Megelin and Old Meddler. No one was set to replace the King. No one knew who an eligible successor might be. Everyone had gotten sick of succession squabbles when the Royalists were still in exile. Once Haroun named Megelin to succeed him the question had gone away. The boy had been young. He had had time to produce an heir. He was still young enough but seemed determined to avoid that royal responsibility—along with most of the rest.

Yasmid asked, "My part in this will be what?" She suspected that Habibullah wanted to make her the next king.

She giggled, startling everyone. Habibullah considered her with narrowed eyes. She drove the hysteria down into the darkness. "You have given me a lot to digest. Permit me to return to my rest. I will say something the moment I'm sure that I've put together a reasoned, rational argument." As an afterthought, she added, "I'll have to talk to my father, too."

That, evidently, was a good thing to say.

Habibullah began to shoo the men out.

Al-Dimishqi would not be shooed. "Lady, I have a matter that needs discussion as soon as possible."

…

Yasmid sat down again. "Adim, I presume this is occasioned by your work in my father's tent."

"Yes, Lady." Al-Dimishqi glanced at Habibullah, who did nothing to conceal his displeasure. "At the risk of offering offense, I'd like to keep this between us two. If you want to include others afterward that is your prerogative."

Ah. So. He wanted Habibullah out of the way. That rattled Yasmid. What was he up to?

She stifled the fear, put on her woman-of-iron mask. "It has to do with something you found over there?"

"It does, Lady. It goes beyond venality and criminal behavior."

"Very well. Step outside, Habibullah. And please don't eavesdrop. But stay close enough to respond if I scream."

"As you wish." The old man showed her the ghost of a bow. He knew she would pass on whatever al-Dimishqi told her.

"He won't go far," Yasmid promised al-Dimishqi after Habibullah stepped out.

"You misjudge me badly, Lady. This truly is a critical matter."

"Please be quick, then. I am feeling…" More than just awful. She was entirely alone with a man who did not approve of her at all. There were no witnesses to her propriety, not even a slave.

"Yes. Of course. I don't want to intrude upon your illness. This, then, is the matter. We found a cache of moldy registers from the earliest days of the movement. Most are in your father's hand. A few were recorded by your mother. And there are two courtesy of the Scourge of God."

"Wow!" She was amazed. Those might be important historical documents.

"Indeed, wow. Though the registers are in bad shape. They'll be more valuable as keepsakes than as records—though I did see some interesting short notes on daily thoughts that did not get into your father's formal writings."

"Did these records produce some remarkable revelation? Or something painfully heretical? Is that your point?"

"Not at all, Lady. What was decipherable only reinforced my faith. The real matter I want to bring up is, what happened to the thunder amulet that your father got from his angel?"

Yasmid frowned, frankly puzzled. She had steeled herself for a confrontation. Al-Dimishqi was rambling about something more legend than… "Oh! *That* amulet! That amulet? The one he could use to call down the lightning or make boulders fall from the sky? That turned the tide at the Five Circles and on the salt pan?"

"That amulet, Lady. Yes."

"It was lost."

"Lady?"

"He lost it, Adim. For real and forever, to a western soldier after he went down outside Libiannin. The plunderers took him for just another dead warrior. My father spent years trying to find it again. He failed. Even his angel couldn't trace it. You'd think *he* could have found it if it had survived. So it must have been broken up and melted down. But why are you asking about it?"

Al-Dimishqi seemed stricken. "The journal… Is all that really true? I was sure I'd stumbled onto something that could change everything."

"You may have, just not the way you hoped. Find out more. But I can tell you this: the real amulet would not have been missed by the thieves who went through my father's stuff. It was gold and weighed a good half a pound. And it had gemstones set in it. The angel didn't want it to be missed."

Al-Dimishqi sagged. "I am heartbroken. I was so excited. I was sure we were about to bring a powerful tool back to the holy struggle."

Yasmid winced, pushed the pain down. "There may have been something. It might even have been given to my father by his angel. My father may have come to believe that it was the original amulet. I know he hated that thing. He sometimes risked disaster so he didn't have to use it… After what happened outside Libiannin—another one of his narrow, miraculous escapes from a situation that should have killed him—my father deluded himself about a lot of things. So Habibullah tells me. He witnessed most of my father's descent. I did not. I was elsewhere. So talk to Habibullah. He may be able to put you on to the real story."

Al-Dimishqi's shoulders slumped further. "I apologize for wasting your time. I will go, now."

"No waste, Adim. Never. You give cause to reflect on secret history. And… Perhaps you did come across something important that you didn't recognize because you jumped to this conclusion. Do keep after it. And do keep me posted."

"As you will, so shall it be."

Yasmid watched him go, hoping that all this would keep him from thinking about her health long enough for her and Habibullah to find a strategy that would get her through this intact.

It would take a miracle. If one occurred it would be the old man's doing. She was capable of nothing but panic anymore.

...

Yasmid was back in her private audience, Habibullah attending, now with women watching from beyond hearing. She said, "I have to go get father's opinion now that I opened my big mouth." She was badly distracted after her discussion with al-Dimishqi. Had Haroun gotten hold of something of great potency? Had finding that been his true purpose for coming to Sebil el Selib?

Her stomach taunted her anew.

"You will, yes. But that is a necessary gesture, the more so because we have declared the Disciple almost recovered." Habibullah watched closely. "Sharper questions would be asked if you did not consult him." He knew al-Dimishqi had rattled her somehow.

"I know. But his advice is useless. He doesn't realize that years have passed. If we bring him out to show off he'll ruin everything by refusing to recognize that the world has changed."

"True. But you have to go through the motions. He had to go through motions himself even when he was his most popular. Those who place their lives and honor at your disposal have expectations and have the right to have them. If you fail to meet those expectations you could face what seems to have caught up with Megelin."

Yasmid grunted, not because she agreed but because her breakfast was making a bid to return.

She controlled it yet again.

So softly she barely heard him, her lifelong friend-companion-guard-worshipper asked, "Is there something you need to tell me?"

He knew.

How long before everyone did? How long till the bad end came?

With marvelous caution Habibullah observed, "All is not lost. You are a married woman."

Who had a husband only she loved, whom her people all wanted to stay dead.

She shuddered, afraid.

"We will cope," Habibullah promised.

She could not believe him. Her hours were numbered.

...

"I'm just not comfortable," Mist said. "But there is no undoing what's already done." She tried to follow three things at once: Scalza manipulating his scrying bowl so he could spy on people at Sebil el Selib; Ekaterina and Ethrian, just staying close enough to warm one another with their presence; and Haroun bin Yousif, who was straining to follow developments in Al Rhemish. Skilled as he had become, Scalza had difficulties due to distance, and had no sound. When they did anything other than vegetate Ethrian and Eka usually only observed the shogi wars. Bin Yousif spent a lot of time muttering and being confused. He was not pleased about the troubles in Al Rhemish but could not form a solid opinion because he did not understand them, either. Nor was he even a little relaxed in the company of so many strangers, some of whom had held him prisoner not so long ago.

Mist was uncomfortable with his presence. Varthlokkur had not been forthcoming on how bin Yousif fit his own form of the Plan.

There were several of those, puffing along in parallel. The upside was, if Old Meddler knocked one down others would keep on rolling. The downside was, she and Varthlokkur kept tripping over one another's feet.

...

Haroun concluded that Varthlokkur was right. Most of these people *were* supposed to be dead. He had been shocked to learn that some were still alive, Ragnarson in particular—though he had gone off to create excitement in Kavelin.

Despite explanations from Varthlokkur and the eastern empress, Haroun remained unsure where he stood. Mainly, he did not understand why they were so determined. Why try to thwart the storm?

The Star Rider was weather. Historical and social weather. You planned ahead and did what you could to endure. Prepared, you could ride it out. You did not tempt fate by trying to control the storm.

Old Meddler was no deity but he was the closest thing Haroun ever saw. The God of his childhood was a god of storms.

He could never be comfortable around so many people, in such a tight space. He did especially poorly with children. They recalled times he would rather forget.

The insanity in Al Rhemish was most worrisome. Angry people kept destroying things, venting frustration caused by years of incompetence. Men of standing kept their heads down and their mouths shut. Beloul barricaded his door once Lalla eliminated outside evidence that the place was occupied by a hero of the old days. He had chosen to weather the storm, then live with whatever coalesced under subsequent rainbows.

Haroun did not miss the parallels between Beloul's attitude and his own.

...

There were no hours of the day when either Mist, Lord Ssu-ma, Lord Kuo, or Lord Yuan were not engaged in advancing some fraction of the eastern plan. Lord Yuan worked harder than any of the others. Their scheme was more complex than Varthlokkur's, which risked little more than self and family, huge enough in his mind but trivial by rational comparison.

Another transfer portal arrived, again by means of the Unborn. It would connect to the transfer stream but none of its parts would be tainted by having passed through that poorly understood realm. So Lord Yuan had decreed.

Grinding her teeth against secret panic, Mist instructed Lord Yuan to key that portal to the life harmonics of Lord Kuo and the Old Man so they could escape but no one and nothing wicked could follow.

A third portal arrived. Mist had it keyed to Nepanthe and Ethrian. Ethrian and the Old Man were her most valuable assets. Scalza and Ekaterina were precious but did not have the power to save an empire. Their mother had to consider countless millions of lives.

She did not suppress maternal emotion indefinitely. When Radeachar delivered the next escape portal she had it keyed to her children. The elderly Tervola executed his instructions sullenly, making it clear that he thought her mind was clouded by personal concerns.

She had the escape portals provided with secondary keys that would allow selected others to use them if their primaries were not. Those designated as secondary did not see much hope for themselves if Old Meddler did launch a sudden thunder and lightning assault.

The mind specialists worked hours as long as anyone. They concluded that forming a useful information inventory necessitated rooting secrets out of minds other than those of Ethrian and the Old Man. There were three surviving witnesses to Old Meddler's raid on the Wind Tower. The Old Man was the least reliable. The others were both available.

Varthlokkur came close to physical confrontation with Mist when those two proposed the research. He wanted no return to that night's emotional storms. The Empress demurred.

Once again Varthlokkur was prepared to round on his allies and chuck everything down a well in order to protect his wife. As he defined protection. In truth, he was striving to appease his own insecurities.

His memories of that night were not pleasant. He thought that Nepanthe had suppressed hers. He did not want them resurrected.

But she snapped, "Varth, stop that right now! Am I an infant? You wouldn't treat Eka or Scalza with the kind of condescension you show me."

Startled, "Darling…"

"Stop! I made it past my fourth birthday. Yes. I'm more emotional than some. I get upset about things that don't bother other people. But I am a big girl." She touched his cheek gently. She did appreciate his concern. "I remember more than I want. But some of it might be useful—if I let the experts dig."

"But…"

"Stop! I won't hear any more nonsense."

He suppressed a flood of the blistering, unreasoning rage that had swept him to the brink with King Bragi. That anger, unrestrained, was the reason today's ugly world had come to be.

He clamped his jaw, went on with his work. He spent time with the mental specialists as needed. They proved deft at panning nuggets he did not know lay hidden in the lowest sands of his mind.

He left Fangdred, though, so he would not have to watch while Nepanthe endured the process.

He was sure he would lose his composure if he stayed.

He took bin Yousif with him.

Chapter Twenty-Six:

Late Autumn 1018 AFE:

Beyond the Resurrection

Ragnarson bellowed, "Silence!"

He had the voice of command still, and it was loud, yet the effect was neither quick nor comprehensive.

"I will have you beaten if you don't stop running your mouths."

Those people knew he was not given to idle threats. They knew, too, that there was no precedent for him doing anything of the sort. Only…

Only this was, clearly, not the man whose arrogance had driven him to disaster beyond the Mountains of M'Hand. This man had been chastened and tempered.

He had a harder feel, and, maybe, a new disdain for past tolerance. He might even have developed a streak of cruelty.

He had been in the thrall of the Dread Empire. Only the shell might be Bragi Ragnarson now. Best not to irk the possible monster concealed inside. Though, still, he was just one man.

Even so, the Thing hall so quietened that the proverbial pin would have sounded like a clash of cymbals. It seemed, almost, that everyone had stopped breathing.

In that desolation of sound a small voice asked, "Daddy?"

The tiny question had more impact on Kavelin than did all the murder and maneuver of the year just passed. Bragi Ragnarson, startled, looked down at the boy in the old-fashioned clothes, who looked back with puzzled hope.

The hard man changed. He scooped the boy up, settled him onto his left hip. He peered into the Sedlmayrese delegation, beckoned Kristen, shook his head slightly when Dahl Haas started to follow.

Ragnarson settled his grandson on his other hip, then declared, "The bullshit will stop." That sounded certain as death. That made it plain who would be in charge. Special pain was in store for anyone who disagreed. All of which he sold without having one soldier behind him.

"I made a big mistake. It cost me more than I can calculate but it cost Kavelin even more. It almost cost everything that three monarchs did to make this a principality where every subject could be proud to live. I will not repeat that error. I vow that here, now."

He was improvising, promising what many wanted to hear but meaning it. His intensity permitted no questions, however much future and established enemies might want to know about his relationship with the Dread Empire.

His piece said, he spoke past Kristen to Inger, "Give them the rest of today to get their minds around this."

Inger managed a nod. She looked to Josiah Gales, who nodded in turn. "Don't we all? Need time?"

Bragi Ragnarson carried his son and grandson down to the floor of the hall, followed by Kristen Gjerdrumsdottir. He set the boys down, took each by the hand, walked out, headed for Castle Krief. He was not armed. Today he had no need.

He was improvising still, going on instinct. For the moment instinct and timing were enough.

The news had gotten out already. People came to see. Most remained quiet and respectful. There was almost supernatural awe in their attitudes.

There was, as well, hope.

Nature had blessed Kavelin. A tide of economic improvement was rising. But the political situation remained calm mainly because the contenders were exhausted and, in Inger's case, impoverished. Ordinary folk dreaded the day she obtained fresh resources.

This might herald the possibility of avoiding all that.

A wondrous hope it was.

...

Inger stared at Josiah Gales as the excitement oozed out of the Thing hall. He said nothing. Neither did Babeltausque, nor did Nathan, who had rejoined them, still shocked. Dr. Wachtel fidgeted but kept his mouth shut.

"What do we do?" Inger murmured. "What *do* we *do?*"

She harvested no advice. Josiah, though, looked like a man who had shed a huge moral burden. Nathan was afraid. His future no longer looked as sweet as it had—that age of bitter almonds. Babeltausque stared in the direction the Heltkler girl went as Ozora Mundwiller led her tribe away.

Inger was worried about the sorcerer. Something was going on with him. Something obsessive. It might be a harbinger of a darkness to come.

She hoped she was wrong. She hoped she was imagining it. She hoped he was not just one trivial mishap of an emotional trigger short of crossing over into the night land that had claimed Father Ather Kendo.

She hoped, but, this morning, she had no confidence that she would ever see anything good again. Hell had become impatient. Hell was coming to her.

Josiah said, "What do we do? How about we go home, hunker down, and see what happens next?"

Bragi was back. He had come in like some natural force, gathering the ley lines of power and expectation to himself. Nothing would happen ever again without his hands being on it, in it, or taken into account. He had managed it so easily, so instinctively.

Bragi was back but he had changed. He was the nostalgically recalled hard case but there was more to him now. Inger thought it might be a new maturity.

She said, "You're right, Josiah. Let's just ride the lightning and see where it takes us." Bragi's behavior suggested that would not be the hell she might have expected.

He was not a Greyfells.

Though the day was advancing and it should have been getting warmer, a scatter of snowflakes fell during the transit to the castle. The flakes melted instantly but did proclaim the imminence of winter.

Inger realized that the trees had shed most of their leaves. When did that happen? She had been too preoccupied to notice. That was sad. Autumn was her favorite season. She loved to see the colors.

"Josiah, the leaves are gone."

"Uhm?"

"We've been missing the good things."

Gales grunted agreement despite having no real idea what she was thinking. He was good that way. Nathan and Babeltausque contributed supporting nods despite being even farther in the dark.

...

After sixteen days in hiding, while rumors of his death abounded—though no body ever surfaced—Megelin made a run for safety, into the desert north of Al Rhemish. He was accompanied by Misr and Mizr, an ancient chamberlain called abd-Arliki, and a grizzled, one-eyed rogue called Hawk in his presence and Boneman behind his back. Boneman was a villain of no special stature. He was involved with Megelin's court through the twins, who had used him to protect their area of corruption. He was dangerous but was known amongst the low mainly because he often bragged that he was evil.

That declaration did not come from the heart. He did it to intimidate.

But for the uprising Megelin would never have crossed paths with Boneman. In the most dangerous hours of the riot, as the good people let themselves vent ancient frustrations, those whose lives might be forfeit had to support one another. The twins brought Boneman in because he was strong, desperate himself, and lacked a conscience. He agreed not just because of the generous pay but because he knew hard men might use the chaos to mask writing a bloody final sentence to Boneman's tale.

Boneman spirited his charges away with considerable finesse. "It's what I do," he bragged, not pleased about having to do it with feeble old men, a weakling king, and a score of donkeys with a mass of cargo.

Megelin wondered why the twins insisted that so many animals were needed.

The party headed north, the direction pursuers were least likely to look. Megelin did not initially realize that they were following the track that his father had taken when fleeing Al Rhemish at an even younger age. Unlike his father, Megelin did not have a horde of enraged Invincibles behind him. There was no pursuit at all. All Al Rhemish thought he had been killed. Even Old Meddler thought him lost and was distressed. Megelin bin Haroun was a feeble tool, blunt, bent, and cracked, but had been, even so, the best blade left in a dwindling set.

All went well for several days. Panic faded. Fear drew back. The pace slackened. The band moved on more through inertia than from a need to escape.

Then the dread returned tenfold, with the king badly shaken.

Mizr demanded, "What is the matter, Majesty?" He and his brother were so worn down that neither attended much beyond their own exhaustion. Abd-Arliki was worse. He was fading. Only Boneman remained strong enough to help him. Boneman did not want to bother. He eyed the old chamberlain like he was contemplating getting rid of the burden.

Megelin gasped, "I know where we are! From my father's stories about when he was fleeing from the Scourge of God. A little farther on we'll find a ruined Imperial watchtower that's haunted by a hungry ghost," using ghost to mean a ghoul or devil. "My father was trapped there for a while. He wasn't ever sure how he got away."

Never saying so, he admitted that he was not the man his father had been. "We're probably dangerously close already. If we camp around here the ghost will come get us."

He thought that was how it had worked. It had been fifteen years since he had heard the story and he had not paid close attention at the time.

"No matter," Mizr said. "We have treasure. No one is after us. We don't have to stick to this obscure road."

"Treasure?" Megelin asked.

"Misr and I brought the household funds. We will live well wherever we settle. I suggest we turn west."

Misr agreed. "Going west will give us a better chance to find help for abd-Arliki."

Megelin looked north. There was nothing there to draw him, really. He thought he could feel the demon waiting, insane with mystical hunger. "West we go. Tomorrow. Or now, even. I want to get farther from the hungry ghost."

Why had the twins not mentioned the household treasury before? Because they wanted it all for themselves? Obviously, but now they understood that they could not get out of this on their own.

The real truth was, Mizr mentioned the money only because he was too tired to remain cautious.

No ghoul came that night but death was not a stranger.

Though Megelin was not surprised he did see something odd about abd-Arliki's eyes. They had the buggy look of a hanged man.

Even Misr and Mizr betrayed guilty relief because the old man no longer hindered them. Megelin was not sure why they had brought abd-Arliki in the first place, but neither did he care. He was busy being exasperated with Boneman, who refused to move on until he interred the old man in a substantial freestone cairn.

"Hey, show the dead some respect…Majesty. The courtesy don't cost nothing. You'd appreciate it if it was you. They's plenty a things out there that'd gnaw on you."

Misr and Mizr helped impatiently. Boneman thanked them graciously, then gave his sullen, nonparticipating monarch a black look. "Nobody can't say I disrespect the dead."

Later, the survivors hit an old east-west trace. Following that, they found some shepherds beside a small oasis. Those people had no news from Al Rhemish—nor did they care. They were not sure who ruled there.

Megelin got his feelings bruised. He was not a hunted fugitive. No one cared enough to bother. He asked the twins, "Did we mess up by running? Should we have stayed?"

"We did the right thing," Mizr insisted. "Otherwise, we would've beaten abd-Arliki into the darkness. They were coming. It is possible that we ran too far, though."

Misr added, "We should have stayed close by and just gone back after everybody finally calmed down."

His twin nodded. "Indeed. Panic is never good. I think that

it may not yet be too late. We should go back. What say you, Hawk?"

...

Megelin felt like a crushing weight lay on his chest. He surged into panicked wakefulness—and found that there *was* a weight atop him. It was a large, flat rock half as heavy as he was. Other rocks surrounded him. He could get no leverage to get out.

A grinning, one-eyed face appeared above, Boneman straining under the weight of another large rock. "Good morning, Majesty." The villain settled his burden onto Megelin's groin. "Looks like it's going to be a wonderful day."

Megelin did not quite grasp his situation. "Please. What? Why?"

"You know I insist on honoring the dead. They deserve all the respect we can give them." He vanished from view. Megelin fought the rocks, without success. His limbs were pinned, too.

From somewhere close by Boneman growled, "Will you lay still?" A squishy crunch followed.

The one-eyed man appeared with another rock. This one was wet and red and had bits of hair and flesh stuck to it. The red was so fresh it had not yet drawn flies.

Something bit Megelin on his inside left ankle.

"That Misr just didn't want to get along. I'm tempted to disrespect him."

Megelin tried to ask what was happening and why. Panic took over. He shrieked commands.

"Now why do you want to get all rude like that? Here I am, busting my butt to do you royal honors, and you're being unpleasant. Relax, Majesty. Your grave will be the biggest and best of all. The foxes and jackals and vultures will never get at you."

Something small took a bite of Megelin. He squealed, imagining things crawling all over him down there. Or maybe he was not imagining things. Another bite followed, then another.

The sun soared higher. It beat down into Megelin's face. Boneman hummed as he went on stacking stones. He confided his plans for a future spent enjoying the treasure in all those donkey packs. "The Disciple's preachers told the truth. If we're patient God will grant us what we deserve."

Boneman said that just before he placed the slab that shut out the sun. That and, "Sleep tight, Majesty."

Megelin wept. He begged. Vaguely, remotely, he heard Boneman humming or chatting as he interred Misr and Mizr. Megelin convinced himself that this was only a cruel practical joke. Boneman would dig him out once his bully streak had been fed.

Despite the pain and terror Megelin fell asleep. Sleep was an escape. He dreamed a dream that recalled his father's adventure when he crossed this same desert, headed north. In that dream Megelin approached the ghost and recognized him, as his father had not done then.

That devil was no spirit. He was not supernatural at all. He was Old Meddler, playing the games he played to keep the world a violent place.

Megelin wakened. The darkness had turned solid. The air had cooled. He could not move. Boneman had done nothing to alleviate his condition. He was lightheaded with hunger and thirst and in substantial pain where insects—small ants, he suspected—had been eating him. Despite all, he felt optimistic. Old Meddler would come for him! He was a valuable resource. Likely the ancient had been on his track for some time.

Panic threatened.

He fought it down. He had to keep an iron grip. A rescue would come. He was the goddamned King. He would show Boneman what Megelin bin Haroun could do. Boneman would, indeed, get what he deserved! Boneman's fate would be the punch line to this cruel joke.

Something began snuffling round the cairn. It grumbled to itself. It tried nosing rocks off the pile. They were too big. Then there were more snufflers. They growled at one another and grunted as they circled, eager to get at the meat. Then there were a half-dozen things all angrily frustrated.

Megelin barely breathed.

But then he began to whimper. The beasts had gotten at one of the twins. A growling, snarling contest exploded as the pack determined feeding order.

A small rock by the left side of Megelin's face slipped out of the pile. Its departure let the slab blocking his view of the sky tilt and slide slightly to the left. Megelin was blinded by the light of a millions stars. Then all he could see was a dark muzzle and cruel teeth illuminated from the side by moonlight. Hot carrion breath burned his face and filled his lungs.

...

The winged steed planed high above the desert. Its brain was that of a horse. Its thoughts were neither complex nor quick but they did work in great, slow rhythms that, in time, eventually executed mildly abstract processes.

It had lived for millennia. It had developed some fixed opinions during that time. Among them was a conviction that immortality was wasted if it had to be spent as the tool of a defective personality.

Ages of slow cogitation had been required to reach that one conclusion. The fabulous beast had begun to nibble round the edges of the notion that it might do something itself to alter its condition, but that concept had not yet solidified.

Meanwhile, it remained a tool and was not happy about that. And it was bored.

Nothing had changed since the time of the Nawami Crusades.

Its rider urged it into a downward turn to the right, headed farther to the northwest. The horse soon saw the vultures its rider had spied already.

...

The tiny ancient dismounted. He revealed nothing but was irked. He had failed to mark his useful fool Megelin so he could be found easily, so he had had to spend days hunting. And here lay the price of laziness. He was just hours too late.

The vultures danced amongst the scattered stones and bones and bluffed a willingness to fight for the little that was left. He swung the Horn off his back, spoke to it, touched it, tapped out a one-hand tune on a battery of seven valves. The carrion birds experienced something neither man nor mount felt. They shrieked and took to the sky so suddenly that there were several feather-shedding collisions.

Swarms of flies fled with them. Ants of a dozen breeds broke off harvesting and skirmishing and headed home to defend the nest.

The Star Rider strolled around playing his mystic Horn. There was evidence enough in the recollections of the air and stones and scrubby brush to sketch out what had happened. "Uhm." A dozen donkeys had left here headed northeast, an unusual direction to travel. Real safety lay closer directly to the west. Maybe the killer felt more comfortable headed northeast. He might be a smuggler or someone who had hidden in the Kapenrungs during the Royalist exile.

The ancient contemplated one incompletely demolished cairn. Once again cruel misfortune, stupidity, and human fallibility had conspired to deprive him of an asset. Never a prime asset, to be sure, but the best in his dwindling arsenal.

It had not been a good year.

Next year might be worse.

He sensed a threat being born. Specifics had not yet proclaimed themselves. No foe had been so bold as to declare himself. But there were signs and shadows and blank spaces out there. That meant just one thing.

Clever death was snuffling along his back trail. It might be lying in wait up ahead, too.

The wizard Varthlokkur would be involved, somewhere. The aftershocks of his activity in Al Rhemish had led to this.

Emotion paled with the ages. Angry and unhappy though he was, the Star Rider set aside his inclination to exact revenge or deliver punishment.

He took to the air, searching for the murderer.

The man could become a useful tool himself, though never so useful as a king.

...

The ruins of el Aswad were so far from Fangdred that there was no communicating between the two directly. Scalza, guided by his mother, fearlessly carried his scrying bowl through a portal to an Imperial border post southwest of Throyes. There he paced the crude rampart, stared at an adobe compound manned by Invincibles. The desert warriors were a tripwire meant to warn of a renewed Throyen effort to occupy the coast of the Sea of Kotsüm.

Scalza's mother was waiting on her lifeguards. The boy did not understand the complexity of her relationship with them. He did understand that she was making a special effort to keep them happy. He wondered why but did not ask.

He was near being a universe unto himself, open only to his sister and, marginally, his cousin. His mother had brought him along because she considered his emotional jeopardy to be greater than the physical risks of the operation.

Though Scalza pretended boredom he was excited. This was his first ever real adventure.

Mist's lifeguards arrived. Soon afterward Scalza was hunched over his bowl, executing simple sorceries meant to inform his uncle-by-marriage that his immediate attention was needed.

Mist said, "I want him here instead of back at Fangdred. That will save him several days."

Scalza nodded, then decided that a verbal response was needed. "I will do that, Mother."

He liked her idea. He would get to stay here longer. The adventure would not end the day it began.

The wizard took longer to arrive than Mist anticipated. He did not look good and was not happy when he did. She asked, "I caught you at a bad time?"

"Any time seems to be a bad time to have Radeachar carry me over the Jebal."

"Ah? So?"

"That's the shortest way to get here unseen by El Murid's friends."

Mist did not understand and said so.

"We came north over the Jebal al Alf Dhulquarneni," he reiterated.

"Oh." Mist recalling that the name meant Mountains of the Thousand Sorcerers. "The thousand resented you trespassing."

"Every last one, and all their children, too. Some of them are really nasty. And some have skills. I mean to reverse my route exactly going back. I'll find out if they learned any manners." He was vexed in the extreme.

"Let me not irritate you further by wasting your time. Scalza, explain. You caught it happening."

That was a good move. Scalza liked not being treated like a kid. "It wasn't all me. I was just the only one around when Lord

Yuan showed up and said somebody was using that Horn thing. He told me where. I zeroed in. Then he showed me how to look backward to see why that man was there looking around."

Scalza was clear and concise with his explanation. He did not need much questioning.

"This is not good," the wizard opined. "Haroun will be… You know… I can't guess how he'll react. He'll surprise us. And me going back by the same route won't be just for fun now. Those people better not mess with me. I won't be gentle and forgiving."

Mist said, "Whatever, you need to rest before you go. You don't want to be so tired that you make stupid mistakes."

"I do believe that, this once, I'll take some common sense advice."

Which let Mist know that his passage up the spine of the Jebal had been more of a challenge than he admitted. He was in a mood to administer another set of spankings.

She stayed put while Varthlokkur did. She had a lifeguard take a patrol to scout the Invincible strongpoint, with Scalza going along. The boy would have something extra to brag about to his sister. His mother would get a read on his character under stress.

The lifeguard reported that he did well.

Scalza was reluctant to go back to Fangdred. He argued, but without spoiled child passion. He did go sullen on being reminded that when he had the bad luck to draw her for a mother he had lost his chance to enjoy a normal life. Some opportunist was sure to snatch him in hopes of gaining leverage on her the instant he tried.

Varthlokkur agreed as he summoned the Unborn.

Scalza said, "I know that stuff in my head but I still hate it… Let's go home. At least I can brag to Eka."

…

The sorcerers of the Jebal had understood Varthlokkur's warnings. He had only two encounters. Both times he overresponded dramatically.

He expected to have no problems ever after.

Bin Yousif had done little during his absence but scout toward Sebil el Selib. He had a young hare roasting, disdaining the dietary laws. "So what was it? And did you have as much trouble as I predicted?"

"I had all that trouble and a whole lot more. There are some testy recluses up there. Mist wanted me to pass on some bad news about your son."

"What did he...? He *was* killed during the uprising."

"No. He avoided that. He sneaked out with some of his advisers."

...

It had been weeks since news of the troubles in Al Rhemish first reached Sebil el Selib. Yasmid's captains had been excited, then. The people would turn the Royalist rascals out... But the rioters punished the Faithful with equal passion.

Yasmid found the distraction useful. If her people were trying to profit from the uprising they had no time to worry about how she might be changing.

Habibullah, too, seized the day. He isolated her, because of her ill health and grief for her son, in her father's tent, where the foreign physicians could attend her. When word came that Megelin had survived after all, and was hiding somewhere in the desert, Habibullah insisted that she remain under Phogedatvitsu's care.

The swami saw no shame in her condition. He manufactured reports about her failing health, which he could reverse given several months. Habibullah carried messages to and from Elwas al-Souki, whom Yasmid appointed as surrogate for her and her father till she came back or El Murid was able to resume his role as first among the Faithful.

Yasmid had been in her father's tent only a short while before she understood that her father would never take up the mantle of the Disciple again. The Matayangans had conquered his addiction but the man the poppy had left behind was almost useless, and had no connection with today's reality. He thought Yasmid was her mother, Meryem. He recognized her condition—and was positive that he was the father. The fakirs could not free him from that delusion.

Which left Phogedatvitsu frightened. If that suggestion got out... He launched a vigorous program meant to keep everyone away from Yasmid and her father. How terrible would the wrath of the Believers be if they thought their demigod had sired a child on his own daughter?

That would be the end of her. That would be the end of him. That would be the end of the Faith.

Again and again Yasmid asked herself why had she been so stupid. Why she had gone so weak the instant that man no longer left her waiting by the door.

Was God testing her? How could this be part of the Divine Plan? How mad must that Plan be?

The essence of the Faith was submission to the Will of God. How to tell, anymore, though, what that Will might really be?

Personal terror became part of life in the Disciple's tent and terror stimulated ever-deepening religious doubt.

Habibullah reported that Elwas al-Souki and his intimates insisted on a direct meeting, whatever her condition. They promised to be brief. They would not be denied.

Habibullah bundled Yasmid into a wheeled chair once used by her father. He brought the Disciple himself in, too, sedated and under intimate supervision by Phogedatvitsu personally. The swami was no longer Elwas's instrument. He understood that his own fate hinged on keeping her condition secret. He had El Murid primed to ramble incoherently about the Evil One.

The confrontation proved anticlimactic, the dark emotion beforehand wasted. al-Souki was in a blistering rush. He arrived thoroughly distracted, having discovered all the thousand grim little truths about being the man in charge. He strained to avoid being brusque. His impatience was fierce. His interest in Yasmid's health never passed beyond courteous form.

He called her "Lady" only, not any of the creative honorifics of the past. "We have an unusual situation taking shape. Details are sketchy but suggestive. It involves the Empire Destroyer."

Elwas went on to relate a confused story obtained from allies developed during punitive expeditions into the high Jebal. The Empire Destroyer had been seen up there. He had skirmished with the mountain people while traveling along the high range. "Because there is nothing we could actually do to keep him from going anywhere he wants, him using a remote route says what he wanted most was not to be noticed."

Yasmid focused. This would be important. That ancient power had shown no interest in Hammad al Nakir before he turned up in Al Rhemish—at a time when Haroun must have been there. Now the old doom was sliding around Sebil el Selib by sneaking through the highest mountains.

She nodded to herself. "Was that Unborn thing involved?"

"It was. Carrying the sorcerer through the sky."

"I see." It seemed plain enough. "Why go that way, and court conflict, when a grand swing over the erg could be managed with less chance of being noticed?"

"Urgency? Swinging out over the erg would take hours longer. Too, the Unborn has made several mountain route journeys without the sorcerer, always carrying something when it was going south."

Yasmid nodded again. She did not fully reflect, though, before saying, "They're up to something at el Aswad."

Elwas seemed fully pleased with his Lady. "Exactly. I have a company of Invincibles headed there, subject to your permission. You can recall them if you want."

She could not back off even if her sifting of facts and speculation left her sure that Haroun was out there, too. "Elwas, as ever, your decision is perfection, and beyond reproach. Just don't waste the Invincibles. We may yet need to cross the erg to Al Rhemish."

That notion startled al-Souki.

Yasmid continued, "Varthlokkur isn't called the Empire Destroyer because he kicked over an anthill when he was seven. With Magden Norath gone he is the most dangerous man in the world. Try to find out what he's up to without starting a war. Just walk up and ask him if you have to."

"I understand. Such was the course I'd hoped to pursue."

"Excellent." Yasmid did not believe him. Brilliant though Elwas might be, he was capable of misleading himself into thinking he was clever enough to outwit and arrest someone like Varthlokkur.

Unfortunately, or fortunately, so far Elwas had not run into any evidence to disabuse him of such a conceit.

...

Haroun bin Yousif was back doing what Haroun bin Yousif did

best. He was a ghost drifting down the wadi that passed close by the Disciple's tent. Luck crawled with him. The wadi was dry. Assured by Varthlokkur that the Faithful here clung tightly to El Murid's ban against sorcery, he did not fail to use his own skills to conceal himself and to probe for trouble lying in wait.

Despite the ruckus Varthlokkur raised in the Jebal, which had a troop of Invincibles headed out to investigate, Sebil el Selib itself was under no special state of alert.

Haroun oozed up to his former point of entry. Repairs had been made. New spikes had been set. But no watcher had been posted. No tripwire spells or actual cords had been installed, nor had booby traps been placed.

How could these people be so arrogantly overconfident? So lacking in justifiable paranoia? Did they really think that they had nothing to fear? Were they that sure of the countenance of God?

Must be. But no sane man ever should be.

God had proven, time and again, that His favor was fickle.

Haroun bin Yousif was not made to trust anything outside himself.

He dithered half an hour trying to find hidden pitfalls. Rational people would have created some in case the invader returned.

Could it be that they never figured it out?

He could imagine Yasmid softening any effort to snare him—but did not believe that she would.

His innards knotted as he finally forced himself forward—not where he penetrated the tent before. This had to be done before there was light enough to show that something strange was happening.

Varthlokkur had convinced him—almost—that his part, successfully executed, would end the torments his kingdom had suffered for two generations. This would reshape everything. It would *compel* the birth of a new order because there would be no old order left. What shape that new order took would be in his hands, too, insofar as he cared to sculpt it.

Varthlokkur would build on what they did here, toward a new order for the rest of the world.

Haroun moved forward. He wanted to believe but could not. Not really. They were still trying to throw a bridle on the wind.

Even so, he hoped. He had a goal again—though he did not quite understand it.

Once inside he produced a wane witch light. By its glow he proceeded to the area where once the foxes had denned. Ha! Here were sure signs that all was not as it had been. That whole wide space had been cleansed down to the bare earth. He would not have to climb over trash once he went to work.

He had brought equipment with him. He hoped the clatter he raised using it would not give him away.

He set out a triangle of witch lanterns for light, then assembled a pole fifteen feet long. He attached a spearhead so sharp that one ought not to look at it directly. He used that to make an eight-foot cut in the canvas overhead, made another cut at right angles to that, then a third parallel to the second, leaving a flap hanging down. Then he cut parallel cut to those to create a six-inch wide strip that might be climbable, making a last resort escape. Only…

Only that canvas was almost as old as he was. His weight ripped a longer strip out when he tested it.

Damn!

He was wasting time. He was behind schedule and falling further back. If he did not get a signal out soon Varthlokkur would abandon him to his fate.

He blew air into a sheep's bladder, attached a mechanical device provided by the wizard, invested the bladder with a levitation spell, child's-play simple but the possibility had not occurred to him till Varthlokkur showed it to him.

His time with the Empire Destroyer had been deflating. He now understood how limited his own talents and imagination were.

Once the sheep's bladder rose a few hundred feet something tripped a mechanical device that sparked a flame. That lasted just seconds and was not showy. No one should notice at that hour. Anyone who did ought to think that it was some strange shooting star.

Too much to hope for, in Haroun's estimation. Much too much.

He grew impatient. The risks were rising now. Others would be involved. He could not keep them from screwing up. Worse, *his* role now consisted entirely of waiting.

Varthlokkur and the Unborn dropped in so quietly that Haroun would have missed them if he had not been watching. The wizard had draped the Unborn in black gauze, rendering it invisible from outside while only slightly impairing the monster's ability to perceive the world around it.

The Unborn deposited the sorcerer, rose against the stars. "There!" Haroun said. "I see a pink glow when I look straight up."

"Aren't you a bit long in the tooth and in the wrong religious tradition to be looking up someone's skirt?"

Varthlokkur could not have stunned him more by whacking him with a hammer. "We're late. We'll have to push it if we're still going to get this done quietly."

Quietly was the ultimate hope. Full execution without ever being noticed. Come and gone undetected, leaving behind nothing but delayed confusion.

The hope.

Haroun considered it forlorn, insane, impossible.

Something would go wrong, if only because he was part of a team. Long experience left him confident that others never achieved his level of competence. They could not maintain the focus.

The wizard asked, "Is something wrong? Is there some reason you're freezing up instead of trying to make up time?"

"No good reason," Haroun admitted. "We can make up time fast if you expand your sleep spells. You were right. No one will notice and no alarms will be tripped. There is no magic here." He used "magic" as a convenience, lacking something more precise.

Varthlokkur understood. "I'll take advantage of that, then. I'll deploy the spells as we go."

Haroun appreciated the fact that Varthlokkur wasted no time on "I told you so." He had argued for a more aggressive use of sorcery. He was less concerned about leaving evidence behind.

Haroun headed into the inhabited part of the tent. Changes were legion. The biggest was the reduction in clutter. Tons of trash had been carried off to be buried, burned, or laid out for anyone who wanted to pick over it.

Someone had done a masterful job. That someone was not yet finished. They passed through an untouched area where clutter was piled as high as a man could reach. Most seemed to be old records, moldy, water-stained, likely useless.

The Disciple's quarters had to be accessed through a cloth-walled room featuring a Matayangan in a loincloth asleep on a pad on the earthen floor. This Matayangan did not like the dark. A tiny lamp wasted oil so the night could be held at bay.

The Matayangans all shared that failing. Lamps burned in the areas adjoining the four cloth walls of El Murid's space. Night had been an evil time while Matayanga was at war with Shinsan.

Phogedatvitsu and his men slept surrounding the Disciple, which made sense because the man had that penchant for wandering off.

The Matayangans were under the sleep spell, but not deeply. Varthlokkur muttered irritably. Why were they not all snoring like the next to dead?

The Disciple was not asleep at all. They found him sitting up, drowsy, on a western-style camp stool, at a little table. He was trying to write by feeble mutton-tallow candle light. His space retained every bit of smell the candle produced. He evidenced no surprise when he saw Haroun. "You're back."

"I am. Come. It's time to go."

"I will not cooperate."

"All right."

Varthlokkur joined them. "I can't push them into a deeper sleep. Don't argue with him. Just get him moving."

The Disciple gaped. He did not recognize the wizard. There was no reason he should. But he had not seen this demon with a companion before, nor could he imagine the Evil One having an accomplice who would tell him what to do.

Haroun moved closer, ready to gag and bind the Disciple.

Yasmid, yawning, sleepily confused, pushed in. "I keep hearing voices, Father… Oh! What…? You?" She froze.

Haroun stopped moving. How weak a sleep spell had the wizard cast? Varthlokkur grumbled, "Maybe it's the geography. It happens where the ley lines are warped. Or they might be partially immune."

Haroun was not listening. Even a blind shaghûn could smell this truth. "We have to take her, too."

"What?" The wizard was at work on the Disciple because Haroun had lost focus.

"She's pregnant. My responsibility. I can't leave her…"

That stopped the wizard cold. He shivered, shook his head. "Fate takes some damned strange channels. All right, do what you have to, but do it now! Do it fast! We're still slipping back on time." He nudged El Murid, who was now grinding to the conclusion that his situation was worse than he had thought.

Haroun told Yasmid, "You have two minutes to get anything you can't leave behind. Don't argue. You know what will happen if you stay. Nothing will save you. Nothing will save our child. So move. Now. The wizard is in a hurry."

"The wizard is in a hurry, indeed. But the wizard has family, too, and understands the compulsions. Will she run screaming if I relax the sleep spell?"

"No." He hoped. He looked his wife, his love, the daughter of his lifelong enemy, in the eye. "Get what you can't live without."

Yasmid's eyes closed as Varthlokkur did something. She bobbed her head. Now she had the emotional freedom to be embarrassed. She did not turn away immediately, though. Haroun grew as frustrated with her as the wizard was with him.

As he started to bark, she said, "Neither Father nor I can manage without the Matayangans."

"What?"

"I don't know why you came for him. Not to kill, obviously. He would be dead and you would be gone. So you have some use for him. But he won't be useful if he doesn't have the Matayangans to manage him and care for him."

Varthlokkur looked like a man who needed a good shriek and a chance to fling furniture. "Get moving!" Haroun's voice was soft but adamant and intense. "Now!" He turned to the wizard. "What can you do?"

...

The Matayangans followed Haroun, Yasmid, and El Murid through the portal, single file, as fast as the device could transfer them. Varthlokkur watched and scowled, shuffled nervously, hearing noises develop as people elsewhere stirred. It was no longer possible to do this unnoticed. Radeachar could not remove the portal unseen. There was no longer any point to repairing the slashed tent roof so the mystery of the Disciple's disappearance would deepen.

Worse, Old Meddler would have what he needed to assemble a portrait of the plot shaping up against him. He had all the tools available to his enemies, and more. He would be able to research this event, decipher its meaning, then would move because of the forces he saw ranged against him. He would strike soon because he was weak, now, and dared not delay seeing to his own protection.

Impatience moved the wizard again. He had to get back to Fangdred. There was much to be done yet to engineer even a chance of brushing away an assault by the Star Rider.

How much was the slight, secret advantage of having the Old Man and Ethrian worth? How much headway had Mist made getting into their minds and memories?

Varthlokkur did not feel optimistic as he placed a foot on Phogedatvitsu's behind and shoved the bulky man into the portal, hoping all of him made it through.

He looked up at Radeachar. "Now you. We'll leave the portal. They may not understand what it is."

The Unborn soared up and away, refusing.

That needed consideration, Varthlokkur reflected. He had a prejudice against portals himself. An outright dread, really, but he would do what he had to do.

He could not recall the last time Radeachar had refused an instruction—if ever it had.

Did it know something? Or did it just share his fears, magnified?

Questions had to wait.

He stepped in, heart in throat, frightened child inside sure that he would not arrive at the other end.

As he did that, tent staff discovered that the Disciple was not in his quarters. The foreigners were missing, too. The Disciple must have gotten away and they were hunting him through the tent again.

There would be no distress till the portal was found. The mood, then, was baffled consternation. No one knew what it was, or what it meant.

...

Mist watched bin Yousif arrive, unhappy but apparently not emotionally crippled. A woman followed, badly frightened. She latched onto bin Yousif. Her movements were strained. She was in considerable discomfort. Damn! She was pregnant? Definitely not smart at her age.

The object of the operation followed, wearing a dimwit look like the one so often seen on Ethrian. He was thoroughly confused. He had no idea about transfer portals.

Brown men followed the Disciple at precise intervals.

Mist approached bin Yousif. "Is this an evacuation?"

"Something like. I could not go without Yasmid. She says she and her father will fall apart without the fakirs to keep them together. We had wasted too much time to argue. We can get rid of them here if they are actually useless."

Mist turned to her garrison commander. "Kei Lin. Feed these people, get them into civilized clothing, and have them physically examined." She turned back to bin Yousif. "How many more?"

"Just the wizard and the monster."

"And the wizard has arrived," Varthlokkur announced, having appeared in time to hear the question. "I'm the last. Radeachar won't risk the transfer stream. Instead, it will go scouting in the northern desert."

She asked, "Can you explain all this?" Making a sweeping gesture.

"Hasn't the King done so already?"

"Why should I believe him?"

Haroun whispered a translation to his woman.

Mist smiled broadly. Fortune had dealt her a royal flush. She had the Disciple and his daughter. There would be no one to hold that movement together, now. And she had the only serious Royalist claimant to the Peacock Throne. His successor was now a scatter of cracked bones.

She said, "We need to move on quickly. We got a fix on our target at the scene of the murders…"

Varthlokkur had a finger in front of his lips. He whispered, "His mother hasn't been told."

"All right. Once we get to Fangdred?"

He nodded.

"I have Scalza, Eka, and Nepanthe trying to track the villain. He doesn't seem concerned. Maybe he doesn't care if we watch. More likely, though, he doesn't know that we can watch."

"That would be a benefit of the Winterstorm. The magic is different. He doesn't understand it."

Mist saw him shiver with a sudden suspicion that he might be deluding himself. That old villain had seen the Winterstorm up close. He had every reason for an abiding interest.

She said, "Kei Lin, one more thing. I want these people free of lice, nits, mites, and fleas before we move. Understand?"

He did not, but, "As you wish, Illustrious, so shall it be."

...

Scalza, with Ekaterina's assistance, had gotten a scryer locked onto the Star Rider's horse. "I started out trying to fix it on him... Ouch! Eka!"

"That's for taking credit for something you didn't do, Worm."

"Yeah? All right. Eka did the brain work. And she's the first one I'm gonna boil in lead after I take over the world."

Which jest ignited an uncomfortable silence. One did not joke about such things amongst the mightiest faces of the Dread Empire. That reeked too much of possible wickedness.

Eka said, "He'd trip over his own mutant feet and fall in the cauldron himself if I wasn't there to look out for him."

That helped, but only a little.

Red-faced, Scalza focused on his task. "Well, anyway, we couldn't lock it on him. He has some kind of protection that keeps that from happening. So we tried to lock onto the Horn thing because he's always got that with him. Same thing, so we tried his horse and that worked."

Varthlokkur said, "It's an insoluble problem with no satisfactory answer. Knowing where the horse is doesn't tell us why the rider went there and it doesn't tell us what he's doing."

Mist asked, "Can the Unborn keep an eye on him?"

"It could. But he would notice. That would cost me my best tool."

"Is he really that powerful?"

"We don't know, do we? And that's the point. There's no telling what powers and resources he has. We do have someone who can tell us, though. Don't we?"

Among the mob jammed in there were Mist's mind specialists.

The senior of the two stuck to the Old Man, talking softly, studying every move he made on the shogi board. His associate focused on Ethrian and Nepanthe, often involving the boy in a puzzle that required him to manipulate wooden blocks in different shapes and colors. After hassling her brother some more Ekaterina went to watch Ethrian fiddle with those. She had trouble not helping but Ethrian was getting lazy, counting on her to make things easier for him.

The specialist let her do nothing but offer encouragement.

She had it bad for someone just getting into the high drama phase of a girl's life. Were Ethrian normal her imagination would not have pushed her into such strong fantasies. His obsession with Sahmaman would have sucked the life out of that.

Ekaterina was brighter than the quietly smart, shy child she pretended. She was more introspective than most girls her age. Further, her little brother was the only child she knew. She owned an unusually adult outlook. That included an appreciation of her own emotional landscape. It headed off nothing before it happened but did make it possible for her to analyze and understand after the fact.

She was scared that the real, secret Ekaterina could become one truly frightening adult.

Meantime, she had her crush on her cousin and it was all she could do to keep that hidden and manageable.

Manageable she managed, but, hidden, not so much. Everyone with eyes and a brain sniffed that out.

The puppy love amused everyone. Folks were kind enough not to torment her, Scalza being the exception. Little brothers have obligations.

The specialist who focused on the Old Man said, "We can now touch the level we needed to reach to get the information you want, Illustrious. If I put him into a deep trance he'll do the rest." He had been preparing the Old Man for hypnosis since he had arrived. The Old Man's memory problems were not the result of physical damage. The emotional scarring, though, was serious.

Mist said, "I'm counting on you, Academician Sue."

"I understand. We need to talk about the desert people, too."

"Desert people?"

"The ones the wizard brought. Neither Lum nor I speak their language. The only available translators are bin Yousif and the sorcerer. The former is marginally capable because he spent time in one of our prisons—unfortunately Lioantung. Those people have an accent so thick they practically speak their own dialect, which he then butchers with an accent of his own."

"I see."

"And I'm not confident of the wizard's translations. He's your ally, Illustrious. You know him best. Is his agenda at variance with ours?"

"I ask myself frequently. And I can't give you a definitive answer. My guess is, he'll be reliable so long as the greater threat exists. He's put himself square on target for that one, possibly deliberately." She looked round, did not see Varthlokkur. He had said nothing about leaving so must be somewhere in the castle. He should not be gone long. He hated leaving outsiders unsupervised in his space. Mist wished he would stay where she could keep an eye on him. "Do the best you can. I'll find an interpreter you can trust."

She looked around again. Scalza was focused on the Star Rider, Nepanthe on events in Kavelin. Ekaterina was beside Ethrian, who had abandoned his puzzle in favor of watching the shogi wars from behind Lord Kuo. When did Wen-chin do any work? She seldom caught him in the act but he was always caught up.

The game ended. Victorious, Lord Kuo abandoned his seat. Ethrian and Ekaterina crowded in opposite the Old Man. Eka began resetting the board.

Old man and boy shared a conspiratorial grin.

Scalza called, "Mother, I need you here."

...

A man with a donkey herd and saddle horses to wrangle ought not to be able to manage much in the way of stealth. Donkeys did not present the nasty challenges offered by camels and mules but they did harken to a unique drummer, in a dimwitted sort of way. They needed close care and inspired supervision. So how could the killer of a king stay out of sight for so long?

Old Meddler was baffled.

Eventually, he decided that someone must be masking the killer from afar. After operating on that premise a while, though, he changed his mind. Even disguised, all those animals would leave a big scat trail and a route stripped of greenery.

The old devil decided that he could not find his man because his man was not out there to be found. He was no longer on the move.

Old Meddler had existed in this world for millennia, and in another for ages before that. His mind was a clutter of ten thousand times the memories of the oldest mortals around. Outside the moment and task at hand that could be a sink of confusion, a cat's cradle of memories mixed and tangled, fragmented and partially lost. He sometimes enjoyed crystalline recollections of events two thousand years gone but modern memories eluded him even when he knew they were there. Till he actually saw it, and considered it from up close, he did not remember the Imperial watchtower.

There were donkeys and horses at a pool in the shade of the tower. They had stripped every plant. The killer was nowhere to be seen.

A faint, almost echoing call came on the breeze, drifting down from the battlements. He looked up, expecting to glimpse a pale white child's face. That left him frowning. *Why* did he think that?

He probed the spell suite that had drawn the killer to the tower. He had done good work back then… He remembered the place now.

His mood collapsed.

He had not shut everything down once he finished manipulating the boy who would become the King Without a Throne.

Troubling, that. An inexcusable lapse. He should review all his recent work, though the blunder was harmless enough—except to the rare traveler who wandered into range of the haunting call.

He tried to get to the tower from above, as in the old days, but his mount shied off. It refused two further attempts. Could it sense something that he did not? Though unlikely, the chance should not be ignored. Silly to force something dangerous.

Could someone have converted the tower into a deathtrap? Improbable, but improbable death had stalked him a thousand times. Death had her eye on him now, and was sharpening her claws, he was sure.

It was the season to indulge in a psychotic level of caution.

He brought the winged horse to earth near the pool. The donkeys still carried their travel packs, the horses their saddles.

The killer had become too entranced to take care.

He did not ease their burdens himself, though it would have taken but a moment to have the Windmjirnerhorn deliver fodder and grooms of a golem kind. The idea never occurred.

Obviously, the killer had been taken by the tower. No mystery, that.

A conjured haunting, crocheted from true, wicked ghosts captured and constrained to carry out targeted missions, could endure indefinitely. Numerous such infested the world, many this same devil's handiwork, abandoned in place once he finished using them.

The old being looked at that ruin, then at his mount. Not a long walk but a walk nevertheless. So much easier just to drop in from above.

Easier. But a stubborn beast made the walk a must. Was there a real threat? Come to think, the original setup made its victim circle the tower several times before the entrance revealed itself. Was the animal just being difficult? Why start at this late date?

He walked. His patience did not last. After one circuit, with his soles and legs aching, he settled onto a boulder and fingered valves on the Windmjirnerhorn while trying to think how best to avoid further exercise.

He spied the dark gap of the entrance, groaned. So. He had to go on in like a regular victim.

He got up. He limped. He ached. How much longer must he endure before his parole finally came through?

†

Chapter Twenty-Seven:

WINTER, YEAR 1018 AFE:

Spiraling In

"I didn't get much sleep last night," Ragnarson announced. "My own fault. I wanted to catch up on the real story around here."

He sat at the same table he had used for small conferences before he went out east. Inger used it for her own meetings. This morning's gathering was the biggest there since soon after Ragnarson's disappearance. The Queen and her main henchmen were present. So were Aral Dantice, Michael Trebilcock, Ozora Mundwiller, and Kristen Gjerdrumsdottir. The tension was less than expected despite Bragi's prior assertion that the meeting would continue till he was satisfied that their conflicts had been resolved.

He tipped a thumb at a corner. Fulk and the younger Bragi were playing with blocks brought in by Babeltausque's girlfriend. The children had no trouble getting along—though Carrie allowed them no opportunity to test anyone's patience.

The newcomers had no interest in the girlfriend. She was furniture, easy to look at but otherwise just there. The Queen's faction, though, considered her an amazement. Carrie Depar was much more than an opportunistic baby hooker. Babeltausque enjoyed their reluctant admiration for his pretty.

There was, however, almost a clang of meeting steel when he crossed gazes with Michael Trebilcock.

Trebilcock felt Babeltausque's attraction to Haida Heltkler. He did not want Haida abused any more than she had been already.

There was quiet lethality in looks Josiah Gales laid on Michael Trebilcock, too. Gales knew the likely source of the maladies he suffered because of his captivity.

Similar looks ran Aral's way from Babeltausque. He was sure that the men who tried to kill him had been sent by Dantice—if not that iron-hearted old Mundwiller woman, whose accent, when she spoke at all, exactly matched that of the would-be killers.

Kristen and Inger, too, often exchanged less than loving looks. Ragnarson knew he had to keep all those conflicts subdued. He dared show neither favoritism nor tolerance. Like that kid wrangling the boys. She tolerated nothing. She had paddled Fulk for launching a sulk, crushing it before it became a tantrum. Fulk had been stunned. Usually he got away with everything because he was sickly.

"So I'm tired," Ragnarson said. "With me that means impatient and cranky, too, so let's see if we can't get through this and start looking toward tomorrow. By which I mean Kavelin's tomorrow, not yours or mine or the literal morning after."

None of these people, nor anyone in town for the Thingmeet, had yet challenged his right to stroll in and take over—though as yet he had garnered not one royal honorific.

"This may be faint praise, Inger," he said. "But I think you did as well as you could once you worked up the gumption to arrest Dane. I hear of no harm done since then."

People stirred uncomfortably. Ozora Mundwiller had a thought but chose to reserve it.

"Kristen, you slipping away after Colonel Abaca passed looks like the best thing you could have done, too. You being away and Inger arresting the Duke let the Marena Dimura back off and just posture while they took advantage of the summer."

There had been a change, down in the bedrock of Ragnarson's soul, more profound than he knew. It had quickened when he stepped through the barrier separating the hidden temple from the kingdom that had conquered his heart so long ago.

His rage at what Kavelin had cost him had evaporated. He was indifferent to the chance that the cannibal state would keep feeding on his heart and soul. "I hear talk about a Kavelin disease. I'm a true sufferer. And it infected you all once the Duke was out of the way. Not so?"

Babeltausque said, "The catalyst was a child named Phyletia Plens. None of us ever met Phyletia but her death touched us way more than the Duke's removal did. It gave us a whole new perspective, maybe because it was inconsequential in a strategic or statistical sense. It shouldn't have influenced us. Children die. But sometimes something is so ugly that it grabs you by the throat and won't let go. It jerks you around till your whole life looks different."

Inger, Josiah Gales, and Nathan Wolf bobbed their heads in agreement, Wolf and Inger slightly red.

Ragnarson conceded, "That was one of the darker situations I ever heard of, and I saw some pretty disgusting stuff when I was young."

"What wormed into us wasn't just the crime's ugliness but the triviality of what drove that priest."

The sorcerer stumbled, his throat tightening. Ragnarson caught the subtle encouragement the Depar girl flashed him as well as the suspicion implicit in the arch of Michael's eyebrows. Babeltausque's secret reputation might not quite fit the actuality but, clearly, even the sorcerer himself feared that it could.

Ragnarson said, "The year is almost over. I want its conflicts and bad feelings put behind. I want us to put our heads together and come up with something we can take to the Thing."

Ozora Mundwiller grumbled, "And quickly. Delegates already think the Thingmeet is just a device Inger can use to get some money coming into Vorgreberg."

Ragnarson nodded. "My mother said that no good deed goes unpunished. For sure no good deed is seen that way by everybody. You can be a saint who is called a saint of all saints by the saints themselves and somebody will be convinced that you're up to no good."

"That would be a somebody who can't live with himself." Josiah Gales, looking like he had fallen asleep, chin on his chest, added,

"Those with wicked hearts make their claims to divert attention from the reek of evil coming off of them."

Silence followed. Everyone eyed the Colonel. Ragnarson figured he was paraphrasing somebody. Gales did not go on, nor did he give credit.

Michael said, "That's true. But it doesn't matter. That kind aren't a problem now and they won't be if they're given no fuel for the fires they want to set."

"We'll find a way."

Everyone looked at Ragnarson. That made no sense. He added, "You wanted to engineer unity by showing off a transfer gate." He looked at his wife. "A good idea, only some Nordmen obstructionist will claim that it was left over from the occupation or when Mist was here."

Gales said, "That point did not elude us. It wouldn't stand up, though. Everyone knows that Varthlokkur has been underfoot. The Unborn has been around a lot, too, and easterners have been seen by people definitely not part of our cabal."

Nathan Wolf offered his first comment. "Most people want an excuse to get along. Today's divisions mostly start right here, with us."

Gales grunted agreement. The sorcerer did the same.

Ragnarson said, "You're right." He waited. Nobody else had a comment. He looked Inger in the eye. She looked back without flinching.

Memories were in the air, not all nostalgic. Sherilee was on both their minds. Ragnarson did understand that his liaison had hurt Inger.

He had not thought that way before. He got caught in the moment… Which was not unusual. People did not think ahead and did not worry about consequences. But now he had positioned himself so that thinking that way was expected. His role demanded it. Making bad personal choices promised bad choices made as a ruler—and had that not shown itself clearly in the east already?

"Understand this. The Bragi Ragnarson you see here isn't the Bragi Ragnarson who roared off through the Savernake Gap. That Bragi's ordeal forged a better man—I hope."

Ozora Mundwiller proclaimed, "Here comes the part you won't like."

Ragnarson scowled. She was not intimidated. He was half her age and a man besides. She had spent the night with him, observing, chiding, once threatening to paddle his behind if he kept on being immature.

"The most excellent lady from Sedlmayr is correct. This won't be popular but it will help you stop wondering about my relationship with Shinsan."

Inger said, "Do talk about that, husband. The Thing will bring it up, I promise."

Everyone wondered how he and Michael could materialize so suddenly. Michael might have been close by all along, yes, but they all knew that he had not been.

"Both… Varthlokkur and Shinsan have joined forces. Haroun bin Yousif and the Disciple are with them, too, believe it or not. They have combined to battle the world's oldest fiend. The prospects don't excite me but I may choose to get in on that, too."

Michael gestured a demand for quiet. "Yes. *Him.* The first step on that path is that we no longer mention him directly. We don't name anything commonly associated with him, either. There are spells floating around that warn him whenever people start talking about him."

Ragnarson said, "Michael may choose to participate, too."

Inger announced, "I don't understand. Why?" The others nodded. Even the sorcerer's girlfriend seemed curious.

"I'm not sure I get it all myself. You'd need to be Mist or Varthlokkur to do that, I guess. It's like the Kavelin disease, only for the whole wide world. On the surface it does seem like a good idea to get shot of the mind behind the world's pain."

Michael volunteered, "We're like soldiers on the line. We're letting the generals do the fine thinking. Maybe we'll fight. They hope we will. They've conveyed their reasoning. We can do our part without grasping the nuance. No one can make a case that this enemy is good for the world."

Ragnarson and Trebilcock understood a fraction of what Mist and Varthlokkur were up to—which was an order of magnitude more than anyone else did. The Star Rider was not just weather, he was weather that happened somewhere else. He was not really real to most people.

Ragnarson stipulated that. "I don't expect conviction from you if we get caught up in this, just that you give us the benefit of the doubt during the struggle." He sounded like he was leaning toward getting involved.

Michael gave him no chance to clarify. "We'll probably participate because it will require the combined efforts of a lot of people—most of whom spend their lives at each other's throats because of him."

Ragnarson added, "If his victims gang up… It wouldn't mean an end to conflict. I'm not naïve enough to think that. But persistent aberrations like Hammad al Nakir, grotesqueries like the Great Eastern Wars and Shinsan's massively destructive conflicts with Matayanga and Escalon, that will all be a lot less likely. That old villain won't be shuffling from faction to faction, stirring the cauldron. He won't be pushing Magden Norath and Greyfells types in where things would stay peaceful otherwise."

Inger said, "You can only put some of what happened off on other people."

"Too true. I paid in pain, misery, and loss, and I'm still paying."

Trebilcock said, "You meant to whip up support by making Shinsan a boogerman. Well, Shinsan *has* been up to mischief involving Kavelin, but nothing wicked. The Empress wanted…" He could not explain just what Mist had in mind. That could be nostalgia at work instead of Kavelin being a cog in the machinery meant to silence the tyranny of the Star Rider. Her invisible engine remained perfectly hidden inside her own mind. Her progress toward assembling its parts remained obscure.

Ragnarson thought he knew all the people and parts but he could not get them to sift down into a recognizable pattern.

He did see that she had stripped the villain of resources—if you called people he used resources, like timber and ore.

Old Meddler must still be whining about the loss of Magden Norath.

"Bragi!"

He started. Inger was barking. "What?"

"You stopped talking in the middle of telling us how Shinsan has become our beloved friend. Where did you go?"

Sarcasm? He had not seen that side of his wife before. "The land of confusion. Boggled by the awesome scope of my ignorance." He paused, chose his words. "I don't trust anybody much anymore. Not even me. Maybe especially not me. But I do trust Mist, on this, as far as I trust anybody."

Michael grumbled, "You're saying the same stuff over, pretty much."

"I'm out of practice saying things out loud."

"He was in solitary confinement."

"Hell, I wasn't even conscious for a long time. Luck and a good turn I did earlier are the only reason my bones aren't scattered across that hillside, too."

He went away again, to that day and the last angry hour of his embarrassment, when men ran at the critical instant, the moment when a touch of stubborn would have claimed the day. For half his captivity his purpose had been to get back here so he could inflict deep and abiding pain on those who had abandoned him.

He was not over that yet. The rage remained but he had a harness on it now. It no longer obsessed him. And, he realized, he no longer recalled exactly who he had scheduled for the headsman's ax. Anger had become habit.

Inger demanded his attention again. "You haven't made clear what you hope to accomplish personally, nor have you given us any convincing reason why we should put up with you trying to do it here."

There it was, on the table, not bluntly, but insistence that he make a case for his right to stroll in and take charge.

The suggestion that he had lost that right caught him on the wrong foot—despite his having spent months wanting to make war on his own people. But that had been a lust for draconian vengeance, not an assertion of a right to rule. Not even his enemies could argue that he was not king. Could they?

He said it. "I am the King."

And Michael said, "There it is. The gauntlet thrown down, without forethought, in an unfavorable venue. Majesty." The latter spoken with an edge.

"Huh?"

Oh.

Babeltausque suddenly wore a bland, inane, innocent expression.

Not good, that.

Bragi had trotted right into a diminutive version of his disaster in the east. Once again he had moved without thinking, never really considering the chance that these people would not accept him.

Well, yes, he had thought about it, some, but not seriously. He did have that blind spot. Why would they resist? He was the King.

But it was clear that Inger's men would resist if she wanted that. They could make this as unhappy a day as the one on that hill.

Castle Krief's dungeon would not be as comfy as the Karkha Tower.

Babeltausque, Gales, and Wolf awaited their cue from Inger. Even the babysitter seemed ready to act. And her potential was entirely unknown.

Michael did not look ready to sacrifice himself. The others, Kristen included, showed little interest in anything but watching. Which was exceedingly irksome.

He tried to remain calm. "I didn't come here looking for a fight."

Inger said, "Of course you didn't. It never occurred to you that anyone would do anything but jump when you barked."

He was perplexed. Maybe Inger was not articulating clearly.

She continued, "I'll take a passive approach. I'll give you your head. A dole out the rope strategy. Will you embarrass yourself?"

She was less frightened and rattled than she had been. She had a plan. She would let him strangle himself. He had shown that he could.

Would her thugs try to nudge him off the precipice?

She said, "I paid attention back when I was your new bed bunny."

That hurt. He had not thought of her as a toy, ever. He never thought that about any woman he loved.

He nearly broke a smile. Some of his lovers might not agree. Women saw things through different eyes.

Inger said, "So I will defer, publicly. I'll be the dutiful wife. I won't make your road any rockier. I'll help where I can and I'll remain blind in the matter of that…girl. Your mistress. Purported."

Kristen hissed. There was no readiness to forgive in her.

Inger said, "I had nothing to do with what happened."

Ragnarson nodded. "I know. I got to interview the assassin, courtesy of Varthlokkur and the Unborn."

Kristen hissed again.

"I've made my peace with that, as much as I can." He had made arrangements to bring Sherilee to Vorgreberg. She would lie not far from Fiana and Elana… Where their ghosts might meet?

Inger's henchmen were more relaxed now. Wolf seemed mildly disappointed.

Inger said, "Let's stay focused on the Thingmeet. You can explain Shinsan's plans then."

"No. Mist wants to be remembered as the one who saved the world from its worst ever plague. We can't just shout out and let him know it's coming."

Babeltausque asked, "Will her feelings be hurt if you don't convince us?"

"I think that if what it takes to win is her having to look like the bad guy lurking in the weeds she'll put on the ugliest mask she can find, then sing weird songs while she prances and postures… Michael?"

Trebilcock was laughing. "Sorry. I was imagining her putting her dignity aside far enough to dance where somebody might actually see her."

"Villain. You have a filthy mind."

"Hey. She is a good-looking woman."

Ragnarson grinned himself once the image got inside his head. "She would be a vision, wouldn't she?"

…

Ekaterina asked, "Do you have a dancing girl outfit, Mother?" deliberately provocative.

Mist glowered.

In her most naïve voice Nepanthe said, "You'd look good. Not like me. Twenty years ago, maybe. Now I'm all doughy."

Lord Yuan was past being interested in women in scanty attire. "Ladies, can we focus?"

Mist turned away from spying on Ragnarson, irked but also arching the back of her vanity like a cat inclined toward more petting. She was disappointed, though Ragnarson had achieved more than she had expected. He could have concerned himself more with her mission and less with her physical form, however.

Even so… No. Good as it felt, the effect would fade. "Lord Yuan?"

"The instrument favored by that one is now in frequent play."

"You said it isn't worth tracking, yet you have been keeping watch?"

"Yes. I have men underemployed because of the peace. It keeps them occupied. The old devil did get busy. For a while he was up to something involving the man who killed the king of Hammad al Nakir." He checked the proximity of the desert people. "Once he finished…"

"He headed east. Scalza has been tracking his mount, which has been giving him trouble. It acts like it's coming down with something." Louder, she asked, "Anyone know if horses get arthritis?"

Swami Phogedatvitsu responded, "Probably. Most domesticated animals do if they live long enough."

Snide Scalza asked, "Does that mean people are domesticated?"

"A strong argument can be made for just that, youngster."

Ekaterina flashed a ha-ha! face from where she hovered over Ethrian.

Mist grumbled, "Worry about that some other time. What is the villain up to right now? Anyone know? Where is he headed?"

Scalza said, "He's already there, Mother. He was headed east-northeast, avoiding towns and cities. He's missing now, but there's no obvious destination out there. It must be somewhere hidden."

"Show me on a map. Varthlokkur has a whole raft of those things around here somewhere."

He had scores. It took just minutes to root out one of a scale small enough to show the world from the ocean in the west to the barren shores of the east. It was particularly detailed where the Dread Empire was concerned. Mist was not pleased.

A dozen people crowded round, Ethrian and the Old Man among them. The latter indicated an archipelago off the eastern coast. "Ehelebe."

Ethrian added, "Nawami."

"Nawami," the Old Man agreed. "That way," indicating the nothing beyond the eastern edge of the map. "Yesterday. Long time."

"Where is Sahmaman?"

The specialists attached to them crackled with excitement.

Lord Yuan had to be the killjoy. "Intriguing matters but not what we should concentrate on right now."

Scalza wiggled his butt and waggled his elbows enough to win some space. He deployed a straight edge, adjusted its lie. "I'm resisting the temptation to mark this out with a pen. The target started here, in the desert. He flew along this line. He's somewhere around here, now, in the steppe in the east of the upper Roë basin. There's a town about here. He probably spent a night there."

Impressed, his mother asked, "He's definitely not moving now?"

"No. He has disappeared. Wherever he got to, we can't watch him there. Maybe it's where he goes when he isn't making trouble. I can't even find the horse, now, so I'm going to look for boundaries."

The Old Man's eyes bugged. His face reddened. Was he choking? Explosively, he blurted, "Wacht Musfliet!" He staggered to the shogi table, assisted the last few steps by his mental coach.

The others strove not to distress him by pressing for details.

Mist demanded, "Where the hell has Varthlokkur gotten to?"

The wizard was home. He had not left since he brought the Disciple in. He had kept Radeachar close, too, once the monster finished scouting in Hammad al Nakir. But Varthlokkur was not in evidence. He did not like the crowds in the Wind Tower.

No one knew where he was. Mist said, "Someone find him. Eka. Someone is you. I expect you know every hiding place in this rock pile."

That caught Ekaterina off guard. She seemed fearful that her mother had penetrated some deep secret. Then she turned bland. "As you wish. No guarantee I can find him if he doesn't want to be found, though."

Mist smiled, nodded. "Anyone know what Wacht Mustflit means?" She hashed the pronunciation. No one noticed, nor did anyone do anything but shake heads.

There were plenty to shake. The Wind Tower was packed with a crowd that now included translators added to help Yasmid and her father get by. The one assigned to the Disciple grumbled plenty because he had so much nothing to do. Today's Disciple was not entrancing. When he spoke at all he preached, without passion or energy, in a mumble. He believed that minions of the Evil One had imprisoned him in the antechamber of Hell.

The mental experts said opium had damaged his mind too much. He would never recover.

"The Place."

Mist looked at Ethrian, who stood over the shogi board, shivering without Eka there to support him or to intercede. He spoke declaratively, though, in a tight voice. Everyone nearby shut up, hoping for more.

"Ethrian? I didn't hear you clearly through the noise."

"The Place of the Iron Statues. Wacht Musfliet is its name in..." Ethrian stopped, perplexed. In what language?

The Old Man made gurgling noises. He agreed but added nothing.

Ethrian went on, "That is a name. It does not mean Place of the Iron Statues. It means Stronghold Lonely. Or Fortress of Solitude."

All right. Mist understood. "Thank you, Ethrian. We should find that useful." Though how she did not at that moment see.

Nepanthe practically pounced on her son, drowning him in hugs of happy approval.

Mist felt the air move. Varthlokkur was beside her. "I arrived in time to hear him."

"Good. Where is Eka?"

The question puzzled him.

"I sent her to find you."

"She's still looking, then. I didn't see her." He pushed up for a better look at the map. "Good work, Scalza."

"Scary good work," Mist opined. The truth of her children had begun to leak through their clever masks.

Mist had carried them inside her for nine months. She could not harm them, however they threatened. Well, she could do no physical harm. Injury of the emotional sort she had inflicted already.

Varthlokkur considered the map as if entranced. His face went through changes, as though illuminated by lanterns shaken by a vigorous wind. He started, muttered, "Whoa. That was..." He recalled that he had an audience. "Sorry. I had an attack of the reminiscences."

Mist eased forward a foot, more directly into his line of sight. "And?"

"I've been there. A *long* time ago. I was someone else at the time. Probably Eldred the Wanderer…though that doesn't feel quite right. It was after the Fall."

Mist waggled fingers at her mental specialists. This might rate a closer look.

The wizard mused, "That may have been when I first met Nepanthe."

A patent impossibility, though no one challenged him. That would have been centuries before she was born. Still, it was no secret that Varthlokkur had discovered Nepanthe in prophetic visions ages before she was entered into the lists of the world.

The idea that he might have been in thrall to Old Meddler once did nothing to comfort anyone now, himself included.

Mist asked, "Can you recall anything else about that?"

"Things are in there, a little rowdy, a little shy, rambling around just outside the firelight. I'll try to lure them in."

"Have these two help." She indicated her specialists. "And don't waste time. I'm sure that the old devil being there isn't good."

"Probably not. But let's don't focus on the past so much that we miss what's happening now."

Ethrian had to be pried loose from his mother and probed while his mind remained connected to realities beyond the usual. Likewise, the Old Man required a closer look. He showed signs of having had memories broach, too.

She wished she had additional reliable mental experts. And she dared never forget that her empire was managed by fractious, powerful aristocrats who did not appreciate the fact that she was female.

…

Ekaterina took the opportunity of being unsupervised to snatch a few minutes with Radeachar. Her friendship for that thing was nothing like her feelings for Ethrian. This was rooted in empathy. The Unborn was far more of an outsider than she was—though her status in that realm had more substance in her own mind than in the quotidian world. The feedback she got suggested an unlikely family pet—as she imagined the devotion of a dog might be.

She had not interacted with an actual dog in years. There were none in Fangdred. The supply situation would not support the luxury of unproductive mouths.

So. Radeachar was, by an order of magnitude, the most alien entity she had ever encountered, yet she was comfortable around it. Even Varthlokkur sometimes got the creeps. Never Ekaterina.

Him. She should give Radeachar that. Radeachar would have been "he" had he been produced by a normal pregnancy and regular infancy.

Radeachar liked being near her. It was a cunning monster, though. It understood that she could not be seen being close or she would suffer. She was too young to sustain the emotional burden of being a great dread.

Too, the thing could not become as devoted as it might prefer. Its abiding obligation was to the Empire Destroyer. Varthlokkur had preserved it—him!—when the rest of the world just wanted the demon-spawn to burn.

Was she under some compulsion to attach emotionally to crippled cousins?

When you zeroed in on strict fact, she and Radeachar were related. Her grandfather was his father, so he would be her uncle if she had her facts straight.

Sudden laughter ripped free.

A glow of pleasure illuminated Radeachar. He was pleased that she was cheerful even though he did not understand.

She brushed her fingertips across the membrane separating the bizarre embryo from the world, then kissed it, too. "Thank you. I feel much better, now." Maybe because she had been reminded that her own situation was far from as awful as it could be.

More pleasure radiant from Radeachar.

She returned to the crowded workroom in the Wind Tower prepared to apologize because she had been unable to find Varthlokkur, discovered that her mission had been unnecessary. The wizard had found his way back on his own.

"Where have you been?" her mother demanded. Like she had some right.

Ekaterina accepted no such claim but offered only an insidiously insubordinate counter-challenge. "I took a long journey to a far place, Empress. A philosophical pilgrimage. An expedition of epiphanic conceptual discovery."

"Wait for it," Scalza sneered, loud enough for half the crowd to hear. "We're in for some vintage Eka." He seemed eager to see how his mother handled that.

"You're gonna get your turn, Worm. And you're gonna love it. Did you realize that Radeachar is our uncle? He's Mother's little brother."

Mist gawked. That was true but it had not occurred to her, ever.

A melodic tinkle of amusement escaped Ekaterina. Something odd, there, though. It started out light but quickly became creepy. "He never needs changing so she still won't have to learn how to deal with babies. She'll never have to get her fingers dirty."

Her tone left all her audience disturbed.

...

Mist realized that Ekaterina's remarks would make no sense even to her if she thought about them, but, still, they served up a steaming dollop of emotional truth. Not once had she gotten her hands soiled serving the needs of her infant children. It had been a rare and remarkable hour when circumstance or deliberation found her in the same room with either or both before they could walk and talk. But that reflected of her own earliest years—and most of the years that followed. She did not remember her mother. Her father had been a huge, grim, infrequently suffered manifestation more fearful than any kami or demon. She had anticipated his rare visits with massive anxiety.

These whiners endured a childhood far more family-intimate than hers had been.

Ekaterina's remarks appeared to amuse Varthlokkur and Scalza while baffling everyone else. Those closest to being in the know, Lords Kuo and Yuan, were indifferent.

They did not care if the blood of Tuan Hoa filled the monster's veins, if blood the thing even had. There was no sign that it ever took sustenance in tangible form. They had noticed that. It did not eat; neither did it shit.

That was scary once a Tervola reflected on the implications. It troubled Mist now that it occurred to her.

Eka had gotten a reaction big enough to encourage her to go on being absurd. "So not only is Radeachar our uncle, he's probably ahead of us in Shinsan's succession. He should be king of Kavelin, too. He has the blood-right. Queen Fiana was his mother. Uncle Bragi only got the job later, by being elected."

Mist snapped, "Eka, stop being ridiculous."

"I know. Nobody would want him, despite his claims. He isn't pretty enough and he doesn't have good social skills." Scalza grinned broadly, enjoying the vintage Eka. "But his legal claim is solid."

Varthlokkur settled a hand on the girl's shoulder, startling her. "Eka, the law, in most cases, isn't what's in compendiums. It's what the man with the most swords says it is on any given day."

Eka countered with a demoniac grin. "Oh, I know, Uncle. I'm just making old people squirm." Another amused tinkle, without the dire finish. She headed for her cousin, frown hatching because he was engaged in an actual conversation without her there to monitor, manage, and protect.

Mist suspected it was time to watch that girl more closely. She herself had started getting into mischief at that age.

On the up side, no one was out to eliminate Eka because her existence was inconvenient, nor did the world include anyone Eka favored for death.

Hell, practically everybody she knew was here, now, and considered her a weird, shy mascot or queer little sister.

No time for all that. Varthlokkur was at the map, muttering with Scalza. The Star Rider remained conspicuously invisible in a region that the Winterstorm, attenuated by distance, could barely touch.

Mist joined them. Lord Yuan, too, caught some etheric cue and came to the map.

Varthlokkur said, "He's gone to ground in the Place of the Iron Statues. My recollections of that are vague but I think they're good enough for me to fashion a baseline strategy."

Scalza said, "I'll bet the Old Man went there lots of times."

"We'll see what he has to offer."

Mist asked, "Are we involved in something that you'll tell us about?"

He smiled. "Suppose I pose the identical question to you?"

Mist forced a smile. "I am striving to move ahead vigorously while not catching the devil's eye. I want him to overlook me till I stab him in the back."

"While he's concentrating on me."

"Stipulated. You haven't kept a low profile."

"All part of the plan, which continues to evolve. Lord Yuan, I have a special need for your assistance."

"Again."

"It's the curse of being the best. Here is my current thinking."

The wizard's strategy was based on his estimation of Old Meddler's character as profiled by the mental specialists. Their assessment rested on what they had learned from Ethrian, the Disciple, and the Old Man, the latter in the main. The Old Man was entirely vindictive toward his one-time comrade.

Varthlokkur admitted, "He keeps doing the unexpected. He may be grinning from ear to ear because I'm about to strut into a big swamp full of crocodiles."

Mist checked the Old Man. If that one got a hold on reality often enough… Old Meddler had lost his allegiance the night that her father died and had worsened his odor with his unhappy actions on that eastern island.

The Old Man did not hate his erstwhile ally. He just wanted an end to his own and the world's torment.

Varthlokkur beckoned the specialist handling the Old Man. "Couple of things. First, get him into a shogi game with the boy. They feed off each other. Once they're engaged try to find out if he ever revolted before. Details don't matter, just the yes or no. Then feed his antagonism. Find out anything about the Place of the Iron Statues. I need to know how to get in."

The specialist glanced at his employer, who nodded graciously. "I'll get on that right away, sir," without asking if Varthlokkur wanted anything else. "Is speed essential?"

"It certainly would be useful." Varthlokkur turned to Mist. "This a good man."

"Those who aren't good men don't get to work for the Empress." She watched her daughter. Eka had heard. She moved closer to Ethrian, presumably to prepare him. Lord Kuo gestured with two fingers of his left hand. He would work on his friend.

After a second look at Wen-chin, Varthlokkur asked, "What's become of Shih-ka'i? He hasn't been around much."

"He has responsibilities elsewhere, including covering for me while I'm involved in this." Which was absolute truth but not whole truth. Nor did the wizard accept it as whole truth. He took a cynical attitude toward such claims. And, of course, his cynicism was justified. Mist added, "He isn't as enthusiastic about this as I am so I'm letting him do what he can to free me to indulge my passion."

"That makes sense."

She observed, "I expect you've prepared for a raid by the old villain."

"Yes. But I'm afraid that won't be good enough. I can't trust anyone but Radeachar to do what needs doing without jumping into the process."

"What does that mean?"

"It means that, if I give you an assignment you would probably decide you saw a better way and would try to use it, which would abort the process. I have to be two places at once to make what I want to do succeed. I haven't figured out how, yet, let alone how to manage supposed helpers."

"You could always attempt the absurd."

"Meaning?"

"Meaning you could explain what you're trying to do so people understand why it's important that they don't innovate. I know obsessive secretiveness is the norm for our kind, usually with good reason. But survival imperatives should trump old habits, shouldn't they?"

"Possibly."

"Particularly when these others are being asked to share the risks."

"It's hard to find the needful capacity for trust."

Mist asked, "How much time do we have? Any guesses?"

"Anywhere from a few days to forever. I think he'll try to end the threat I represent directly and forcefully. I don't think he'll waste time. He has to believe he's vulnerable and can't afford to be subtle. He operates inside a cloud of ignorance. I'm counting on that to make him vulnerable."

He surveyed his surroundings, added, "He doesn't know about these people and can't possibly be prepared to deal with every secret they might give up. But he does know about the Winterstorm and I expect that he's given that lots of thought."

"Two days might be enough, just barely, to drag in an arbitrator-director to manage the crisis. I'm thinking Bragi even though he doesn't like either one of us much right now and is probably convinced that he has weaseled out of his turn in the barrel."

She watched him swell with resistance.

"Exactly. And you can expect plenty of attitude from him if either of us comes out ahead because of this."

The wizard took nearly a minute. "I am repelled to the point where I suspect that you have identified a workable design."

"It needs only persist for as long as it takes to succeed or be flayed."

She expected the latter to be the more likely outcome. Once reason placed her eyeball to eyeball with that she just got more obstinate. There would be a grand showdown. Potential hurdles rolled off the duck's back of her determination.

What had become of that Poles of Power project meant to identify them and locate them? She had handed that off to Kuo Wen-chin, had she not? Then she had not followed up. Wait. No. She had not given that to Wen-chin. She had not given it to anybody. She had gone and forgotten the whole damned thing herself. It was too late to work that angle. The crisis was just around the corner, beyond her ability to delay.

Old Meddler would operate from inside a miasma of ignorance but would know that survival was table stakes. Weak, he would shun cat and mouse diversions. He would attack with ferocity and vigor.

She peered hard at the Old Man, then Ethrian. Could they really provide the tools she needed?

Doubt declared otherwise.

Doom was on its way.

†

Chapter Twenty-Eight:

WINTER, YEAR 1018 AFE:

Run in Circles

Al Rhemish remained chaotic. Whenever the confusion began to settle, some fresh dollop of rumor brought the turmoil back to life. The King really was dead. His remains had been found. The site was grisly but there was evidence enough to identify the dead. One man, with the pack animals and mounts, was missing. Anyone who knew Boneman had a good idea what had happened.

Then came news that Haroun bin Yousif and the Empire Destroyer had carried off El Murid and his daughter.

How anyone could actually know that never got explained. Varthlokkur's participation was based on circumstantial evidence, Haroun's on less. That there had been kidnappings at all remained uncertain. The Disciple's medical team was missing, too. There were no actual witnesses.

Those left behind were determined to believe what they wanted to be true.

The chaos at Sebil el Selib beggared that at Al Rhemish. The Faithful were not accustomed to life without established leadership—though that might be as corrupt as any on the

Royalist side.

Elwas al-Souki and his intimates did what they could, though they suffered continual sabotage by Adim al-Dimishqi's clique. The latter saw a God-granted chance to push the Believers onto a more traditional path.

The situation was juice-dripping ripe for exploitation by Old Meddler.

...

Old Meddler was preoccupied. He had wind of a huge threat, possibly the worst in fifty generations. He had pushed too hard. The push-back had devoured his resources. He was weak. He had no friends. Without, he was close to blind.

Too much happened beyond his ken. There were a thousand places he could not look without spending hours and vast reserves of energy. There were some into which he could not look at all, however hard he tried. A thousand glittering spears were headed his way but he could make out the shimmering razor edges of only a few.

He could not recall when he had felt this uneasy. And malaise rested entirely on intuition, not on facts already determined.

He could not sit tight and let events unfold, improvising responses. He had to act. His character demanded preemption.

His only real choice was what direction to strike.

Once he started he would, ironically, operate through improvisation anyway.

It might turn grim. He lacked allies. His arsenal had been depleted. The Poles of Power were beyond his control. One had vanished completely, as though Fate itself had chosen to tamper.

All effort would be wasted, anyway, whatever the world looked like on the other side. Success would win neither reprieve nor parole. Death itself might be no escape.

Even so, it was time. Definitely time to go shove his hands into the pie. After all these ages he could do nothing less.

...

Ragnarson delayed his appearance before the Thing for as long as he dared. Days and days, till Michael warned him that Haida said the delegates were out of patience. The rumor accusing the castle of stalling out of greed had gained considerable momentum.

Haida Heltkler made friends easily. She moved amongst people comfortably, taking the popular pulse. She could be flirty when she wanted, which was no handicap amongst the unwashed.

That did not become a problem amongst the more frequently washed of the castle once Carrie Depar and Michael Trebilcock each took a moment to counsel Babeltausque. That gleam in his eye had best disappear. No telling which Babeltausque heard more clearly but he did take the message to heart. Haida was too ripe, anyway. And he was damned happy with Carrie. That was going far better than he had any right to expect.

Ragnarson's main reason for stalling had been a hope that Babeltausque would discover a working transfer portal. A live one would provide the impact he wanted.

The sorcerer had one hell of a time finding one, though, despite knowing that it had to be out there somewhere. He found one at last, in Fiana's tomb, fourth time he looked, when Ragnarson insisted that he try it yet again.

The Thing met in full, with numerous native and foreign observers crowding into every otherwise unclaimed space. That whole end of the world, kings and commons, wanted to watch history in the making. And history *would* be made. History happened where King Bragi went.

First order of business, declaration of a requirement for order, manners, and good behavior inside the Thing hall. Misbehavior would not be tolerated. Following his minute of stolen glory each transgressor, whatever his station, should expect harsh penalties, from the stocks to public whippings. Colonel Gales would enforce good manners at his own discretion.

Ragnarson expected to make examples. People did not believe you till you hit them hard enough.

Silence gathered quickly once Ragnarson moved past his grim prospects cautionary speech.

He leaned on the rostrum, surveyed the assembly. Inger and Kristen were with him, a step back and one to either side, Inger on the right. Neither was happy. Each had suffered abiding disappointments. Each felt humiliated and betrayed.

Neither Fulk nor the younger Bragi were present. Each woman still wondered if she could fully accept what Ragnarson meant to announce.

Neither saw any other choice. The legal monarch was back. No one else minded him asserting his rights. Popular sentiment was plain. Common folks were thrilled. He had screwed up, back when, but the kingdom had enjoyed unprecedented internal security before that, and ferocious chaos in his absence. Things could only get better.

Nostalgia always ground off the bloody, jagged edges and wafted away the bad smells. The old days were ever better times, ever sweeter than the hells folks were slogging through nowadays.

Even so, Ragnarson sensed resentment. The people here were sure he was wasting their time. But they wanted the measure of the new him. They were no longer stunned beyond calculation. They were about to start knitting conspiracies tailored to whatever strengths he betrayed.

He offered a brief, brisk, insincere apology for the delays. "What I'm going to show you was more cunningly hidden than I expected. But, before that, I want to deal with the succession, which has caused too much friction and confusion."

That got their attention. Scores, possibly hundreds, had perished in those squabbles, rancor stirred by Dane of Greyfells and traditional prejudice. Though weary of the fighting the survivors all retained strong opinions.

"When it looked like I was gone for good this assembly designated my son Fulk to succeed me, a cynical choice pushed through in hopes that Inger would prove a weak regent, easily manipulated, while Fulk's constitution would betray him quickly."

That caused a stir. Some thought the Queen appeared stricken by the bald statement, though Dr. Wachtel's prognoses certainly supported it.

"I confirm the will of the Thing. Fulk will be my successor, with his mother as Queen Regent."

A buzz began. Elation. Disappointment. Wonder. Surprise that he would favor Fulk over his grandson. That emotional connection was stronger.

"However," Ragnarson said, portentously. "Practically, though,

I must face the fact that Fulk is sickly. He probably won't enjoy a long, peaceful reign. An intercession of evil won't be necessary to end the disappointments he may cause you who have black hearts. So, though I want Fulk and his mother to follow me, I also want my grandson, Bragi, and his mother to follow Fulk—even if Fulk produces his own son. And, Kristen, you will be patient. Michael has assured me that you will." He paused to allow reflection, then, "I want this made law. The Queen will herd it through and Michael Trebilcock will enforce it."

Ragnarson stood silent momentarily, then boomed, "The Crown will not tolerate any more squabbling amongst its subjects."

He did not say how he might enforce his will with no income or army. He had no idea how he could. He was winging it again, but reminding them that Michael was out there, watching. Few Kaveliners did not dread Michael's ire—though there were, in fact, few certain instances of that ire having been expressed directly.

Michael Trebilcock, the terror, was mostly perception.

Since the Great Eastern Wars perception had been enough. For most people, perception and truth were identical.

Trebilcock had arrived with Ragnarson but had disappeared right away. He was a spook now, rarely seen as he prowled the Thing. His eyes were hard. He was looking for something.

Which was Michael doing what Michael did, while hundreds sensed him watching, calculating, noting faces and names.

Ragnarson lifted a hand.

A tall, wide swath of canvas swept aside. Babeltausque clomped onto the floor of the Thing leading a tired-looking donkey and cart. The animal looked like it had mange. The cart carried a tall black box which, at first glimpse, resembled a one-hole outhouse. It produced a faint hum and random tweets. The tweets followed crackling sparks like those snapping between your fingertips and cold metal on a dry winter day.

Some onlookers knew it was no shitter, though it could scare the crap out of someone of questionable courage. It was a Dread Empire transfer portal and it was alive. There was, in fact, something wrong with it. It should not crackle and hum while on standby.

No one, including Ragnarson, actually understood that.

Ragnarson explained, "This was concealed inside Queen Fiana's mausoleum, masked by one that we deactivated before." He tried to sound more distressed than he really was. He was willing to exploit his own pain and vulnerability.

He experienced a tweak in time with a tweet. He was becoming an apprentice Greyfells, cynical and pragmatic. He wanted to look back but feared what he would see reflected in the faces of the women.

Babeltausque worked his cart round so that the donkey faced back the way that it had come. Four garrison soldiers lifted the portal down, settling it where all the delegates could see it, a dark, oily, interstellar black thing that the gaze either fell into and lost focus or slipped off and did likewise, partly why it had been so hard to find.

Ragnarson made random comments during the unloading. He wanted the onlookers distracted while the soldiers grunted and strained.

The portal seemed heavier than it should be.

A bear of a man in black armor emerged from the black, oily face. A twin came after, followed immediately by two more. Three of the four garrison soldiers demonstrated the better part of valor. The fourth fainted.

Yet another pair of giants emerged. Heart pounding, near panic, Ragnarson nevertheless did note that the Imperial Lifeguards were not arriving with their weapons bared.

He noted, as well, Babeltausque drifting away, eyes huge, leading donkey and cart at a glacial pace, stricken by this ugly turn of events, no doubt desperate for something to do and failing to think of a thing.

Had Mist's gang chosen to infiltrate when their portal was in exactly the worst possible location for their purpose?

The Empress herself stepped into the Thing hall. No doubting who she was. Most delegates remembered her from her exile. Her visual impact remained immense. The rising panic peaked. The screams and curses of men clambering over one another to win first escape eased up immediately.

Why, in the names of all devils and gods above and below, had that woman chosen to step into the heart of this kingdom at this moment?

Ragnarson did not doubt her move was as calculated as a public beheading. She wanted to be seen with Varthlokkur, who emerged from the portal behind her.

Those two approached Ragnarson.

Inger quietly told Josiah Gales to do nothing, an instruction he supported wholeheartedly. He signed, "Steady on!" to Nathan Wolf and Babeltausque. Both relaxed. They were not expected to commit suicide.

Mist came as near as the layout permitted. "Bragi, you're needed."

The wizard nodded. "It could be just hours, now."

Mist asked, "Where is Trebilcock?"

Ragnarson did not trust his tongue. He shook his head. He did not know. Around somewhere, probably in disguise.

He had seen Haida Heltkler moments ago, making eyes at Bight Mundwiller, but not now. Like Michael, she was out there listening.

That kid had a cooler head than he did, he feared.

He did croak, "He'll turn up." Or he might do something weird that nobody would notice right away. Or something that everyone *would* notice, and regret forever. Something they could tell their grandchildren thirty years from now.

Mist said, "Come. We have no time. We can collect Trebilcock later, if need be."

"You're shitting me, right? I got stuff to do here. And I don't think I care much about what you got yourself into out there."

Varthlokkur said, "We need you. We expect your help. We will take you back with us."

The Thing hall had gone silent. Those few delegates still moving did so slowly, randomly, like their minds had shut down.

Mist had come prepared, no doubt about that. Bragi would be going where she wanted him to go. And he had all too terrifying a notion where that might be, though not why. What could he possibly contribute? His whole experience with the Star Rider was a single glimpse, years ago. What could he actually do but get himself dead along with the rest of them?

However much they believed, and were committed, it would not be enough. He was not prepared to die for their fantasy.

Haroun was right. Old Meddler was weather. You lived with it, and you hoped you survived it. You hoped that it did not single you out.

How his attitude had shifted after just a brief romance with freedom!

"It's nice to be needed. But I can't imagine how I can help you die any less ugly than you're going to if you keep this up."

Babeltausque had not been overcome by the spell dulling the delegates. He turned loose of his donkey, straightened up, headed for the portal.

Had he decided it was time to die?

Ragnarson began to turn away, but not before Babeltausque's baby fluff, equally unaffected, latched onto him, whispering urgently, trying to get him to stop.

For the ten thousandth time in his life Ragnarson was amazed by the surprises the human animal could spring.

The child really did care. And the little pervert cared right back. He was trying to explain. But he did not stop moving.

Mist and Varthlokkur both reached up as though to beckon Bragi down to the Thing hall floor.

Michael Trebilcock appeared, approaching. Michael, who could be intimidated by so little, was unaffected by the calming and clearly meant to intercede. "Perfect," Mist said, clearly enough to be heard by everyone.

Babeltausque and his friend, of a single mind now, kept on toward the transfer portal. Trebilcock shifted his course, heading there, too. Break that damned thing and this villainy would die unborn.

There might be a lot of flash and burn afterward, though.

The invaders did not seem especially concerned.

Ragnarson could not imagine what Babeltausque hoped to accomplish. No way he would get past Mist's lifeguards.

The girl darted left, then forward. The sorcerer shot a spell through the space vacated by the bodyguard who moved to intercept her.

Clever, but a second lifeguard deflected the spell with his body. It knocked him down but he grabbed at the fat man as he collapsed. His effort shoved Babeltausque right into the portal.

Carrie Depar dove after him.

Mist cursed. Varthlokkur laughed.

Ragnarson figured those two would be dealt with in the Karkha Tower, or wherever they emerged. They had just plain jumped into deep shit.

He stepped down. His mind had begun to fog, too, though as yet less completely than most—though some remained unaffected. He forced his head round enough to follow Michael in his muffed attack. Trebilcock ended up getting tossed into the portal at a gesture from Mist.

She spoke to the men helping the lifeguard who had gone down. One boomed back, his tone not at all pleasant.

Another grabbed Ragnarson and dragged. He went, heels skidding.

...

Nepanthe dropped to her knees beside Bragi. He had the pale, sick look of a man with a ferocious hangover. He made sounds that probably were not efforts to communicate. He made no sense. Elsewhere, others treated other arrivals. Eka and Ethrian were fascinated by a girl only slightly older than Eka. Nepanthe needed a moment to recognize her. She did not look the same in person. She had come through better, physically and mentally, than any of the adults. She was unnaturally calm for someone suddenly snatched into an improbable situation.

Nepanthe got the creepy sensation she often felt while watching Ekaterina. This Carrie could grow up to be something dark and special.

The affection she showed her pudgy companion seemed bizarrely inappropriate.

After a quick look round, to see if they were in danger, the girl concentrated entirely on him.

Curious Eka was indifferent to any other arrival. Ethrian stood close by, shaking till Eka slipped her left hand into his right. He came alert immediately. The change was remarkable. His mind had turned on. He began assessing the situation.

Nepanthe suppressed an urge to charge over and start mothering. Ekaterina's warn-off look was unnecessary.

It made her ache but the evidence was in. Ethrian improved when she refrained from fussing. She did not understand but would take the pain if that meant her baby might come back.

Speaking of babies.

Smyrena charged through the crowd, fearless, hands shoulder high as she toddled at best speed toward the Winterstorm for the hundred and eleventeenth time since she figured out how to get up on her hind legs. Thank heaven Varthlokkur had adjusted the magical construct to be indifferent to her intrusions.

Nepanthe pursued her anyway. As she passed Ekaterina, she asked, "What is it?"

"Nothing. I never met a girl my own age before."

"Oh." But it was not like Eka knew nothing about Depar. She showed a limited interest in what was going on elsewhere but she had seen enough. You could be surprised how much Eka knew if you made her hold still and quizzed her. She probably knew exactly what went on between Depar and her keeper, though understanding it might elude her.

One more thing to worry about.

Worry was Nepanthe's ground state.

Smyrena wiggled and babbled, then twisted and extended her arms toward her brother, whom she had begun to manipulate already.

Ethrian noticed, focused, grinned, said something in his own dialect of baby, and reached back. Nepanthe surrendered her daughter. Smyrena was good for Ethrian. He would stay connected and focused for as long as Smyrena remained interested. He might have trouble concentrating on much else if she was in a demanding mood, though.

His mind-wrangler was there in a moment, ready to take advantage. Nepanthe was amazed by the gentle, tolerant skill the man showed. Right now he wanted to reinforce Ethrian's connection to this world.

He knew patience and put that ahead of any desire to root out useful information, even after Scalza squeaked, "He's back! I've got him again! He's on the move again!"

Too many people crowded the boy immediately. The nervous surge his way even got Ethrian leaning. Ekaterina took his arm, held him in place. She melted some when he smiled down at her.

Scalza's announcement struck deep into the Old Man, too. He

joined Ethrian, positioning himself at the youth's right hand, across from Eka, with both mental specialists behind, making calming remarks despite not being calm themselves.

Varthlokkur chivvied the crowd back. "Come on, people. All you can do is make this harder for those of us who have to..." He stopped talking, not because his remarks were not fair but because he had caught something over Scalza's shoulder. "All right. He's back out where we can see him. But where the hell is he going?"

Scalza said, "The horse is headed east. You should try your own resources on this, Uncle, just to see if this isn't a diversion."

"Clever boy. Yes. Get back farther, people. I need room to swing my elbows." He climbed inside the Winterstorm and started manipulating symbols. Old Meddler was near the limit of its reach already.

It took only two minutes. "Gor! It's him for sure and he's headed east. And he isn't alone. He has four black winged demons with him." He did not add that each demon carried a metal statue.

"Why is he headed east? Because he knows I'm watching and wants to be out of range before he lines up his attack?"

The Old Man had a one-word explanation. "Ehelebe."

Ethrian nodded. "Still secrets there."

Varthlokkur stepped out of the Winterstorm. "Lord Kuo. Can you tell us anything?"

"Nothing useful. I was there for months but only saw part of one fortress on one island. I know that Magden Norath had labs there at one time."

Ethrian said, "Nawami," as the Old Man repeated, "Ehelebe."

Varthlokkur looked from one to the other, forehead creasing. Both, with Sahmaman and the Great One, belonged to what they had to say about the deep past, so old that the names, which they never explained, were lost.

Mist stepped up close. "Lord Yuan. Lord Kuo. Can you set traps that he might trip once he gets there?"

Tin Yuan replied first. "That could be arranged, Illustrious. But please understand that the efficacy of any hasty booby trap will be problematic—and he might think that he was expected."

Wen-chin did not fully agree. "Only if the snare is clearly targeted. A generic trap, set to take anyone…"

"That's what I want. Obvious one place, subtle another, with a hope for nailing him if he's too sure of himself or just doesn't pay attention. Magden Norath proved that anybody can stumble."

"Worth the investment," Varthlokkur opined. He stepped back inside the Winterstorm, hoping to find out how fast the devil was moving so he would know how long they had to build traps.

Old Meddler had passed beyond the Winterstorm's range.

Paranoia embraced him. There was no way, now, to know what that devil was really doing.

He tried being amused by the fact that the Star Rider did this to everyone. He was fear incarnate, pure and simple. Millennia had gone into establishing that perception in the foundation assumptions of the world.

There was a hint of panic in the air.

Lord Yuan said, "We cannot manage what you want from here, Illustrious. The resources aren't available."

Lord Kuo nodded.

Varthlokkur thought Mist was surprised that the elderly Tervola had not deferred to Wen-chin. Would Lord Yuan become directly involved?

...

The winged horse settled to a battlement walkway on the mainland-facing side of the island fortress. Its muzzle drooped. It released an unambitious, exhausted whicker. Its rider lapsed into a moment of drowsiness that could have become sleep if nothing had happened.

Equally exhausted demons settled nearby but stayed only long enough to shed their burdens. Then they made a concerted attempt to escape, despite a staggering weariness.

The Star Rider dismounted as they soared. "We will rest here." He did not want to waste time on rest but his companions were almost used up. He was on his last reserves himself. He swung the Windmjirnerhorn round, began tapping its valves.

A demon screamed in angry despair. The Horn's power dragged it back down. The other demons found new energy and flapped harder.

The captive demon lacked any sense of sacrifice. It gave up

right away rather than mount an agonized rearguard struggle that would give its fellows a chance to get away.

Old Meddler was too tired to work fast. He was able to recapture only one more demon.

The others were not beyond recall, however, whether they wanted to respond or not. But he would need several days' rest before he tried, then would need an additional two more days to complete the recall.

He refused to invest the time.

His enemies would not be resting. They never slept.

One instant of relaxed incaution had cost so much already.

Less haste, more rest, before commencing the journey east, and he would not be in this predicament.

He eyed the horse, bitterly inclined to blame it. Somehow. Would it flee, too? Its behavior had been strange lately. Its desertion would be a disaster of the first water.

No. It would not forsake him after all their ages together.

That just could not happen. Its recent behavior had to be just time catching up.

The animal was getting old despite being immortal.

He stared across the strait. There lay a long trek back to civilization along a harsh route. That boy, the Deliverer, had managed it but the devastation he had left behind guaranteed that no one would again until the complexion of the earth changed and a new climate embraced this part.

Star Rider's scheme was springing leaks. Only two demons remained. Success could require all four iron statues. Two might not be enough to dilute Varthlokkur's strange sorcery. And the wizard would not be alone.

Improvisation had become imperative.

He was not good at making it up on the fly, despite so much experience. He was a master of the long, slow, complex machination, shogi with a thousand pieces.

He no longer knew real fear. Nothing had threatened him mortally in so long that he had lost the emotions surrounding the event. Last time of maximum risk had been during the Nawami Crusades.

He was uneasy, though. Definitely uneasy.

Little had gone well this past year, up to and including the last five minutes. There was no reason to expect his luck to turn around.

The new year was close, though, and the changing of the years always brought new hope. That was what new years were for. Not so?

He made sure he had the remaining demons under absolute control, then herded his companions down a long stair to a weathered court. A stiff-stepping iron statue missed its footing and tumbled, grinding and clanking, taking the fall alone. A human in the same straits would have grabbed at anyone and anything to save itself. It rose from the flagging wearing only a few new scratches. It waited on Old Meddler and the rest, then followed, creaking worse than before.

Old Meddler surveyed his surroundings. Curious. These fortifications had existed when first he had come to Ehelebe. Time had inflicted few changes. The dust was thicker. The sandy decomposition surfacing the building stone was just a little crustier.

Nowhere had so much as one plant taken root. Other abandoned places suffered the assault of vegetation beginning the moment its caretakers went away. In a few generations a mighty city could subside into jungle entirely, vanishing before its legends could fade.

Plants did not strive to reclaim this place, nor did any animal. Birds refused to nest, yet swarmed the cliffs across the strait. Every species of mammal but Man shunned the place. Bugs and spiders were rare. The few were warped compared to their mainland cousins. Only scorpions and some things with a thousand legs appeared to prosper.

Once inside, Old Meddler caught a scent that did not belong, body odor from someone who ate mostly rice and smoked fish. An ascetic, perhaps, who had visited recently.

His nose had saved him before. He trusted it completely.

The odor was unremarkable. He associated it with older Tervola. It had been there last visit, not as fresh, dissimilar enough to have been left by a different individual.

Tervola must be frequent visitors. But which? And why? Was the place being scouted as a possible secret base? It had served that purpose before. Some middle-level Tervola conspirator? The only access was by transfer portal. Only the Dread Empire owned those.

Yes. The woman ruling there would be a red flag to half the Tervola. Where better to plot an end to that abomination?

Too bad he was locked into this, which demanded swift resolution. Otherwise, he could sit here like a trapdoor spider, snapping up conspirators, adding them to his inventory of fools. Tools.

He heard a humming that could only be a live portal.

He headed for the kitchen area. It was there that he had seen workable portals last time. Could someone be there? Those portals had been too small to pass an adult. The man-size ones, in theory, could only be activated from the other end.

The racket his crowd made would have to have been heard. The hum might be somebody making a getaway.

He sent a demon ahead, backed by an iron statue. The demon, shrunken down to a beetle of human size, entered the kitchen walking upright on unnaturally robust rear legs, feeling the air ahead with antennae half as long as it was tall. Its wings lay on its back like fitted plate, polished purple-black. The statue, the one that had fallen earlier, clanked behind clumsily, right leg squealing as it dragged through the first few inches of each step. It had not been maintained. Old Meddler wished there had been time for an overhaul. There had been no time for years. Not a minute to invest in routine upkeep. Too often, not a minute for desperately needed sleep.

This task had become impossible once he lost his ancient associate.

A bad choice made, that time.

Old Meddler seldom acknowledged mistakes, even to himself. He did not make mistakes. He was who he was. He was what he was. He could not make mistakes.

Even so, that sloppy choice had cost him like none other since the cluster that got him sentenced to this hell. It had, worse, cost him the closest thing he had to a friend.

So now the Old Man was dead. All that he had done to help, when he had been awake, had piled itself onto Old Meddler's weary shoulders.

So. There was no time for maintenance. No time for anything but handling the crisis of the moment.

Retina-blistering emerald light flared. A green shaft ripped through the demonic beetle, hit the iron statue in the right abdomen. Chunks of demon chitin flew, revealing the inside of the thing's wing case to be orange and the body beneath as red and orange. Stuff flew off the iron statue, too. It staggered back a long step, leaning slightly, like a man kicked in the gut.

That flying stuff might have been globules of molten metal. They splattered, then hardened quickly.

This was not possible.

Blindness came.

He did not panic. He knew flash blindness was not permanent. He had lost vision this way before. He would recover, not as quickly as he might like. But…

That bolt, however generated, had immense power behind it, of a level not seen since… No, even the Nawami Crusades had produced no blast savage enough to pierce the frontal armor of an iron statue. Had it? This world had seen nothing like this. Someone had tapped directly into…

He could not concentrate. His eyes hurt. The pain threatened to become the focus of his existence. Despite past experience he had trouble managing his fear of blindness—though he *must* remain calm and controlled. He was deeply vulnerable at this moment, even with demons and iron statues to shield him.

The event had not been an attack. He understood that when no follow-up came. The demon had triggered some trap. Maybe there was competition for this place. Underground movement often wasted energy on internecine murder rather than battle the object of rebellion.

Or maybe he had been expected. That would explain the magnitude of the blast.

Unlikely, though. There was no way anyone could have predicted his visit. Some overly bright Tervola was determined to make a convincing statement to any fellow Tervola who stumbled onto his handiwork.

One of those master sorcerers had found the golden key, a way to suck power off the transfer streams. Must have. The dream had been out there for ages. No lesser source could have delivered that emerald violence.

Had he truly seen molten metal fly? He did now recall a similar instance in one rare moment where the Great One had chosen to inject himself directly into the Nawami conflict.

The Great One had used power stolen from the transfer streams. He had made himself a god by finding the way, and later became a denizen of the transfer streams, existing in all eras simultaneously while also constituting a parallel, prior entity in the world outside. The Great One inside had been the Great One the Dread Empire defeated in the eastern waste. Shinsan had gone on to root his fetch out and engineer its annihilation—though not before it reached back and fathered itself in an age long gone.

Those absurdities should have claimed devoted examination ever since. How could that happen? It had despite the logical implausibility. Could there be an even stronger ascendant coming now? Ssu-ma Shih-ka'i, whose ingenuity brought the Deliverer down? No! Not some ridiculous farmer grown too big for his trousers! But who else? There was no other significant name associated with those events. Not amongst the living.

Clearly, he had not looked where he should. But that was too hard when you were alone. Tactics devoured your time, leaving none to linger over the meaning of what might be happening behind what was distracting you at the moment.

His vision began to clear. He discerned frozen shapes. Disinclined to trigger another trap, his companions awaited his instructions.

The stricken demon had settled to the floor. Its birdlike skinny legs projected into the kitchen. Its through and through wound still produced wisps of black mist. Greenish ichors streaked the color where a wing and wing case had been ripped away. It was trying to reinstall something that had fallen out of its chest.

It was a demon. Its wound should not be mortal, in this world, but to survive it dared not flee to its own realm even though here it could survive only as a cripple.

The stricken iron statue remained fixed, almost unbalanced, in the process of taking an awkward step. The green shaft had not driven through but there was a six-inch circle of bluish purple shine on the statue's back, bulging, where the light would have emerged had it not spent so much energy skewering the demon first.

Old Meddler's vision continued to improve. He eyed that bulge. How could anyone set random traps that powerful? Where had they gotten the know-how?

Better question. More important question, right now. Were there more such traps? It was not reasonable that his evil luck should be so foul that he would trigger the worst trap first stumble. Far more likely that it was one of a battery.

"The perfect response to an improbable event," he said, softly, punctuating with a tired sigh. "Stay put." He readied the Windmjirnerhorn.

So. Yes. There were more traps, impressive in number, but with disposition and trigger choices that seemed naïve. Once you knew they were there you could deal with them easily. People as sophisticated as the Tervola ought to have built a network so cunning that the triggering of one instantly rendered the rest more sensitive.

Suppose they had been set in haste, to deal with an anticipated intrusion by mundane burglars? The traps could polish off a battalion of regular bandits. Unless that notion was what the trap builders wanted put into the head of a more sophisticated intruder.

Unless…

The curse of being Old Meddler was overthinking and seeing everything through the murky lens of his own twisted character. Of assuming that everyone was as warped of mind and motive as he.

He eliminated the most obvious traps. Even so, the iron statues triggered several more, better disguised, as they assisted his futile search the next few days.

Old Meddler grew increasingly disgruntled. He had one healthy demon left. The statue smitten by the green light had not moved since. It still communicated but that made it no less an oversize, man-shape heap of scrap.

He had planned to spend a few hours recuperating once he arrived, before investing a few more recovering weapons and tools from hiding places beneath the fortress. Magden Norath had left a lot. Old Meddler had hidden his own reserves here and elsewhere across the archipelago.

He had come to the emergency against which all that stuff had been cached.

Only… The hiding places were empty. Covert after covert, whatever had been hidden was gone, as though someone who knew every cache had systematically rid them of anything that might ever be of use to the Old Meddler.

Hours burned gathered into days of despair. What the hell had happened? *Who* had happened? Varthlokkur was not plausible. Had some incredibly clever Tervola matured unnoticed while developing the skills to root out the Star Rider's hidden treasures? That reeked, too, but not as badly as the possibility that the bitch Tervola Mist might be responsible.

No. None of that was credible. Those were not people who could resist the temptation to use what had been hidden here. Tervola were dark of heart by definition, nor could Varthlokkur possibly be as goody-goody as he wanted the world to think.

All men did evil when they saw a chance to get away with it.

The Star Rider was a stubborn old beast. Yet another thirty hours of daylight and lamplight went into his search before he surrendered to the fact that every filthy tidbit was gone. The fortress had been stripped.

He had to get back west. Time was fleeing. "Enemy never rests," he reminded himself, over and over. "Water sleeps, but enemy never rests." He was not ready to spend the time necessary to look back and find out who had done this and what all they had done. That could cost another week. Meantime, leakage from the small freight portals had begun to weaken the Horn.

He could not destroy those. He needed them—unless he wanted to return to the Place and start over, which would take ages because he had conscripted the best iron statues and most tractable demons already.

Perhaps the universe itself was out to thwart him.

The hours fled on. He should have launched his attack long since, crushing resistance instantly using weapons which even Varthlokkur's weird sorcery could not withstand. He should have passed through the final fire by now, and be headed back to the Place for a long rest, not still be out here with a stomach gone sour.

By grace of the Horn he learned that his missing treasures were not lost forever. They were out there, in the waters of the strait, thrown there by whoever had robbed him.

The Horn brought several relics ashore. That was a waste. Anything that had been unbroken when it went in had been damaged by the brine and battered by surf and current. Everything had been in the water a long time, not just days. His weakening had begun even before the Deliverer crisis commenced.

"Only one option left. The other islands." A feeble hope, there. Little of value had been cached elsewhere. There had been no clear need for the redundancy.

His remaining demon hauled him hither and yon, from barren outcrop to empty sand pile. Each cache was as pristine as could be hoped. His enemy had either not known about them or had been unable to reach the lesser islands. His mischief had been incomplete.

Sadly, what he recovered was useless now—though, sweet miracle, he did discover copies of Magden Norath's research records. Those would be invaluable later.

He would make time for those after he finished. He would go to ground for a generation or two, maybe three, letting his fields lie fallow. New generations would produce ambitious men willing to disdain the lessons of history. And he could rest up and get ready to leap back into the game.

He had done it a hundred times before.

But first he had to push through this.

He realigned his strategy to fit the tools available and what he suspected about the people ranged against him. He brooded over the role of the Dread Empire. He had no concrete evidence but felt certain that Shinsan's ruling class were actively working against him. Too much cleverness had gone to make him stumble.

His nature compelled him to waste time rehashing every little episode of the past year, looking to tie unrelated events into one cunning campaign, but his grand capacity for conspiracy theory could not pound some events hard enough to make them fit a unified hypothesis.

If it was all connected, he lacked some critical piece of evidence.

He had no time to winkle it out. He had to strike.

As it stood, his enemies—with everyone entangled in the year's events—appeared to be victims of plain old-fashioned "Shit happens."

He announced, "It's time. We begin."

His pitiful army raised no cheers.

...

Breathless, Josiah Gales said, "It won't take a sell to convince them that Shinsan might be a problem."

Inger nodded numbly. That was pure understatement. The spell suppressing emotion in the Thing hall was fading. Chaos was breeding, though the delegates no longer wanted to flee.

Kristen Gjerdrumsdottir stepped past, vaulted the rail, rushed the transfer portal, flung herself at the last Imperial lifeguard. She was half his size but her momentum knocked him sideways.

Dahl Haas shrieked at her to show some goddamned sense! He got there two steps behind her, hammered the man's helmet with the butt of his belt knife, cracked the nonmetallic material. The blow stunned the man. Several Thing members piled on. Class and ethnicity were not factors.

"Stop!" Inger's bellow pierced the excitement. "Let him get up."

The easterner grasped what was expected. He rose slowly, looked around carefully. He had been disarmed. Half his armor had been torn away. He would enjoy a fine crop of bruises if he survived.

Inger said, "That's enough, people. Josiah, take charge of him. We'll hear an exchange proposal soon."

Its nature and details should be revelatory.

The Empress was interested only in Bragi and Michael. She might not know who Babeltausque or the Depar girl were.

Delegates eased away from the captive, awed and wary alike. The easterner submitted. He knew he needed only be patient.

Inger announced, "Stay away from the gateway. It might take you somewhere you really don't want to go."

The portal tweeted and crackled. It now canted slightly. The angle was visually disconcerting.

"Josiah, once you have him safe, see if you can't come up with a way to communicate if they don't contact us."

Gales inclined his head. He did little talking anymore. Dr. Wachtel said he was in continuous pain and did not want to take it out on anyone.

Maybe she could exchange the lifeguard for treatment for Josiah. They were good at fixing people in the Dread Empire. Bragi should not have survived. And look what that woman had done for herself… Flash of jealousy. To look that good at her unnatural age!

The gate still hummed. Could she shove Kristen and Haas through, then work a deal to keep them over there?

Probably should not try, sweet as that sounded. Bragi would not approve. And he would be back.

"Josiah, don't take him far. I need you handy." On reflection, if she had to trade she would ask for Babeltausque back. Though Bragi might argue, the sorcerer was invaluable.

"Gentlemen, the interruption is over. Take your seats." She had to milk this while it was fresh.

†

Chapter Twenty-Nine:

WINTER, 1018–1019 AFE:

Fire and Maneuver

Other than an exotic half-breed girl-child, whose beauty nearly unmanned him, no one paid attention to Babeltausque or Carrie. Most were too busy, even when all they did was look over one another's shoulders. The couple tried their best to stay small and unnoticed, day after day.

The exotic took it on herself to see that they touched nothing in what she called the Wind Tower, a place Babeltausque felt should exist only in fairy tales.

He and Carrie were free to come and go so long as they touched nothing and did not get underfoot. Slyly, the exotic girl explained that they could leave whenever they wanted—if they could find a way out and were ready to cross the Dragon's Teeth in winter.

The girl was curious about Carrie, jumpy around him, and reluctant to chat. She seldom left her young man long enough for a conversation, anyway.

She impacted Babeltausque like a kick to the heart of his fantasies but he managed his weakness.

Carrie murmured, "She is incredible, isn't she?" No doubt to remind him that in this place self-control came under the heading

Life or Death. "I saw her once when we were little. I envied her so much."

"I won't lie, darling. She is the most beautiful girl I've ever seen. But she is more dangerous than a bushel of cobras." She intimidated him in more than just the survival mode. The girl had a sinister psychic air that no one else seemed to notice.

The eastern Empress emerged from a transfer portal. Lord Yuan followed. Mist and her Tervola henchmen had vanished shortly after their return from Kavelin, leaving King Bragi in charge. Varthlokkur had gone soon after they did. Ragnarson seemed confused. There was nothing for him to do. He hung around with a dour, dark man from Hammad al Nakir, also supposedly a king, and with that man's wife. That marriage seemed totally bizarre. She was in the throes of a difficult pregnancy. She was too old to be carrying a child. The three spent hours at a time gathered together not saying a thing.

Varthlokkur's wife kept things going.

And that man, yonder, was the Disciple? Truly? And *that* one was the Old Man of the Mountain? And that other one was Kuo Wen-chin, who was once Lord Protector of Shinsan?

Fortune had delivered him into such company?

Carrie murmured, "And this is her mother, which explains so much."

Yes, indeed. Even he was smitten, though his need insisted that they be so much younger.

The Empress announced, "That's done. Now we wait."

Babeltausque had little real idea what was happening. Nobody explained. What he knew he figured out from what he overheard in the few conversations in languages he could understand. He was not asked to contribute. He had nothing to do. He and Carrie were putting in hours till Mist had time to swap them for a lifeguard who had gotten left behind.

Carrie was more daring than he. She tackled the crowd, engaged in conversations where she could. Her luck was limited. Few spoke her language. Those who did were inclined to shy away because she was intimate with a sorcerer.

The Ekaterina girl had implied that she and her brother had spied on their private moments. Scalza thought it a great dirty joke. Ekaterina was troubled.

These people had bigger worries. At some level each was working to end the tyranny of the Star Rider.

Just the thought sparked terror. It showed more hubris than would mocking the gods themselves. The gods did not meddle in mundane affairs anymore.

Babeltausque surveyed the crowd while hugging Carrie close, her proximity offering reassurance. If he understood correctly, these misfits had generated all the information Varthlokkur and the Empress needed.

Where had the wizard gone? He had spent time close up with the Old Man before leaving. Babeltausque thought he was on a spoiling mission unconnected with Mist's operation.

...

Radeachar carried Varthlokkur over and around what had to be the Place of the Iron Statues. There was little to be seen: rocky hill country spotted by scraggly oaks, stunted pines, breaks of scrub brush, and dried brown grass. Varthlokkur saw no running water. He saw nothing manmade. He looked in from a variety of angles in changing light and never saw anything remarkable.

And yet he sensed the presence of something there.

No angle showed him the entrance he had been told to seek.

He saw nothing even vaguely familiar. If he had visited before, that had been erased from his memory.

The echo of a memory that did haunt him was of something resembling a crowded old Itaskian graveyard, behind grey stone walls wearing lichens and creepers. There should be massive wrought-iron gates. Inside, there should be forests of monuments. Amongst those would be iron statues and statues in noble stone.

Varthlokkur could see no ground that looked suitable for such a graveyard.

He did discover redundant protective barriers unlike those associated with other masks for reality, such as the one surrounding the temple Ragnarson had found outside Vorgreberg.

He decided that his memories must have been distorted by an outside influence.

As Radeachar settled to earth Varthlokkur began to entertain a new concern: How to get inside if the Place had gone through a makeover and the Old Man's recollections were obsolete?

That one had been sure that the Star Rider would have changed nothing. There had been no need. Old Meddler was lazy. He lived in permanent crisis mode, concerned only with the disaster of the moment, seldom bothering with preventative work or the grand scale equivalent of housekeeping. When Varthlokkur asked how that gibed with the vast, complex, generations-long schemes the Star Rider wove, the Old Man just shrugged. Those were something else. They interested the Star Rider. Someone who wanted to bother could work out the psychology.

Radeachar had its own sense for the magical, if little inclination to report it.

Once Varthlokkur set his feet down he saw what he sought so exactly that he knew it must be his expectations reflected, yet could be taken as real for today's purposes.

The one expectation the place did not meet was an aggressive defense. It did nothing even when he touched the gate. The Old Man had said that the entrance would be the most dangerous part. Once he was inside he would belong. If he did not belong he would not have been allowed in, would he?

Carefully, by the numbers, hoping the Old Man had lost nothing during his prolonged mental holiday, the wizard executed the rituals that would let him enter. The Unborn floated behind. Varthlokkur wondered if it owned a sense of time. He could recall no situation where it had become impatient.

Screaming, the gates swung in a few feet. Rust chunks broke off the hinges. Old Meddler had not come and gone here.

Inside, the Place conformed to his recollections. It *was* a cemetery—where the tombstones and stelae told no tales. Time had erased most every inscription. The rare partial survivors were incised in alien characters. There was no reason, in fact, to conclude that this was an actual burial ground. It simply resembled familiar cemeteries—and was a product of his own mind, anyway.

There were mausoleums, too, more weathered than the simpler monuments, suggesting that they were older. He was curious but did not step away from his mission. Foolish to open a box, the contents of which were unknown and might be deadly.

The few iron statues all appeared to be damaged. Several were down, overgrown, and sinking into the soil. The most damaged were also the rustiest. Those with the least rust nevertheless lacked a hand, a foot, or showed signs of having been hit violently by something at least as hard as they were.

Varthlokkur had seen iron statues in action only once. Nothing had stopped or slowed them, but that time their advent had been a total surprise. Still, even forewarned, he feared sorcery would not slow them. On the other hand, the efficacy of natural law was persuasive here.

He selected the least-impaired-looking statue and told Radeachar to proceed as planned.

The first challenge was to find out if Radeachar could shift one of the damned things.

They looked heavy.

Not too heavy for Radeachar, though it did strain.

The Unborn soared till it and the statue were a speck. The Place's boundary membrane seemed infinitely elastic from inside.

The statue ended its plunge on granite flagging, surviving better than Varthlokkur expected. No pieces flew off.

The Unborn repeated the cycle again and again, enjoying itself. It wore down quickly, though. That was not good. They had to get back to Fangdred once the damage was done. Old Meddler would attack soon. The trap had to be armed and set. This was just to make sure the villain would remain hamstrung after that dust settled.

Radeachar had dealt with the soundest statues. Varthlokkur had hoped to achieve more. Had hoped to come across better opportunities to do mischief. Loss of the iron statues would have to do.

Still… He probed gently, cautiously, everywhere, but learned very little. This was all beyond him and more mechanical than his mind was equipped to handle. His inclination was to loose a storm of generally destructive sorcery to rip the place up, on a scale not seen since the Fall. Totally liberal vandalism would ruin the Star Rider.

The graveyard feel restrained him. The uneasy sense that he should not. Destruction could break things open.

There might be more here than appearances suggested. It now

felt like not all those graves might be empty. Like some contained tenants who were wakening.

Could the Place be a prison for the restless dead as well as Old Meddler's home base?

Could be. It might contain some of the world's oldest horrors. Or enemies Old Meddler had conquered in ages past.

There might be places here reserved for Varthlokkur and the Empress.

That such an alien notion entered his head left him more wary. It did not feel like original inspiration. Something wanted him worried and scared.

It was an old, old world haunted by countless secrets. Sorcerers built themselves by using evils claimed from colleagues who had gone before them, who had grown fearsome in their own time by taking from the dead who had preceded them.

This was the fate of any sorcerer of attainment. One accepted it as the price of power today—or shied away from, whining, by those who would deny the inevitable.

A thousand Magden Noraths, and worse, had come, then gone. Ten thousand more would follow, every one cannibalizing his predecessors. The Great One demonstrated that a horror clever enough and stubborn enough could persist beyond death by establishing itself in the very skin of reality.

That was another idea that he would not have entertained in the normal course, but it felt completely true. Could it have leaked out of that membrane, across Radeachar's consciousness, its path opened by his own sense that these graves might not all be empty symbols?

For a moment he thought he felt the amusement of a distant something that had been tasting his thoughts. He shuddered—then blanched as he sensed another something, screaming mad and starving to get at the world, this one a terror at least as powerful as the Great One had been.

He headed for the gate immediately, summoning Radeachar as he went. They dared not tarry. He might be one of the most powerful men alive but he was too weak to resist what wanted to control him here. He beckoned the Unborn again, impatiently. "Let's go! Now! We've done all that we can do here." Which was not nearly as much destruction as he had hoped, but might already be more than could possibly be good for the world.

Pressure that he had not fully recognized stopped once he passed through the gate.

The boundary definitely kept in as well as kept out.

With Radeachar's help he resealed the gates, then rested with hands on knees, panting. He had not been worn down like this for ages. "That was harsh." A few breaths. "The man might not be entirely wicked after all." Assuming Old Meddler *did* restrain things like whatever it was that had reached out…

Radeachar did not comment. It was not feeling chatty. Not that it ever did.

"We've done what we can. Back to Fangdred. The hour is coming."

…

Ragnarson asked, "When the hell will all this go down? I've been here a week. I've got stuff to do back home."

Mist gave him a look of exasperation. She had grown impatient herself, especially with those who could not understand how important her mission was. Old Meddler's attack was overdue. The villain must have something up his sleeve.

It seemed an age since Lord Yuan had reported one of his booby traps tripped. He did not think the Star Rider had been hurt but did believe that the event had led to the delay.

"We can't make the man hurry, Bragi. We're the ones sitting on a static defense."

Though Mist looked at him she was talking to herself. She surveyed the gathering. Her sister-in-law looked particularly haggard. Bragi just looked bored, like everyone else. There was no sense of urgency here.

So. Nepanthe had taken everything on her shoulders. Bragi had done nothing. The effort to collect him and Michael had been a waste.

Speaking of… The pudgy sorcerer and his child-whore-spouse. What had become of them?

She asked.

Eka responded, "Probably out on the wall. They spend a lot of time there, looking at the mountains and holding hands. And talking lover stuff, Scalza says."

Did she sound wistful? She did glance Ethrian's way.

The boy was much recovered, though still not what he had been before his stint as Deliverer. He had become less dependent than his cousin liked.

"Careful what you wish for, eh?"

"Mother?"

"Nothing. Find them, please. I want to send them home."

Eka loosed the long sigh of the teen who was expected to do everything around here. She did as she was told, though.

Mist headed for Scalza, to find out what he was watching. The Winterstorm caught her eye. There was something odd about it. Something not quite right. She turned away from her son, toward the shogi table, pushing Matayangan kibitzers aside. "Lord Kuo..."

"You spotted it quickly." He did not look up. His opponent was destroying him. There could be no doubt that the Old Man's mind was back, though his ability to remember still left much to be desired.

"Something is wrong with Varthlokkur's artifact."

"Ekaterina was tinkering with it. She tripped a security routine she didn't anticipate. It was there to protect the baby. She did the damage trying to undo and cover up. Don't get too upset. Kids do that kind of stuff. And he can put it right."

"I *will* get upset but maybe not the way you expect. What does it tell us that she had the daring and confidence to mess with that thing? And to think she could get away with it, in front of all these people?"

In as portentous a tone as Mist ever heard from him, Wen-chin replied, "To me it says we'd better hope that her Aunt Nepanthe did a good job shaping her values."

What could she say to that? Whatever Wen-chin was thinking, that was a bold statement. Letting ego drive a response would be of no value whatsoever.

"You're right."

"Is it frightening? I have no children myself."

Many Tervola did not, on the right side of the blanket. Family created complications. They became hostages to fortune, Mist knew too well.

"She didn't do any permanent damage. She stepped away as

soon as she saw that she could only make things worse."

"Good to hear that."

"She's sensible and responsible, given her age and situation."

Mist suppressed a surge of irritation.

Wen-chin said, "I expect he'll be understanding."

"Varthlokkur? Let's hope." He was unpredictable, emotionally. Where was he, anyway? "Shouldn't he be back by now?"

Wen-chin shrugged. "Check with Scalza. He's trying to keep track." The Tervola added softly, "Be pleased that it wasn't the boy."

She did not acknowledge but she understood.

Kuo Wen-chin found Scalza worrisome.

Mist did, too, but less so than Ekaterina. Scalza only thought he was clever and secretive. He was talented but he was like every other talented boy produced by Shinsan. If he became trouble he would be predictable trouble. Eka, though, could be a menace less fathomable than her mother had been. She would be as unpredictable.

Could it be a sex-linked thing?

Female Tervola were rare. So rare that Mist knew of only two. Ekaterina was the other one.

Her toenails felt likely to curl in dread.

She leaned over Scalza's right shoulder, so close her hair brushed his and her breath heated his cheek. She saw what might be the Unborn, in his scrying bowl. The view there was obscure but the color was right.

He jumped. "You startled me, Mother."

"Sorry."

"When did you get back? Did it go well?"

"I've been back for some time. I'm wondering if my feelings should be hurt because you didn't notice."

Scalza made a visible effort to process her meaning before he responded. He reached the right conclusion. "I was preoccupied. Sometimes I get too focused."

"Yes. You do. But don't we all? It went well enough. The target tripped some of the traps."

"But you didn't get him?"

"Naturally not. It couldn't be that easy. What's the wizard's story?"

"I don't know. He's back in range, barely, but he isn't in any hurry to get here."

She harrumphed.

"I think he's going as fast as he can. It must not have gone right. The Unborn acts like it's hurt. It has to rest a lot."

That was new. She considered the monster infinitely indefatigable.

Eka brought the Itaskian sorcerer. She and he were blushing. The girlfriend wore a smirk. Had Eka interrupted something?

Mist found the girlfriend's composure as disturbing as she did Eka's potential for chaos.

She glanced from Eka to the Winterstorm and back. Her daughter went on defense immediately.

Mist told the sorcerer, "We're sending you home while we have time to do that."

Babeltausque's relief was almost pathetic.

His companion brightened considerably, too.

"Excellent!" the sorcerer said, then said no more, as though he did not trust himself not to jinx it.

The girl asked, "What will we need to do?"

"What you've done all along. Stay out of the way while they ready the portals." She beckoned Lord Yuan, who was conferring with some specialists. That was good. He should have everyone he needed on hand.

Tin Yuan responded with what was, for him, alacrity. He pushed through the press. "I understand what you want, Illustrious. But there are problems."

"How so?"

"The portal we used before is no longer operational. We haven't been able to reach any of the others. They aren't out of action, we just don't have the codes or capacity to access them from here. You should shift these two to the Karkha Tower and send them on from there. Tang Shan has constant access."

"I don't like that idea. They don't need to see things they don't need to see. Have Tang Shan bring the codes here."

The old man disapproved. He thought her choice was wrong but said only, "As you command, Illustrious."

She did not ask why he thought she should do it differently. She faced the odd couple. "It's going to take longer than I hoped."

The sorcerer shrugged. "It's all right. Waiting is better than walking."

That was a jest. Even his girlfriend was surprised.

...

Babeltausque was lightheaded with joy. The Empress really meant to let them go!

The excitement faded when Mist explained, "We tried again. Even with the right codes we can't connect from here."

Cynicism set in.

"I'm as frustrated as you are," she said. "I want you out of here before the storm breaks. Lord Yuan says there's only one way. We send you to a place where we have permanent connections with our Kavelin portals. You'll move on from there as fast as Tang Shan can manage." She waved at the portal bank. The man she meant had just disappeared. Someone she called Candidate entered the cabinet next door.

Babeltausque said, "We're ready," as Carrie slipped her hand into his. That was hot and shaky. She squeezed.

Mist said, "One of you follow Tang Shan. The other one, go after Lein She."

Babeltausque did not like the separation but knew that these portals would pass only two people in succession before they had to be reset.

Mist continued, "Good fortune attend."

She sounded disinterested now she was about to be shot of them. He was tempted to ask to stay.

But doom was coming. The end of the world was coming, for some. Old Meddler would arrive in a mood for destruction. Soon everyone here would be dead. The best plan of all time would be to get the hell gone before the shitstorm descended.

He and Carrie followed the easterners, Carrie first murmuring, "You thought about staying, didn't you?"

"For the two seconds it took me to realize how much I'd miss you if I was dead."

"You say such sweet things, Bee. I'd miss you, too. I wouldn't stay. I'd follow my skinny guy anywhere he wants to take me."

"Carrie!"

"You know what I mean. I don't plan on getting downwind of Death for about nine hundred more years. Longer if I can work it."

"Then I'll stick tight and help you get what you want." Though Carrie could have stated it with more clarity Babeltausque understood that she wanted him to remain evasive in the matter of deliberate self-risk.

She gave him a big grin, a peck on the lips, and popped into her portal, a master traveler after only one previous experience. The portal hummed. She vanished.

Babeltausque stepped into his own destiny.

Darkness. Then terror like none he had known before.

He was not alone in there.

Something had been lurking at the boundary. Something that had a yearning beggaring his own sad need for Carrie.

He stumbled into a place where half a dozen easterners gabbled at Lein She like frightened geese. Something was happening that should not be. Lein She rushed Carrie on toward a portal making feeble teakettle whistling noises. Someone plunged in ahead of her, a boy with a rusty short sword.

Tang Shan bums-rushed Babeltausque toward another portal, this one quiet. Another armed boy preceded him. Lein She pranced like he had a bad need to pee. The instant that portal reset, he followed Carrie. Behind him, babbling technicians settled into combat poses behind long swords, facing another portal producing especially hideous noises. Babeltausque experienced a weird sensation suggesting labor pain.

Tang Shan shoved him so hard he feared his shoulder had been dislocated. He spun, staggered into the portal backwards, glimpsed several unsettling things before the darkness embraced him.

Carrie's portal tore itself apart—in total silence.

Black smoke emerged from the portal making the ugly birthing noise. The technicians harried it with their blades, which began to droop like overheated candles but caused much worse noises each time they slashed the smoke. Something was in extreme agony. Then a disembodied face pushed out of another portal. Babeltausque knew it without ever having seen it before. Old Meddler. And he was furiously unhappy.

Babeltausque suspected that devil found himself in the slow, painful process of arriving at a destination other than the one that he wanted.

Darkness.

The yearning engulfed him. It felt more familiar, now. It had become a friend after one brief connection. He thought at it, *Crush that wicked old devil.* Or something of the sort, never really articulated but enough to distract it briefly.

Then he felt Tang Shan coming, frightened by the inexplicable presence.

The passage dragged. Tang Shan remained close. Too close? Almost… They could not merge, could they? The receiving portal would not spit out some eight-limbed vertebrate spider-monster, would it?

He tumbled. Momentum brought him up against someone.

Carrie. She was seated on a dusty stone floor, laughing wildly while making no sound he could hear. Behind her, on hands and knees, the youth who had preceded her was puking his guts up while crawling toward his sword. Lein She lay curled on his left side, clutching his abdomen. The easterner who had preceded Babeltausque also lay in the fetal position, his blade eight feet away. He did not appear to be breathing. The sorcerer headed his way, to help, only belatedly realizing that he was suffering less than anyone else.

Tang Shan began ridding himself of his last several meals.

One thump and Babeltausque had the boy gasping. The pudgy man dizzily struggled to keep his feet under him. It was all on him, now. Whatever it was. He was the only one able to do anything.

The portals. There were three. Two still hummed. He had to make sure nothing followed…

Would Old Meddler bother? Who here was of any value?

How could the devil know that?

Someone stirred in the portal that Babeltausque had used. He hesitated, caught between the urge to snatch up a sword and the desire to fling an attack spell. Then he recognized a portal technician, another boy, maybe fifteen, armed but terrified and desperate to escape.

Something pulled him back.

He disappeared with a pathetic puppy yelp.

The calm nurtured during his association with Dane of Greyfells came over the sorcerer.

He had to silence those portals. They looked delicate. They should break easily. What to use?

Obviously, the sword that had gotten away from the youth who had come through ahead of him.

While stooping to recover the sword he became aware that every muscle and joint he owned now ached. He might not be puking up his soul but he had acquired a world of hurt all his own.

Carrie tried to say something.

He promised, "Nothing will get you. I won't let it." And he meant it.

He shuffled toward the portals.

Someone began to emerge from that same portal where the panicked boy had been pulled back. This one wore shreds of clothing similar to that boy's but was more nearly naked than dressed. Babeltausque did not recognize that pale face. That was not anyone from Karkha Tower.

He raised the sword like a club. He had no idea how to employ the Eastern weapon.

The newcomer desperately dragged two-thirds of her body length out into the cold. Her? Oh, definitely, yes! Though she wore tatters of boy's clothing, there could be no doubt. She had been well-blessed by Nature.

She could not get any more of herself free of the transfer's grip.

Her desperation touched Babeltausque. Blade held high in one hand, he extended his other, let her grab hold, pulled. Out she popped. Well, most of her did. Part of a fine right leg, from just above the ankle down, did not emerge. There was no bleeding. Babeltausque noted that she wore scraps of a boy's clothing.

Carrie gasped, "Bee Boss, you got to wreck them damned gates!"

Well, yes, he did have to get on with that, even if he and Carrie were way down on Old Meddler's list, if just to deny that villain a possible escape route from the Karkha Tower.

Carrie was up now, hunched, in pain, muttering about hoping being pregnant was all in her head because no fetus ought to go through what they just had. Babeltausque did not quite grasp that right away. He dragged his attention away from eternity's most marvelous set and attacked the portal whence their owner had come.

The one called Lein She said, "Strike lower, to the right. Your other right. The right side of it. Hit the orange and yellow hashes." Babeltausque understood every word. At the moment he did not wonder how that could be.

Carrie stumbled to the stranger, helped her remain upright. The girl stared down at herself, plainly thrilled. She cupped her breasts, then commenced a slow blush. Carrie said, "One of these perverts will give you his jacket."

Babeltausque was not alone in being thoroughly impressed.

His sword stroke fell where Lein She said it should.

A whine went out of the world, a sound the sorcerer had not recognized was there till it went away.

Tang Shan gasped, "Silence the others, too!" He was on his knees, now, eying the footless girl, baffled.

As a boy Babeltausque often fantasized himself an unstoppable swordsman, even then knowing it would only ever be a fantasy. He was not an athlete in any sense. But here he was, swinging a long eastern blade like he knew what he was doing. *Clang! Clack! Ring!* It was a magic blade, a singing sword!

"Enough!" Tang Shan yelled. "We want them damaged so nothing can come after us, not busted beyond repair."

"Working off some fear energy," Babeltausque admitted. "And now I'm exhausted." He understood most everything Tang Shan said. Lein She, too. Was that a byproduct of their passage through the transfer stream? Instead of them being mashed together into a two-headed human crab?

"Settle down. Relax. Sleep if you have to. We're safe. Its dark out. We can't go anywhere now, anyway." There would be no more transfers. They were on foot for now.

Babeltausque settled beside Carrie, snuggled in for the warmth, physical and emotional. He slid the sword across to its owner. It was in bad shape. The nicks might never get polished out. Carrie teased, "I saw you lick your chops when you saw those boobies."

"I can't help being alive. But your sweet booblets are the only ones for me."

"It's all right. They're so excellent I'd want to get my hands on them myself if I was that kind of girl."

Babeltausque looked at the mystery woman. "Who are you?" As though she might understand. Hell, she might. Tang Shan did.

He was sure she was the presence he had felt in the transfer stream.

...

Ragnarson joined the crowd looking over Scalza's shoulders. People babbled in several languages. Old Meddler had found some way to get at the Karkha Tower through the transfer stream. That was unexpected. The Tower was lost, no doubt about it. Those who had not gotten out quickly had become part of the red layer now coating everything inside the transfer chamber.

The Star Rider sent a demon through, somehow, though that should not have been possible. It killed everyone, opened the way for its master, who made adjustments to a freight portal and brought an iron statue through. But not the Windmjirnerhorn. Passage through the transfer stream would destroy that.

Old Meddler had to do without while his winged mount made the long real-world journey from the farthest east.

Mist said, "Lord Yuan, it's gone well enough, so far, despite the surprises. Dare I hope that something there might nail him?"

"No, Illustrious. But he won't be able to transfer out."

"Then with Varthlokkur's help we might be able to smash the place with him inside. Where *is* Varthlokkur?"

Scalza said, "Almost here, Mother. But he won't be much help till he and the Unborn recuperate."

Ragnarson glanced at Mist's daughter. She seemed unhappy about the Unborn's situation.

Lord Yuan refused to be distressed by the disaster. He said, "Let's locate those who managed to get away."

Scalza snapped, "Want to tell me where to look?"

Lord Yuan did have suggestions. He knew exactly where each Karkha Tower portal should have taken someone before having been sabotaged by his lost technicians. He was quite proud of his "children."

He did admit, "This will take time. The strange couple wanted to go to Kavelin. But..."

The boy said, "I checked our old house, Mother. They didn't go there."

Ragnarson lost interest. He joined Haroun and Yasmid against a wall. Haroun had withdrawn completely. Yasmid was almost as remote. Their hosts had no interest in Hammad al Nakir anymore. Anything could have happened there.

The same was true for Kavelin.

It was all about Old Meddler, now, and only about Old Meddler.

Haroun asked, "Have we been hornswoggled?"

"Huh?" Bragi could not recall his friend ever using that word before. "How so?"

"Were we collected just to get us out of the way of the Dread Empire's grand design?"

"Not intentionally. This is real." The effect might be the same, though, if Old Meddler miraculously lost the round. "She's probably just gotten everything from us that she wanted."

Yasmid stirred but said nothing. She clung to Haroun constantly now. She had nothing more to do with her father. Ragnarson had not seen El Murid for days. His handlers kept him isolated somewhere, safe from the specialists responsible for Ethrian and the Old Man. Curious, that. If the Disciple had given Mist anything useful Ragnarson had missed the transaction. The only positive contribution El Murid made anymore was to stay the hell out of the way.

He could shut the hell up, too.

Everyone else would happily deal with God's concerns once they met Him face to face—including the Disciple's presumptive heiress.

"You going to fight when he shows?" Ragnarson asked.

Haroun gave him a look that asked if he was stupid. "The choice is between dying fighting and dying whimpering." He was not happy about being caught in those jaws.

"Ideas?"

"None. But I have an advantage. I know he's coming. I didn't have that with Magden Norath. And he won't be expecting me."

Ragnarson did a slow turn, ended up staring at Mist as she bent over Scalza. "He doesn't know about most of us." How deliberately had that woman worked to make this come together the way it had?

She sensed his regard, turned, frowning slightly. He shifted his attention back to Haroun. His thoughts had begun to drift away from business. "I need to make peace with Inger."

Bin Yousif was as monogamous as any creature that ever lived but he understood. "At your time of life? That would be smart. Not to mention an act of political wisdom."

"Yeah." He glanced at Mist. The charge had gone neutral but the curve of her behind still reminded him of Sherilee. He shivered. "There a cold breeze in here?"

"Actually, yes."

Varthlokkur had brought it. The man appeared to have aged two decades. He was exhausted. He had failed to close the door behind him.

Mist's daughter touched Nepanthe's boy lightly, then made a quick departure. No one paid any heed.

Wen-chin and the Old Man gave up their seats at the shogi table. The wizard collapsed into a chair. Mist settled opposite him. He eyed the Winterstorm, noting that it had been altered but showed no excitement about that. Mist said something that probably explained.

Haroun asked, "You going to go eavesdrop?"

"They won't use a language I understand. They'll let me know what they want me to know when they figure I need to know it."

"Hell of a way to run things."

Ragnarson responded with a sarcastic snort. "It's the way we all run things. Transparency is against the rules."

Haroun actually chuckled. Yasmid smiled. Both were responses more positive than most Ragnarson had heard lately. He told no one in particular, "It can't be long, now. Even if I don't really get what's going on."

"You aren't out in the wilderness by yourself, my friend. I'll bet nobody involved in this really knows."

Yasmid whispered, "God Himself must be confused. No two of His creatures are pulling in the same direction."

Haroun did the bizarre. He demonstrated affection publicly by kissing his wife's cheek. "Precisely the truth, heart of my heart." His expression dared his friend to even note such remarkable behavior.

Ragnarson winked.

†

Chapter Thirty:

YEAR 1019 AFE:

New Year Begun

Kristen watched the boys play. Fulk had a snobbish streak. He tried to lord it over his nephew. Bragi would not have it. He protested with punches. Fulk's streak was fading.

Still, they got on better than did their mothers.

The women shared a small room with the boys and a maid whose principal task was to referee. Josiah Gales, Nathan Wolf, and others came and went as they dealt with routine business.

Kristen felt awkward but knew this was more so for Inger. Inger sprang from a rough and tumble political tradition. No doubt she was still trying to come up with ways to twist things to her advantage.

Kristen saw no chance of that—unless Fulk fathered a potential heir. Bragi's succession solution had broad support. Even the Estates had signed on—with limited enthusiasm. Ozora Mundwiller had decreed that the tapestry of tomorrow would be woven in accordance with the King's will. Sedlmayr and its commercial allies would guarantee that. The monarchs of several neighboring kingdoms had recognized the arrangement formally, too, perhaps made nervous by the interest the eastern Empress had shown toward this side of the Mountains of M'Hand.

Kristen and Inger also suspected the influence of Michael Trebilcock.

Whenever anything not easily explained took place Michael usually got the blame—mainly in situations likely to produce a net positive result.

Old Meddler or assorted devils and witches got blamed when a worse tomorrow seemed likely.

Kristen read the letter Inger had brought, for the third time. Not a word had changed. She had to speak to its contents eventually, though there was little enough to say. "This does prove that Liakopulos survived."

Inger grunted. She was not happy. She had the Greyfells taint, which meant that she resented having any option denied her. "Any thoughts?"

"Not much to think, is there? We just need to not act like brats."

The letter was from General Liakopulos, supported by the old men of High Crag. The Mercenaries' Guild meant to guarantee Kavelin's succession, as established by King Bragi, who was still a Guild member. He had left the Guild but the Guild had not left him.

"No choice," Kristen said. "Liakopulos was as much the King's man as his Guild status let him be."

Inger muttered something that included several virulent Itaskian swearwords. In a more composed voice, she continued, "I imagine the old men are concerned about Shinsan's ambitions, too."

"Maybe they know something."

"They know history."

Kristen read the general's letter again. It was not ambiguous. "It is what it is. Fussing won't change it. It sets limits on how the tapestry of tomorrow can be woven."

"I just hate… Forget it. You're right. We've been told. Only Bragi can change it." Inger put her embroidery aside, rose, paced, eventually wondered, "When will she send them back? She said she would."

Mist had made no demands other than to ask that her lifeguard be treated well. He had a family. They looked forward to his homecoming.

Inger was concerned more about her sorcerer than her husband. Without Babeltausque or money she was just an impoverished noble who had not yet abandoned her airs.

Having others acknowledge her status meant everything to Inger.

She had a full ration of the Greyfells inferiority complex.

"She's probably too busy staying alive."

"Understatement. You're good at that, aren't you? Of course she's busy! That happens when you're dim enough to try to play on the same field as... Ah! You almost got me to say it. That would be one way to get around those dire warnings about what will happen if..."

Kristen did not argue. There was no point. Inger was stressed. She would be who and what she was, only more so.

Inger punched herself in the forehead. "Stupid! Why do I go all whack job when it's time to be sensible?"

"Suppose we get Ozora back?"

Inger stopped pacing. "Are you serious?"

"If she was here, neither of us would mouth off without thinking first. That dragon would lean on us so hard..."

"I couldn't take it. The pressure would build up and I'd do something stupider than anything Dane would try. What I'll do, though, is ask myself, 'What would Ozora do?' when I butt heads with something really tough."

"I'll try that, too. What about your cousin? Is it really safe to send him home?"

Inger shrugged. "His time in the cellar won't have changed him much but he might've grasped the fact that he has to at least fake it to survive. Plus the family needs somebody in Itaskia. Their problems are so awful, he won't ever have time to bother us again."

"That makes sense." And, she was sure, Greyfells would get his own unambiguous communiqué from High Crag. "I've had a letter myself. From Abaca Enigara."

Kristen watched Inger think, realize, harden, but consider, *What would Ozora do?* before she asked, "Would that be the Colonel's daughter?"

"That would. Being a girl, custom won't allow it officially, but, practically, she's chief of chiefs of the Marena Dimura now. Some good soul let her know all about the Thingmeet. She wants to follow the path her father tried to blaze."

Inger drew on Ozora again before she suppressed her prejudices enough to observe, "This poor hagridden kingdom. I pity it if Bragi and Michael don't come back."

"Really? My whole life women have been telling me how much better the world would run if the girls were in charge."

"Pardon my cynicism. Show me a couple of examples."

Kristen shook her head. The only women she knew of, who had gotten famous, had been really serious kickers of ass.

...

Babeltausque found himself second-in-command to his thirteen-year-old girlfriend, who could be precisely decisive even when she had no clue. She was one of those people who got things done.

"Lein She, we need firewood." In seconds she had determined that the Candidate was the line officer while Tang Shan was only a senior technical specialist. "Send someone to find some. Then we'll inventory our resources, including skills, before our ability to communicate goes away."

It might. The easterners were becoming harder to follow.

"Keeping warm is our main project for now."

Dawn came. They watched it from the portico of what seemed to be a temple. The world sprawled below was grey and white with tufts of brown weed showing through crusty old snow.

Carrie said, "Let's figure out where we are. And find something to eat. I'm really hungry." Fire was no problem. A forest lay at the foot of the hill. The easterners had tramped a path already.

Tang Shan spoke slowly. The sorcerer said, "I can't follow him anymore."

"What he said last night. He's been here before. Only now he says if we head straight south we'll come to a road."

"You still understand him?"

"You have to listen hard."

Tang Shan said something more.

Babeltausque listened hard. This time he caught a few words. Something about small game. Rabbit and bird tracks marred the snow. The crust had weathered till those were featureless depressions, but they did suggest that a clever hunter need not starve. "I can help with food."

"We're going to get cold," Carrie said. "Them worse than us. They're not used to our kind of winter. But we can't stay here—unless we want to make it to spring by eating each other."

Babeltausque asked, "Why do you say things like that?"

"Gallows humor? All right. It wasn't funny. But it was true. If there's a road we need to find it and let it take us somewhere warm."

The sorcerer could not argue with that. "Let's get out of the wind and get a plan worked out." Carrie was right about them going to get cold. They had barely enough clothing amongst them to preserve the new girl's modesty and their own. And they would have to help the woman travel. She did not do well on one foot.

She was a strange one. The oddest things amazed her.

Carrie said, "Bee Boss, we could outfit you and send you for help while the rest of us stay by the fire."

Him because he was most likely to get serious attention, of course.

"Wouldn't work. This place can't be found from outside, remember?"

"Are we sure this is the place where the King came back?"

"You heard Tang Shan. And how many secret temples, with transfer portals in them, can there be near Vorgreberg? So we all have to go and we all have to be miserable and I really, really hate that. I really don't like winter. And right now it feels cold enough to cause frostbite."

The easterners kept whispering amongst themselves. Near as Babeltausque could tell they were trying to follow what he and Carrie were saying. He and she spoke deliberately, for their benefit, and for that of the woman, who seemed able to read moods well, if not follow their actual speech. Tang Shan focused on Carrie intensely, working hard to maintain communication. Survival might depend upon it. She reported, "He says they can create a heat exchange bubble big enough to keep three people warm. We can take turns."

"That should help." He had no idea what a heat exchange bubble might be. Definitely not something within his own skill set. Food he could help with. He could call game to the slaughter if he could see the animal before he started the draw. "How far to that road?"

"He says it's a matter of time, not distance."

"That's right. It took the King and them hours and hours to cover three or four miles."

"We'd better get started. There's less daylight this time of year."

...

Scalza shouted, "Mother! I found them!"

Mist closed in quickly, wondering who. They were looking for more than one… Ah. The sorcerer, his girlfriend, and some of the Karkha Tower garrison, with Tang Shan, all crowding a bonfire beside a dirt road in a snowy forest. So a few had gotten away, probably because they had been moving the couple along when Old Meddler arrived. They looked totally miserable now.

"Who is that woman?" She could not be from the Karkha Tower—unless the boys had had a prostitute in. No! That level of indiscipline was unimaginable after the stronghold had been compromised before.

Ethrian said, "Sahmaman!"

Silence descended as though some grand spell had been cast. Those farther away caught it from those close enough to see into Scalza's bowl.

Ethrian glowed.

Ekaterina looked like she had been slammed with an emotional hammer.

Not good, Mist thought.

Lord Kuo was right. Pray that Nepanthe had instilled her own values.

But once the first moment of pain was over Eka crowded in beside Ethrian. She stared, face stony. "Is it really her?"

"Yes," stated in such a way that everyone understood that Ethrian was his old self again—complete with recollections of being the Deliverer.

He yielded visibly to an abiding sorrow.

Eka put her arms around him and squeezed. Had the moment not been poignant it could have been amusing, she being half his size.

Ethrian accepted the comfort. He took deep breaths, said, "Pulling it together now." Mist met his gaze over Eka's head, was startled.

This boy—who had crushed half an empire and had commanded hordes responsible for having slain thousands—this crazy boy not only adored the woman pictured in Scalza's bowl, he had a fierce affection for Eka, too.

But were his feelings what Eka wanted them to be?

Were his feelings for Sahmaman what Eka did not want those to be?

Eka asked, "What's wrong with her foot?"

Ethrian shrugged. "I don't know. She wasn't like that before."

A darkness began to take Ethrian after the first joyous flush. He was troubled, wondering how this was possible. Sahmaman had been a ghost before. That ghost had grown quite solid, but was a ghost even so. And that ghost had been stilled again at the end of the Deliverer wars, evidently forever. She had given herself up so Ethrian could survive.

But there she was again, in the flesh, interacting with the sorcerer, his girl, Tang Shan, Lein She, and some apprentices from the Karkha Tower.

"Check this," Scalza said. He had drawn the bowl's point of view back.

Michael Trebilcock said, "They went through the same temple that the King and I did. That's where we hit the Sedlmayr road."

He saw nothing remarkable, otherwise. Neither did Bragi, who observed only, "Looks like they're freezing their butts off."

Mist asked, "Scalza, is that drover the man who killed Megelin?"

"Yes, Mother. Exactly. Intriguing conjunction, isn't it?"

"Old Meddler might be a more clever manipulator than even I was willing to credit."

Varthlokkur announced, "That devil has run out of patience. He's on his way."

"Shit," Ragnarson murmured. A dozen others agreed with that sentiment.

Haroun and Yasmid forced their way in for a look at the donkey drover. Neither spoke. No one contested their demand for viewing space. The black emotion steaming off them impressed even the Empress.

There was a great chance that Boneman would not live happily ever after should his path intersect that of King Megelin's mother and father.

...

Varthlokkur was wrong. Old Meddler had not been about to launch his attack. Instead, he had slipped out to visit a fellow conspirator from the Pracchia days who had survived the subsequent purges. The man was a merchant-sorcerer-gangster of modest means, talent, and attainment, but of expansive ambition, who believed that he should be the successor to Magden Norath. The Star Rider agreed. That was what the man wanted to hear. Old Meddler needed the borrow of his equipment, and his assistance, to gather more demonic help.

It might be days yet before the winged horse came with the Windmjirnerhorn. He for sure had to be ready to go when it did.

First order of business, though: more demons. He could not improve his position with iron statues, but there were countless demons out there. His old associate owned the means to call them and was eager to help. His once-upon-a-time attempt to capture the Karkha Tower, undertaken without approval and with secret, malicious ambition, had gone awry. Further, it had let the Tervola know that some of their secrets were not secret at all. There would be no chance for a surprise again.

The attack also told the Star Rider which underling believed that he dared hijack his master's tools and powers to further his own ambitions.

He did not pursue the matter. He did not have the luxury now. He needed every advantage he could pull together.

He could indulge his vindictive streak later, once his survival was assured and the world had been cowed again.

...

Ragnarson grumbled, "Going crazy over here! When in the h…" Nepanthe's child stopped maybe eight feet to his left and stared at him with eyes gone big, trying to decide if he was entertainment or if she should run away shrieking and get herself some big-people comforting elsewhere.

"Ah, damn," Ragnarson muttered. "Don't scare the kids and

horses, man." Wouldn't do any good, anyway. Neither time nor the gods cared how much you whined.

It was late. The usual crowd, including Varthlokkur, had gone to bed. Mist and her main associates had gone off to some Imperial military headquarters to catch up on business having nothing to do with the Star Rider. There was plenty of that. Insofar as anyone could see, Old Meddler meant to spend the remainder of his days in Throyes conjuring demonic reinforcements.

He was marking time, waiting for his horse and magical Horn. The farseers could not locate the beast, whose dallying had the ancient more frustrated than did his enemies.

Nepanthe was playing with a scrying bowl. Now that Ethrian was mostly recovered she seemed to be in an even more troubled place. Bragi was unsure whether that was because the boy no longer needed mothering or because she was afraid that he might become the Deliverer again.

Ragnarson would not worsen her concern by mentioning it but was confident that Varthlokkur and Mist, independently, would have arranged that the boy should never don the cloak of darkness again.

Mist's daughter was there, too, piloting her brother's scrying bowl, as were several low-level easterners, monitoring transfer portals and farseeing devices of their own. The girl was having trouble staying awake. She noticed him looking, straightened some and glared. He got the feeling she wished he would go away.

Smyrena came closer now. She was fearless lately. He had seen her crawl into the Old Man's lap. She had put the baby hoodoo on Kuo Wen-chin. Now she was trying to conquer a king.

Not that difficult. Ragnarson loved the little ones. He had only Fulk left. Fulk had passed the cute and cuddly stage.

Another glance at Ekaterina. Yes. She definitely wanted him gone. Why?

He caught her fleeting look at Nepanthe.

Ah. She wanted to talk to her future mother-in-law, in private.

Almost funny. It was all drama at that age, particularly for girls.

Maybe she was worried about becoming an old maid.

She could have been married by now had she been born in his northern homeland, or in Hammad al Nakir, where they married them off even younger but recommended that they not be used as women before they turned nine.

He could not help a judgmental sneer, which the girl caught and, probably, thought had to do with her.

Nepanthe squeaked, half in surprise, half in distress. Ragnarson, Ekaterina, and Smyrena all headed her way, the little one clambering into her lap, then having to have her hands restrained so she would not splash in the bowl.

There was the winged horse, airborne, streaking over a vaguely discernable river. Nepanthe had adjusted her bowl to see in limited light, but there was little of that. Ragnarson thought he saw ruins and a substantial wood that had been ripped to kindling.

"That's right outside Lioantung," he said. "What's going on?"

"It's running from something. It gets away but then when it tries to hide the thing that's after it always finds it again. There! That shadow."

It was dark out there. Ragnarson saw nothing but the night.

"That's a demon," Ekaterina said. "One of the… Serving the one we aren't supposed to name."

"So," Ragnarson mused. "He's lost all patience."

"Varth was right," Nepanthe said. "He has a problem with his horse not doing what he wants." She backed off the point of view. The horse became a white toy flapping desperately toward the shattered forest. The demon, a sprawl detectable only where it masked whatever lay behind it, followed. It had trouble staying locked onto its quarry.

A bit of red light, just a point but so intense it hurt the eye, appeared at the edge of the bowl. It moved toward the demon at an absurd speed. A second point, paler but more intense, ripped toward the winged horse.

Ragnarson blurted, "What the…?"

Neither Nepanthe nor Ekaterina managed that much.

The easterners on duty crowded round, excited. They knew what was happening but lacked the language skills to explain.

…

A startling amount of progress had been made toward restoring Lioantung. Lord Ssu-ma Shih-ka'i, however, had established himself in the worst of what remained unreclaimed. He led a company of specialized artillerists. They had a dozen transfer portals in support, against a need for hasty redeployment. There was no obvious sign of their presence, from ground level or the air.

A runner approached. "Message from the Empress, Lord."

"Another one?"

"Yes, Lord. Another one."

She would drive him crazy if she did not stop. He wished he dared cut communications completely so he need not waste time keeping her reassured.

He had sent one message bluntly asking her to stop. She had apologized, then had kept right on fussing.

She would be watching now, he knew. She kept sending updates, repeating what his own people had reported already.

His second for the operation, Lord Chu Lo Kuun, announced, "The target has changed course and put on speed, Lord." It had been drifting lazily, out of range, going nowhere. "It might finally come close enough… Something odd, here. Ah! It isn't alone!"

Lord Ssu-ma stepped over. "I see." He saw more than the obvious, in fact. "Sixty miles separating them."

"But closing fast."

"Total alert. Stand by for action." He wanted to step out where he could see the eastern sky but there was no point. It was dark. He would see nothing but stars and a sliver of moon too slight to dust the ruins with silver. Winged horse and demon both would remain invisible unless right overhead.

A demon, though—and one of considerable power—was after the winged horse. Only the Star Rider was calling up devils these days. The horse had been shunning its master. Must have disappointed him hugely to have generated such a cruel reaction.

Lord Chu saw it, too. "What do you think?"

Shih-ka'i's response would not be popular in some quarters. He removed his boar's mask so Lo Kuun could read his lips, which he shaded with his right hand. "Target lock them both and calculate their probable closest points of approach." Unstated, do all that before higher authority intervened. Before the Empress decided to take the Windmjirnerhorn for herself.

Lo Kuun might have some slight ambition, too, though only Old Meddler had ever been able to control the Horn. His body language suggested that he did not like his orders. Nevertheless, he executed them. Nor did he remind his superior that angles of fire and points of approach would change by the moment as horse and demon maneuvered. Lord Ssu-ma Shih-ka'i had written the doctrine for extreme range use of this artillery. He had proven that doctrine against the Great One.

That Lo Kuun would do as instructed was why Lord Ssu-ma had chosen him as his second.

Coming events would be choreographed to serve the empire, not individual ambition. Thus did the pig farmer's son will it.

Shortly, from nearby but out of sight, Lord Chu announced, "All set, Lord. They are in range, targeted and locked."

"Launch one on each."

"Launching now, Lord."

Came a roar like the combined release of a hundred heavy ballistae in barrage. The ruins shook. Rubble fell.

"One is away," Lo Kuun announced.

The roar repeated itself. So did the shaking. Somewhere not far off a brick wall groaned and collapsed.

"Two is away. Three and four are targeted and locked."

"Stand by. Reload one and two."

"Reloading one and two, Lord."

Shih-ka'i stepped over to where farseeing specialists were tracking the shafts. They reported both flying true.

He whispered, "She will be extremely unhappy," inside his mask, not moving his lips.

She might dismiss him. Though she had not given specific instructions she would expect him to preserve something with the potential of the Windmjirnerhorn. And, as certainly, he knew that this attack would tell Old Meddler a great deal about what he now faced.

The shafts were no secret, though. They had been employed in number against the Great One, then against Matayanga to the extent that any remained in inventory after the struggle in the east. But Shih-ka'i's ability to target them precisely, against objects in motion… The Empress would rather that neither the Star Rider nor the world know her artillerists were able to do that.

But what point to owning an unknown power never deployed?

Shih-ka'i believed that success tonight would be worth the secret. Loss of his horse and Horn would cripple the Star Rider forever. He would be reduced from demigod status to the level of a Varthlokkur or Magden Norath—except for his command of the iron statues. Which advantage might be lost to him already.

Shih-ka'i watched the fiery points of his shafts cross the scrying bowls at speeds difficult to encompass. Somewhere, Old Meddler might just now be realizing that something was terribly wrong.

"Shield your eyes!" he barked.

He protected his own as shaft one came on target fifty miles away. The flare overwhelmed that quarter of the world.

Shih-ka'i gave it a half minute before saying, "Targeteers, report."

Two men replied, "Hit, Lord!" Two more declared, "Standing by to launch, Lord."

"Did we actually accomplish anything?"

"The demon is burning, Lord."

Lord Ssu-ma scooted over while the other targeteer reported, "The animal is going down, Lord, damaged but still struggling."

"Launch number four." This follow-up was the shot that would irk the Empress most. He moved in behind the specialist tracking the demon. "That is impressive."

A vast patch of sky had become a thunderhead of hazy, oily fire.

The technician, so excited he failed to maintain his composure, declared, "That is screaming amazing, Lord! We caught it completely by surprise!"

"Yes. If he sends another, though, expect it to be prepared."

Shih-ka'i was nearly as awed. He had not killed a demon before, nor had he watched one die. And this was a major demon. This would get attention across this world and on other planes. Could Old Meddler watch without the Windmjirnerhorn? If not, he would be lost. He had sent a king demon, yet would hear nothing back.

No. Wrong. He would hear, eventually. The demon's kin would clue him in when he decided to send another. They would show him, when they refused to be condemned to an identical fate. Maybe they would be intimidated to the point where they would abandon the weakened him altogether.

Compulsion could be counted on only so far.

There would be no powerful demonic urge toward revenge. Revenge was not, generally, something that drove demonkind. Socially, they interacted more like crocodiles than primates.

Shih-ka'i moved to the man tracking the winged horse in time to catch the second weapon in its final approach. "Shield eyes!" he barked.

The winged horse was only twenty miles away now, and just two hundred feet up. The flare even generated a mild shock wave.

"Hit again, Lord. It was more ready... Oh! It crashed. I'll zero in when my eyes adjust."

Shih-ka'i studied the downed horse. Its one wing was partially crisped and probably broken. Its right foreleg was broken for sure. It tried to walk but could not. Neither could it get airborne. The farseer conveyed no sound so Lord Ssu-ma could not hear its screams. He observed, "I don't see the Horn."

"Underneath it, Lord. And damaged. It started smoldering after the first shaft hit." The technician backed the viewpoint off. A scatter of debris stretched along the animal's line of flight for half a mile. It looked like all the goods of a grand bazaar had been spewed across the rocky countryside. Some scrubby bushes wore tattered silk. The mess would be more striking once the sun rose. "It appears to have puked tons of random stuff."

Shih-ka'i nodded. "How far? I'd like to go see—if it's reasonably close."

"That's just across the river." The technician drew the view back. "It's there. We're here. Six miles?"

"Fine. Excellent, in fact. Lord Chu. Let's go meet a legend face to face."

"As you command, Lord." Lo Kuun lacked enthusiasm. He preferred to use another shaft and make absolutely sure.

...

Ragnarson demanded, "If you've got weapons that ferociously powerful why use them way out there instead of throwing them at himself? You could..."

"Exactly the sort of point the Tervola would raise to argue that a girl shouldn't be in charge. Ignoring the practicalities. Like there were only nine shafts available and all of those were on the frontier, whence they would have to be transported close enough to shoot at himself. He took a shortcut getting to Throyes. We can't shortcut those things. Normally, in fact, they're made where they're going to be used."

Ragnarson was not mollified, nor was he ready to take that at face value. She had known she had those weapons from the start. Had she not? She should have started moving them months ago…

Maybe she had not known. Such weapons might be hoarded jealously by those who controlled them. Plus, there would have been no way to know where they would be needed before the need arose. Right?

He needed to think more before he barked.

…

Old Meddler sensed disaster even before his attempt to conjure another supernatural soldier produced a demon messenger who delivered visual proof.

He watched his hunter burn. He watched his old friend, twice hit, go down so violently that no protective spell was enough.

Nor was the Windmjirnerhorn engineered to survive such punishment. Chunks came off, some aflame. A gout of miscellany, literally dozens of tons, spewed out, including sparkling new coins, casks of wine, clothing, a carpet fifty feet long and twenty wide. Weapons. Shoes. Several living things. A fine art sculpture the size of an iron statue.

It was his own worst disaster since his condemnation to this horrible plane, happening almost casually. Absent the Horn…

He had to stop it. All of it. Now. He had to take time out to reflect seriously, not just about how to survive in times to come but about what this all meant in the grander scheme.

He was not watching a chance encounter go foul. That was an ambush. Tervola had been in place and waiting, armed with the most ferocious weapon in their arsenal. That they had been waiting told a hundred tales—none of them happy for the Star Rider.

The product of the combined equations was that that the Star Rider needed to leave the stage immediately, abandoning the play while it was in progress. Any other course would lead to the end of everything.

They would be waiting at Fangdred, Varthlokkur and the she-Tervola. They had been ahead of him most of the way. They had immense resources, some of which he had remained unaware.

All that was obvious. He did not send demons to spy. There was no point. They would be prepared for that, too.

The messenger demon brought word of Varthlokkur's raid into the Place of the Iron Statues, further proving that the enemy had exceptional resources and impossible knowledge. Varthlokkur might reasonably remember that the Place existed but how could he possibly know how to get past the safeguards to do the damage that he had done? Could it be that the Unborn was that much more powerful than anyone had imagined?

Old Meddler sighed. He slumped. The long struggle might be over—with him as the loser.

Not yet! No. He had options. Again, the best was just to hide till today's devils died and their knowledge faded. They always did die. The knowledge always did fade—though this time could be the exception.

Was there any real point? His enemies had eliminated his last few tools. With no Horn, no horse, and the Place in shambles, he had nothing left *but* time.

There was one final refuge, beneath the Mountains of the Thousand Sorcerers. He had not gone there since his effort to ready the Disciple for his role. He could head for the Horned Mountain now and let himself be wrapped in the arms of his lover, Time, underneath, till he could emerge and amaze and terrify tomorrow with his return. He would have to do so armed only with Magden Norath's grim journals, because there were almost no resources cached in that deep labyrinth. He knew not why. Those choices had not been made by him.

But. The Horned Mountain was a long way south, through deserts and mountains, a harsh passage for a man several thousand years old.

Also… Varthlokkur really had invaded the Place. How much damage had he done? Had he broken any chains? Had he cracked any confining walls? If he had done more than just finish off already damaged iron statues, things could begin to come apart in a huge way. And the warder in charge, the warder once able to handle it all with ease, no longer possessed the powers or tools to do his job effectively.

"Be careful what you wish for. There are always unforeseen consequences."

He could not just walk away from what might be coming.

...

Babeltausque murmured, "What did he say?" He no longer understood anything Tang Shan said.

Carrie wiggled like she wanted to snuggle closer, though the fire was huge and she was damned near inside his clothing already. She had been creeped out by the donkey drover from the moment the man used sign and broken Wesson to beg leave to share the fire.

She breathed, "He said this is the man who murdered the King of Hammad al Nakir."

"Oh."

There had been a lot of talk about that in Fangdred because Megelin's parents were underfoot. Babeltausque had paid attention only because there was nothing to do but monitor the gossip getting kicked around in the few languages he understood.

"Your heart just started beating faster, Bee Boss."

"Yes."

"Be careful. He's deadlier than a cobra."

And sensitive to personal danger. He knew the instant the attitude of his companions changed from indifferent to calculating.

"What?" Babeltausque asked after Tang Shan added something.

"He says Shinsan could earn a debt of gratitude from both sides in Hammad al Nakir by delivering this monster."

"I know I wouldn't want to be in his boots. I don't know about the Lady Yasmid but that King Without a Throne ain't a very nice guy."

"He needs delivering, Bee."

The drover casually thanked them for sharing their fire. Carrie thanked him for having provided tea. Babeltausque donned his "handling a Greyfells in a fury" bland face. He felt the killer calculate his chances and dislike them—even unaware that he had fallen in with sorcerers.

Babeltausque was not that sure of the easterners himself. He chose to assume that Tang Shan and Lein She were at least his equals.

He said, "Sit down. You won't be leaving us."

Carrie added, "We know who you are. Don't make it hard on…"

Babeltausque snickered.

"Bee Boss, you aren't twelve."

The killer was not amused. He fixed on Lein She now. Lein She had donned his mask. He was just a Candidate. His mask was simple but it was what it was. The killer knew what it meant. This would be an excellent time for that devil who saved him from the hunger in that desert tower to pop up again, to keep the scheme he wanted played out from aborting.

"Sit," Babeltausque said again, gesturing.

The man understood. He sat. His options were few.

Carrie asked, "What's the plan?"

"Hunh?" He did not have one.

"Be a lot of money on those donkeys."

"Temptation, you're saying."

"Big time, Bee. *Big* time."

"Carrie, this will sound bad. It might not even make you happy."

"Surprise me, love."

"The last temptation I gave in to was you. I'm not interested in anything else anymore. I'm especially not interested in grabbing some money and trying to outrun a lot of people who want to take it away."

Carrie giggled and pretended to tickle his chest. "You lie like a dog, Bee. You'd be all over Haida Heltkler if you ever got the chance."

His heartbeat increased. She would feel it. But it was not the pounding that would proclaim him a liar. "I don't think so. I'm happy with what I have. Really. You and my job as the Queen's wizard. That's all I want. It's all I need."

"Wow. All righty, then. Know something, Bee? I can live with that."

Tang Shan said something the sorcerer had no need to follow closely. He wanted the love stuff shelved. He was hungry. It was cold out. It was time to move on. The boys from the Tower were up and bouncing, getting their blood flowing. They could stay warm by jogging.

Babeltausque looked down. His belly was a specter of its former glory but it had not gone away completely. He would do no jogging anywhere.

Lein She understood prisoners management. He lashed the killer's right hand to a donkey pack, added a cantrip that would keep the knot from untying till he told it to let go. Then the cold march began.

†

Chapter Thirty-One:

YEAR 1019 AFE:

Knots at the End of the Rope

Nathan Wolf leaned into the Queen's sitting chamber. His breath misted. "The sorcerer just turned up, Majesty."

Inger pulled her hands back from the brazier that was the best even Kavelin's Queen could afford. "Babeltausque?" Unable to believe.

"Yes, ma'am."

Ma'am? Nathan must be thoroughly rattled.

"But... How...?"

"Ask him yourself. I came as soon as I heard. It's him and his girlfriend, some Shinsaners and a couple of others, plus about twenty donkeys and horses. They strolled in a couple minutes ago with their butts frozen off."

"But... How...?" Oh. Yes. Ask Babeltausque. "All right. Let me grab another wrap and some gloves."

She strode so briskly that Nathan had trouble keeping up. Everyone in the castle was headed in the same direction. Inger almost trampled Dr. Wachtel and Toby.

Josiah was there already, with blankets and hot tea. The constant babble eased briefly on the Queen's arrival, then redoubled. Even the easterners seemed compelled to talk to her.

She watched a desert man be led away, his hands bound behind him.

The sorcerer's sex toy quieted the foreigners while her lover explained to his sovereign.

She, of course, heard only, "The entire treasury of Royalist Hammad al Nakir," and nothing about the Star Rider or deadly attacks.

"No. He cached some a few places before he banged into us. You should probably get that gleam out of your eye."

Greyfells blood would tell. The moment she knew there was money to be had she thought that anyone who knew of its provenance ought to be silenced.

Babeltausque told her, "These people are Tervola. They're alert. They won't cooperate. And neither will I."

"Excuse me?"

"I won't be used as a black sorcerer anymore. Majesty. I'll be the royal wizard, but not the kind that does dirty deeds. I have responsibilities, now." He looked at his baby whore. She looked back with adoration that Inger feared was real.

"Good heavens," the Queen said. "Good heavens."

Kristen, with Fulk and Bragi swirling around her, asked Carrie, "Are you all right with that?"

"Bee growing a set and wanting to be a decent guy? Yeah. I'm loving it." Not a hint of acknowledgement of Kristen's status.

"That, too. But I meant…" She looked at the girl's waist and nodded.

"Oh. Sure. Yes. It happened…"

Inger grasped the truth as Carrie realized that her lover's transformation had happened because he had figured it out, too.

The Queen shook her head, surprised by her own good feelings.

Josiah had men unloading donkeys already. Those poor animals were bedraggled. "Nathan, appropriate enough to buy firewood for us, the staff, and the stable, then get some decent food in here. Decent. Don't go crazy. Then you and Josiah join me to go over our books."

She owed a lot of money. Good people and bad, no one who had seen the El Murid Wars would have trouble rationalizing confiscation of wealth from the desert. Most of that would have gotten there as plunder, anyway.

"Babeltausque, I could bear your children myself. Conning you into signing up with me was the smartest thing I ever did."

The sorcerer had trouble understanding when people were joking, especially when they were droll or sarcastic but kept a straight face. He coped by remaining unresponsive till he gathered cues enough to guess what was going on.

Carrie said, "I bet he'd jump at that. But I'm selfish. I won't share."

Inger was stunned. Did the girl think she was amongst her own street people? She managed, "I'm heartbroken. Who is that forlorn cripple?" The woman did not look like much but seemed important even so.

Babeltausque said, "I'm not sure, Majesty. Something supernatural. She came out of the otherworld used by Shinsan's portals. She took control of a boy who tried to follow us and transformed his body into that. The bad foot was the last part out. Maybe the boy wasn't big enough to let her make a complete new body. Don't offend her. She might look lost but still be a goddess or devil."

He knew more than he was saying. He believed what he did say. Complying with his suggestions would be sensible.

"Doctor Wachtel, take charge of the young lady. Help her if you can." She had forked branches for crutches. Lein She had made those for her.

Wachtel approached her, made himself understood by grunts and signs. Too, she understood a few Wesson words and phrases—which astonished everyone.

Inger said, "Toby, take our other guests to the empty quarters. Garyline, help him. Miss Depar, you seem able to communicate with them. Go with Garyline and Toby. Kristen, contribute wherever you can."

That earned her a grim look—followed by a curt nod. Things did have to be done.

Inger added, "The lifeguard that got left might be helpful, too. Where is he? You'd think he'd want to see this."

Kristen said, "You asked him to stick to his quarters."

Of course. It was honorable behavior to the point of obnoxiousness. Centurion of the First. Something like that. She was ashamed. She could not recall the man's name.

"Tell him I said he can come out and help. We should hear from his boss again soon, shouldn't we, Babeltausque?"

"As you say. Some of them are important officers."

The Depar girl engaged the one Inger thought might be called Tong Shand. Inger said, "Get them settled, then join Josiah, Nathan, and me. We need to decide what's next."

"As you will, Majesty."

Damn. He *was* having serious moral difficulties.

She understood. He had delivered what might be the one tool she needed to turn completely nasty, at a moment when she had Kristen and her brat in grabbing range.

That move would alienate Babeltausque—and, possibly, Josiah and Nathan, too.

"Everyone, please handle your assignments."

Inger took herself to the wall. She stared westward, toward the part of the kingdom least likely to support her if she seized this day.

The Kavelin disease stirred. Anything she did to aggrandize herself could succeed only after savage cost to the kingdom. It would mean a return to the situation of a year ago, when Kavelin had been ready to indulge in a suicidal frenzy.

She reflected briefly. Ozora Mundwiller would not suffer what she was tempted to try. Neither would Abaca Enigara. The Guild would stick a few spears in. And Bragi would be out there somewhere, unpredictable, with supremely dangerous allies.

Michael Trebilcock was with him, wherever. Aral Dantice had turned invisible but rumor had him nearby and watching.

So, layer dire practical considerations atop the Kavelin disease and one might even overcome one's own worst nature.

...

Mist told her daughter, "This isn't something I'm qualified to help you with, dear. I've never been in your situation. I've never even seen anything like it." She would not devalue Eka's trauma. Puppy love or not it had to be taken seriously. It could shape a girl who might torture the world later on, trivial as this might seem to a jaded adult right now. "Talk to your Aunt Nepanthe." Hardly an expert herself, of course, but Nepanthe had had more than one man in her life. She had navigated some fierce emotional waters.

Mist added, "Don't be angry. I do want to help. I just don't know how. The only man… Only your father… I was just hopeless."

Ekaterina delivered a tortured sigh worthy of a girl a little older and much more put upon by an indifferently cruel world. "I guess I understand."

"I do know that you can't force things to be what you want. The harder you try the worse they get."

"I know that much, Mother." Another millennial sigh. "So when will all this stuff be over? I'm sick of this place. I want to go home."

Mist maintained her composure. She did not ask where Eka thought home might lie. "I can't even guess anymore, dear. Our opponent might have accepted defeat."

"He's up to something. Scalza and I can both tell that."

"That's his nature. We're as prepared as we can be."

She saw Eka grasp the loophole, then choose to ignore it. "I'm just tired… No, I'm really depressed."

"Here's a thought. Just blue-skying. Did you ever tell Ethrian how you feel? Yes. I know. It's dangerous. He might say what you don't want to hear. But he might surprise you, too. And if the wound is waiting, putting it off won't help."

Eka's response was instant outrage that gave way quickly to her dangerously grounded, deadly rational core.

Ekaterina set free a different species of sigh, the sort that eased tension before one commenced a risky venture. She went to where Ethrian was playing a sleepy game of shogi with Lord Kuo, whispered into his left ear. Puzzled, the boy excused himself. He let Eka lead him outside.

Dread rising, Mist whispered, "She's too young." Then started.

Michael Trebilcock was scarcely a yard away, one eyebrow raised. He shrugged. "I don't know. The body may be. But it feels like there's a very old soul inside."

She nodded. She understood, though she did not agree. Eka could be unsettling to adults who expected her to be like others her age but half as bright and raised in ordinary family circumstances. "She'll be all right, though. Nepanthe is a good mother." Which was painful to say. "Can you do me a modest favor?"

"Within reason."

"Keep an eye on Eka till she comes back."

"Any special instructions?"

"No. You'll know if something needs doing. Just be Michael You till it does. If."

He bowed slightly. "All right." He went out.

Mist turned back to her personal war, having realized that Eka was better liked than either of them had believed.

She leaned on the back of Scalza's chair. He tended to be off-putting. Other than Ethrian people had to work at liking him. Ethrian liked everybody. Oh, and the Old Man. The Old Man considered Scalza a kindred soul. They both felt isolated but that isolation was self-induced. Scalza was young enough to be lured out. People here would care for him if he would let them.

...

Yasmid felt lost in space and time, and culturally, too. Maybe she was too old to adapt. She had been flexible when she was young. Look what she had survived...

Now she clung to Haroun, watched Sebil el Selib through the enhanced scrying system Lord Yuan had generously created, and waited while the child within her grew. The daughter within.

She knew. There were many months to go but she knew. And Haroun was not pleased, though he never admitted that. He hoped she was wrong.

Elwas was holding it together at home, better than she would have thought possible. He had harnessed Ibn Adim ed-Din al-Dimishqi, somehow. Jirbash and Habibullah added their own genius. Overall, the movement remained healthy. With no sound Yasmid could not determine how Elwas kept the reins on a people who now lacked their Lady and Disciple. That he did so was pleasure enough.

Old Lord Yuan had observed, "There did have to come a day when you and your father passed the mantle."

She had been surprised the first time he spoke her language, then learned that he had been one of Varthlokkur's teachers when the wizard was young. He had discovered a few truths about the mechanics of the world and time.

"True, but it isn't something we face well."

The old man offered a slight bow and moved on.

Her husband found nothing to encourage him when he took his occasional glance at history in the making in Al Rhemish.

That city remained chaotic. It looked like the Faithful meant to stay away till the insanity of factionalism devoured their enemies. Al-Souki and his ilk would move only after those idiots spent themselves, bringing welcome order.

Yasmid asked, "Can we just forget everything? Leave it to the next generation?"

She was not pleased by his answer, which was no answer. He was not yet ready to step away, though his struggle had been poisoning his soul for two generations. But he did not reject her suggestion, either.

...

Ragnarson tracked events in Kavelin when he could get a seat at a scrying bowl and help from somebody who knew how to work it. He strove to be nicer than was his nature. These folks knew him now. His strained smiles and schooled friendliness were suspect, but still they helped. The combination of close quarters and external threat had created a camaraderie unlikely to survive the threat's conclusion for long.

Mist joined him as he followed developments in Vorgreberg with his oldest surviving friend. Bin Yousif was as animated as Bragi had seen him since their reunion.

Hunger for a killing was upon him.

Ragnarson grunted his acknowledgement of her presence. She said, "We'll be sending you home soon. Lord Yuan has made a connection with a portal out there."

"So you don't need me to..."

"None of this went the way I expected. Nothing ever does conform to plan but this has been... unusual."

She seemed distracted. She kept looking around, nervous about something.

Ha! Daughter and boyfriend had disappeared. As had Michael.

Could that be a big deal? Had he missed some big change completely?

"I'm not sure I'm that excited about going back. There'll be a lot of work waiting."

Bin Yousif said something softly, without turning.

"Yeah. I know. It's my fault so it's my job to fix it."

Ouch! That seemed to tweak Haroun's wife.

...

Haroun made his decision. "Light of My Heart." He beckoned Yasmid, indicated the scryer Bragi Ragnarson was watching. Centered was a one-eyed man in a cold and dirty cell: Boneman. "There is one more thing that I need to do."

Her face hardened. "I understand." Some seconds later, she added, "The Evil One has found a home in my heart. I cannot forgive."

...

Micah al-Rhami no longer considered himself anyone or anything else. What he had been was lost, nor could it ever be recovered. The Evil One had done his wicked best. But God had won His point as well. The Message had been brought to the world. There were Believers who would carry on. He hoped God would let them remember him as el Murid, not what, in unconquerable weakness, he had become afterward.

His entire world was a tiny, icy cell. He was not quite sure where that was. The air was thin. He had never been so cold. He sniffled constantly. He could find no good in anything there. But he had gained something he had lacked for years: a friend. The heathen Phogedatvitsu, who had no agenda and no desire to use the Disciple to further it.

They spent a lot of time discussing mutually alien philosophies. And Micah was content to be this new, unknown worm of a worn out old man. He was content to have the world think that the Disciple had gone to his reward, if it was so inclined, because, in a way, that was true.

And, if he understood right—things were always confusing—he had a grandchild coming at last.

...

Michael did not get close enough to hear what passed between Ekaterina and Ethrian. The latter looked startled and confused. He stood there with mouth agape, unable to respond—especially not the way the girl hoped.

Michael had played both roles in this scenario in his time, most recently, *in absentia,* with Haida Heltkler. He had not had serious designs on the girl but he had taken her for granted. Had thought Haida the perfect mate, other than that she was so young. She was Michael Trebilcock in a gender mirror, all he was and a girl besides. But, as with what had been happening between Eka and Ethrian, theirs had been a dance of the clueless and the deluded exacerbated by militant mutual dread of the potential consequences of straightforward communication.

In his absence and perceived indifference Haida had been swayed by the determined and bluntly declarative courtship of Bight Mundwiller—to the not entirely uncompromising despair of Bight's great-grandmother.

There was every chance that Eka had stated her case the most oblique, arcane, and confusing way possible in order to minimize her own emotional risk.

Would the possibility that the relationship she wanted had not occurred to Ethrian hurt Ekaterina more than outright rejection? In the names of all gods, let the boy not make a joke of this.

Thanks be, he did not. After several stunned seconds he extended a hand, took Eka's, that she had raised uncertainly, and drew her into an embrace.

This part Michael did not follow. This was what he should have done with Haida, if he had wanted her, but he had not done it. Nor did he hear what the boy whispered to please the girl.

It might not have been what she wanted to hear but it was close enough. For the moment.

Everything would be all right. For the moment.

Michael headed for the chamber in the Wind Tower. He would report one less threat likely to arise at this most inopportune of times.

He found Varthlokkur fixated on the Karkha Tower and in a state of agitation. The wizard expected Old Meddler to do something ugly any minute now.

Haroun bin Yousif, his bride, and King Bragi were gone. "Home," Nepanthe told him when he asked the air. "You and I and Smyrena will go after the portals cycle."

Another glance at the wizard explained why Nepanthe and the baby were to leave. Varthlokkur expected big trouble. The symbols floating in the Winterstorm danced as though stirred by an unseasonable whirlwind.

Michael asked, "Where is Mist?"

Nepanthe said, "We don't know. She got a wild hair and took off. Said she'd be right back. Where are Eka and Ethrian? We have to get them out of here, too."

The other living clutter had begun leaving soon after the Karkha Tower went.

...

Mist's wild hair lured her to Lioantung, where night had fallen already. Lords Ssu-ma and Chu were startled when she turned up, unaccompanied by lifeguards. Lo Kuun could find no words. Shih-ka'i babbled, "Illustrious?"

"You captured the horse. And the Horn. I couldn't stay away. I *had* to see them, up close, before..."

"Before?"

"The grand old villain is finally ready to attack. I wanted my successes fresh in my mind beforehand."

"I see." She meant that she did not expect to survive the night. She wanted to go into the darkness sure that she had come closer to victory than had anyone before her. She wanted to go out believing that she had damaged Old Meddler so badly that he would not be able to go on for long. "What did you do about the children?"

That, she sensed, might be the most important question that this man had ever asked her. Somehow, it held personal meaning.

"They will go to Kavelin for now. They will not be at risk when my doom arrives."

"Very well. I shall stand behind them, then." Meaning he would become their guardian should she truly be taken.

"Thank you, Shih-ka'i. You can't imagine how much that means to me. I'll face the night with much more confidence."

"Come, then. I'll show you."

They had the winged horse suspended in a custom harness on a huge wagon. Hanging there, it could not escape. Neither would it suffer further damage as it traveled west toward the heart of the empire. A senior Tervola veterinarian had treated its injuries. The animal was half hidden inside casts and bandages. It was awake despite having been given medications for pain. It eyed Mist intelligently.

"Has it tried to communicate?"

"No, Illustrious. I believe it is content, though."

Lo Kuun said, "As content as any creature can be after having been rattled by the blast from a thaumaturgic long shaft, followed by hitting rocky ground going fifty miles an hour."

She considered the beast. "Yes. I suppose. What about the Horn?"

Shih-ka'i said, "Over there. You'll be disappointed."

He was right. The Horn was mashed, broken, burned, and melted in places. What had been recovered lay strewn about on one long table. Beyond and around it lay tons of random material that it had spewed across the countryside after it was hit.

"They're still bringing stuff in by the wagonload," Lo Kuun said. "I doubt we'll ever find it all."

Mist said, "I am disappointed but I understand. I'd better get back. Just to make sure my orders are unambiguous and being carried out exactly." Her children might not be entirely accepting of their new role, which was to get out of the way and stay alive.

"It is truly that close to happening, Illustrious?" Lord Ssu-ma asked.

"It is. It may have begun already, though I hope he delays for a few hours more."

"That being the case, I have to get a move-on myself."

Mist wondered what that meant. He volunteered nothing.

...

Ragnarson stepped out of the portal feeling giddy, with an inclination to throw up. A voice said, "Keep moving. You don't want to be in the way when the next traveler arrives."

Ah. That antique, Lord Yuan, was managing this exercise personally.

Ragnarson stumbled a half-dozen steps before he realized where he was—because when he focused he found himself looking at Fiana in her casket, radiant as ever she had been in life.

He wanted to be mad because they were still using her tomb to hide their portals, but he was too sick and there were too many things that had to be done. He kissed his fingers, laid them on the glass over Fiana's beautiful face, then staggered toward the light.

One of Yuan's henchmen had the door to the mausoleum partway open. It was late afternoon in Vorgreberg. Bragi stepped out far enough to look westward. The descending sun had settled behind the hill already.

Haroun and Yasmid emerged. Bin Yousif said something about the milder weather.

Minutes passed. Ragnarson began to frown. The others should have come through by now… Ah. Here came Scalza, indignant about having to miss the impending battle, but without much real vigor. Michael Trebilcock was two minutes behind the boy, patiently chivvying Ekaterina, who *was* thoroughly put out. Nepanthe followed, with the baby. Smyrena was terrified.

Nobody looked like they had come through without feeling terribly ill. Yasmid appeared especially sick, and troubled by concerns about how the transfer might have affected her unborn child.

"All right," he growled. "We're all freaking unhappy to be here and we're all hung over. But we are here and they aren't going to let anybody go back till the excitement is over. I'm going to be hungry when my gut settles down. I reckon the rest of you will be, too, so let's go someplace where we can find food and fire."

Lord Yuan came outside. "Please hurry, Majesty. To the castle. And send our people back out here. We have a task for them." He paused several beats before adding, "And we will do our best to leave this memorial in at least as good a condition as we found it."

He sounded quite sincere.

"Thank you. I'll send them right away."

…

Josiah entered Inger's private quarters using the secret passageway. He seemed particularly uncomfortable. "Josiah? Are you...? Should you be with Wachtel?"

"Ah...probably. Though I think this is more mental than physical. A rider just came in. The King is back, with a party that appears to include..." He suffered a spasm of some sort. He pulled himself together, offered several unlikely names in addition to that of Michael Trebilcock. "They could be at the gate by now."

"Damn." Said without any real fire. "We can't run them off so let's bring out Nathan and Babeltausque and deal with it."

...

Mist felt ill and was nearly exhausted when she left the darkness for the orderly quiet of the Wind Tower, where Varthlokkur was half lost inside the Winterstorm. The others were just waiting. The Disciple and his Matayangan friend, whom she continued to pretend not to recognize, crowded a shadowed alcove, shivering. Ethrian, Lord Kuo, and the Old Man sat around the shogi table. A game was in progress but nobody was paying attention.

She asked, "They all got out, then?"

Lord Kuo: "Some took more convincing than others. Ekaterina in particular. But we got her to understand that she would go regardless of what had to be done to make that happen."

Mist eyed Ethrian, one eyebrow raised.

Ethrian said, "I was too big for even Michael Trebilcock to shift since he already had his hands full with your wildcat daughter."

Mist could not restrain a smile. "She has potential."

"Scalza only argued a little."

The Old Man said, "That one calculates."

"Yes." She eyed Varthlokkur. The wizard was so busy he had yet to acknowledge her presence. "How soon? Do we know?"

Wen-chin said, "There are demons in the air now, carrying iron statues. We can't track himself so we'll have to wait for him to get inside visual range. Always assuming that he comes in person."

Mist nodded. She did not doubt that Old Meddler would want to stand witness to his wickedness. She was counting on it, in fact. She turned to peer into the darkened end of the chamber. The stasis sphere from long ago, resurrected and refurbished, awaited

Old Meddler there. She hoped that phase of Varthlokkur's scheme worked out.

Ethrian said, "All we can do is wait."

She agreed. "We wait."

"Not long," the Old Man said. "And this time will make an end."

...

Old Meddler finished instructing the demons that would attack Fangdred. Thirteen would go, in two waves, none pleased to be involved. They expected nothing good to come of this. Great demons had died already. *Dead,* for real and forever. That did not happen on this plane. Not credibly. Never before.

The old villain had constrained them completely, however. They could do nothing but go forward and execute his will, so long as he survived. And he had made sure they could not seize on that loophole, even by aiding his enemies through inaction.

They would go, those lords of the demon plane, carrying two iron statues, neither of those especially overwhelming. They would attack Fangdred. Some would get hurt, perhaps badly. He had not lied to them about that. But he was confident that they would end this latest threat for all time.

His ka would go with them while his flesh remained in the Karkha Tower. Demons would come for his flesh once Fangdred fell and its thousand booby traps had been disarmed. He would then appropriate the magic of Varthlokkur and his bitch Tervola ally. Both would be invaluable in ages to come.

He settled himself, left his flesh, entered the smallish demon that would carry his consciousness northward. They set out.

Scout demons soon reached the Dragon's Teeth. They were linked to all the others. What one saw, all could see. The scouts were particularly important. Fangdred's exact location remained mysterious.

Yes, Old Meddler had been there before but Fangdred was hidden now, behind sorcery of both Dread Empire weaving and of Varthlokkur's creation. A visual search was unavoidable.

Last time a furious storm was raging. This time the sky was nearly cloudless, though there was moisture in the air that captured and scattered the light of a moon that was almost full. Only the brightest stars stood out, against a background that was blue indigo rather than black.

The demon scouts stood out, too, as bleak absences of light snaking about like serpents swimming, dragon-size, sniffing for Fangdred's unnatural warmth. The enemy would not betray himself with outside lights.

There. A fierce peak where stone had been shaped and piled by Man.

The scouts circled, waiting for the rest of their wave. Old Meddler eased in closer, wondering if he had not found the hidden fortress too easily. Were they trying to lure him in?

He encountered a limit beyond which his demon steed could not pass.

No. Definitely not trying to lure him. But they knew he was coming. And they had not run. They meant to make a stand. They did want him to attack, maybe to spend his strength getting through to them.

He prowled and probed. He would give them what they wanted. They could not survive the power he had brought to the game.

There was a momentary lapse in Fangdred's protection. He darted through, only beginning to feel uncomfortable after he had. Had they let him in?

No. Someone had used a transfer portal. Evidently the barrier had to go down while that happened.

His vision grew fuzzy nearer the fortress. He approached cautiously, wondering why he was afraid. He doubted that he could be done any harm. Should his guide be hurt he could just break loose and be pulled back to his flesh.

He aimed for the Wind Tower, which rose above the bulk of the improbable fortress. His demon could not penetrate solid stone but it found a place where a lack of mortar would let it slide a tendril between blocks. Old Meddler took his consciousness through, crawling along that slender thread. The viewing inside was more vague and distorted, still. He pulled demon, stretched demon, took his consciousness down a floor, then drew back and went up to the level where his enemies had gathered.

What? No! This could not be!

The Old Man pushed a shogi piece forward. The Deliverer made a comment about the move.

Lord Kuo Wen-chin shrugged and shook his head sadly.

The bitch Tervola looked almost directly at Old Meddler's viewpoint, frowning, as though sensing something uncertain. Beyond her the specter of the salt trader's son stirred and said something possibly cautionary.

So many dead men. That Matayangan… But the Old Man was the worst. Because of him this might yet get dicey indeed.

Varthlokkur stood surrounded by glowing symbols. Old Meddler spied dark worms representing each of his demons—including the one limpeted to the outside of the Wind Tower, permitting him this access. The second wave would arrive before long.

There was no sound. He could not hear what the wizard shouted. His henchmen crowded in to see what had him excited—which was not, as Old Meddler supposed, the proximity of the demon that he himself rode.

The wizard's wand tapped four viciously brilliant points of light moving through the Winterstorm, two toward the shadow dragons swarming outside Fangdred, one toward the squadron in transit, while the last and most intense streaked toward Throyes.

The bitch Tervola, facing his direction, mouthed, "It's Shih-ka'i! The sneaky bastard brought the last four shafts up from Matayanga. He must have started them moving weeks ago."

Old Meddler did not know what that meant but he was sure that it boded no good for the Star Rider.

He began to pull back. To get out. Not because he was in danger here but because danger was afoot somewhere else and he ought to be there to handle it. He had a huge crew about to deal with this place.

He had entered a trap after all, but not a crafted one.

The barrier was back. He and the lead troop were inside. He had to get out.

How?

He would have to wait out the first squadron's attack. That should open the way.

Points of blinding light came out of the south at a velocity almost unimaginable. The barrier troubled them not at all. Each found a demon carrying an iron statue. Blinding blasts of light, separated by a second, shredded the night. They boiled snow off the mountains below. They set both demons aflame. The iron statues, molten on one side, fell away. The explosions threw off blazing sub-munitions like the biggest fireworks ever created. Those took out several other demons. The sky over the Dragon's Teeth filled with burning serpents but Old Meddler's demon was not among them.

An identical firework burst in the distance, amidst the second wave.

The violence here cracked Fangdred's barrier. Old Meddler's demon dashed through and headed south.

There had been four points of light moving through the Winterstorm. The brightest was headed for Throyes.

He had stumbled into an ambush that even surprised his enemies. Varthlokkur and the bitch Tervola had had something else entirely in mind, he was sure.

What had they been waiting for? Knowing that he was coming?

The Old Man was with her. That would be root and core and foundation of all his difficulties, now and forevermore.

He might not make it through this time.

The dead might pull him down.

He was surprised at how much he wanted to go on living, even after ages of pain and disappointment.

His demon ripped past the second squad. Four were on fire. He sent the strongest call he could: *Abandon everything and come with me!*

Despair. His consciousness was out here. But his body was…

A blinding point moved across the night. He was moving faster. He was not a material entity. He and the point were converging. What would one of those things do to the Karkha Tower? What would it do to the people inside, of whom he was the one who truly mattered?

Slam! Like hitting a wall at full gallop he reentered his flesh. And was still trying to harness it when the world went white.

…

Lein She was first to burst into the transfer chamber in his home base. He had insisted he be the man once Lord Yuan made sure of the connection. The Karkha Tower was his responsibility. If need be he would go down first in the effort to reclaim it.

He stepped into heat that stunned him, though it was fading. It dried his eyes. He kept blinking, having trouble seeing. He spotted a shape scuttling with one arm across its eyes, making mewling sounds. None of his men, nor any of Tang Shan's, had survived the earlier attack. He thrust his blade into the whimperer's back.

Tang Shan arrived, then—as the world surged and shifted and icy darkness flooded the chamber. Lein She felt a presence so sudden and vast and abiding that he lost control of his bowels.

The demon was not interested in him. It had work to do. It was gone when the next man arrived to find Lein She and Tang Shan leaning on one another, gaping at surroundings notable for the absence of a little old whimperer.

The new arrival observed, "Damn! Everything is all runny melted like candle wax!"

...

Varthlokkur stepped out of the Winterstorm and collapsed, though he remained conscious. "We won. Sort of. And without having to spend much of our own capital."

Mist said, "He got away. Again."

"He'll be no threat again in our lifetimes. Or in many lifetimes to come. And him surviving may not be an all bad thing."

"You'll have to work hard to sell me that."

"We'll talk about it later."

"All right. Meantime, I do know where to look if I want to keep after him. El Murid was good for that much."

Varthlokkur fell asleep before he could ask where, thinking that that old devil always had one more trick. But today they had played a few of their own and had gotten several steps ahead.

†

NIGHT SHADE BOOKS IS AN INDEPENDENT PUBLISHER OF QUALITY SCIENCE-FICTION, FANTASY AND HORROR

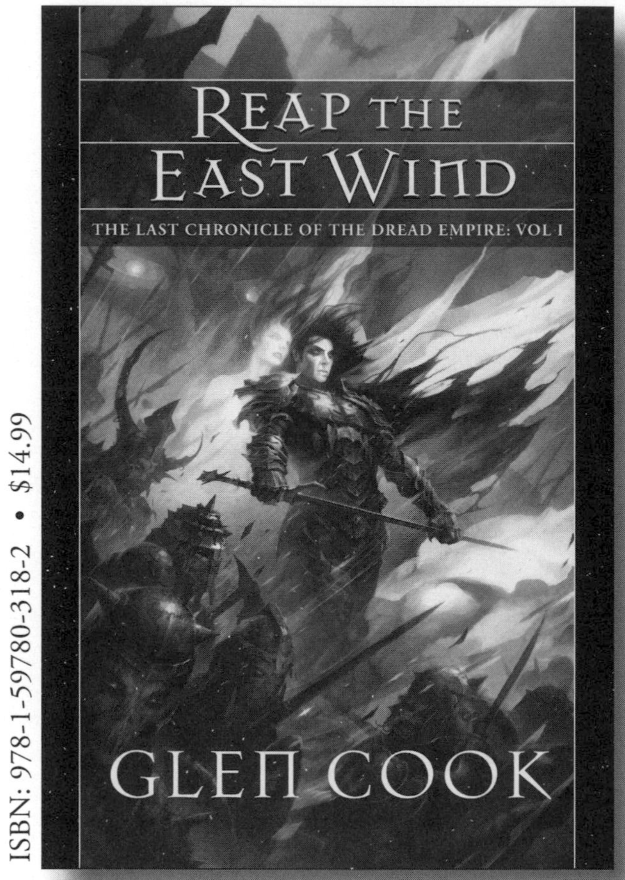

ISBN: 978-1-59780-318-2 • $14.99

VOLUME 1 IN THE LAST CHRONICLE OF THE DREAD EMPIRE

It has ended. It begins again. In Kavelin: Lady Nepanthe's new life with the wizard Varthlokkur is disturbed by visions of her lost son, while King Bragi Ragnarson and Michael Trebilcock scheme to help the exiled Princess Mist re-usurp her throne - under their thumb. In Shinsan: a pig-farmer's son takes command of Eastern Army, while Lord Kuo faces plots in his council and a suicide attack of two million Matayangans on his border.

But in the desert beyond the Dread Empire: a young victim of the Great War becomes the Deliverer of an eons-forgotten god, chosen to lead the legions of the dead. And the power of his vengeance will make a world's schemes as petty as dust, blown wild in the horror that rides the east wind.

NIGHT SHADE BOOKS IS AN INDEPENDENT PUBLISHER OF QUALITY SCIENCE-FICTION, FANTASY AND HORROR

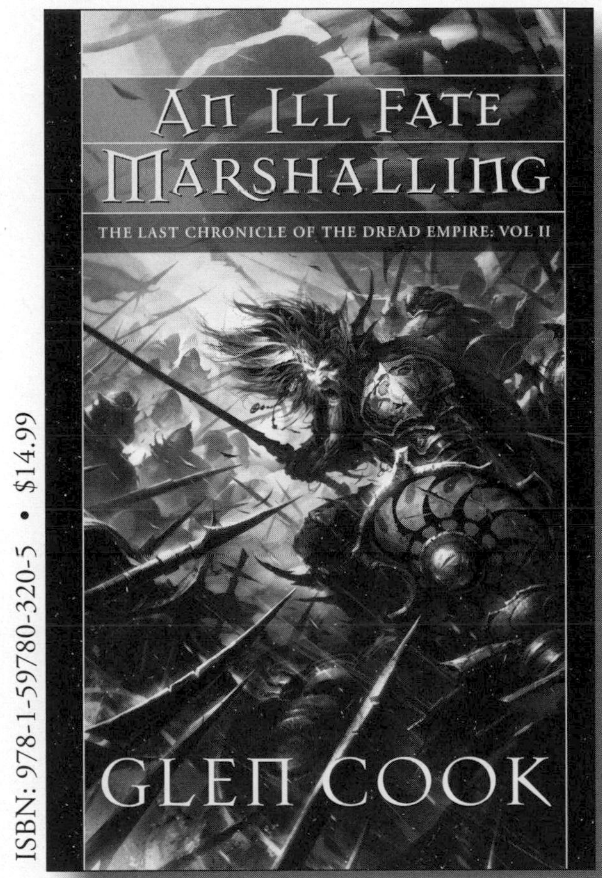

VOLUME 2 IN THE LAST CHRONICLE OF THE DREAD EMPIRE

King Bragi Ragnarson decides to join Chatelain Mist's coup against the Dread Empire. Varthlokkur—the King's wizard—tries to dissuade Ragnarson from this chosen path, but only the drum-beat of war is heard. The King's Spymaster Michael Trebilcock joins with the wizard to stave off The Ill Fate Marshaling, to no effect.

Many of the characters from past volumes take center stage, and the climatic events of this book shake the world of the Dread Empire to its very core, creating *A Path to Coldness of Heart.*

ABOUT THE AUTHOR

GLEN COOK is the author of dozens of novels of fantasy and science fiction, including ***The Black Company*** series, ***The Garrett Files***, and ***The Tyranny of the Night***. Cook was born in 1944 in New York City. He attended the Clarion Writers Workshop in 1970, where he met his wife, Carol. "Unlike most writers, I have not had strange jobs like chicken plucking and swamping out health bars. Only full-time employer I've ever had is General Motors." He currently makes his home in St. Louis, Missouri.